ALSO BY J. ELLIOTT

Haint Blue Series:

Monkey Mind

Spooky Short Story Collections:

Ghost Lite

Tales from Kensington

Uncanny Stout

Monkey Heart

Hedonistic Hound Press

This book is a work of fiction. High Springs and Gainesville are real towns and there are some real or hinted at landmarks. Names and characters are all creations of the writer's imagination and any resemblance to actual persons or events is entirely coincidental. It's fiction, folks!

Hedonistic Hound Press 

Book cover and interior artwork by J. Elliott

Printed in the United States of America

Acknowledgements

I am indebted to the Writer's Group of the Alachua Branch Library—you are the best! Many thanks to the Writers Alliance of Gainesville for supporting me and taking me seriously and to my "pod" group who allowed me to stay in the sci-fi group—hey, there are lots of cryptids here, it almost sort of counts! Dan South, James Singer, Mike and Betty Kite and Calvin Gregg—many blessings and much success to you all, always.

Special thanks to Jordan Borstelmann and Kathryn Whipple for technical suggestions and support.

Much gratitude to the book club within the Adventure Club of Gainesville for supporting Haint and her friends.

JoAnn Lordahl, Elaine Young, and Peggy Cogar, my brave beta readers, this may never have gotten finished if you hadn't had your pom poms out. I owe you everything.

Kathy Passman, you just have no idea how much your enthusiasm and kindness has meant to me. Maybe I can write an alpaca into the next one!

Special thanks to Rick for your love, encouragement and support. I could not have done this without you.

Jessica Elliott 2020

Table of Contents

OFFICE

Max: All I know is that when I'm not with you I'm a total wreck.

Nora: And when you are with me?

Max: I'm a different kind of total wreck.

—*White Palace* (1990)

Retreat Map

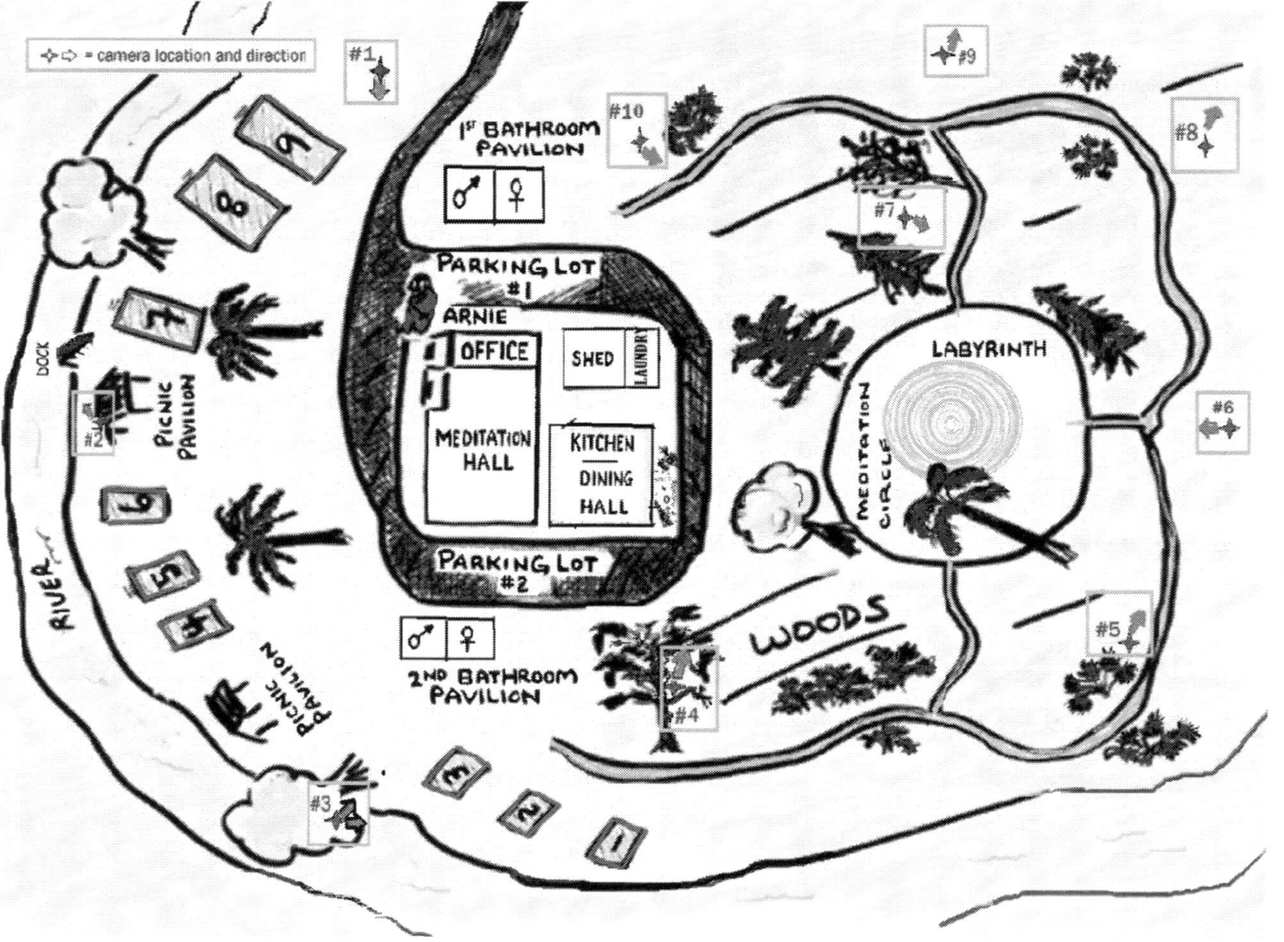

= camera location and direction
#1
#2
#3
#4
#5
#6
#7
#8
#9
#10
1ST BATHROOM PAVILION
PARKING LOT #1
ARNIE
OFFICE
SHED
LAUNDRY
MEDITATION HALL
KITCHEN
DINING HALL
PARKING LOT #2
2ND BATHROOM PAVILION
LABYRINTH
MEDITATION CIRCLE
WOODS
PICNIC PAVILION
PICNIC PAVILION
DOCK
RIVER
1
2
3
4
5
6
7
8
9

The Guest List

The Cryptozoologists
George Burgwyn "Buster" Shadetree
Shane Ouellette
Rebel Saggory

The Wiccans
Vida Glossimer
Theadora Nutterberg
Boo Nutterberg
Fawn Nicole Janus
Rose Water

The Burlie Boys
Chet Lewis
Aubrey Sinclair
Various Others

Preppers
Jim Calhoun
Julie Calhoun
Cog Wheeler
Various Others with similar names like Jerry, John, Joe Harry (maybe?)

Take It Off
Prudence Blackwell
Annie Woddell
Serena Lippincott
Magnolia (Maggie) Beth Burgess
Belinda Wheeler

Chapter 1

The Country Song of My Life

The perimenopause elves, Hot Flash, Moody, Bitchy and Put-on-Pounds kept me company as September handed over the baton to October 2014.

The name on my passport is Helena Bluszczski, but since childhood I've been known as Haint Blue. I was born in Charleston, South Carolina, premature and albino. The nurses in the preemie ward took one look at me and said I looked like a "haint" and, since they weren't going to attempt Bluszczski, they went with Blue.

God willin' and the creek don't rise, next September would usher in my fiftieth birthday. Just observing, not complaining. Too much to be grateful for, but even so…I wasn't exactly *over* the hill, but I'd reached the peak and stuck my flag in the rocky soil. The view was unfamiliar.

I count my blessings, really, I do. I've got a few solid friends, enjoy mostly good health, have a house in need of repairs, but a house all the same. Thankfully, I've got little drama in my life. The fact that most of my family tree up and died has a lot to do with it, plus I'm on the introvert side of the teeter totter. A Basset hound named Naughty Britches rules my world. She has a friendlier-than-average Russian blue/gray tabby cat named Mischief. She adores him.

The country song of my life at the end of September lacked the catchy riff and toe-tapping beat that makes a top-ten hit. I'd name the song, "Misfortune Got her Foot in the Door and Now I Can't Get Her to Leave." I was getting edgy.

My latest endeavor, opening a meditation retreat, was so far, a nightmare. The unofficial opening of the retreat earlier that September should have been fun and relatively stress-free. It had been disastrous. I had expected difficult guests, yes, but not a homicidal one; double murder all but killed my business, so to speak. I felt more alone and vulnerable than I had since my husband Dillon died.

And that was another thing. I've been a widow for some years with scanty dating prospects to speak of. Sure, I was lonely, but I'd rather be alone than stuck with anyone less than Dillon. That was a tall order. Would I ever find someone? That had been wearing on my mind, as my mother used to say.

As you might imagine, after the murders, the few bookings I had called to cancel. The rest of the month crept along. The only fresh reservations I got were out-of-towners who'd missed the news. It kept me afloat and from total panic, but a funk of unease and worry began to consume me—a funk further nourished by a rapid series of savings-sucking events.

For starters, there was the chemical assault. One day while I was out, migrant laborers contracted by the power company arrived. They sprayed every green plant under the power lines along the road that led into my meditation retreat. Ginger. Beauty berry. Palmetto. Plants that had no intention of growing tall enough to deny access to the power lines. It's bad enough that Florida doesn't experience much autumnal color. Nothing road trip or photo-op worthy.

This swath of indiscriminate brown death looked post-apocalyptic. To add insult to injury, they just left it. No coming back to chainsaw or mow to remove the crime scene. My gaudy Blue's Lotus Lodge sign might as well say Welcome to Withering Heights.

My well pump up and died one Saturday night, no chance of repair until Monday so I was without water. I got that annoying *blee-dee – BLEE sound and* "we're sorry, but the number you have reached is no longer in service" when I called my trusty well pump folks. So much for being a loyal customer; they'd gone out of business without a word. Again, not a crisis, but inconvenient. The well guy recommended by a friend actually rubbed his fingers together as he declared my pump was shot and I needed a new one.

Ka-ching!

That same week Mischief ate a lizard or something mysterious that put him off his feed and made him listless. After a hefty vet bill, he recovered, thank goodness.

Ka-ching!

The funk turned into panic when my computer succumbed to a deadly virus and blacked out. Kaputsky. Despite the alleged backup, I lost *everything*. Even my computer guru, Tony couldn't recover it. The ironic silver lining was that with the new business barely running, and my old-school, paper backups, I could recreate most of what was lost.

New computer: *Ka-ching!*

All of the inspirational messages "follow your dreams" and "find your passion and abundance will follow you" did not seem to apply to me. I'd had virtually no social life while throwing my all into the retreat. I worked my tush off fixing up the old fish camp only to gaze out at empty cabins. My gorgeous new meditation room sat unused.

Tired and floundering, I prayed for an upswing in my business. I needed some good news, a blast of something uplifting. Some sign of being on the right path.

Often in my morning meditations, I would recite "Advice from Atisha's Heart". Venerable Atisha (982-1054 AD) is credited with bringing pure Buddhism to Tibet. His advice is excellent but deceptively simple—easy to comprehend but not so easy to put into daily practice. For example, "Friends, the things you desire give no more satisfaction than drinking sea water, therefore practice contentment." While I understand that attachment to things is samsaric♥, my contentment was pulverized when my computer crashed.

"If from your heart you practice in accordance with Dharma, both food and resources will come naturally to hand."

Obviously, my practice was lacking.

♥ Samsara is the cycle of suffering birth, struggle, pain, death, repeat. The only way out of this cycle of delusions and suffering is enlightenment through virtuous thoughts and actions, releasing all attachments of the world. While this is primarily a Buddhist/Hindu belief, enlightenment is not limited by religion. Anyone of any faith can become enlightened.

"If the things you desire do not come, it is due to karma created long ago, therefore keep a happy and relaxed mind."

Somehow the thought of burning off bad karma with all these setbacks was not granting me bliss.

And this menopause business blind-sided me. Forty had come quietly enough; I'd loved that people assumed I was closer to thirty. A non-smoker and an albino, I enjoyed clear alabaster skin and an ageless, almost comic-book-character mystique intensified with tinted contacts. But, as if an alarm went off on my biological clock, I began noticing significant changes. One morning the skin on the back of my hands looked crepey and whoa! Whose hands were *those*? They looked like my mother's hands, not mine. My feet started hurting in strange places. And since when did I need a few steps from the couch to get fully upright? What was up with the stiffness?

And hello, hot flashes! I'd heard of them of course, but no one said it was akin to self-combustion. Was this my new superpower? My vision has always been bad, but recently even my close-up vision was fading. I couldn't see my armpit hair to shave it anymore, and I found rogue, catfish whiskers sprouting on my chin with my fingertips, not my eyes.

As the first full week of October unfolded, I tried to rally my spirits and get excited for the cooler weather of autumn, for Halloween and Thanksgiving. That was challenging as the daytime temperatures were still close to ninety; the humidity was still much as it had been in August. My bank account was heading toward the red…and that was *not* a festive, feel-good color to see.

You have to be careful what you wish for.

I asked the Universe for prosperity and love. My prayers would be answered soon enough but not in any form that I would have imagined.

Wednesday, October Eight: Blood Moon

My brother Iggy and I aren't twins, but we share the extraordinary connections that twins often share, a telepathy and completeness, a knowing which we've both relied on since childhood and more keenly since my husband died a few years ago and Iggy's girlfriend Running Deer left him.

But lately, my calls had either gotten no answer, or a quick and edgy, "call you later, okay?" He had a new girlfriend, Louise Swanson. Sure, he was distracted by new love; I got that. They'd met during the disastrous meditation weekend and hit it off. But he was avoiding me for some reason beyond distraction. Maybe I'd catch him that night at his martial arts studio.

Iggy and Joe Chow own Crouching Blue, Hidden Chow Studio in Alachua. The memorable name, a mashup of their surnames and a classic martial arts film plus some clever window art, was a winning gamble. Even though some people mistook Hidden Chow for a restaurant, Iggy and Joe had a solid client base and a steady influx of newcomers.

I often dropped in on Iggy's Wednesday night advanced tai chi class. I'd even substituted for him in a pinch if he was called away in his capacity as volunteer fireman. When I showed up a few minutes early in yoga attire, Joe was at the front desk stacking rolled complimentary towels. No sign of Iggy.

"Hey Joe," I waved as I entered, appreciating the air conditioning. In the few moments it took to park and cross the sunny parking lot, I'd already begun to sweat. "Remind me. It's now October, right? Aren't we supposed to be enjoying cooler weather?"

"Not with global warming," Joe said, shaking his head. Joe is in his forties with the body of a martial arts instructor, shoulder-length black hair with wisps of, gray tinsel around his temples. Easy on the eyes and the spirit.

"Iggy not here?" I asked before bending to take a quick slurp of water from the water fountain.

He twisted his mouth. "No, he asked me to sub. Said he was busy."

I frowned. "Hunh. Joe, has he been avoiding you lately, or is it just me? Have you seen him? Is he okay?"

"Think so, but he does seem distracted. He's got that lady friend, you know."

"No, there's something else. I can tell."

Joe shrugged. "Guess he'll tell when he wants to. He's a big boy."

"Yeah," I said with disappointment. I'd hoped Joe had the inside scoop.

Class attendees began arriving; I trailed along with them toward the exercise room. Most of the students were considerably younger than me with perfectly tight thighs and butts encased in trendy yoga pants. I removed my shoes, set my bag down and found a space in the back corner where I couldn't see myself in the mirror. Joe entered, greeted everyone and the session began.

My body was grateful for the stretching; my mind settled into concentrating on the movements, making my hands float, shifting weight, exaggerating my steps: heel… arch…ball…toe. Shift weight. Step. Heel…arch…ball…toe. Shift weight. Step.

"That's it. Light and purposeful. You are butterflies, gossamer butterflies," Joe encouraged.

I watched the lithe students balancing and shifting. Their upper arms were taut, not flappy wings like mine. Most of them could sweep from snake to rooster without losing their balance, like I did. I've known for some time that I'm past my prime and that's fine. Mostly. But some days, I feel old and clumsy. This was one of those days.

After class, I was slipping on my shoes when Joe announced, "Hey folks, be careful out there. Blood moon tonight."

As if receiving a cue, a young female student began singing "Shine on Harvest Moon." She strutted and swayed, touching each of us as if working a dinner theatre audience. She had a dancer's body and bounce, but her most notable feature was her shaved head. Her tanned scalp, visible through the sturdy protrusions of dark hair, reminded me of potting soil encouraging chive sprouts.

She changed the lyric from "for me and my gal" to "me and my Al." Like a seasoned performer, she was able to show most of her teeth and sing at the same time. Her voice was clear, her pitch, perfect. She finished with a flourish and a bow to our applauses. "Thanks, sorry, I just had to. We did that song in a play last year." Hefting her bag over her shoulder, she sighed, "Another engagement, I'm needed elsewhere. TTFN." She slid her feet into her flowery flip-flops and flip-flopped out the door.

"Bitch," a class member muttered as she got her things and left with another classmate.

Joe rolled his eyes.

"Who was that?" I asked.

Joe and I were near the door as people began trickling in for the next class. Joe has a tendency to get right up in my personal bubble making me very aware of his maleness. It doesn't bother me, but it is a bit distracting.

"Her name's Nicole. She's a senior theater major at Saint Faith College," he said, moving closer in an enticing, mostly-hollow flirtation that reminded me that I'd been alone for a long time. He was happily married, but a natural flirt. Since he and Ig were friends and business partners, I saw him a lot. We had a comfortable rapport.

"She's talented. A bit of an attention seeker, as you see."

"Gotcha."

"Hey, Haint. I'm having a moon watch party tonight around 9:30 PM. Come by if you like. Soak up some moon magic."

Unsure if I was having a hot flash or too close to his pheromone force field, I stepped back. "Thanks. Blood moon sounds ominous. What does it mean, Joe?"

He narrowed his eyes to slits. "Just because I'm Chinese doesn't mean I know jack shit about astrology or horoscopes." He swirled his hands before my eyes like a magician, his voice now pidgin-English. "This is the year of Wood Horse…wood horse strong, run very fast, very wild. Means must take great care. Because the blood moon…full moon…very strong, very powerful." He sounded wise and mystical. I was entranced. His hands floated for another beat, then he clapped and said, "it's just…an eclipse!" His hands flew apart as if releasing an invisible dove, ending the spell. He stepped back, watching for my reaction.

I was startled but pretended to shrug. "You know, with that expression, darker eyebrows and the right mustache, you'd make a great Fu Manchu."

"Ah!" His eyes flashed then narrowing to slits. "You've seen through my disguise. " He swirled his hands as if beginning another imaginary magic trick but morphed into a wave goodbye. His next class was arriving. "Hope to see you tonight," he called over his shoulder.

Joe has a lighthouse effect--the kind of magnetism that gives you a buzz when you are hit by his attention but feel let down when that attention moves away again. Leaving him to drive back home alone, I soon felt dejection settling back on me.

Iggy, where are you? What's going on?

As I drove home through Alachua, I noticed a team of city employees with a cherry picker putting fall decorations on the streetlamps. Autumn is my favorite season and Halloween is hands-down my favorite holiday. The cheery reds and oranges perked me back up a bit. This year's fall theme was scarecrows and cornstalks. Each lamp post was wrapped in cornstalk bundles with decorative orange ribbons. Banners hung from the tops of the posts with pictures of pumpkins and cornucopias wishing everyone a Happy Fall Y'all!

I'd noticed decorations in Catfish too. Most of the shops

had made their own displays. The Whatcha Need Mart—a tiny building part jiffy store, part hardware store, part feed store, had a family of scarecrows walking out of the store with a shopping buggy filled with supplies; Blondene's Beauty Barn had a little scene of a seated scarecrow wrapped in a smock getting a haircut; and the laundromat had a clothes line under its awning with red and orange children's shirts and coveralls hanging on it anchored by small crows instead of clothespins. Even Skeeter's Garage had a risqué tableau out front: two figures leaning into the hood of a derelict car exposing rotund pumpkin butt cheeks from their jeans. The dive shop had pumpkin faces wearing dive masks staring out of their window through cornstalks.

I should explain that Catfish Springs is a tiny town that still survives and maintains its charm thanks to its proximity to local springs. Divers come from all over the country to practice cave diving here. The city commission wisely refuses to allow any chain stores into Catfish. While nearby towns like Alachua have vacancy signs in their downtown windows while the chains pop up like weeds along the highway, Catfish remains sleepy Catfish.

Maybe I should put up a seasonal display by my road sign, I thought.

My retreat, Blue's Lotus Lodge was off the beaten path, but that didn't matter. I should dress it up, make it look festive. Corn stalks and a few pumpkins would be easy enough to set out. Was that really necessary? Was it worth the bother? Did it take pumpkins and kitsch to get people to come to a retreat? Hadn't I already put in enough effort? Obviously, I wasn't in the right frame of mind for decorating.

I lost the rest of the day to mindless cleaning: sorting junk mail, vacuuming and checking emails. No new booking requests. Great.

Needing to talk to someone to get me out of my head for a while, I tried calling my best friend Lorraine. After three rings the call went to voicemail.

I tried calling Iggy again. Voice mail. Fine.

When Naughty Britches began her I-need-attention antics, I was happy to play with her.

The half glass of wine with dinner made me feel sedentary and sulky. I could have gone to Joe's moon party to see if Iggy showed up but doubted that he would. Instead, I donned my jammies and watched Alan Ladd in *Shane* with NB and Mischief.

I fell asleep and had bumpy dreams about blood and moons. A prairie woman in a long dress was luring Iggy away to a wagon. It was the middle of the night, but the wagon was clear in moonlight tinged with red. She was pushing him to climb onto the buckboard. He looked back to me with a helpless expression. Standing in the doorway of my little cabin, I called out to her, "No, you can't take him, I need him! He's all the family I have. He's my brother, my blood brother."

She ignored me and continued to prod him to take the reins. He moved like an automaton and shifted his gaze over the two dark horses that strained to get their burden in motion.

"Iggy!" I cried, "You can't leave, I need you…Iggy!"

Chapter 2

October Ninth: Gadwaddicking or Molly Hatchet Omen?

Early that Thursday morning, the sky was clear, the air coolish, and I needed to get moving. Forget worrying about Iggy and get focused.

My word-of-the-day calendar word for the day was:

gadwaddick: verb: (old English): go on a pleasure trip, wander.

Perhaps a nature walk would rejuvenate me. My Basset hound, Naughty Britches, NB for short, was still stretched out on the bed, head on a pillow.

"Let's go 'gadwaddicking' in Chastain-Seay and look for the bobcat," I suggested. Chastain-Seay, my favorite park is about eleven miles away in Worthington Springs.

NB opened an eye. I'm quite sure that "Chastain-Seay" is one of her vocabulary words. She seemed to be waiting for a signal that I was serious.

"Go for a walk?" I asked, picking up my keys. She leapt off the couch and bunny-hopped down the hall ahead of me.

I needed to see some wildlife. I needed a symbol, a totem,

a guide for the lost feeling closing in on me. Normally, we see a young alligator, a convention of turtles sunning themselves, some egrets or a heron. Once I'd seen a bobcat--a quick glimpse as it scampered silently across a log and disappeared up the opposite creek bank.

Coffee in one hand, leash and wallet in the other, I locked the house and we loaded into my F-150. Naughty Britches draped herself over the console, head up. I took a swig of coffee and clicked my seatbelt. We were off.

Chastain-Seay is a free, town-owned park on the Santa Fe River, in nearby Worthington Springs. One of my favorite parks in Florida, it features extensive boardwalks and nature trails, concrete picnic tables and a boat launch. Not well-known, this gem is all but deserted, even on weekends.

We had County Road 236 to ourselves and arrived at the empty park in good time. Naughty Britches bounded out, soon sniffing and marking her progress across the parking lot to the first boardwalk. The water level was low. There were gullies of sand where tributaries normally hosted water bugs and small fish. The logs usually occupied by turtles stuck out of dry earth. The woods were unnaturally silent in an ominous static.

We worked our way around to the frayed rope swing suspended over an eroding section along the river, near an overgrown picnic area with two concrete picnic tables and a perpetually burned spot in the ground speckled with broken glass shards. The metal garbage can, ripped from its chain mooring, was wedged in the river bottom. Its bulky broadside acted as a barrier island collecting floating grass, twigs and trash. One of the concrete benches seemed to have been the victim of a jackhammer demonstration. Broken bottles and paper trash were strewn about the whole picnic area.

Such a beautiful park; such a shame. I regarded the scene with dismay. I wished I had a trash bag with me; I'd clean up what I could, but I had nothing.

Naughty Britches worked her snout into a dirty Doritos bag. I pulled her away and hurried her from the scene. Was this a sign? Destruction? Waste? Was my meditation camp a lost cause? We were both panting from the humidity.

"Here's some water, girl," I said, pouring some water from a bottle into her travel water bowl. I finished the rest of the bottle as she slurped and dribbled her share.

I needed to cheer up. Keep driving. Where? Ah! We could visit my favorite nursery in Gainesville. Working with plants and dirt nourishes my earth-sign Virgo soul.

"Let's load up!" I said, lifting her into the crew cab. Soon we were turning south on County Road 121. I flipped on the radio.

The honeymoon with my F-150 is over. Eleven years and two-hundred-thousand miles since we drove off the sales lot, it suffers minor annoyances like sporadic loss of window power and no digital display on the radio. With no way to see what radio station is playing, I just "seek" until I find something I like.

Sort of sums up samsara, in a way. Seeking and avoiding.

Jackson Browne's voice called out to "Take It Easy." I sang along for a few lines, but it was too upbeat. I punched "seek" a few more times. James Taylor's smooth voice crooned "You Make It Easy" and I mashed the button hard. My former husband, Dillon and I used to slow dance to JT records late into the evening then fall into bed with slow kisses and long love making.

Scheisse. It's so jarring sometimes, the way a song can transport you in time. I sniffed and blinked back the tears that wanted to come unbidden. Seemed like we were barely married and then his ticket was punched by a ravaging cancer and I was single again and alone. I could feel a pity party starting in the grief room of my heart; the tables were being set up and crepe-black paper streamers were getting tacked to the walls.

Nope.

Not doing that.

A stray tear made its way down my cheek as I punched the radio through a political rant and a bunch of commercials. A peppy song on the classic rock station popped up. Oh yeah, I remember this, what is it? I never could catch the lyrics. My foot was tapping. Words flew by until we got to the chorus and I realized the song was called "Flirtin' With Disaster." I exhaled a nervous laugh hoping it wasn't a bad omen.

It's just a song, the Inner Critic grumbled.

I hoped so. But moments later, entering LaCrosse, I checked the gas gauge and decided I'd better stop. LaCrosse, Florida, is a tiny town with a post office, town hall, the remnant of a long-closed pizza joint, one gas station and one major intersection, County Road 235 coming in from the east.

Just shy of the intersection, I flipped my turn signal to make a left into the gas station. Call it instinct, a guardian angel, my fondness for Coachman RVs, or perhaps the roaring engine sound that made me hesitate. A Coachman Prism had approached the intersection towing a lemon-yellow Jeep, followed by a silver SUV towing a fishing boat with an oversized Mercury engine mounted on the stern. The driver of the Coachman had stopped at the light and begun to accelerate into a left turn, misgauging the speed of a vintage black car roaring toward us.

The north-bound, sixties-era Ford Thunderbird zoomed closer: bad-ass, glossy black with dark tinted windows and fat muscle car tires, like a demon car with diabolical intention.

The gravelly Molly Hatchet song bebopped along.

The Coachman lurched to a stop halfway across the northbound lane. The SUV behind it slammed on brakes, missing the lemon-yellow Jeep by a fingernail. The black bomb careened around the Coachman, swerved hard just in front of me, back tire bouncing up on the curb as it pitched into the gas station parking lot, and slid into the free spot next to the pump like an Indy 500 car hitting a pit stop.

Molly Hatchet was back to the chorus.

The Coachman edged forward again and completed the left turn, followed by the SUV trailing the boat. The road was clear again.

I smacked the button to shut off the radio and made my left turn but hung well back from the pump. The spot on the other side of the island was occupied. I was just as happy to wait, keep my distance, an eye on the lustrous Ford.

I've dated guys who were car buffs, and I've enjoyed car shows, gravitating towards farm trucks from the forties and fifties. This dark monster was souped up, the beast of muscle cars. One good roar of the engine and I felt it in my root chakra.

The passenger door opened, and a man's foot touched down on the concrete. Several beer cans rolled out, and something that looked like a homemade bong. Then the driver's door opened, and an attractive man with a full head of hair, hurried into the store.

The overweight, balding passenger hoisted himself out, tossed the bong-looking thing back into the car, and in doing so, revealed two inches of plumber's crack. He stumbled around the gas pump and picked up a nozzle. He fumbled with the car's gas cap, swiped his card, and began to pump gas. He shuffled from side to side like an elephant as he waited. His faded jeans had holes and stains; his T-shirt was wrinkled, giving the impression he'd been wearing the same outfit for several days.

Perched on the console, ears flared, head up, eyes focused, NB's lips parted ever so slightly to release a prolonged warning growl.

The driver emerged from the station with a supersize coffee, walking briskly.

He barked something to the passenger that sounded like either "Cool, man" or "Coal man" and "Let's roll!"

"But it's not full yet. The pump is slow," the passenger answered.

The driver's door slammed.

The passenger disengaged the nozzle and returned it to its cradle and flipped the gas door shut. The car growled to life as his derriere hit the seat. A cascade of detritus spilled out from the passenger's floorboard as he pulled his leg in. The force of the spin out closed the passenger door with a *wham!*

The Thunderbird rocketed off eastbound on 235, right in front of an oncoming farm truck loaded with pumpkins. The driver's arms locked on the steering wheel bracing for impact, eyes wide, mouth open as the muscle car blurred clear. Two medium-sized pumpkins tumbled off the truck and splattered *puh-KUSH! puh-KUSH!* on the pavement.

NB's ears were wide as semaphore flags.

I exhaled and blinked, wondering with unease if this wild episode wasn't the foreshadowing of a dark and menacing energy coming into my life.

I edged up to the vacated area beside the pump. As I filled the truck with gas, I glanced down at the rumpled candy wrapper, lottery tickets and pennies left by the passenger. There was something else just under my truck. I bent over for a better look. A filthy driver's license. I picked it up and flipped it over.

The name read Leroy Mackinsaw. Odd. That wasn't the name the driver had yelled. The photo was of a long-faced man in his twenties with short red hair. Not the driver or passenger. Had there been a third passenger in the back seat? Not my business. I decided I'd leave the card with the store clerk just in case the T-bird came back.

I had hoped to just pass the ID card to the cashier, but she was waiting on a large and loud woman with faded pink hair named **Brenda**, or at least I assumed it was her name as it was tattooed in large letters on her chest, framed by her bathing suit straps. She was putting away her debit card and shrieking at her daughter. "Put that down! Lord, child, you got the Devil in you. Get over here."

The sullen girl chucked a packet of peanuts back onto the shelf. Her scowl made me hope she wasn't pyrokinetic or we might see Brenda catch fire. She dragged her feet back to her mother's side as if she was fighting an undertoe. Brenda grabbed her purchases and the girl's arm. "Come on. I'm not havin' it. Not today."

I pressed myself up against the counter to get out of her way as she bulldozed the girl out of the store.

"Next," the cashier said in an I-can't-get-more-bored-than-this voice.

"Hi," I said, stepping forward, "I found this driver's license out by the pump. Thought I'd bring it in, just in case the person comes looking for it."

"Okay," the clerk said, taking it reluctantly. She didn't even look at it before she slid it into a drawer. Her half-lidded look and slumped shoulders suggested that I had just added one more straw to the endless pile that was breaking her.

You ever do something that you feel is virtuous but somehow it doesn't come with any reward, thanks or recognition? You feel deflated? I remember a girl in a prayer group back when I was church shopping. She described having to practice the piano for hours and hours. It was tedious. There was no one to clap when she played particularly well. But she knew, and God knew, and that was all that really mattered. Good karma to do a good deed with good intention regardless of the outcome. I had to let the let-down feeling go.

I was relieved to be back in the truck with NB. "You are one lucky little girl; do you know that?" I said kissing her head. Her tail spun wild figure eights behind her.

We drove into Gainesville and stopped at my favorite nursery. The staff is friendly and knowledgeable, the selection is terrific, and they love Naughty Britches. She and I browsed the display of orange and yellow mums in oversized pumpkin-shaped planters. They'd be perfect in front of the office and meditation hall all season into Thanksgiving.

The Muses of Decoration descended upon me. Soon I was picking out corn stalk bundles and pumpkins. NB was contemplating little gourds as potential chew toys when three little boys ran to her.

"Aww, a wiener dog!" The oldest child said.

"Well, sort of," I said. "This is a Basset. Dachshunds are usually the wiener dogs," I said.

"I love wiener dogs!" he said. "Mom, look-it!"

NB dutifully rolled over, so the children could pet her.

The bleary-eyed mom watched them with sleep-deprived attention. Her eyes roamed the scene as if in search of her pack of cigarettes.

"Does your dog do tricks?" another child asked.

I pointed. "The roll is it."

They seemed disappointed but patted her head and belly anyway.

"Come on, boys," she said.

NB was still on her back hoping for more petting.

"Okay, let's go, little girl," I said, "Uncle Max is waiting for us."

"Bye, wiener dog!"

As the sales assistant helped carry our purchases to the

truck, I heard the family behind us.

"Mommy, how come that dog didn't do tricks?"

"I don't know," she answered with the fatigue of a parent who has answered two-hundred questions by lunchtime.

I bungee-strapped my purchases in the truck bed as best I could I wondered why people needed pets to do tricks. Isn't it enough to have the pet as a loyal companion? It pains me to see pets with treats on their noses waiting for a signal that they may eat the treat. What is that about? On the surface, it's cute, I guess. But in reality, isn't it a power trip?

NB took her place on the console and soon we were back on the road. I looked forward to decorating.

For the first time that day, my spirits lifted.

Chapter 3

Crazy with Second Guessing

Instead of heading north, I gunned it across busy 43rd Street to duck into Fresh Fresh Foods for coffee. I left the engine running so NB had the air conditioning and trotted into the store. Passing the fancy candy section, I thought of Max, my friend and former owner of my meditation center, back when it was the Stinkin' Skunk Ape Fish Camp. Knowing his fondness for gummies, particularly the tart fruit wedges, I grabbed a couple bags, beelined for dark roast coffee and off to the checkout. I pulled out my cell phone and punched Max's number. He picked up on the fourth ring.

"Hey Haint. How're you?" he asked in a sleepy voice.

"Did I wake you?"

"Naah. Just dozing in front of the boob tube. Wazzup?"

"I'm on my way home and thought to stop by. I've got NB with me though, so you'd have to meet us outside. Are you up for company?"

"Honey, you are always welcome. I'll put some pants on and meet you outside. Cripes, it's probably cooler out there anyhow. They's somethin' wrong with the air, it's hotter than hell stewed down to a half pint in here, even with the fan goin'. When d'ya reckon ta be here?"

Scheisse. I should get him a cold drink then too, I thought. I gestured to Wendy, the checkout girl that I'd be right back, cradled the phone in my neck and told Max "about a half an hour" and began sprinting to the refrigerated drinks aisle.

"It'd be nice to have company, especially you," he said. "I might even shave."

"Don't go changin' to try to please me," I said, a bit out of breath, grabbing two large bottles of his favorite upscale, fizzy, orange drink.

Max added, "Hey, can you bring me some o' them gummy candies I like?"

"It might happen," I answered, sprinting back to Wendy. "See you soon."

"Are you jogging or something?"

"No, no," I said, panting. I set down the drinks on the conveyor belt and dug out my debit card. "All good. See you soon."

"Okay, Sweet Cakes," he said and hung up.

Card swiped, items bagged, I was out the door.

Naughty Britches was reclining on the console watching a flock of children walk by. I got in, received a wagging fanfare and, after a moment of deliberation, one lick on the nose.

Purchases stowed, seatbelt fastened and zoom, we were on the road again, heading north to the Old Oaks Retirement Home.

I was having hunger pangs and realized neither of us had had breakfast. I called the Latin café in Alachua and placed a take-out order, two breakfast sandwiches involving eggs, steak and Cuban bread, with an extra portion of steak for NB.

We were almost to the Old Oaks when my phone rang again.

"Hello, this is Haint."

"Haint? Sorry to bother you…this is Louise. I feel so stupid asking this, but…oh, crap, never mind."

"What, Hon?"

"I know you and Iggy are close and…I don't mean to seem like I'm checking up on him, but he's been really weird lately. Evasive. I thought we were good, but now I'm not sure. He says we are, but then he seems to be avoiding me. I'm going crazy with second guessing. We were supposed to meet at Joe's moon party last night, but he didn't show. He texted me later with a lame excuse. Is he dumping me? Be honest. Has he said anything to you?"

"Oh…"He was avoiding Louise too? Oh, not good.

"What? What is it?" She asked, dread in her voice.

"I was hoping *you* knew. I've only talked to his voice mail lately." I didn't want to tell her my nagging fears that maybe he had some health issue he wasn't telling us about. Freaky disease? AIDS? Cancer? I wiped those words from my mental movie screen and took a deep breath. "Whatever it is, he'll tell us when he's ready. He's not usually one to hold it all in."

She exhaled. "That helps…some. I got so paranoid last night at the party. There was a dark-haired man who kept staring at me. Then he and two others were whispering while watching me. I was sure they were talking about me. It was straight out of high school. It made me uncomfortable, so I left."

I tried to picture who she was talking about and mentally flipped through my rolodex of Joe's friends. "Did you happen to catch a name?"

"It was some animal… Beaver? No. Badger? Does that sound right? The music was kind of loud, I may be mistaken."

"Oh, it's Badger," I said, hoping to strain the dislike from my voice. Badger was Running Deer's older brother, a sullen and edgy man with advanced martial arts skills. Like Running Deer, he tended to move around every few years. Unlike Running Deer, he had the energetic signature of a storm cloud. I felt easier when he was gone on a walkabout or whatever it was that he did, disappearing for a long stretch and then showing up again like a lint-covered sock creeping out from under the dryer. I always hoped he wouldn't find his way back to Catfish, but evidently, he had.

Joe maintained a paternal friendship with Badger that hinged on an incident from years ago when Badger had gotten himself in with the wrong crowd and Joe rescued him.

I didn't want to worry Louise and was at a loss for what to say.

"Hello?" she asked. "You still there?"

"Yeah, sorry. Yes, Badger. He's a…friend of Joe's." I didn't want to tell her he was Iggy's ex-girlfriend's dark-shadow brother. "He's been out of town for a while. He probably just heard about you and Iggy and was checking you out, that's all." I tried to sound breezy, but I was sure she saw through it.

"Well, maybe. But it wasn't pleasant."

"Yeah, well, he wears morose like some men wear Old Spice. Look, I've arrived at my destination, so I need to sign off. Try not to worry. I'm sure whatever is up with Iggy is not anything about you. I know for a fact that he really likes you."

Mercy and Mickey Rooney, this *did* sound so high school. *Just stop talking!*

"Okay, I guess. Sorry to be such a ninny," Louise said.

"No, you're not being a ninny. I'm sure he'll break his silence soon and we'll have a good laugh about it."

No, I'm not. I think he's got leukemia, needs me as a donor and is afraid to ask. Or he has developed a serious gambling problem he is ashamed of, and now owes gobs of money to a thug named Ox… Stop!

"Oh, I hope so. Would you…ask him to call me if you hear from him?"

"You bet." I hung up, parked, and turned off the engine.

I knew that worrying and second guessing was a waste of time. But knowing that Iggy wasn't talking to Louise amped up my worry. Why was he avoiding her too?

I had to talk to Iggy.

Max, The Trickster

As promised, Max was waiting for us at a picnic table outside in an area adjacent to the nursing home that looked like a parking garage with seating and ceiling fans. There were a few potted plants to offset the otherwise impersonal, concrete atmosphere. Nothing could break, blow away or tip over here; it could be kept clean with a garden hose.

Max's white hair was combed, his face looked smooth and

I caught a whiff of aftershave. He was wearing long tan cargo pants and a loose-fitting cotton shirt. Even spiffed up, he looked older and more vulnerable than I wanted to acknowledge. Since his wife Charlene passed away almost four years ago, he seemed to be on an aging fast track that made me heartsick. *Be in the moment,* I told myself. *It is what it is. He's still here, feisty and able to shave. Be glad.* I waved and dropped NB's leash so she could run to him. She did, launching herself at his lap, planting her front paws on his leg so he could pet her head.

"Hey you two," Max said, eyes bright. "Thanks for coming by."

He eyed the to-go bag as I set it on the table. I fished out a foam container and set it in front of him then pulled out the fizzy drinks and handed him one.

"You are a blessed angel," Max said opening his box. "Honey, pardon my French, but I'm so hungry I could eat the ass end of a rag doll. I can't eat the slop they call food here." He took a huge bite of his sandwich, closed his eyes and moaned. "Mm-mmm!"

The Buddhists advocate that one of the best things you can do to bring joy to your life, is to do something beneficial for others. Watching Max enjoy his food made me happy. I enjoyed my sandwich too, passing some meaty bits to NB that she chomped down.

"Hope you're okay with sitting outside. They won't let dogs in the cafeteria unless they're licensed and bonded support dogs. And cripes, after being cooped up in there all the time, even this heat is worth the fresh air and sunshine."

"It's not so bad with the fans," I said, though my bra was

sticking to me and I felt beads of sweat sprinting toward my waist from somewhere around my bra line. I reminded myself that *I chose* to live in Florida, land of humidity in October.

"Honey, what's wrong? There's a look in your eyes like you've been funeral hoppin'. When was the last time you kicked up your heels and had some fun, or just laughed yourself off the couch, eh?" He pointed his orange drink at me. "Get yo'self laid! Go dancin'! Road trip somewhere and blow the funk off ya, for cripes sakes."

I chewed my breakfast sandwich and pondered. Yeah. When *was* the last time I got a little wild? I couldn't remember. The retreat had sucked the fun out of me for longer than I wanted to think about. "Well, fixing up the camp took a lot—"

"Bull crap!"

"The retreat's soft opening was a debacle and business has turned up its toes since then."

This was a slight exaggeration. Truthfully, I'd had a few bookings to keep me from despair. A Girl Scout troop from Jacksonville booked a weekend to work on outdoor merit badges. Turned out the troop leader hadn't heard about the murders and had picked Blue's Lotus Lodge as an opportunity to sneak away and visit an old boyfriend in High Springs. A scuba group had booked for a week and had offered scuba certification with day trips to several of the springs in the area. A group of retirees staged a mahjong tournament over a few days. But none of these groups requested yoga, tai chi or meditation instruction; they just rented the compact cabins. I wasn't exactly raking in the bucks.

"Hogwash! You don't need to spend a fortune to gussy up

and have a night out! Cripes, Charlene and I used to have fun just joy ridin' to Bell for the livestock auction, even though we weren't buying nothin'. She liked seeing all the animals. She did talk me into getting ducks...you remember when we had ducks?"

Vaguely. I was thinking one would have to be mighty bored to joy ride to Bell, Florida. I couldn't recall if they even had a traffic light in Bell.

Frail retirement home Max had vanished, and feisty, bossy Max was in full throttle which both pleased and annoyed me. Even though he was absolutely right, I wasn't feeling receptive to his admonishing. But then, as if he'd remembered something, his tone shifted, and that naughty gleam came to his eyes.

He fished in his pocket and pulled out a roll of bills. "Here." He thrust the wad at me. "Get yourself a pedicure and a new dress. Go on, take it."

I pushed his hand away, but he insisted. "Promise me. I want you to spend it on yourself."

"Max, it's not like I have anyone to get glammed up for..." I glanced at Naughty Britches who wagged, nosing at a bit of Cuban bread left in my to-go container. "She doesn't care what I look like or what I'm wearing."

His eyes still twinkled. "Just do it, okay, Honey? Trust me."

"Max, you remember the old line from Phyllis Diller? She said she wasn't sure she'd know when the right one came along, but then she didn't have to choose because only one came. I had the one. We were happy. He died on me. I just haven't met anyone that—"

"Hush up now, just do it. You're beginning to piss me off." Max scowled like he meant it, too.

I half-heartedly said that I would and pocketed the bundle. In return, I passed him the bags of gummies. He did a seated dance of joy and blew me a kiss while he ripped into the fruit slices. He popped two in his mouth. The effort of chewing and extreme sourness of the candy soon distorted his face in a comical display of stretching, chomping, blinking and puckering. He coughed a few times and rasped, "God I love these things." He coughed again. "Thanks, Honey."

We packed up our trash, finished our drinks and said our goodbyes. As an afterthought, I wondered if he'd see Iggy.

"Hey Max, has Iggy been in touch lately?"

"Oh, let's see now," he blinked and coughed again. "No, come to think on it, I reckon it's been a while. Why, is he all right?"

"I don't know. He's been avoiding my calls."

Max shrugged. "I'm sure he'll sort it out."

"Sort what out?" I asked.

"Oh, ah…whatever it is." He waved a dismissive hand in the air, looking away. Bassets and Bulldogs! Once again, he seemed to be withholding information, and like an oyster with a pearl, was not about to give it up without a fight.

"Did you know that Badger is back in town?"

This time, his head swiveled, and he looked me in the eye. "Is that so? Hmph."

"That's it? Just hmph?"

Max started to speak then shook his head, his lips tight. He patted NB goodbye and turned toward the sliding glass door. Over his shoulder he hollered, "When you come next time, I want to see you in that new dress."

I tried calling Iggy on the way home. It went straight to a message that his voicemail box was full. I texted him when I got home and got a response about an hour later, "Just busy. Will call you soon."

That evening, I drove over to his house to find his truck was gone. I scribbled a note and tacked it to his door:

Ig!
What's going on?
Are you dying of cancer
or on the lam?
Worried. Call me.
Love you.
-H

Chapter 4

Friday October 10: Answered Prayers like Ketchup from the Bottle--First Nothing, Then the Big Splut!

I'm not super-savvy about astrology, but a planet must have moved out of retrograde or a cosmic defibrillator had been applied to my lifeless phone. The calls came in a wave…and there was the letter. I'll get to that.

I had just let Naughty Britches out back when my best friend, Lorraine called with good news.

"Hey, Haint. How are things?"

"You know. Could be better, could be worse. You?"

"Same. Listen, thought I'd give you a heads up. Aunt Moira called this morning. She's got a Wiccan group looking for a place near Gainesville for a Samhain celebration. She gave this woman named Vida your number…she should be calling you. She's interested in access to the river and your meditation circle."

"That's great. Is Aunt Moira coming too?"

"Don't know. You know how she is."

"Right."

"Gotta go. Got a new dog sitting job this week. Seven Chihuahuas. The female, Lulabelle is pregnant, ready to drop puppies anytime."

"Better you than me."

"Ha!" she said and hung up.

I love Lorraine. She's practical, unsentimental and a straight shooter. We've been close friends since we met at a cocktail party about eight years ago. She's younger than I am, spunkier and wise for thirty-five. Usually. And good with animals. I'd probably help her hide a dead body if need be, but no way I'd take on a houseful of Chihuahuas.

Her Aunt Moira kind of scares me. She's attractive, friendly, very easy to like, and a professional psychic. The few times I've been around her, she's had a habit of looking me in the eyes and then examining my hairline. The first time she did it I thought she was looking for head lice, she was so focused.

"She's studying your aura," Lorraine had said.

Somehow that made me feel only marginally better.

She cocked her head, squinted, nodded and ended her examination with a curious "interesting."

"What?" I'd asked.

"Oh, just…" and a shrug was her response.

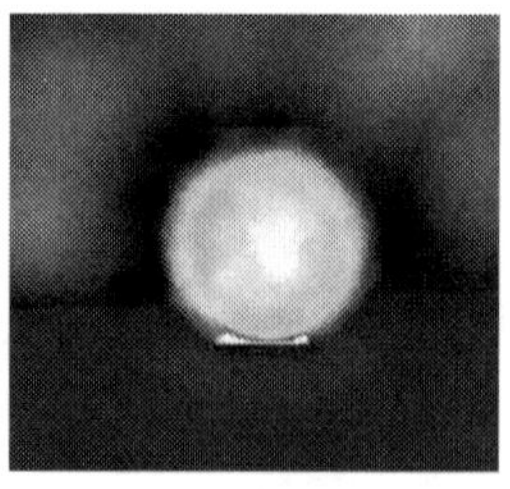

As promised, Vida called me later that day.

"Hello? Is this Blues Lotus Lodge?" a woman with a moneyed-Mississippi drawl asked.

"Yes. Haint speaking. How may I help you?"

"Moira Redding suggested I call you. My name is Vida Glossimer, I'm the leader of a ladies' group—Wiccans, actually. Your website doesn't have photos of your meditation circle, but Moira says that you have one. Is that correct?"

"Yes."

"Are you all in woods, and do you have a view of the moon at night?"

"Limited view from the circle or the dock."

"Fine. You're on the same road as Blondene's Beauty Barn aren't you, just farther down past the cemetery? On Snapping Cooter?"

"Yes, but there's a culvert that caved in and a detour. You can't come from Catfish, you have to go out to Route 27 and turn in on Night Swamp Glen, then turn right on Cooter."

The culvert had collapsed just before the opening of my retreat. Since the initial flurry of activity of barricades and machinery, I'd seen no actual repair work.

"Glad you told me. I'd like to come meet you and have a tour if you don't mind. If we find the property suits our needs, we'll want a reservation for five, with exclusive access to the circle. We'd like to come Thursday October 30th through Sunday November 2nd. Would that be a problem?"

Vida was clearly a woman who knew what she wanted and with that luxurious, Tupelo-honey voice, she probably got what she wanted often. We arranged to meet the following afternoon.

About to turn the phone off, I noticed a voice message from Iggy, "Hey Sis, sorry to worry you. I'm not in jail or dying. There was a heavy sigh. "There's just…a problem. I'll tell you soon. Promise."

Shimatta!♥ Missed him again! I was relieved he was not in crisis but annoyed at his reticence. I reminded myself that anger was based on fear, so what was my fear? I wasn't sure. I felt my psyche squirming as I thought this through. Iggy was under no obligation to tell me a darned thing, but we were close and always shared our innermost problems. So, the issue was that a) I was worried about him. He claimed he was fine. What then? I resented that he was holding back. Ah! b) my ego was hurt. And the antidote for this would be…patience, allowing him to be himself and share or not, as he chose. And to send him love and clarity to resolve his issues.

That evening I moved Mischief off of my meditation cushion and realized it had been a few weeks since *my* tush had occupied the cat-hair-covered seat. I balled up the worst of the fuzz and threw it out, then lit some candles and incense, sat down, and focused my thoughts on universal compassion and sending love to Iggy. While holding the visual image of my heart radiating out loving pink light, I also imagined a phone cord stretching out from my head to Iggy. *Call me. Talk to me. What's going on?*

♥ Japanese: Damn!

Saturday October 11, More Ketchup

I popped into the High Springs branch of the Alachua County library. An old man sat in a chair reading the paper, and I heard voices from the children's section, but otherwise the library seemed empty. I browsed for a half an hour, deciding on some CDs of cello music and a DVD of *Dancing Lady*, a 1933 film with Joan Crawford and Fred Astaire. As I approached the checkout desk with my selections, Prudence Blackwell, the branch manager greeted me.

"Haint! How are you?" She was wearing a light blue sweater with a giant cat face across her chest. Tall and on the rotund side, Prudence's adoration of cats clearly trumped fashion sense as on her frame, the cat stretched fat and saucer-eyed.

"Oh fine. You?" I answered, setting my materials down on the desk and fishing for my library card.

"I've been meaning to contact you, but I've been so busy. Listen, I've joined a group of women in a weight loss club called Take It Off, and we were thinking about having a getaway weekend. Of course, our first choice would be the Biggest Loser resort getaway on Amelia Island—they have golf, swimming pools, tennis, personal trainers…"

Oh boy.

Her face sagged, looking dejected. "That would be so great, but most of us can't afford it, unfortunately. Then we were going to go to Camp Laquacoo—that's local of course. That was our next choice, but they're booked solid." She sighed and slumped her shoulders.

Wow. Next, she'll say "And you're not too freaky looking for an albino," the Inner Critic said. How many times had I heard that one?

Steady. Patience.

"The only time most of us are available is the last weekend of October. I'd hoped for the weekend before, so it wouldn't conflict with the church Harvest Festival, but well, thankfully I'm not on the committee this year, so as long as I can be there on Sunday, it'll be fine." She paused for breath and lowered her voice. "Frankly, I'm a little relieved too. I'm doing a booth at the downtown Fall Festival first weekend in November and I'm a little behind on my afghans. I've got some darling designs in orange and blue for Gator fans." She fingered her gold cross necklace. "Anyway, someone suggested that your place was probably available since you haven't had much business since the uh, ...well, the tragedies...what with it being all in the paper. Such a shock to happen near this little town." Her fingers tightened around the cross.

I closed my eyes, grateful there wasn't an audience to appreciate this broadcast of my misfortune. *She didn't mean anything by it. Be kind. Just listen.* I opened my eyes.

"...they suggested that we might have it at your place since you offer yoga sessions, right? We'd like to try that." She beamed for a moment, then added, "None of that meditation stuff though. We're Christians."

"Of course. Is that for Friday through Sunday?"

"No, we'd like to arrive Thursday night to get settled. That way we have all day Friday and Saturday and part of Sunday. Of course, I won't be there Sunday. I'll be at church."

"Great!" I said and pulled out my phone to add Take It Off to my October calendar.

She narrowed her eyes at me.

"I mean, great about the booking," I said. She must have thought I meant great she wouldn't be there on Sunday. This made me nervous and a bit clumsy. I only got the phone for my business, and I was still learning how to use the features. It looked like I had entered it correctly. I'd get it on my paper calendar later. I'm hopelessly old school and rely on Lorraine for tech help.

"Do you have a weight room?"

"No, I don't, sorry. Is that a problem?"

"No," she said, though I could see she was disappointed. "I think Serena is bringing a personal trainer from her gym who is going to help us with an exercise program. His name is Javiar--she says he's really hot. You know, to be honest, I'm not sure I want to work out with some hot Latino trainer feeling sorry for us middle-aged old things. Of course, Serena doesn't care, she's probably sleeping with him—Oh! I shouldn't gossip like that..."

"Do you want all meals?" I asked.

"What?" She gave me an irritated, how-dumb-are-you look. "Yes--breakfast, lunch and dinner." She said this slowly as if English was not my native language.

"And what kind of diet are you following?"

"Paleo."

I wasn't familiar with it, but I'd do some research. "Do you know how many people yet?" I crossed my fingers hoping for at least eight, enough to fill a bunk house.

"Well let's see." She counted on her fingers, "Me, Serena Hot-to-Trot, Maggie Beth, probably Annie Woddell, and possibly Belinda Wheeler, so that's five."

Hmm. Not a bunk house. Family cabin. Still a booking that sounded firm. "You can book it online if you like, we've got our website up and running. Sounds like you'll want a family size cabin; they're for four to six people. They're close together but with slightly different décor. You can pick which cabin you want when you book it."

Another library patron carrying a pile of DVDs stepped up behind me and sighed heavily.

"Good to see you, Prudence," I said, moving aside. "Looking forward to hosting your group."

"Bye, Haint. Take care."

I was about to leave but then thought, wait a minute, maybe they've got a Paleo cookbook or two. I circled back to the computer and did a search. I was in luck; they had quite a few including one for preparing paleo meals in a slow cooker. Jackpot! I found the cookbook section and soon was back in line with four more books.

With relief, I noted that Prudence was helping another patron, so Joanne helped me check out. This meant Prudence wouldn't know that I was doing homework on the paleo diet and I didn't have to admit that I wasn't familiar it. I sensed my vanity puffing out with satisfaction like a preening cockatoo. Why was I being like that?

The cockatoo faded away as my Inner Critic spoke up. *It's your ego, dear. You don't want to give her the upper hand. You are afraid she'll think less of you. Tsk. Tsk. All you had to do was say you were looking for ideas.*

Yeah. I know.

As I walked to my car, my mind replayed her guest list. I wondered if she'd said Serena Hot-to-Trot on purpose or if she'd slipped. Serena's real last name was Lippincott, but she earned her nickname after her fourth marriage to a snowbird from New York City who sported a Rolex and chauffeured her around in a Maserati. The first time Iggy saw it, he asked Lou Lippincott about it. Serena snuggled into Lou's arm and said, "Don't you *love* the color? It's called *Blu Passione*. Isn't that *romantic*?"

When Ig related the encounter to me, I ran a showroom hostess hand over a streak of dried mud on my ten-year old F-150 and cooed, "It's *Lime rock Passione*. Isn't it *sexy*?"

I like Serena; she fascinates me. She's loud, dramatic and pouts a lot to get her way, but she's also got a good sense of humor. To her, life is like a cruise buffet and she's going to sample everything. She flaunts fake boobs, readily greeting the world tits out. A smoker since her teens, she has a husky late-night radio voice that, combined with the perfect pout, can get her anything she wants. She's a cougar and a sorceress in animal print sandals.

I hoped Maggie Beth Burgess would join them. Maggie Beth reminded me a lot of the comedian Melissa McCarthy: a lively woman, always laughing or giggling. She was built like a Highland games weight-tosser yet was flexible and nimble, always the first to jump out on a dance floor and rock the house. She elevated any gathering. I didn't think I knew the other two women, but the name Wheeler rang a bell.

Modern Conveniences

Late Saturday afternoon found me in my laundry room cussing at my new washing machine.

This was my second washer in two years; the replacement for a machine with no agitator that was supposed to wash clothes with the latest and greatest technology while saving water. Great. The latest and greatest technology feature of this machine, a marvel really, was that no matter how you loaded the clothes or sheets or towels into the machine, they would be swept up and molded into a giant mushroom. I twisted my back something awful trying to pull the wet mushroom up out of this machine. So, I wasn't entirely pissed off when this modern wonder needed replacing when the house got hit by lightning. All my major electronics got wiped out, including the mushroom maker. I called Smashing Appliances, our local appliance shop run by an ex-pat Brit named Conor Reid, to find out about getting it repaired.

"Well, it'll cost you $200 to have a serviceman come out and tap the first mother board. This'll tell you if the second mother board is fried or not. If the second mother board is fried, it'll cost you $650 for a new mother board. Plus labor. And then there's still the possibility that other components got fried, and it still won't work, even with the new mother board."

"That's ridiculous! The machine only cost me $475 to begin with."

"Yes, I know, Love."

"But I got the limited warranty."

"Yes, I know, Love."

I trekked down to Smashing Appliances and explained to Mr. Reid that I wanted a simple, mechanical, no mother-board-involved, old-fashioned, agitating machine.

"Follow me," he said, and we walked down the washer aisle. "I know just the one."

"*The* one?"

"Yes. They don't make them anymore. They've gone out of style. They all have computers. If you get an app, you can control your washing machine with your phone."

"Why would I want to do that?"

"Most appliances are getting this feature."

"But I can do the laundry by myself when I'm at home. Why do I need my phone to run the washer?"

"You could start a load remotely. From the grocery store, or from your car, say, on the way home."

"But if I'm in the grocery store, I'm shopping for groceries, and if I'm in my car, I'm focusing on driving.

"But you could, if you wanted to."

"I don't want appliances running when I'm not home. What if the washer malfunctions and overfills?"

He shrugged. "I'm just telling you the special features, Love."

I arranged to have the new one installed and the old one carted away to the graveyard of unwanted machinery.

This new model was touted as a great energy and water saver. Does anyone actually test machines anymore before they put them on the market? I doubt it.

To be fair, this machine cleans clothes, but I don't know

how, as it never seems to have water in it. The wash tub is not level. In the first spin cycle, the contents are heaved over to one side of the tub, wadded up and knotted together. The machine lurches and heaves like a bronc at the rodeo, slamming into the dryer, bucking away from the wall like it wants to hump my hot water heater. To piss me off further, there's a safety mechanism. I can stop the cycle but have to wait a whole minute for the lid to release so I can unsnarl it for the next rodeo event.

I've named this gift from sadistic engineers Patience. Well aware that screaming and yelling at a machine is irrational and a sign of an unsettled mind, it helps to tell myself that if I can master my anger and frustration with Patience, I will advance forward along the path to perpetually happy mind. If there were a Buddhist version of Monopoly, say, I'd pull the Community Chest card that said, "Advance to go and collect extra karmic merit."

Some days, I fail. Jaw clenched, spitting tacks, I wrestled with a thick macramé twist of pajama bottoms and sleeves stretched to twice normal length. I felt like one of those guys in the reality shows pulling a snake out from under a mobile home. My phone chirped in the other room. It was the melody I'd set up for the retreat.

A booking perhaps!

Making a Reservation or a Date?

I released the pajama anaconda to find the phone.

"Hello? Haint's Lotus Lodge Retreat," I answered, forcing myself to sound breezy and pleasant despite my tense jaw. "How can I help you?"

A dreamy male drawl began, "Howdy! Ms. Blue? Buster Shadetree here, from the Southern Cryptozoology Society." With his accent, "cryptozoology" rolled out sounding like it had double the syllables and was in his mouth like a candy gobstopper. "We spoke a coupla weeks ago 'bout a reservation for a cabin. Figure we'll be up your way on the twenty-fifth and stay round 'bout a week, mebbe more. Kinda depends. Mightcha got one o' them small cabins available for three guys?"

Wow. This guy had a whopper of an accent but with one of those voices like Sam Elliott or Matthew McConaughey that I could listen to all day long.

"Not a problem," I said.

He exhaled as if he was relieved. "That's set then. Lookin' forward to it. And to meetin' you."

Huh? My insides did a flip. I remembered that Max, as the former owner of my retreat knew Buster. Had they talked about me?

"You too," I said, not at all sure if I meant it.

"Lemme give you m' number," he said in a way that sounded more like a date than a reservation. I scrambled to find a pen and a paper scrap to write it down on just in case it wasn't the number he was calling from. He rattled it off. Each number had multiple syllables, as for example, three was "tha-raye"and five was 'fi-yeve".

"Got it. And do you have an email address?"

"I sure do. Are you ready?" he asked in a provocative way.

Ready for what? Oh yeah, his email.

I swallowed.

"Capital B, capital D, lowercase a-z-z-l-e-r at g-b-s-b-i-z dot com."

"BDazzler?"I repeated with a laugh. What an ego on this guy!

"'at's right," he drawled. "At g-b-s biz-dot-com."

"Got it."

"Good." He managed to draw "good" out in a way that made me want to put on red lipstick. I thought he was going to ask about payment. Maybe he was digging out a credit card.

I opened my mouth to say "you can register online" but he cut me off.

"Say, you like Creole or Cajun food?"

"What? Yeah sure, I guess."

"I mean, you okay with spicy food?"

"Sure, why?"

"Hmm-mm." His voice charged up my lower chakras. The way he said the simple "hmm-mm" implied that I'd said the right thing. Passed the test. "Just checkin'. See you in a week, Ms. Blue." Then he hung up.

What was that? I hung up the phone feeling all high-school tingly. Had we just confirmed a reservation or made a date?

I went back to untangling the heap in the washer. I

fantasized just pulling out a huge knife and hacking it out.

A long-buried memory of a painting bubbled to the surface. A studly hero in royal red holding a sword over a wagon wheel and a prophecy that the one who could undo the knot holding the cart wheel would be the next ruler. Alexander the Great didn't waste time, as I was doing, picking at the knot. He whacked it with his mighty sword and cut it off. In the painting, Alexander looked magnificent--wise and regal surrounded by bowing townsfolk.

My Inner Critic mumbled, Yes, l*ike the Gordion knot*♥,.b*ut in this case, that would be stupid; you'd hack up your clothes.*

Naughty Britches appeared in the doorway. She looked upon me with disapproval that my attention was diverted from her. Mischief wandered up to her, pushing his head into her shoulder. She wagged and licked his head. He popped up on his hind legs and cuffed her around the neck with his front paws in a quick hug and scampered away. NB turned back to me and sauntered out of the room.

I calmed down and returned to the washer. I treated the snarly mess like a meditation in patience. Tugging and pulling a little at a time, I got the wad separated from the agitator. Rolling and twisting the heap helped loosen it up. With much effort, I finally got it all apart and arranged the garments back in the washer for round two: the final rinse.

♥ Refers to situation that appears impossible from one angle but a simple solution from another. Comes from the legend of Alexander the Great as explained in following paragraph.

Crunching sounds from the kitchen. I rounded the corner to find a NB's hind legs and tail sticking out of the cat food bag. She was walking and eating, pushing the bag across the floor as she ate.

"Little girl!" I yelled and spanked her butt. Naughty Britches backed out of the bag and wagged. Her expression was "Well, it was on the floor and you were busy, so I helped myself."

I snatched the bag up, put a clip on it and set it back where it belonged. She trotted out to the living room. I could see her over the counter. She threw herself on the floor to rub her back. All four feet took swipes at the air as she waggled and growled with pleasure. Ha ha! Pulled one over on Mommy, her dance seemed to say.

Chapter 5

Vida

Vida was punctual to the minute. I wasn't sure what I expected when I saw the silver Honda Civic hybrid pull into the parking lot. Not knowing much about Wiccans, I'd tended to clump them in with empaths, astrologers and psychics—a mistake, I know, but I didn't really know any Wiccans. I knew that like Toaists or Celts, they had a focus on nature and the changing of the seasons that I could appreciate.

Lorraine's psychic aunt Moira is flamboyant, dramatic and unpredictable. I'll confess I was expecting the head of a Wiccan group to be adorned in scarab necklaces and pentacles, perhaps with a prominent nose, hawkish eyes and a flowing muumuu.

Vida Glossimer was in her sixties, dressed in a fashionable cotton pantsuit. She had thick curly hair and a trim figure on the thin side. The only hint of the mystical was the raven-headed cane that she set on the driveway for support before getting out of the car. She put the shoulder strap of a bag over her arm, shifted her weight and stood.

"Mrs. Glossimer? I'm Haint Blue. Please to meet you," I

said, offering my hand when she was stable.

"Please, call me Vida. I wish you'd mentioned that Night Swamp was a dirt road. Tore up my little car!"

"I know, I'm so sorry. It doesn't look like they'll get to fixing that culvert any time soon. Every time I check on the progress, I find a guy with yellow teeth napping in his truck. 'We're workin' on it, ' he says. Drives me nuts."

Vida swept her hair back over her shoulder as if she were dismissing all of our problems. "I can imagine. Well, thank you for meeting with me. Moira said you'd had some trouble here recently. Hope all is well now?"

"I hope so too."

Vida pivoted slowly, looking around at the cabins, the river, the office, and Arnie, the concrete Skunk Ape statue leftover from the fish camp era. Arnie was holding a rustic "welcome" sign.

"Who's this?" she asked with a chuckle.

"Arnie. The last owner named the place The Skunk Ape Fish Camp. Arnie is so retro, old Florida, I had to keep him. It'd be better if he were sitting in a meditation pose, but he is what he is."

"Oh, I'd keep him too," she said. "He's tacky, sure, but makes me nostalgic for the old days. He's a perfect greeter." She set her cane as if readying for a mountain hike. "I'm ready for the tour and eager to see the meditation circle."

"Sure! Let's go," I said, leading the way. "The retreat has nine cabins along the bend in the river here. The first three are eco/honeymoon suites designed for two to three people; the next three are family-style for up to six people; the last three towards the entrance are bunkhouses able to accommodate up to eight people each. I thought for your party of five, you'd like the family-style cabin. It has room for up to six, with a small kitchenette and sitting area. Unfortunately, none of the cabins have bathrooms, but there are two pavilions with toilets and showers." I gestured to both.

Vida's face fell. I glanced at her cane, hoping the bathroom situation wasn't a deal-breaker.

Whether she saw my glance, or read my thoughts, she said, "Sorry to be so slow. I had a knee replacement a few months ago. I hoped I'd be back to normal by now, but I still have some swelling, and feel safer using the cane."

As we approached the porch of cabin four, a rabbit darted from under the steps, ran a safe distance away, stopped, stood on its hind legs and sniffed, then hopped behind a log.

"Rabbit. That's auspicious," Vida said. "Rabbits are a good sign for fertility. The obvious meaning relates to sex, of course, but can also be about fertility in planning a project."

Maybe that would sway her to make the reservation.

Vida took the step up to the porch and looked at the two rockers and a small table with a throw rug. She pointed with her cane. "Cozy. Nice touch."

I held the door for her, and we went inside. "As you can see, the kitchenette has a microwave, coffee maker, refrigerator, toaster, and stove. Stocked with cups, plates, pots and pans. You have the option of bringing in all your own food; we do have delivery from a few places in Catfish Springs or I can provide meals. I'll give you a brochure of our options."

Vida eased down on one of the beds and moved into a lying

position. "Hmm. Comfortable. And I *love* these beautiful quilts." She rolled to her side, supporting her head with her hand. She looked like she was posing for a pin-up photo for the over-fifty crowd. "Do you quilt?" she asked, tracing the pattern with a hand.

"No, I wish I had the talent or patience! My best friend Lorraine made these."

"It adds a very homey touch." She eased back to a sitting position. "Oh, I hate to have to get up, but let's see the circle."

We made our way to the office. Vida's breathing was getting louder, and her hesitations lengthier.

"May I offer you a lemonade? I have some in my fridge. It's a bit of a walk to get to the circle."

"Lovely, dear." She took a wide stance and leaned back, stretching her back. I trotted into the office, grabbed some drinks and a retreat brochure. Back outside, I offered Vida a lemonade, and showed her the site map.

"We're here at the office, and the circle is back that way. The path wanders a bit to get there, but it's shady. Will you be able to walk that far and back?"

"Oh yes, don't worry about me." Vida gestured with her lemonade at the pumpkin planters on either side of the office. "Very tasteful. Love the pumpkins. And mums are a symbol of joy. We use them in our practice. Excellent choice."

I cocked my head, remembering an *ikebana,* or flower arranging class from long ago. "In Japan, they represent the sun, and the opening petals represent perfection. They can be used as objects of meditation, just like the lotus."

"Is that so? Interesting. I've heard that a single flower petal flower placed at the bottom of a wine glass will promote a long and healthy life."

"I'll definitely try that!"

I was warming to this woman and hoped she'd decide to book with me, not just for the money, but I hoped for another opportunity to spend time with her.

Talk of colors and symbolism reminded me of the black car and the ominous feeling I'd had about it.

I asked, "What does the color black mean to you?"

She swallowed some lemonade, lowered her bottle and studied me. "In what context?"

"Oh, I had an encounter with a black muscle car recently. It gave me the weirdest sense of foreboding."

"Well, for starters, Westerners believe black is bad and a sign of death. It certainly can be, but that's just one aspect. In Wiccan culture, it is a powerful color for change, protection and deeper consciousness. We often light a black candle to enhance the intention of a prayer. I'd say, if a fast moving sleek-black vehicle got your attention, then perhaps there is a big change coming for you. What kind of car was it?"

"A mint-condition, classic T-bird from the sixties."

Her gaze shifted from my face to my aura, her eyes moving slowly over my head then back to my face. "A Thunderbird? Interesting." Her eyes wandered off as if trying to dredge up a memory.

"What?"

"Well, it's probably nothing at all, but the Thunderbird sits at the top of the totem pole. Connects heaven and earth, life and death. It's *extremely* powerful, all the other animals in creation bow down to it. It is the creator of storms—thunder by flapping its wings and lightning that shoots from its eyes. Representative of an indomitable spirit, determination. Sometimes even the harbinger of war."

"Oh, *merde, alors*,"♥ I mumbled.

Vida continued. "As a sky creature, a vehicle of wind, it has dominion over earth. I seem to recall the Thunderbird in an epic battle with a snake…something like that. Sorry, I don't remember the details anymore. It's been a while since I've been out west."

The Thunderbird killed snakes? The snake was my major totem animal. That didn't sound good.

Vida's eyes inspected the top of my head again; I assumed she was checking my aura. Her features softened with apparent approval.

"Don't fret. Something is coming," her eyes roamed my head again. "A shift. You'll be fine."

I winced. Now she did remind me of Lorraine's psychic Aunt Moira, who sprinkled cryptic hints about future events and then disappeared.

"Please don't be cryptic and mysterious. Please tell me." I touched her arm like a pleading child.

"Listen, Sweetheart, I'm not a psychic. I can't see details, but I do have a sense that you've been in a rut lately, and that's about to change. Like a powerful wind is gonna blow the

---

♥ French for "shit then!"

stagnation right out of you."

"*Rut*? What rut? I went out on a limb and bought this retreat and have worked like a dog—"

"Yes, yes," she patted my hand and moved away from me. "But that's not it. You have expanded your career horizons...this is more about...personal growth, dear."

We had just reached the corner of the building when I heard a familiar rumble on the driveway. Patriotic Pete, the mailman waved from his Jeep, pulled up beside us and idled. He's a little guy with wild white hair usually in a patriotic bandana and matching star-spangled gym clothes.

"Hey Haint!" He shouted, stepping out of the truck. Tipping an imaginary hat towards Vida, "Ma'am." He held my bundle of mail upright with both hands like a bouquet of flowers. "Sorry so late today. Them damn Chihuahuas over ta Mrs. Collins charged out from around the shed and liked ta've gnawed my ankles to the bones."

"Oh my," said Vida.

I thought of Lorraine and her new dog sitting job. I prayed it wasn't the same mob of dogs, but Catfish is a small town. How many packs of Chihuahuas could there be?

Pete handed me a bundle of mail bound with an elastic band then yanked up his pant legs to show wide bandages around his ankles. "Tore me up six ways to Sunday, they did."

Vida put a hand to her mouth.

I blanched.

The bandages were stained; it was obvious the wounds were still oozing.

"*Motka Bosca*!♥" I blurted, as Pete released his pant leg sparing us from the gross wound. I kicked myself for displaying poor impulse control. I've been trying to stop swearing. I weaned myself off the worst ones by swearing in foreign languages, a habit my brother and I cultivated in our teens. This one was a favorite of our Polish/Russian mother.

Vida glanced from the bandages to me. She was about to comment when Pete got a fresh wind and began again.

"Hey, listen, I'm so glad I caught you. I was talkin' with my buddy Jim Calhoun a coupla days ago. He was askin' me if I knew a place for him and his buddies to have a regional meetin'."

"Oh?" I asked. I wished he'd leave. I could tell that Vida was uncomfortable with the intrusion and her leg was probably bothering her. Nothing against Pete, but he's profoundly deaf. Attempting conversation is an exercise in frustration. The less said, the better.

Pete's dentures waggled until he got them back in place. "I told him about this place. Told him to contact you." He nodded in a wobbly, roundy-roundy-way reminiscent of Jerry Lewis readying to swing at a golf ball.

"Thanks!" I nodded. I was curious about what interest group they were from that needed a place for a regional meeting but was reluctant to attempt asking. Lion's Club and Rotary Clubs had their own lodges. Who'd need mine?

♥ Pronounced with more of an 'o' sound at the end: mottco bosco. This Polish phrase means "Mother of God".

Curious.

Vida's eyes moved slowly from Pete's face to mine. She bit her lip to conceal a rogue smile of amusement. He was a lot to take in. I'd had lots of practice.

"Jim said he would," Pete said with more controlled nod. "He was thinkin' for a place round about Halloween time. I said you had plenty of space, no problem, you hadn't been busy at all. He'll be in touch." The dentures lost their mooring again and clacked around, then settled.

I pinched my ear hard and focused on the pain to keep a straight face. Vida looked away, lips tight.

I made the okay hand signal and put my thumbs up. "Okay. Great. Thanks." I waved, stepping away.

"Have a nice day!" Pete yelled.

As the blue Jeep rumbled away, Vida's mouth opened and closed, as if she couldn't decide whether to speak or not.

"I know," I said, "He's a good guy but refuses to wear hearing aids. He's afraid the government would get into his head. You know, mind control." I hoped this little tidbit would distract her from his comment about my lack of business.

Vida arched her eyebrows. "Oh, I see."

I tossed the mail onto the porch, and we set off along the path. We were in the hottest part of the afternoon and my deodorant quickly threw up a white flag. Vida pulled out an honest-to-God cotton handkerchief and wiped her forehead. As I had promised, the path was shaded with hickory and oak trees. A northern flicker called and flew out in front of us. Several zebra butterflies spiraled around us and drifted upwards into a ray of sunlight.

Vida stopped for a rest, leaning on her cane. "It's so peaceful here." She looked up as if embracing the sky and all creation with a huge inhale.

"Usually," I agreed, pleased with her appreciation. I didn't want to tell her about my neighbors occasionally pooling their funds to have all-day target practice which lasted until the ammo ran out.

Witches in a Hot Tub

She turned to me. "Haint, what do you know about Wicca?"

"I have a hazy idea. It's a religion that embraces connection with nature and seasons, cultivating inner strength and connection with the universe. A long time ago an acquaintance invited me, well, coerced me to attend a circle with her. I got the weird feeling that my albinoism made her think I had some supernatural powers. She and her friends seemed expectant somehow, like lightning would fly from my fingertips or frogs fall from the sky to my feet. Anyway, they seemed disappointed and almost angry at my wallflower attitude. While they talked up nature and love, they focused on the accoutrement, the wands, robes and medallions. They took great glee with manipulative spells to punish lousy boyfriends. Not very spiritual."

Vida shut her eyes and thinned her lips to a pencil line as if holding counting to ten to avoid cussing. She inhaled deeply and fully exhaled before opening her eyes. "You know I hate that. But, just as there are the show-up-for-Easter-service

Christians, there are the once-a- month club Wiccans who chant about oneness, but then go back being petty and rude until the next gathering. I'm sorry you had that experience."

I shrugged. "Me too."

We arrived at the circle, a mostly shady area where I had mapped out a crude meditation circle with sticks. There was mottled sunlight to mostly shade around the meditation circle. Perhaps because it was deeper in the woods, it felt significantly cooler here than along the path.

"Here it is," I gestured. "I hope to get the meditation walk filled in with rocks soon. I just haven't had time. The walk takes longer than you'd think. It's about ten minutes to get to the center."

Vida stepped over the sticks on her way to the center. Once there, she let go of her cane, held her arms overhead and looked up to the rectangle of sky. She closed her eyes and mumbled what I hoped was a prayer. When she opened her eyes again, she turned and looked at me with that wide, warm, all-knowing smile. Her eyes glimmered.

"How did you find this spot? Was it like this before you got it?"

"I'm not really sure. It was woods, but there was a natural clearing here. I thought it would be perfect for a circle."

"It is. There is a positive, healing resonance here. I suspect it has been used for this purpose before."

I thought about Lorraine's Aunt Moira. When she visited a few weeks earlier, she had told me of a clan of Native Americans who had lived and died here. She also told me that the ghost of a mother and her two boys lingered at the camp.

Once or twice I thought I'd glimpsed a woman at the edge of the circle but when I looked at her full on, there was nothing there. Once when I was placing rocks, I thought I heard children laughing. The laughter moved behind me such that for a split second, I thought there must be children playing tag. Where had they come from? Perturbed, I turned to look. Nothing. It could have been bird chatter and my imagination. I thought about mentioning it but decided against it.

Vida picked up her cane and stomped back out of the circle.

"Yes. This place is perfect. Please plan on five of us. I hope my request for exclusive access to your circle wasn't too cavalier. It's just that we would want to occupy the space for some time without interruption. I've been a Wiccan for a very long time, and I've had to navigate a lot of judgement, ridicule and intolerance. We just want peace and privacy."

"It's all yours." I said.

As we walked back along the path, I felt a zing of excitement about having the Wiccans as guests. Being in Vida's company gave me a feeling of peace. For the first time in a long stretch, a knowing came over me that everything was going to work out just fine.

It took a while to get back, but Vida seemed to be holding up. As she settled into her Honda, she rolled her window down. "I enjoyed meeting you and look forward to our weekend here."

"Me too. This may sound outlandish, but I feel like I've known you for longer than just today. Like I just forgot that we used to be friends or something." I shook my head, realizing how stupid that sounded.

Vida surprised me though, responding, "Maybe we have. Oh say, you know what the best thing about having pagan friends is?"

"Not a clue."

"They worship the ground you walk on."

It took me a second to realize she had told a joke. She was so earthy, the joke surprised me. "Oh, I get it!" I said with a dopey-me slump.

"Know what you call thirteen Wiccans in a hot tub?"

I shrugged, prepared this time.

"A self-cleaning coven."

Chapter 6

M.O.: 1) noun : short for Modus Operandi : procedure or method
2) Money Order: method of payment, like cash, requires no bank account

As Vida drove away, I picked up the pile of mail and walked into my office. In with the usual junk mail was a typed envelope with a Fort White post office box for a return address. I couldn't match this with anyone I knew. Curious, I ripped into it. A money order flitted to the ground as I opened a typed note on plain stationery.

> Please accept this money order to reserve a bunkhouse cabin for a party of eight checking in on Wednesday 10/29, checking out on Sunday 11/ 2. Breakfast only. We will need dining hall or similar space for lectures during the day.
>
> Please advise at once if conflict.
>
> Jim Calhoun

I picked up the money order. When was the last time I'd

seen one of these? I couldn't recall. Many moons to be sure. This must be the Jim that Patriotic Pete had mentioned. No mention of his organization. Whatever it was, they had lectures. I thought I'd heard something about preppies. Well, a group of students prepping for college should be easy enough to handle.

Later that day when I got home, I fished a thin pile of postcards from my grandmother's secretary desk. I selected a card, a remnant from a trip out West, featuring a teepee and wrote:

> *Reservation for party of eight cabin plus breakfast receved. Dining hall yours except during mealtimes. Advise if presentation equipment or additional meals required.*
>
> *Look forward to meeting you.*
>
> *Haint Blue.*

I addressed it to the post office box, affixed a post card stamp to it, and set it out on the round marble receiving table near the front door.

With one thing and another, the frustration with the washer, meeting Vida, the quaint reservation with a money order, by the end of the day, I'd forgotten all about the call with Mr. Shadetree. It wasn't until I was fading into the dream world that night that it came back to me. In the dream, I was sitting at a table for two with a stack of cookbooks in front of me. I was trying to find the caveman recipe for rock soup. Bright lights hit a stage in front of me. Elvis Presley came out gyrating in the white Evel Knievel jumpsuit. The song looped "Goes by the name of King Creole" over and over. A smoldering voice behind me asked, "you okay with spicy food?"

Late the next morning, I handed Pete the postcard to Mr. Calhoun.

"Hey Pete. Thanks for the reference." I pointed to the envelope addressed to Jim Calhoun.

"Fence? What fence?" He looked around my yard.

"Ref-er-ence. Jim made a res-er-va-tion."

"Reservation?" He looked confused and readjusted his dentures. "There was a powwow in Chiefland a while back…don't know of a reservation though." His mouth twitched again, and his teeth clacked.

I grabbed the card back, pointed to Jim Calhoun's name and pointed to the ground. "Coming here! Made a res-er-va-tion!" I gave him a thumbs up, all set sign.

He squinted. "Jim Calhoun. Yeah, I know him. Oh! I get it. He made a reservation?"

I nodded, then placed my hands in prayer position above my head, offering thanks.

"Ol' Jim and I go back a-ways. Yessir, known him almost m'whole life." He swallowed, and his teeth plates floated about. He worked his jaws. "Salt o' the earth, that man. Mm-hmm. Good people, his bunch."

Not sure if Pete was referring to Jim's family or the party of eight in the reservation. Seemed kind of a small number for college preppies, and odd that they didn't want meals besides breakfast, but I didn't dare ask for clarification from Pete. Maybe it was a special group from a church. Oh, well. I'd find out soon enough. Backing up, I waved bye-bye.

"Don't look like they're makin' much progress on th' road," Pete called out. "They need to get the grader out on One Fourteen. I'm tearin' up my Jeep." He shook his head and *tsk-tsk*ed, which dislodged his teeth. With a frown and some tongue work, Pete got them back in place. "Felt almost cool first thang this mornin', didn't it?"

I nodded.

Pete shook his head. "Didn't last long though. Woo-wee, it's warmin' up again. Dang. Was hopin' we'd get some rain, or one o' them cold fronts. Heard it was snowing in Missouri this morning. Wouldn't that be somethin'? Instead we got daggum love bugs. Went through a bad patch of 'em and could hardly see out my windshield yesterday."

I scrunched up my nose and nodded.

"Well, good talkin' with you, Haint," he waved. "You take care."

I pointed at him and held up two fingers.

"Me. Two. Oh! Me too! Yeah, thanks." He nodded, allowing a wild white wisp of hair to escape from his star-spangled headband. "Say listen, what do you think about this business with—"

Just when I thought I was clear of Pete, he was launching into a one-way discussion on some meaty topic. Luckily, I had my cell phone in my back pocket. Naughty, I know, but I acted as if I'd heard it ringing. I held up a hand to wait a moment, pulled the phone out and punched at it.

Pete was still talking, "...Donald Trump running for President, now wouldn't that just be something! Don't that beat all?"

"What? Oh no," I said, frowing. I pointed at my phone and mouthed, "I have to take this."

Poor Pete looked deflated.

I made apologetic faces, waved goodbye and stepped toward my door.

"Oh, okay then. You take care, Haint. I'll see you." Pete said behind me.

I nodded. "Oh, no" I said into the dead phone. "Yes, I understand." I waved once more and went inside, closing the door behind me. Safe at last, I dropped the phone to my side and leaned against the door feeling guilty for the masquerade, but it was quicker than trying to extricate myself. I wasn't up for a political debate in the midday heat.

Surely even enlightened beings avoid getting sucked into sticky conversations. I wondered how. Next time I would try honesty. "Thank you, but I must go now." Why was that so hard?

Yet More Ketchup, Righteous and Fierce

I was contemplating this when my phone rang for real. My guilty conscience conjured up a creepy voice coming through the phone saying, "You create your own negative karma with your lies!"

Yes. Dear Divine Universe, please forgive me, I thought.

I answered on the third ring. "Hi! Blue's Lotus Lodge. This is Haint. How can I help you?"

"Hey, ah, we were looking at your website and wondered if there was any chance me and some of my friends could book one of the big cabins for a Halloween party on the 31st. I'll be honest, it might get kind of wild…not destructive or anything, but see—" The caller paused, I could hear a heavy drag on a cigarette, "it might be best if we could get a cabin away from everyone else."

Oh boy. Closing my eyes, I had flashbacks to horrid apartment complex living with sleepless nights compliments of the neighbor's stereo, the bass pounding the pictures off the wall.

Complaining only aggravated the situation. Pajama-clad, I banged on the door, "Hey! It's too loud! Turn it down!"

The drunk swaying on the door answering, "Hey, Spooky! Come party! Too loud? Really? Soo sorry. We'll turn it down imm-eee-diately." The door slammed. There was laughter. The volume amplified twofold.

I opened my eyes. I wanted to say no, but he sounded sweet and had that pleading tone, the equivalent of a sad-eyed Labrador thumping its tail against a counter, you can hardly say no to giving him the treat. I weighed the choices. Say no, say goodbye to the money and word-of-mouth reference. I could envision scathing social media reviews featuring the word "unaccommodating".

I could demand a deposit and make some tight ground rules and hope for the best. "How many people?"

"Twelve…no, maybe sixteen…uh, not sure yet."

"Tell you what," I said, pacing the floor and visualizing the retreat. "Cabins eight and nine are close to the road, kind of away from everyone. Sounds like you expect more than eight. Pay a deposit up front, I'll reserve the two side by side."

What about the preppers? The two groups would co-exist for the one night, and fortunately cabins eight and nine were set apart by the three-hundred-year-old live oak between cabin seven and eight. If I put the preppers in number seven, they should be far enough away from music in cabin nine. Fingers crossed; problem solved.

I continued, "I've got a group for cabin seven. If you can contain the party to cabin nine, and swear to keep the noise down after midnight, it should be fine. I'll be checking IDs; absolutely no underage drinking. No smoking inside; you can smoke on the porches. If I can hear the music from the bathroom pavilion after midnight, I'll shut you down. If I don't get any complaints from other guests, you get the full deposit back. Deal?"

"Totally!" He answered in a gosh-thanks-Mom tone. This was followed by a muffled, "Righteous and Fierce!"

"I'm sorry?" I asked.

"Sorry. I wasn't talking to you," he said. We discussed cost further, and he gave me his name, Aubrey Sinclair, and credit card information for the deposit. He ended the call saying he'd call back as soon as he had the final head count for his festivities.

It was a few moments after we hung up that I noticed I was humming Gershwin's, "Things Are Looking Up."

Chapter 7

Monday October 13: Lorraine Trips Up, Ig Trips Out

I was working on the first cup of coffee when Lorraine rang.

"Hey, Haint. Sorry I've been a bit out of touch..." There was a disconnected, ethereal quality to her voice.

"How did the Chihuahua gig go?" I asked.

"Ha! Yeah. Well, won't be doing that again soon. I'm going to be fine, but I broke my ankle yesterday tripping over Sparky while trying to get away from Lllu-labelle."

"Oh, *scheisse*!"

"Could you..." There was a pause. It seemed an effort to get the words out and stay focused. "Could you come pick me up? I'm at Regional hoss-pital. They've stabilized it and I'm outfitted with crutches. There's scary scaff-ff-folding between my foot and my leg, I'm skewered with old-fashioned television antenna implants. No reception. Well, there were pain receptors, but I've got some lovely pain killers. Oh. But I will need to pick up a prescription. I'm not going to be able to walk for a while."

"Stabilized?"

"It was ugly." There was a pause. She sounded exhausted. "I tripped over Sparky and fell down a short flight of ssstairs. Lucky for me, they were carpeted, so I'm not as banged up as I could be."

"Holy Donald O'Connor, Lorraine! Yes, why didn't you call sooner? You had to spend the night for a broken ankle?"

"Long story. I was in line for an x-ray, but they kind of forgot me, then I was next, but I got bumped by a car accident…"

"Yikes! I can be out the door in a couple of minutes. Hold tight, I'm on my way."

"Hey, one more little thing."

"Yeah?"

"The dogs. They need to be fed and let out the back door. It's super easy, you just--"

"Oh, no way." Of course, I'd do anything for Lorraine, but that didn't mean I looked forward to it.

"Just this once? It's on the way to the hospital, it'll take just five minutes."

"The same dogs that tried to kill you and are the reason you're in the hospital?"

"I just tripped. They're sweet. But they've been inside a long time now."

"You're fooling no one. I saw Pete's leg."

"Pete's leg? What are you talking about?"

"He got attacked by a pack of Chihuahuas. Showed me the bandages."

"If you throw treats out, they'll be distracted while you get in the door."

"Yeah, right. Look, I threw out my shin guards after eighth grade field hockey."

"Please? The owners won't be back for a couple days. They've got a substitute lined up, but he can't come until this afternoon."

I set my cup down a little too hard. The mug clunked the counter; coffee splattered. "Oh! I see! You're lonely and need a roommate, is that it? If I break my leg or have a chunk ripped out." I envisioned myself lying on the ground with dogs on me like hyenas on a gazelle.

"Please?" Her voice was higher than normal, probably due to pain killers. She sounded like a cute little girl.

"*Kurwa mać*!"* I snapped, eyeing the fridge contents for a bag of bagels.

"Thought you gave up cussing. It's unprofessional." She may have been high on meds, but her sense of humor was intact.

"I'm not working at the moment. My business has been deader than King Tut."

"Cussing in Polish is ssstill cussing." I was sure she was waggling an index finger at me. "Someone might understand you."

"Not Chihuahuas," I countered, finding the peanut butter.

Lorraine begged, "Pleeeassse?" "I swear you'll be in and

---

* Pronounced "coorvah mahtch." Translates literally as whore, but used as general expletive, "For f** sake!"

out in five minutes."

"Fine. You know I'll do it 'cause I love you, but you'll owe me big time. If I live."

"Of course."

She gave me directions to the Collins house with detailed instructions and we signed off. I slathered half a bagel with peanut butter and chocolate honey spread and choked it down with coffee. I shooed Naughty Britches outside to pee, put in my lavender-tinted contacts, and ran a brush through my hair. I wriggled into the pair of jeans and T-shirt I'd been wearing the day before and called NB back inside. She sensed I was leaving and started barking and throwing herself at the bedroom door.

"Not now, sweetie. I've got to go visit the killer Chihuahuas and get Lorraine. I'll get you breakfast when I get back. Assuming I live."

She was still barking when I got into my truck. I was halfway down my driveway when Iggy's truck pulled in. He pulled up alongside me.

"Hey Haint, you're off early."

"Iggy! Bad timing! I'm on my way to the hospital to pick up Lorraine. She broke her ankle and needs a ride."

"What? Wait. Can I go with you? I was hoping to talk to you."

"It's about time. You haven't returned my calls."

"Yeah…sorry 'bout that, I—"

"Come on. You can help."

He drove up to the house and I backed up to get him. He

climbed in and shut the door. His whole demeanor was wrong. For starters, he wouldn't look at me and he just stared forward at my dirty windshield. His eyes looked puffy and dark, and he hadn't shaved or brushed his hair. I wondered how long he'd been wearing his clothes.

"You look like you were in the outhouse when it got struck by lightning," I said, tickled to use one of Max's more colorful expressions.

Iggy didn't laugh, he just said, "Gee, thanks."

"Well, what's up, Ig?" I swatted his shoulder with my fingertips. "You've been avoiding my calls. Joe said you dropped a class, and no one's seen you lately. This isn't like you."

I knew as soon as I said it, it was a stupid thing to say. No one is the same person all the time. We are all a kaleidoscope of good, bad, witty, thoughtless, energetic, exhausted, kind, rude and confused.

He didn't respond.

"Okay, well, I haven't heard any rumors about a mob hit taken out on you. If you are ill, I can swap you out for Lorraine at the hospital. Come on, bro, what's the deal?"

When he spoke, his voice quivered on the edge of a crying jag. "I really like Louise. We've been seeing each other, and I know it's just been a month, but I feel a connection, like we could be really good together. I think I'm falling for this woman."

My hands twisted on the steering wheel. "You know, most people in love are giddy like Gene Kelly dancing in the rain! To borrow from Max, you look like the dogs been keepin' you under the porch. What's wrong? Are you afraid of falling in love?"

"No. It's not that. I *was* Gene Kelly dancing in the rain. Louise is great. We *get* each other and have lots in common. She's even got some martial arts experience and is interested in more classes. We laugh a lot. She's got so much heart...like a Labrador: loyal, true, open, ready for anything. Fully present, no holding back, no pretense."

"Okay...I know I'm female, half-Polish and left-handed, which makes life challenging beyond the albino thing, but I'm not seeing the problem here."

"It's great, only..." He sighed and shook his head.

We arrived at the dreaded Chihuahua kingdom.

Iggy looked up. "What are we doing here?"

"A huge favor for Lorraine."

I explained the situation as I searched for the key hidden in a fake rock by the door. I straightened and summoned courage before opening the door. The dogs, corralled in a mud room at the back of the house, set up a yipping frenzy that was like ice water down the back. Chilling as the disembodied calls of hungry coyotes.

"We get the treat bag from the kitchen," I said, moving toward the kitchen, "...ah, here it is good. Then we open the door, throw treats and pray the little demons don't shred our legs before we get the sliding door open."

"You're exaggerating a bit, aren't you?"

Before I had gotten the treats out of the bag, he had opened the door. The yipping peaked then waned as he said in a baby-soothing, woman-melting tone, "Oh, look at you guys...aren't you cute?"

Using Iggy as a shield, I lobbed a handful of treats to the floor. Some of the little terrors went for the treats, while others fell under Iggy's spell. He slowly bent down and offered a hand. The yipping cacophony faded to mute as the foodies went for the treats and the rest inspected Iggy, eyes bugged, noses wiggling. A white tea kettle with bug-eyes tottered over on tiny legs, the last to scrutinize Iggy.

"Good God, that looks uncomfortable!" I said.

Iggy lost the trance voice, his body and tone tensed. "Oh. She's pregnant." He patted her head. "Got yourself in a bit of a fix, huh girl?" She gazed up at him with trusting eyes. "What's her name, do you know?"

My mind searched the memory rolodex and it popped up. "Lulabelle."

Cooing again, he said, "Hey Lulabelle? Can we make it outside, huh? Isn't that a great idea? That's it. Good girl. Come on everyone."

I slid the door open, and like dutiful little devils following their master, the dogs trotted after my brother, Lulabelle staggering behind. Spotting the grass, they fanned out to do their business.

"Is there *anything* you can't do?" I asked.

"Yeah. Figure out what to do. My life is a total mess." He covered his face with his hands.

We emerged from the Collins house unscathed and were soon zooming south on I-75, making good time, since we were early for rush hour.

"So...what's the *crise, mon chèr frère*?"♥

"It's Indigenous People's Day."

"What?" Oh wait. Columbus Day. Now I remembered. Running Deer, Iggy's former girlfriend used to call it Indigenous People's Day, as it was offensive to Native Americans to honor Chris C. who indirectly brought about their destruction. Doubly stupid really, since it's now assumed that the Vikings made it to North America long before Chris was in short pants.

"So...?"

"Running Deer called."

"Oh, *kurwa*." I about swerved off the road looking at him.

"She's in Alabama, on her way to Tampa for a huge pow-wow festival. She'll be here Wednesday."

"Whoa! As in two days from now?" I felt my face go slack and my chest tighten.

"Yeah. Two days."

Running Deer was Iggy's true love and soul mate, a beautiful and talented Navajo who chose a nomadic life over Iggy's marriage proposal two years back. Iggy, normally confident, breezy, an all-around glowing and beautiful being, had been devastated by her leaving. Louise was the first woman he had dated since Running Deer moved west.

"But she's just passing through then?"

"She asked if the proposal was still offered."

♥ French: what is the crisis, my dear brother

"Oh, *Matka Bosca*!"

I reached out my hand and squeezed his. "But, she...she doesn't want to settle down, right? That was the deal breaker before, she didn't want to be tied down. What's different now?"

"She's pregnant."

"*What*?"

"Yeah."

We were silent. The hum of the truck on the road and the air conditioning too loud all of a sudden.

"Uh, what about the father of the baby?" I asked.

"She said the father wasn't in the picture."

I looked at him. What did that mean? She wasn't a one-night stand kind of woman. Did she find a guy who bailed on her? Or died? Reports of drugs and rape in Rainbow Gatherings came to mind. Shit, had she been raped? Iggy's haggard expression staring at the windshield suggested his mind had gone down that road as well.

"Louise and I are supposed to go to St. Augustine for the weekend...she's made reservations in one of those historic B&Bs."

"Well, you should go."

"How can I? I'm a wreck."

We pulled up to the hospital and saw Lorraine in a wheelchair chatting with some other patients and a nurse holding a set of crutches. Her leg was elevated in a footrest. She looked relieved to see us. I stopped the truck and Iggy got out. I flagged the car behind me to go around, got out and walked around.

"Is that an erector set on your leg?" Iggy asked.

"Yes, I thought I'd play with it when I got home," Lorraine answered in a too-merry, probably pain-killer enhanced tone. "Ack-shually, it freaks me out. I'm trying not to look at it. I can't believe that is in my leg, so I'm pretending that it's not." She spoke at an almost normal rate, but her whole face seemed slack, her words sounded like she was on a third martini. "But Iggy, look at you! You look with-th-thered like a mid-January poinsettia. What's the matter? Are you sick?"

He shrugged. "Sort of."

I couldn't stop staring at Lorraine's leg. I'm very squeamish about even minor medical stuff like blood and stitches. I passed out once just getting an x-ray to check my bladder function.

I felt light-headed. There was a fuzziness in my mouth. I leaned against my truck and focused on a palm tree near the entrance. A heavyset woman with purple-black legs was wheeled through the automatic doors. I told myself to get a grip.

Breathing in happy thoughts, breathing out all jitters, barfies and faintness.

The nurse helped maneuver Lorraine out of the chair and propped with the crutches. Lorraine took a few awkward hops towards the truck. Iggy moved the seat back to give her more leg room and helped her into the front seat. I was relieved to move back to the driver's side and focus on driving. Iggy took Lorraine's purse and the crutches and got in the back.

Lorraine exhaled. "Thanks so much. I'm exhausted." She caught Iggy's eye in the rearview mirror. "So? What's up?" She tried to narrow her eyes and look stern but went a little cross-eyed instead. "The Chihuahuas didn't get you too, did they? You didn't have any problems with them, did you?"

"No. I'm okay," Iggy said without conviction.

"No, he's not. Running Deer is back," I blurted. "She's pregnant."

"Oh, shhhit!" Lorraine looked at Iggy again in the mirror. "What about Louise?"

"Exactly," Ig and I said in unison.

I waited for a Subaru to pass me then eased the truck into the flow of drop-off and pick-up traffic. "Are you hungry? Want to stop somewhere? Do we need to pick up any prescriptions or do a grocery run?" I asked.

"I want to go home and go to bed…although, I think I have to sleep in the recliner. But some bra-breakfast to go would be grand. I'm s-s-starving."

"Does Lerlene know about your ankle? Do you need me to call her?"

"She knows. She's busy but coming over later. I've s-s-sworn her to see-crecy, Saint Eleanor can't know about this or she'll drop everything to come stay with me. Ugh!"

"Saint" Eleanor, her mother, was a sweet woman with the can-do spirit of Eleanor Roosevelt, Florence Nightingale and Joan of Arc all in one.

"She loves you. She'd be happy to help," I said, teasing.

She smacked my arm. "Yes, and she'd s-s-swoop in, smother me in kisses, hold my hand and fret. Then she'd prop me in a medical bed downstairs, oversee a m-m-medical staff to visit on high rotation--"

Lorraine's eyes were half-closed. She was tumbling her fingers around each other, imitating rotation. With difficulty. She got a second wind and began again.

"She'll comman-nan, woops, I mean comman*deer* my kitchen, direct a con-struction team to construct a handicap ramp to the front door…" Her flat hand floated up and away like a runaway sleigh. "Let's see, what else? Oh yes, al-alphabetize my pantry, and color coordinate my closet."

Iggy's mouth made a silent O. He canted his head to look at me sideways, "Not like our mom, eh?"

"Hardly," I said. My nose scrunched up involuntarily. Our mother had provided food, clothing, shelter and discipline to us as children. After puberty, we were on our own, practically dismissed. Well, I was. I was pretty sure she'd considered smothering me as an infant, shamed by having an albino child. I was grateful that she allowed me to live. But even with Iggy, her baby boy, pride and joy, she wasn't the model of motherly love.

I called in a to-go order at the Street Deli, which was ready when we got there. The parking lot was full, so I did a K-turn and we waited while Iggy trotted in to pick up the order.

"I've got some good news," I said. "The Lotus Lodge is going to be hopping for Halloween. So far, I've got a weight loss group, a small group of Wiccans and Max's favorite, the Bigfoot Researchers, a huge Halloween party made up of a bunch of twenty-somethings, and some mystery group that promises to have lectures."

Lorraine lolled her head over to look at me and giggled like an elf on helium. "So, witches, monster hunters, fatties and hedonists, eh?" She snorted. "And a team of stuffy lecturers. Sounds perfect."

We drove in silence for a mile or so. I thought Lorraine had fallen asleep, but she perked up and tapped Iggy's shoulder. "So what are you going to do about the Louise and Running Deer situation?"

Iggy stared out the window. His reflection against the glass was like an anguished ghost. He said in a voice brimming with despair, "I don't know."

Chapter 8

Nicole to the Rescue, Tickety-boo

Not that I'd had clients begging for yoga classes, but the week of Halloween was looking pretty busy, and Lorraine normally taught yoga for me at the Lotus Lodge. She also taught classes at several of the Alachua library branches, and a senior center. Or she had, pre-Chihuahuas.

I bit my lip and glanced over to Lorraine, "I hate to bring up the obvious, but you won't be teaching yoga anytime soon. Do you have someone in mind to cover for you?"

"Ac-shually, I do. I have a student who just got c-c-certified and is looking for work. She's young, insanely flexible, energetic and eager. I think she'd jump to pick up my classes. I'd almost be worried that she'd steal them from me…"

"Why do you say that?"

"Oh, nothing. I hate to say it, but there's something about her I can't quite exshplain. Just a feeling. Not sure it's founded. Could be I just have issues with women named Nicole."

"Would that be the Nicole in Ig's advanced tai chi class?"

"Probub-bub-ably."

I glanced in the mirror. Lorraine had nodded and her head remained lowered. Poor thing. I thought maybe she'd fallen asleep, but she stirred and her head popped up again. "Ex-shtrovert, pretty, too perky, theee-atre major?"

"Yup. That'd be the one," I confirmed.

"Ah. I let her teach one of my clashes when I was a bit under the weather. She went through a solid routine, moving smoothly from one position to another with very good di-rection. She even… kept an eye on the class to make sure they were keeping up and doing the poses correctly. She offered great--encouragement." She waved her hands around. "She was a natural. That's why I en-couraged her to get certified. I figured she could teach right out of school."

She sounded so loopy, I wondered if she'd remember this conversation later. "Okay. With your endorsement, I'll give her a try. I'll take one of her classes first. Bob sure taught me to vet anyone I hire."

Back in September, I'd hired Bob in desperation to do some last-minute yard work without getting references first. Both his person and personality were on the grimy side, in fact, I winced remembering Sheriff Dave Marshall saying, "If I'd ha' order a dozen bastards, and they'd sent me only Bob, I wouldn't ha' felt short changed."

Lorraine scrunched up her face. "Bob. Bob was not a nice man."

"No."

"Why are we talking about *Bob*?"

"Nevermind. We were talking about Nicole."

"Oh. Yes." She waved her hands around again. "She'll be

fine. You might want to replace me and take her on full time."

"Never."

She pointed at her leg. "Hey! Who knows how long it'll be before I can even walk normally again? You know *all* of my jobs depend on me being able to walk. Even baking cakes, I have to stand up."

I thought about her fabulous cakes and the restaurants that depended on her for their desserts. "Surely you know someone with a bored teenager to get out of the house, who could come over and do the standing, mixing and whatnot while you looked on…like a baking apprentice?"

She raised an eyebrow. "You know, I jussst might. That's not a half bad idea. I like it! Indentured servitude! Maybe I could get them to do laundry for me and take out the trash, too."

We got Lorraine home and helped her get settled. It took a while. We set her up in the recliner in the living room with her leg propped up.

"Lerlene's coming soon…she's picking up my prescrib—prescription. You guys can go. I just want to shhleep. Couldn't get any… shhleep in the hospital. They're always poking at you and beeping."

I got Nicole's contact information before her head rolled to the side and she began snoring.

Back in the truck alone with Iggy, I hoped to have a fuller conversation, but he looked like Death eating a pickle. "What are you going to do?" I asked.

"I can't not see her."

"She broke your heart. I was *there*. It was ugly. Are you sure you want to open yourself up to that again?"

"No. But I can't turn her away without seeing her."

"What about Louise?"

He passed his hands over his face. "I don't know."

We drove in silence back to my house. We could hear NB barking inside. "Wanna come in?" I asked.

"Naah. I gotta get some sleep," he said, getting out of the truck.

"And a shower," I said, hoping to add levity though seeing him so tortured was breaking my heart. I got out and walked around to meet him by his truck.

"That too. Jeez, I don't know what I'm doing."

"Get some food. A shower. Some sleep. Take care of yourself, or you're going to get sick. Okay?" I gave him a long hug. "And please call me. Leave a message. Send a text. Something. Anything."

"Yeah. Love you."

He got in, waved and soon was gone.

Oh, Iggy.

Once I walked NB and got her fed, I called Nicole. I expected to get a voice mail since most millennials won't answer their phones. I was presently surprised when she did.

I explained that Lorraine's situation and asked if she'd be available to pick up some daytime yoga classes.

"Sure! I'll have to check my schedule, but yeah, I'd love to!"

I was grateful for her eagerness and flexibility, timewise.

"Would you mind if I took one of your classes in advance, just to get a feel for your teaching style?"

"Of course!"

She gave me some session options and welcomed me to sit in on any of them. Her Thursday morning class seemed promising; I told her I'd shoot for that one.

"Great! See you then."

Thursday October 16: Release the Flying Monkeys

Lorraine was right; Nicole was a very competent teacher. I arrived late thanks to NB having some stomach issues. I woke to the wup! werp! yerking in my closet, so after walking her around, spooning liquid Pink Stuff for Tummies into her and making sure she would live, I rooted through my closet for some yoga wear. Too late I discovered that my best stuff was still in the laundry, so I threw on what I could find and dashed out to Nicole's class.

Nicole taught a vigorous yoga style, with repetitions of sequences that left me breathless. As she introduced new poses, she'd begin with a basic form, then say, "and if you want more, you can do… and if you still want more, you can try…" On the small side and with a dancer's body, she made the moves and transitions appear effortless. Her almost-bald head made her seem extra vulnerable, yet she was lithe enough to be a Cirque du Soleil performer. In one lissome swoop she moved her body from a downward facing dog to a hanging cobra, sweeping her chest across the floor and up into an arc. When I attempted this move, my arms gave out and my boobs ground into the mat. I bottomed out—or would it be boobed out? There's road rash and then there's mat rash. The girls did not appreciate being mashed.

I panted my way through the class, eyeing the clock. I felt sluggish and out-of-shape. I tried to remember the last time I felt truly *genki. Genki* is a terrific Japanese word that doesn't translate very well into English but means something like healthy and vitalized. In polite conversation, one may ask, *Genki desu-ka*? Are you *genki*? Loosely translated, it just means "are you well?" but it's subtle and deeper than that…more like are you energized, or, are your batteries fully charged?

Mine were not.

By the time Nicole settled us, supple and whooped, into a relaxing shivasana, or corpse pose, I was sending up silent prayers that I had survived the class without a stroke.

As her students departed, I helped Nicole pack up the straps and foam blocks she had provided. She held the gym bag while I pushed the blocks down inside. Standing close to her dainty frame, I felt like a lumbering giant. She had run the class with a confidence and authority that belied her size. She reminded me of someone, but my brain couldn't make the connection. Sinead O'Connor? No, close but that wasn't right…

"How was it?" Nicole asked.

"Great!" I said, "Guess I'm used to a slower pace but I'm all loose and melty now."

Her dark eyes flashed up at me. "Thanks."

She didn't have any signs of sweat or fatigue. In fact, she looked like she could start another class, fresh as a daisy.

She glanced at my outfit, a scowling cartoon ghost print on a faded, honey-mustard-yellow shirt, an old gag gift from Lorraine. Soiled diaper yellow is a disgusting color on someone with no pigment; it makes a healthy person look jaundiced. My yoga shorts had snags and an unravelling hem.

"Sorry. I don't usually make public appearances looking quite this bad. My dog was sick. I was running late."

"Is your dog okay?" She asked, tilting her shaved head, accentuated by her exposed neck and delicate pearl earrings. Again, there was something familiar about her face, but I couldn't place it.

I said, "She'll be fine, thanks. Listen, I'd be pleased, no, *honored* to have you teach at the Lotus Lodge. At present, I think I just need a few morning classes over the weekend. I've got some ladies who wanted yoga classes."

"Awesome! That'll be so perfect! You know I'll be staying there anyway. I'm with the Wiccan group. I'm pretty sure they'll do yoga."

"Oh, really? How cool is all that? Perfect." Vida was considerably older than Nicole. Somehow, I'd expected her group to be all middle-aged. "Well, that is perfect."

"Yeah! See Vida and Mrs. Nutterberg are bffs from the Stone Age, and Boo Nutterberg's my bff from kindergarten. This'll be so awesome! We shouldn't be too busy in the morning, after our greet-the-day routine, so it'll be no sweat to do a class or two, like maybe before breakfast. Tickety-boo."

"Sorry?"

"Oh, I have a British friend who's always saying these brilliant things. It means easy-peasy."

"Ah. tickety-boo. I'll try to remember that."

I held the door for her as she turned sideways maneuvering the awkward gym bag.

"I know, it's weird. I just love words. I was going to be a linguistics major if I hadn't gotten into theatre," Nicole said, squinting. The bright sunlight reflected off the white sidewalk.

"Really? Then we have may have something in common. I'm a polyglot. Not exactly fluent in many languages, but I've picked up phrases. Love interesting vocabulary; got one of those obscure word-a-day calendars."

"Yes! I especially like fun-sounding words like 'mugwump' or 'quagswag'."

"Yes!" I clapped my hands with enthusiasm. "I can be quite scaturient♥ on the subject!"

"Nice!" she said, laughing.

Standing by front of the door like boulders in a stream, we were blocking the flow of gym patrons coming and going. We went outside.

"Well, we'll work out a schedule. Talk soon, eh?" I said.

"Yeah, great." She said, with a goodbye wave.

It turned out that her purple Honda Element was parked close to my truck. As I walked past it, I noticed the two bumper stickers:

IF THE BROOM FITS, RIDE IT!

♥ over-enthusiastic

DON'T MAKE ME RELEASE THE FLYING MONKEYS

My initial reservations about Nicole vanished. I liked this girl. She had spark, intelligence and a sense of humor. I thought about the nasty comments I'd overheard at the tai chi class and decided it was jealousy. How unfortunate.

Almost home, just coming up on the road to my retreat, I passed Urliss Oakey's Super Duty F-150. Hollis, his twin, was in the passenger seat. As I waved, I could have sworn I saw Max ducking down in the back seat. When I glanced in the rearview mirror, there were only two heads visible beyond a new metal hunting dog crate in the truck bed. The odd thing was, I was pretty sure they had just turned out of my retreat driveway.

The Oakeys were friends with Max, but why would they go to the Lotus Lodge without letting me know? They hadn't called. My first thought was they were just showing Max all the improvements I'd made since I bought it from him, but I'd brought him out and given him the tour myself. And what was with the crate? What were they up to? No telling.

NB greeted me at the door. She darted out to do her thing then romped back inside demanding cookies. She snarfed the cookies then chased the cat around the coffee table as if she'd just become aware that he was there.

I made myself a cup of orange spice tea, grabbed the cookbooks and nestled into the couch. Soon, Naughty Britches was next to me, pawing at the pages.

"Settle down, hon. Mommy's got to do some recipe homework."

She scooched up closer and popped her nose under my hand for a pet. I complied. Mischief hopped up to join us. The two nosed each other, then Mischief curled up by my feet.

"Let's see about this paleo business," I said, turning pages.

Chapter 9

Stone Age Menu Plans

The first book I picked up had a great cover: a size-zero cave woman in a skimpy Flintstones-style dress casually holding a turkey leg. She's cool and *en vogue*. The title is *Cave Women Don't Get Fat: The Paleo Chic Diet for Rapid Results*.♥

The premise to the paleo diet is that prior to agriculture, humans hunted for meat and gathered fruits and nuts. They got exercise and maintained a balanced weight. In modern times, we've introduced grains into our diet and become more sedentary. Heaven knows, corn is hard to avoid: corn flakes, corn muffins, creamed corn, roasted corn, corn on the cob, corn nuggets and popcorn. Remember the old food pyramids that advocated lots of carbs? Bread, pasta, rice and cereals? I fell for it; we all did. We ate cereal and granola and thought it was good for us.

♥ This is a real book, folks, look it up. Author = Esther Blum, published in 2013 by Gallery Books, a division of Simon and Schuster. Fabulous cover designed by Kyoko Watanabe. Love it!

The book went on for several chapters on the health benefits of protein and how a body responds to good fats vs. bad fats. As I read, guilty thoughts about the package of biscuits in my fridge intruded. Nuts.

Oh, look! Nuts are good for you. That's a plus, I like nuts. Grilled bananas? Yum. Coconut brownies? Seriously? Wow. I could pass up biscuits if there were brownies to be had. Scrambled eggs, avocado and salsa? Stuffed peppers?

My mouth was watering. This didn't sound too hard.

I reached for my tea slowly so as not to disturb the harmonious snoozing taking place against me. The tea was strong and good but now I was craving that coconut brownie.

You should never flip through a cookbook on an empty stomach.

I'd look at this one in more detail later. I dropped this one to the floor and picked up the next one, *Big Book of Paleo Show Cooking* by Natalie Perry. The slow cooker is right up there in the top inventions after the wheel, hot water, sliced bread, coffee and chocolate. I love my slow cooker—such a brilliant idea to have food cooking by itself while you're off doing something else! Come back and voila! Dinner!

Ooh…pomegranate glazed chicken wings! Yeah, baby. Strawberry balsamic chicken… good golly, the pictures had me drooling and wanting strawberries…cauliflower rice instead of white rice…hmm. Okay. I like cauliflower…Oh no, a whole section on pork and lamb. I love lamb…

A recipe has to be good when the book falls open to the page, right? Chocoholics unite! The next book fell open to page 188: Dark Chocolate Sauce. Ingredients: 100% cacao bars, coconut cream, honey and salt. I might have to get a copy of this *Idiot's Guides: As Easy as It Gets! Paleo Slow Cooking*, by Molly Pearl,♥ I thought. *Got this Paleo business covered, Prudence,* I thought with satisfaction.

With great care, I extracted myself from the couch and the two sleepers to go in search of a chocolate fix and some sticky notes to flag recipes plus a notepad to make a grocery list. I returned with my goodies to find that Naughty Britches had stretched out covering most of the space I had vacated. No saved seats in this house. Fine. I sat on the floor in front of them and was soon lost in a foodie reverie, jotting and flagging.

Drowning Sorrows to Pandora's Top Sobber Hits

I heard my phone chirping somewhere in the kitchen. Shoving the cookbooks aside I trotted in to find it, catching the call too late, it had gone to voice mail.

A sniffy female voice sobbed, "Haint? Haint, are you there? I'm sorry to bother you again, it's Louise. Would you call me as soon as you get this? Just be honest. He doesn't want to see me anymore, right? Or…is he bi-polar or something? Is this an off-his-meds thing that I should know about? I just don't understand. Everything was fine, or so I thought. We were supposed to go away this weekend, and suddenly he's avoiding me. Just tell me. I just want to know why. What have

---

♥ Idiot's Guides are apparently a series of books published by Penguin Group (USA). This particular book by Molly Pearl was published in 2014.

I done?" She hung up mid-sob.

Dammit, Iggy, you've got to talk to her. She deserves the truth.

Naughty Britches had followed me into the kitchen and looked at me with the long-suffering expressions Bassets have perfected.

"Come on, little girl. We're going to do an intervention."

I leashed her, and we took a quick tour around the driveway. She did her business. I loaded her into the truck where she took her position draped over the middle console, looking forward.

Apprehension muddled my stomach as we drove to High Springs. Seeing Iggy's truck in his driveway was a mixed blessing. He should be at work. I wasn't sure what we would walk in on.

I lifted NB out and set her down. She trotted towards Iggy's door, tail wagging. His stereo was on high, the whole house was pulsing with a steady subwoofer beat. Pointless to knock since he wouldn't hear it, I unclipped her leash and turned the knob. The door opened, and NB charged in to find him.

The song blasting through the house was Michael McDonald's *"I Keep Forgetting (We're Not in Love Anymore)."* That sure didn't bode well. I heard a woof from the master bedroom and followed, turning down the volume of the stereo in the living room before heading down the hall to Iggy's room. I found him in his underwear, sprawled on the floor against his unmade bed, a framed photo of Running Deer in front of him. His hair was rumpled, he hadn't shaved in days and his face was wet with tears. NB pawed at him, insisting on attention. He patted her absently.

Easing myself down next to him, I put his head on my shoulder. His face contorted as he gasped, cried and snorfled—my word for that super-snotty type of crying. I let him go knowing he'd talk when he could. I just held him, my shoulder getting wet. I thought about finding a box of tissues, but guessed that being a guy, he didn't have any, and I didn't really want to break away. I tried to wipe his face with the corner of my grumpy ghost shirt but couldn't quite stretch the fabric far enough.

"Ig…what happened?" I coaxed.

"She's here. She came over last night." More crying. "It was a shock to see her so pregnant. She's so little. She has that radiant look people talk about. Her face was so beautiful. But it's not mine. Not my baby. I just can't…" He sobbed again. I waited, my heart breaking with his.

Before Running Deer had broken off their relationship to head out west, Iggy had been so in love with her, sure she was the one. He'd planned to propose to her and was making plans for their future. He bought this house with her in mind. He talked about it being a great school district for when they had children. The night he brought her to the house and proposed, he imagined her excitement, expected her to want to pick out furniture and curtains, talk about where the garden would go. Instead, she kissed him sweetly and shook her head.

"Oh, my Iggy, I was coming here to tell you that I'm going away. I will always love you, but I feel a deep connection with the Native American community I've discovered. They've invited me to travel with them. They travel seasonally up north into Canada, to the Pacific Northwest… I leave on Monday."

I had seen him like this then. Utterly broken. He'd spent a few weeks barely getting out of bed, not eating.

"It was like no time had passed. Like I dreamed that she left, and we were still together and happy. She told me she still loved me and wanted to get back together." Wracking sobs.

"Tell me about the baby," I said. "What about the father?"

He pulled his head up then and sniffed hard. His jaw clenched. "She went out west and met a shaman she fell in love with, Lone Elk. She travelled with him. Got pregnant. They even got…married in an Indian ceremony as well as a regular legal one. She married *him*. She was *his wife*. They travelled to a big powwow in Reno, Nevada."

"Oh, Ig," I said, putting my forehead to his for a moment.

He snuffled, "Lone Elk was asked to perform a healing on this woman with cancer. During the ceremony, he travelled to the underworld and spoke with a spirit who told him that she did not want to live, and he should not try to save her, it was her path to be released from the world. He spoke to the woman's spirit; she confirmed it was true. She wanted to let go. It was the most difficult ceremonies for Lone Elk because so many people were expecting a visible outcome, a shift, a sign, tangible proof of healing taking place. He would not lie and 'perform'; he told the people that he was helping her to fulfill her wishes, but they didn't understand. The woman's brother was outraged that Lone Elk would not heal her. The brother got drunk, returned to the powwow late that night and knifed Lone Elk in the back." He covered his face with his hands, then wiped his eyes.

"Oh Jeez," I said.

"Yeah," Iggy said, wiping his face again. I felt a shift in him, an increased awareness of himself. He was travelling back from a great dark void into this room with me, back into his body. He pulled his legs up under himself and stood up. "Sorry I snotted all over you. I'll get you a clean shirt." His voice was distant and flat, but I was glad he was coming around. He walked into the bathroom. While NB and I waited, we heard the toilet flush then water running in the sink. When he returned, his eyes were still red, but his face was clean. He moved to a dresser, pulled out a T-shirt and tossed it to me.

He continued his story as I peeled off my shirt and pulled on his T-shirt.

"So…you haven't talked to Louise, Ig. You have to. Just tell her something, anything. She doesn't know what the hell is going on with you. She thinks she did something wrong. Or maybe you're a bi-polar psycho and this is the other side."

"Maybe I am. Sure feels like it." He sat down again next to me.

"So…if Running Deer will take you back, are you going to take her back?"

"It's killing me, Haint. I love her so damn much, just seeing her again my heart busted wide open and I wanted to just scoop her up, cover her in kisses…"

"But?"

"She married someone else, Haint. *Married.* Left me and married a guy and got pregnant with a kid in less time than we saw each other." His voice dropped to a whisper, "She was on birth control when we were together."

"Oh." I said.

Ouch.

The refrain from Bruno Mars's "Now She's Dancing with Another Man" trailed in from the living room.

"We talked about getting married, having kids, Haint. Why did she run away from me to find some other guy? How could I trust her again? I wasn't good enough for her before, I'm so scared she just needs me because she's pregnant."

"What did she say, Iggy?"

He drew in a breath and held it. "That's just it. She says she loves me, always has, always will. But when I asked her about Lone Elk, she said she loved him too, it was just a *different love*."

"Okay…" I said. Part of me understood this: if love came in types of food, I'd say I've had the chocolate cake love: sweet, delicious but totally bad for me; the meat loaf love: not *la grande passione*, but solid and steady; and then the spicy Thai stir-fry: incendiary, tasty and fresh, a bold array of feelings with a secondary burn at the finish.

"And I do love Louise, I think," Iggy said. "She's not my soul mate, though."

Chords from Pink Floyd's "Comfortably Numb" drifting down the hall. "Do you think you always have to marry your soul mate?" I asked. "I mean, in the big scheme of reincarnation, if we come back time and time again, do we have to keep getting married over and over? Somehow, I don't think that's all that it's about. If you and she are soul mates, truly, maybe you just spend some time together this time around."

"But what if she just made a mistake and this time the dream would be real. We'd get married, settle down, have children…"

"Did she say she's ready for that? Did she say she wanted to live here, in this house with you?" My gut said that she didn't. She was full of wanderlust when she left, and she just floated back into town again. Was she staying this time? Somehow, I doubted it.

"Not exactly," Iggy said, looking down.

"Is she back for good?"

"I don't know," Iggy said, sniffing. "Badger called her; their mother is in Hospice. She's not expected to live much longer."

NB's stomach let out a Yeoowwwwarpppp! which summed up the situation, I thought.

The Pink Floyd guitar and drums were reaching an agonizing climax.

"Jeez, Ig, what the hell channel are you listening to?"

"It's a mix of top breakup songs."

I was about to get up and turn it off when NB's ears alerted to a car door closing. She barked and bolted out of the room. I followed. She threw herself against the door. There was a knock and then the door swung open. Naughty Britches leapt up, pawing at Louise. She wore jeans, white sneakers and a scrubs top with an ID lanyard around her neck from Quick Fit, her physical therapy job in Gainesville.

"He's here, isn't he?" She asked, wiping her face, which resembled Iggy's earlier. A sheen of tears covered her cheeks; her mascara was smeared. "Are you ghosting me too, then?"

"Oh, hon, no," I said, pulling Naughty Britches away from her. "I got your message. I came out to talk to him. I didn't want to say something that wasn't— " What a hollow, pathetic excuse for not calling her. *Merde*. But she wasn't really registering what

I was saying anyway.

Across the room, Bonnie Raitt was building up to the chorus of , "I Can't Make You Love Me."

"Right," she said, looking past me.

"He's in the bedroom," I said, nodding my head in that direction.

"Okay," she said, moving past me.

Bonnie was singing her sad heart out as if she was directing it at Iggy on poor Louise's behalf. *Just what they need.* I crossed the living room and hit the power button.

I leashed NB and we left, closing the door on sounds of crying and talking coming from the bedroom.

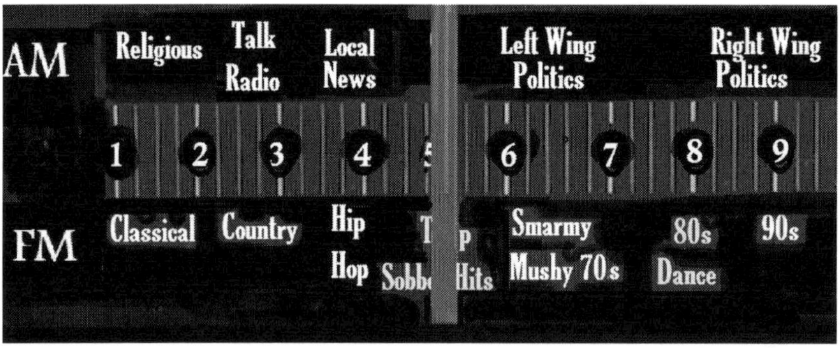

Chapter 10

Friday October 17: Will He Run from Running Deer?

I had choppy sleep Thursday night; a looping dream where Nicole was leading vigorous repetitions of sun salutes to a packed yoga class. On the fourth repetition, I noticed with shock that when Nicole stood up, arms stretched over her head, an enormous belly protruded before her. She was profoundly pregnant. Her face morphed into Running Deer's and she began speaking in a rapid mantra:

"Coming and going, I love me, I love you, I love everyone. We are all one and I will go where I want when I want with whoever I want in the circle of life, coming and going…"

She cascaded forward in a bend and with a sharp cry gave birth to a baby boy with a feather in a band around his head. The boy looked up and began to cry.

The feeling of the dream was positive; the baby was fat and healthy. There was a sense of well-being about the baby, despite the crying. He needed attention.

I pulled my glasses on and looked outside. A layer of fog clung low along my back fence, hugging the trees, a hint of cool, dry autumn in the air. Thank goodness. The summer seemed endless; I almost forgot we got some change in seasons.

I padded to the bathroom, put in the lavender contacts, my favorites, and rubbed my face with a cold-cream-smeared washcloth. Looking back on the bed, NB and Mischief were dead asleep, butt to butt, in a furry paisley pattern.

I headed for the kitchen and Mr. Coffee. As the machine gurgled to life, sending out the first promising aromas of dark roast, my phone rang. A little early for the telemarketers, I thought. Suspicious, I wandered over to the caller ID.

It was Iggy. I snatched up the receiver.

"Hey, you," I said, "How did it go?"

"I didn't wake you up, did I?" he asked.

"Nope. Dish. Wait. Let me get caffeinated." I trotted back to the kitchen and fixed myself a cup with what was brewed already. I added a splut of milk and dashed back to the phone.

"So?"

"We had a long talk; I told her everything and apologized a thousand times for being an ass and not telling her sooner. I told her I was really stuck and terrified of making the wrong choice."

"How did she take it?"

"We cried a lot. I told her I love her and would never want to hurt her or deceive her. I told her my fears about getting burned again or losing her. She was amazing. She said she loved me and really thought that I was THE ONE. You see that she's in the same position with me that I'm in with Running Deer. It sucks, Haint! She's afraid I don't think she's good enough for me, and I'm hurt that Running Deer didn't think I was THE ONE. I hate this!"

"You are turning this into a black and white, all or nothing, Ig. What if there is no THE ONE, and there is, instead, the right one for right now? Remember the bit about 'everyone you meet along the way is your teacher'?" I took a quick gulp of coffee. It bordered on too hot but was delicious.

I heard him exhale. "I have to make a choice. I'd like to make the right choice. Louise understands. Meanwhile, she made these B&B reservations and it's too late to cancel, so we decided to go to St. Augustine and chill out. It'll get me away from Running Deer, and the beach might help clear my head. We can keep talking."

"Talking is good," I said, taking another sip of dark heaven. "Besides, didn't I hear that it's homecoming weekend? Good time to be out of town."

"Oh, right. The Gators are playing Missouri tomorrow. Sure hope they get their act together. The LSU game was just upsetting."

"Oh, Right. Yeah…upsetting," I said, not having any idea.

"Oh, shut up, I know you don't care. Anyway, we're leaving as soon as we get done packing. She's in the shower. We're going to stop for breakfast on the way. I just wanted to call you while I could talk alone."

"Did you get any sleep last night?"

"Oddly, yes. It was a huge relief to get it all out in the open. After we talked, I took a long shower, then she gave me a massage that put me right out. I'm still really confused, but it's like I'm so exhausted, I don't care right now. I don't have the energy to struggle."

This was favorable news, especially on the heels of the weird dream I'd had of Running Deer blathering about "do what I want with whoever I want" that had sounded self-serving to say the least. I was pleased that Louise had a calming effect on Iggy.

"Glad to hear it, Ig. Hope you two have a mellow, restorative weekend. Call me when you get back, eh?"

"Love you, sis."

"You too, *brat*," I said, using the Polish/Russian word for brother like brat in bratwurst, a reversion to our childhood.

Naughty Britches wandered out and gave me that subtle look that indicates I can either let her outside or she can go pee on a rug somewhere. Or go investigate in the kitty litter snack tray and come back later.

"Let's go potty, little girl," I encouraged, and opened the kitchen door. She swaggered outside and stood for a long moment assessing the day. There were hints of fall coolness in the air and the lack of humidity was luscious. I eyed my hot tub and contemplated a quick but relaxing soak.

NB looked back at me then moved a few steps forward, yawned and squatted.

"Good girl," I said, pulling my tired old bathrobe together. It was actually coolish. How lovely! Definitely a hot tub morning.

NB shuffled back inside, and I poured a bowl of kibbles for her. She stared at the bowl and looked up at me. "Where's the good stuff?" Her eyes asked. Meanwhile, Mischief wandered in, stretched and yawned. NB licked his face and looked back at me. Mischief peered at her bowl and turned away.

"Fussy, aren't we?" I asked, pulling a leftover Chipotle roasted chicken from the refrigerator. "Here. Will this do?" I pulled some chickeny bits off and dropped some in each of their bowls. This was the game-changer. They tucked into their respective breakfasts.

I grabbed a towel and headed outside. After a few turns under the outside shower, I pulled back the hot tub cover and hit the jets. I stripped down and climbed in. The temperature was perfect—cool air on my face, welcoming womb-like temp on my body. Leaning my head back, I closed my eyes and began a meditation on gratitude.

Dear Divine Universe, thank you for this day, and all the blessings in my life, the ones I'm aware of, and the ones I completely take for granted. Blessings to all those who are physically suffering, those languishing in hospitals, those who are alone and suffering mental disturbances…

Something soft caressed the top of my foot. *What was that?* My eyes popped open, I jerked upright, and levitated out of the tub. I hit the jets button so the water would settle. A nebulous green blob swirled slowly around the bottom of the tub then caught a current and floated upward.

It was the remnants of a poached frog. As it rolled over, the dead eyes looked at me as a bit of back leg drifted away from the main body.

The peace and gratitude vanished in a wave of anger and revulsion. Revulsion because, yuck, bathing with a dead frog was not part of my meditation plan, and anger because I am constantly chasing frogs away from the hot tub, but they keep slithering up under the cover for warmth then drowning and becoming frog soup.

I said a quick prayer for the frog, wishing it a good journey and better life in the next go-around. Using a cup for tub chemicals, I scooped the carcass out of the tub as best I could, flipped the cover back on, dumped the carcass in the shrubbery and went inside. The moment of relaxation was gone.

I was toweling off when my phone rang. It was Lorraine.

"Hey, you, how are you doing? How's the ankle?" I asked.

"Just great. It's starting to itch; it hurts and I'm cranky and lonely. What are you doing today? Can you come over? I could use some help. Lerlene is busy."

"Of course."

"Oh! Guess what? Lulabelle gave birth to eight puppies."

"Oh?"

"Five girls, three boys."

"Wow."

"They offered me one, if I wanted. They feel so bad about my ankle and all."

"You want a Chihuahua?"

"No, but I bet they're adorable puppies."

"Puppies are always adorable."

"Want to go visit?"

"Dying to, but not with this ankle. Mrs. Collins is texting me videos. There's one with a skullcap. They've named him Yamaka."

"You aren't thinking of getting one, are you?"

"I might."

"Hunh. I'd never figure you for a Chihuahua momma. I'll

be over in half an hour. Let me get dressed. I just took a soothing bath with a dead frog."

"*What?* Gross!"

"Yeah. See you soon."

The day slid by visiting with Lorraine and doing simple chores for her like cooking and laundry. It felt good to be helpful.

When we are well, we completely take for granted the simple things like the ability to get dressed, take out the trash, make a bed, haul laundry out of a washer. With metal rods in her ankle, significant pain and crutches, Lorraine's day-to-day activities had been reduced dramatically.

"Bookings are picking up, eh?" she asked with enthusiasm. "That's great."

"Yes. I've got a retired couple and a few divers coming in tonight for the weekend and a folk band on their way to the Keys coming next week. It's not much but it's something. But Halloween is looking really good."

We were working on our second round of happy-hour margaritas (hers was alcohol-free) when she said, "Of course, if I got two puppies, they'd be able to play with each other and keep each other company."

Sunday Night: Just Say No

The weekend drifted by. My few retreat guests had been easy maintenance which had allowed me more time to hang out with Lorraine and help her around the house.

It was about nine o'clock on Sunday night. Sitting on the

couch in my pajamas with Mischief and Naughty Britches snoozing beside me, I was engrossed in a peculiar old black and white movie from the forties called, *The Ghost Train* when Iggy called.

"Hey *brat*."

"Yo, Sis."

"How'd the weekend go?" I asked, hitting the pause button on the remote.

"Good. Real good. We talked a lot. You know, Louise is just so comfortable to be around…"

"Not like Running Deer?"

"I think I always felt, well, I'm not sure what the right words are, but edgy, fearful…I loved Running Deer, you know that, but it felt like she was gliding along like a champion skater and I was stumbling along the rail trying to keep her in sight. She'd glide past me and laugh and glide away again. I never felt like I was gliding with her; it was more like wishing, pretending I could keep up."

"So, things are more balanced with Louise?" I said, trying to disguise the excitement in my voice.

"Yeah. It's solid. Comfortable. Honest."

"Sounds like you've made a decision."

"I think so."

"Have you told Running Deer?"

"No…"

I waited. The frozen scene on the screen was of the silhouette of a train engineer carrying a lantern down a misty train track. He was purported to be a ghost, but I doubted it.

But it was a great effect. Spooky.

Silence.

"You are going to, right?" I asked.

"Yes, but—"

"The sooner you do it, the better—"

"I know, but—" He sighed. "How do I tell her?"

"Well, I wouldn't text, that's for sure," I said.

"You know I wouldn't do that... it's just that when I see her in person, I lose myself. Like I just can't close that door, you know? Like I want to leave it ajar. Like I just can't watch her face when I say no."

"Call her."

"Yeah."

"Iggy, I know it's hard, but you've got to."

"I know. Maybe tomorrow..."

"Iggy!"

He sighed again. "Right. You're right. I will. Tomorrow. G'night sis."

"Love you, *brat*," I said.

Chapter 11

October 20: Monday, Monday

I was in the middle of a dream about a ghost tour in St. Augustine. Iggy, Louise and I were in the Tolomato Cemetery which, covered by a canopy of oak trees, is unnaturally dark and quiet at night. The guide was telling us about the ghost of a little boy sitting way up in the granddaddy oak and how his ghostly thin legs dangled down and the dark spaces where his eyes should be were often described as giving one the feeling he was radiating menace. I couldn't see him, nor did I want to. I was wishing myself out of the cemetery when the frightening silence was stabbed by loud, mournful shrieks coming from so close by that we all jumped and screamed.

I woke with a start, disoriented in darkness. In the middle of the night, a few days from a new moon and without my glasses, I might as well have been locked in a safe; I could see nothing.

And the wailing shrieks from my dream were, in real life, moving across my back yard. I felt Naughty Britches jerk upright, shoot off the bed, fly down the doggie steps and bark her way to the back door.

Woah woaharr-wooh! Wooo-ooo – oor! Something was crashing through underbrush ahead of the wild baying. Some part of my mind fought the fear and panic with logic. Not screaming banshees or phantoms coming to get us. Dogs. Dogs chasing something like a deer through the woods.

Yarp! Yarp Yarp! Yarp! Naughty Briches barked a continuous high C.

I fumbled for my glasses and the lamp switch.

Tha-wump! came from the porch as NB threw her body against the door. *Tha-wump!*

The wailing grew fainter as it moved east.

I got to the porch and flipped on the flood lights. NB was frantic, hurling her body at the door.

I looked outside, not sure what to see, not entirely sure I wasn't still dreaming. Nothing. My back yard as normal. No marauders or ghosts, just the bird feeder.

Naughty Britches looked up at me with frenzied eyes, bouncing, "I'll track 'em! I'll get 'em! What's the hold up? Let me GO!"

"I don't think so, little girl. You'd never come back, and mommy would be so sad."

I bent down and petted her. She bucked in protest, but eventually she decided that getting petted was better than chasing monsters in the dark.

My pulse was slowing, and my breathing was getting back to normal. "Let's go back to bed, Miss Naughty B."

NB glanced at the door, to me and back to the door.

"No way, kiddo." I pointed to the bedroom. "Go."

Her head and tail drooped; she ambled toward the bedroom like a fat old woman using a walker: lots of side to side, not much forward momentum.

As we passed the kitchen, I turned on the light and looked at the clock over the sink: 3:53 AM. Various traditions have it that 4 o'clock in the morning is an optimal time for meditation. Still keyed up from the adrenaline rush and confusion of the dream world folding into my waking world with yowling distress, I plopped myself down on my meditation cushion in the corner of the bedroom as NB tromped up the pet stairs, did a few circles and settled on the bed with a sigh. I lit a few candles and pushed the button on my meditation timer, pre-set for twenty minutes.

I mentally sent love to Iggy and Louise and hoped they could sort out the Running Deer mess. My breathing got deeper. I concentrated on one of my favorite meditations, a form of shavasana in which you send love and gratitude to your body starting from the head and work down to the feet, sending love to joints, skin, organs and the various systems: digestive, circulatory, nervous, respiratory, etc. The timer chimed while I was sending love to my knees. By the time I finished thanking my toes, my yawns were syncopating with NB's snores. I blew out the candles, got into bed and took my glasses off. I was beginning a dream as my head hit the pillow.

It was a little after eight o'clock when my land line rang. I listened as my answering machine went through its spiel in the imitation voice of Jack Nicholson, finishing with "...and if you turkeys don't wanna leave a message, it's no big deal just...don't ever call here again."

Urliss or Hollis, I wasn't sure which one, spoke. "Haint? You there? Uh, we was wonderin' if you've seen Willie or Waylon?"

I swallowed my coffee and picked up the receiver. "Hello. It's me. You aren't seriously calling this early in the morning to ask if I've been to a Willie and Waylon concert, are you?"

"Oh hey, Haint. Naw, not that. The dogs, Willie and Waylon? Oh yeah, maybe you ain't met them yet. We got these two bloodhound brothers. Heh-heh. They look almost identical, just like us, 'cept Waylon's got an ear that ain't right, just like me! Ain't that somethin'?"

Ah. I was talking with Urliss. Urliss and Hollis are middle-aged identical twins who tend to dress alike, usually in overalls or hunting garb. Urliss is missing his left earlobe resulting from a bar fight in Daytona.

"Somethin'," I muttered.

"But we just got 'em 'bout a week ago, and they dug out o' the pen we built for 'em. Run off sometime last night."

"Well, there was a ruckus in my yard last night around four in the morning, Urliss." I'm so bad. I mimic people easily, and somehow talking with the twins, quaint words like 'ruckus' pop into my vocabulary. "I thought it was a banshee howling, but I'm guessing it was your dogs chasing a deer. They were running east."

There was a bit of cussing back and forth as Urliss relayed this information to Hollis. Then Urliss came back on the line, deflated. "Well, would you call us if you happen to see 'em again?"

"You bet."

Don't get me wrong, I'm a dog lover. I was sure Willie and Waylon would melt me in a heartbeat, assuming they came home and were unharmed. But the idea of living next door to baying bloodhounds while trying to run a meditation center didn't exactly butter my biscuit.

I sighed and finished my coffee.

One can get used to anything, the Inner Critic said.

The phone rang again; the caller I.D. came on with IGGY B. I swept up the receiver.

"What's up?"

"Haint?"

"Were you expecting someone else?" I asked. I didn't mean to be snarky, but he sounded surprised. Or uncertain. Uh-oh, that wasn't a good sign.

"I tried to call Running Deer. Suggested that we meet at a coffee shop to talk. Before I could say all I wanted to, she asked if I would go with her to visit her dying mother."

"What? This sounds like a trap to lure you back."

"Well," Iggy said in a squirmy way, "she knows that I really liked her mom and what with her being pregnant—see, her mom wasn't thrilled when she took off—"

"As I recall, you weren't either."

"I know, but she feels vulnerable— "

"Well, she's the one who made that choice."

"I know."

She's sucking you in, *brat*," I said.

"But maybe I *should* go say goodbye to her mom. We were kind of close."

It was my turn to sigh heavily. "Iggy. It sounds like you are asking me for permission to go visit your ex's dying mother. I can't and won't make that call. You have to do what your heart tells you. My concern is that Running Deer is manipulating you, luring you back into her life by playing the pity card."

"I know. Running Deer said her mom asked to see me."

"Oh."

I waited, expecting more excuses. He was silent.

"You're going, aren't you?" I asked.

"I think I have to."

I honestly didn't know what to say. "I love you, Iggy. Do what you need to do but be careful. And don't forget about Louise."

"I know, believe me," he said, sounding utterly miserable.

"When are you going? Today?"

"This week some time. Not sure. Running Deer wants me to help her take her mother on an outing to the beach to see a sunrise one last time."

"Sun*rise*?" That meant an overnight. "Please tell me she doesn't expect you to share a room."

"Haint, please. No. I'll have my own room. The hospice caregiver will stay with her mom--assuming it can be arranged.

She'll have her own room. So will I. And Badger. The whole plan kind of depends on Badger's schedule. He's working out the details with Hospice."

"Oh." Badger again. "Where?"

"Flagler. They want a dog-friendly place so her mom can bring Hawk Eye, her German shepherd."

"Wasn't that dog part wolf?"

"Yes. The Lapis is super cool about dogs. She'll get a downstairs room; she can be wheeled right in from the parking lot."

"Sounds like they've thought of everything."

"Haint, don't be ugly. Her mom was more of a mother to me than ours was."

I chuckled. "That's not much of a stretch. Bears could be--"

"Haint. I'm not stupid. But her mom specifically asked that I come."

"Okay, I get that. And I get the last wishes and peaceful departure and all. Just don't lie to Louise. Or yourself."

"Yeah."

"I'm here for you."

"I know. Love you." He hung up before I could say, "Love you, too."

Chapter 12

Saturday October 25: Who Are You, Buster?

After a bumpy night with twitchy legs and anxious dreams, I woke to the *wurp-wurp-WURRACK* of Naughty Britches throwing up on the rug. A real oriental rug, just inches from the tile. I pulled my glasses on, got her outside, and found some carpet cleaner. The pile she left for me had lots of grass in it.

"Wish I knew what's bugging you, little girl," I said, even though she was still outside.

It was still dark outside, but there was no point in trying to go back to bed, so I finished swabbing at the stain and moved on to making coffee. I heard the doggie door bang in the bedroom. A moment later NB sauntered into the kitchen. No tail wag. She plopped herself down by her food bowl.

Werrp! Reeeeep! Her stomach was making alien noises again.

"Got into the kitty litter, did you? Or some nasty thing in the yard?" Had I given her something she couldn't handle? She had a bit of chicken breast in her dinner, that shouldn't be a problem. I got the The Pink Stuff for Tummies out of the fridge and spooned a dose into her mouth.

"That should help, sweetie."

She regarded me with the saddest version of sad eyes. She shook her head and pink droplets flew side to side. I felt wetness on my lip.

"Thanks, but I think I'll have coffee," I said, wiping my hand over my cheek.

I tried a sit on the cushion, lit some incense and candles and set my chime timer for fifteen minutes. I sipped coffee and focused on gratitude. Okay, so my business was flagging and that made me anxious, but I had my health, good friends, a roof over my head, and a peaceful house, even with NB's alien belly commentaries. But when the chime went off, my mind was still antsy. *Do something physical. Clean the house. Better, work in dirt. Repot something. Plant something.*

I pulled the grumpy ghost shirt from the top of the clean laundry pile, and a working-on-threadbare pair of jeans. Ratty and unsightly, but super comfy.

I fixed a bagel with peanut butter and got a coffee refill. "Let's go out in the yard," I said, opening the back door for NB. She found a cool spot in the shade of the potting shed while I potted loquat seeds in starter containers. That done, I got out the clippers to hack at some grapevines that were taking over a cassia tree. It felt great to liberate the strangled tree. I found another patch of overgrowth to attack. Despite the heat and sweat, it felt great to make such progress.

Glancing up, for a moment, I regarded a walkway rapidly disappearing under a creeping groundcover. I'd need a shovel, an edger and a broom. It wouldn't take long. Then I'd call it quits. *Psiakrew!* ♥

The edger was in the shed at the retreat. I'd go get it when I finished this last little bit of vines. I was straining to reach a thick stem when I got jabbed in the eye by a branch that poked over the rim of my glasses.

Wow. You know, the austere religions that promote self-flagellating have one thing right. Pain sure gets you to focus.

I dropped the clippers and put pressure on my eye. As the pain reached its crescendo, I waited, taking slow breaths. I pulled my hand away and opened the eye. Blurry at first, but yes, I had vision. Whew. Lucky girl.

Perhaps this was a reminder to pay attention to what was right in front of me.

NB followed me inside while I took a short break to rinse the eye and get a drink of water. A small but angry red spot hovered to the left of the eyeball. Lucky miss.

I noticed the lack of alien growls in NB's belly. Hooray! The The magical pink elixir was working.

"Wanna go for a ride? We've got to run next door a sec."

A glimpse of myself in the full-length mirror on my way out made me laugh. I had a thin scratch over my nose and some angry red scratches on my arms above the glove lines. Madhouse hair was icing on the fruitcake. Some witch hazel

---

♥ Polish, pronounced "sha crev" literally means "dog's blood", but it's a very mild curse word, the sort your parents or grandma would use, even in the presence of children.

and a long bath would be grand when I finished.

Keys, dog, coffee pot off, back in a sec. I didn't lock up or even grab my purse.

I pulled my F-150 into the retreat parking lot, parked, and peered at the vehicle in front of the office. It looked like the forensic unit van or the county animal control truck, but this bad boy had all kinds of bells and whistles and sat atop an F-350. Special Ops black, with off-road tires and rims with spikey rivets and several antennae sticking up from a box on the roof, I half expected this monster to breathe or the antenna to twitch and swivel to face me.

But wait, there was more. Attached to the trailer hitch was a shallow-drafted camouflaged fishing boat covered with a camo tarp. This was no ordinary boat trailer. Painted black to match the F-350, the trailer also had matching heavy-duty tires and riveted rims. I guessed I was looking at well over $450,000 worth of equipment.

I picked up NB and set her on the ground. We walked around the imposing intruder, a self-proclaimed Bengal Tiger 4x4 or so it said in a large font over the right rear tire. Despite the dark window tinting, the driver was clearly not in the front seat. I walked completely around the vehicle, wondering at the outer compartments, some padlocked. The menacing T-bird from the other day came to mind, but was a Mini Cooper compared to this behemoth.

I trotted up to the office and stepped in; no one waiting for me there. Odd.

"Stay here, little girl," I said, coaxing NB into the office and closing the door. I walked to the meditation hall and opened the door to find a handsome man, eyes closed, in full lotus position. His bare feet, high on his thighs, on *my* cushion in front of *my* butsudan, or Japanese altar. My CD player was running softly, sounds of gentle rain and flute music filled the room.

"Hello? Excuse me?" I said.

No answer.

I took off my shoes and walked over to him. His posture was perfect, his face serene and relaxed, his eyes just slits of exposed brown.

"Hello?" I asked again.

His shoulders twitched. He exhaled a contented moan. No answer. Was he faking this or was he really zoned out? It looked real.

Okay…a strange Special Ops fishing guy stopped in unannounced, took over my meditation hall and was now unresponsive in a nirvana bliss out. I wasn't sure what I felt. Should I be angry? Should I just leave and come back in half an hour? Should I call the sheriff and report an intruder? That seemed extreme.

And this guy was quite appealing. I know, I know, a major lesson in Buddhism is equanimity, don't be distracted by looks…delusion of the mind, yadda yadda…serial killers can be handsome too, right? I was wary but felt no threat. His coloring was all Indiana Jones brown, from his full head of wavy hair going back to a short ponytail and the precision beard that traced a thin line along his jaw, to his tanned skin, brown shirt and cargo pants.

His lips parted to release that faraway contented moan again.

Wow.

I couldn't just keep staring at him, it seemed intrusive. Pull up a cushion and join him? How did he *do* that anyway? My meditations were often productive, my thoughts subsided, and time slipped away, but I didn't get deep like *that*. A wave of doubt and inadequacy hit me. This stranger could meditate better than I could. But hang on, it wasn't supposed to be a competition, so, why did I feel so dopey all of a sudden? *Schiesse!*

Oh, for pity's sake. Get a grip. I pulled over a cushion and sat, allowing the music to fill my mind. Relax. As my breathing slowed, I smelled something pleasant that took me back to childhood. Waiting for my Dad to get a shave and haircut in a barber shop. My feet dangled from the chair and I swung them in lazy circles, smelling soap, Barbasol, pomade and bay rum. That's what this guy smelled like, if you add a woodsy musk.

He was still surfing the bliss. I closed my eyes. Slow breath in, slow breath out. Thoughts like clouds passing. Breathing in, breathing out. I was just getting to an empty place—

"Aww, you must be Ms. Haint, right?"

My eyes popped open. I recognized that voice, that slow, take-your-time drawl, where picking the next word was like selecting a ripe peach at market.

His gorgeous greeny-brown eyes took me in. The mustard ghost shirt, mussed hair, the holey jeans. More than my ponytail was coming undone.

"Are you, Mr. Shadetree?"

It couldn't be! I expected Buster Shadetree to be some redneck crackpot with bad breath, a lazy eye, a limp and body odor. *This*? This man was a Bigfoot hunter?

"Buster, please," He said, offering a tanned hand. I shook it. Firm. Muscular. Callouses on the tips of his fingers. "I know I'm a mite bit early. Hope you don' mine, I came by hopin' you might be here. You warn't, but I thought I'd have me a look aroun'. You've done one heckuva job fixin' up this ol'place!"

"Thanks," I said, feeling tongue-tied, and painfully aware that I hadn't brushed my hair, applied deodorant, had no make-up on. There was a red spot under my eye from almost blinding myself, which was likely magnified by my thick glasses. Sweat stains in my arm pits, not to mention the scratched-up arms. My mother's harsh voice came to mind, "You look like something from the rag bag!" Worst of all, I was caught in the baby puke-yellow shirt. *Figures!*

"I peeked in here and saw them cushions," he continued "it's been a coon's age. Too long. Thought I'd just set a spell an' wait for you." His eyes dropped momentarily to the grumpy ghost on my shirt front.

"Shall I leave you to it then?" I asked.

"Oh, shoot no," he said unfolding his legs. "Reckon I'd like to get checked in and whatnot...find out what cabin we're gettin'. I kinda like cabin one on account of it's close to the woods and the shars, but it don't rightly matter. Figure the boys'll be here in a little bit."

Still adjusting to his accent, I was momentarily thrown until I realized he had meant "showers." My mind caught up, snagging on the last part of what he'd said. "Boys? You have sons?"

"Oh no," he said, shaking his head in a reflective no, "I jus' call 'em that. They're my assistants, Shane and Rebel." The radiance in his face dulled a bit. "Naw, no children…of my own. My ex had a boy from a previous marriage, but a'course she took 'im with her when we divorced."

I haven't been in the retreat business long, but I've gleaned from other retreat owners and bed and breakfast managers that people tend to unload all kinds of personal baggage when they go on vacation. I've done it too. Overshare. Reveal painful secrets. You think, hey, these folks don't know me from Adam's house cat, and it feels cathartic to let go of the angst.

In my short time as hostess/manager/owner of Blue's Lodge, I've had people confess to affairs, drug problems, as well as provide me with a laundry list of the medications they are on and surgeries they've had. It doesn't bother me. I assume it means they feel comfortable talking to me.

In this case, though, I was pretty sure he was signaling that he was available. I felt my face redden.

"So, it's Saturdee…you got a lot of folks comin' in…busy weekend, is it?" He was watching my face closely for some reason. I looked away.

"No, not exactly…"

He rubbed his thumb over his precision beard, "So…mightcha be available, or have ya got plans for dinner this evenin'?"

I blinked and I'm sure I blushed. Other than Buster and his crew, I had one couple and a family of four booked for the weekend. They had signed on for breakfast only. I was hardly busy.

"When the boys get here, we'll set up the cameras in the woods. After that, we'll have a regular cook fest. See, we all like to cook, and Shane's from Bayou country, he's all about the boil, and Rebel, well, he's The Grill Master. Cookin' for them's about as natural as breathin'. Can't say 'xactly what's on the menu, but it'll be good, no doubt. Sure'd be glad if you joined us."

I hesitated, wondering what I was getting myself into, picturing a possum head sticking up from a pot of carrots. With caution, I run on faith that a new experience will expand my horizons, and this one didn't seem too foolhardy. I heard myself answer, "Sounds intriguing. No, I don't have any particular plans. I'd be happy to join you, if it's really no trouble."

"Perfect," Buster said with a dimple-popping smile.

He was distracted by something in my hair.

"What?" I asked, instinctively touching my head.

He pointed, "You got a small pink blotch. I'da guessed you were growin' out a hair color expurment, but it's just in one place—"

"Oh, yeah." I felt my face flush. "No, not hair color. My dog was sick this morning. We both got medicated with the magic pink elixir."

"Ah-ha." He pointed to my arms. "Ya got a cat too?"

"Well yes, but he didn't do this, he's a sweetie-pie. No. Yard work earlier pulling greenbrier and wild strawberries. They would have won, too. We were both determined, but I had sharp clippers with long handles. In fact, I came over for the edger--"

He was nodding but not really listening. He was looking at my eyes.

"The red spot? Yeah. Accidentally poked myself in the eye. Should be fine."

He nodded again with an amused twinkle in his eyes. "Interesting shirt."

"Yeah, well, it's a work shirt...gag gift, you know me, grumpy ghost. Albino. I don't usually look like I rolled in the leafpile— "

The theme song from the X-Files startled me for a split second. Buster reached behind him and pulled his phone out of a pants pocket, still emitting the eerie *doodley-doodley bong, bong, bong* tones.

"Y'all here?" He asked into the phone. "Yeah. Be right out." He stood up, pocketing the phone. He reached down to me and offered his free hand to pull me up. I took it. His grip was warm and solid. His lifting me up chest to chest made me keenly aware of his maleness and that pleasant woodsy-musky smell. Nervous, I stepped back to create space between us. We walked outside and around to the parking lot. Hoping to hide the pink blotch in my hair, I walked a little behind him, patting at my head.

Chapter 13

Roamers and Tigers, Oh My

A whopping silver vehicle lumbered to a stop next to the Bengal Tiger. This was Earth Roamer according to the slanted black font over the driver's door. Whereas the Bengal Tiger was all black-ops-bad-ass down to its spiked wheels, Earth Roamer looked friendly: a field researcher's fantasy vehicle, with similar exterior compartments and antennae. I half expected Jane Goodall to step out of it. Earth Roamer was not towing any extra toys—no boats, no cages. I heard NB barking wildly in the office.

Buster raised a hand in a half-hearted wave.

The doors opened, and two men stepped out. The bald, muscular driver in a black tank, jeans and hiking boots, exuded confidence. With wide-set eyes, a slightly flat face and brown skin, he looked like a darker version of Yul Brynner. The passenger looked like a happy hippy with thin white hair in a ponytail, and matching beard and mustache. He wore thick round glasses that gave him a spooked gopher look. They stared at me.

I could've felt grubbier if I'd wallowed in a mud hole. As it was, my armpits were telling me I needed another coat of deodorant and the baby-puke-yellow shirt was beyond embarrassing.

"Where y'at?" The bald man asked moving toward me to shake my hand.

I blinked. *Why would he ask where I'm at? I'm standing right in front of him.*

"He's Creole. From Louisiana. He means hello," Buster said.

"Oh. Hi," I said, looking from Buster to this buff warrior, Yul Brynner/Michael Jordan mash-up.

"Your eyes are so pale…like moonlight," the bald man said taking my hand. He held it and caressed my palm with his fingertips. "*Belle*, I'm falling in love wid you."

Feeling not even remotely libidinous, I folded my arms across my chest. "You *must* say that to all the girls. I look like I climbed out of a dumpster.""

"No, *chere bebe*,"he said looking stricken. "I speak from de heart."

Buster beamed. "Her eyes *are* like shimmery moons. Boys, this is Haint Blue. Haint, your droolin' admirer here is Shane Ouellette♥. Don't pay him no mind, he's a reg'lar ol' charm machine. He'll put the romance on yer grammie. He cain't hep it. He's the 'riginal Grizzly Adams of the South, he can disappear in the woods for years just fine, not only survive, but thrive, and man-oh-man can he cook! Hoo-ey! You won't

---

♥ Pronounced "Willette"

believe how fine a cook he is. If this man serves up poison ivy stew with oak leaves and squirrel tails, you'll love it and come a-beggin' for more. He's hidin' a magic wand somewhere in his cookware. We've searched, but we ain't found it yet."

The hippie nodded. "It's true. I'll eat anything that man puts on a plate and be a happy camper." He patted his Buddha belly harnessed in overalls, straining the bib buttons.

Shane waved his hands towards his chest like a ground crew worker directing aircraft forward. "Shower me wid praise if you must. I can take it."

Buster gestured to the hippie. "And this shaggy beast here is Rebel Saggory. Don't let his Droopy Dog face fool you, now, he's a crafty ol' weasel and a damn fine cook, too. I'd trust him with my life. And he summons the angels from heaven when he plays his dulcimer."

Rebel took a bow.

"So how was the trip?" Buster asked them. He turned to me, "Shane came from Louisiana, lookin' into new reports of a rougarou. Unfortunately, it turned out to be a big ol' hoax, as we suspected."

I raised an eyebrow. "What's a rougarou?"

"Well 'at depends on who ya ask. Some say it's a variation on a Bigfoot, others believe it's more like a chupakabra."

Baffling. *How could these grown men talk about this stuff as if it were real?* I needed to stare at something to keep from laughing. Unfortunately, my eyes landed on Shane's watch, which had a large face and lots of inner dials. It was probably a watch, compass, barometer, stun gun and walkie-talkie. This did not help. These were adult-sized kids playing camp out. A huge giggle was cresting and about to break.

In desperation, I jammed my knuckles against my lips.

Buster must have sensed my disbelief. He added, "The stories of the rougarou don't have much foundation or evidence. Most likely, it's a legend, passed down since the French settlers to keep their children in line. Originally it was lou-garou. Like lupus. Wolf. A werewolf."

"Surely you don't believe in werewolves." I pressed my lips together harder, fist still in place.

Buster shrugged, his face pulled back in an I'm-not-telling expression, but there was a sadness to his eyes I couldn't interpret. Was that disappointment in my skepticism or something else?

"What we do now?" Shane asked.

"Let's park closer to cabin one, unpack and set out cameras," Rebel said.

"You said you were setting up cameras?" I asked. "Shall I show you around when you're ready?"

"No need." Buster's eyes twinkled. "We been here before. Come to think on it, you have the house next door, don'tcha? Could we put some equipment up in your woods as well?"

It was unsettling that Buster was familiar with my camp, and now he wanted to get to my home property too. It was clear he and Max had talked about me, but Max hadn't told me anything about Buster. Everything about this man was putting me off balance. I wanted to say no, but I couldn't see what harm it would do. If they were lucky, they'd get pictures of a few deer, a bunch of armadillos and maybe my fox.

"You aren't planning on killing anything are you? No

hunting here, Shane." A vision of a stew pot with a fox tail sticking out of it distressed me.

"Photo shoot only," Shane answered, with a Boy Scout salute.

"Then I guess it's okay. Watch out for snakes and poison ivy. And leave the meditation circle alone. I've got a group of women who…ah…will be using it exclusively. I've promised them total privacy."

I winced. That sounded mysterious and kinky, didn't it? I had tried to not identify them as Wiccans, but now I couldn't think of another explanation, especially when all three of the men were looking at me askance.

I shook my head, "No, no, it's not what you're thinking. It's Halloween or Samhain. They're Wiccan. They want the circle for their ceremony…honor the dead…celebrate the season. I'm not really sure."

Their faces relaxed.

Buster said, "Shouldn't be a problem. We can still put 'em on the trails, right?"

I nodded.

"Fine. We'll unpack, set up cameras, then Shane'll get his magic dinner wand out. What time is chow, man?"

Shane looked at his gadget watch. "Somewhere 'round candle lightin' time. Let's say…eight o'clock. Hope that's not too late for you, *Belle*?"

"I'll be there. Want me to bring anything? Dessert? Wine?"

"We got it. Just bring yo'self," Shane said with a wink. "You'll be dessert enough." He wiggled his eyebrows. This could have been oily and repulsive, but as he didn't seem to take himself seriously, it was charming.

Rebel said, "Don't listen to him, he's a natural born flirt. He probably smarmed the nurse who first diapered him, and he'll charm little old ladies until they twitterpate their pacemakers. He can't help himself."

Shane and Rebel got in the beastie-mobiles and drove to cabin one as Buster and I walked over. We walked in sync. I noticed that our gait was even. His gentle woodsy smell had my attention and my thoughts were again wrapped up in his maleness when he broke my reverie.

"You've got a four-wheeler with a wagon, don'tcha?"

"I do, do you need it?"

"It'd be great for settin' up our observation stations."

"I'll get it and pull it around."

I turned away and began walking, disgusted with myself torn between desperately wanting to run home and gussy up and delighted to have the excuse to hang around. My attraction to Buster had butterflies emerging from dormant cocoons in my stomach while a schizophrenic argument took place in my head:

Scheisse! Get a grip! Don't make an ass of yourself, for pity's sake!

I'm not, I'm being helpful.

Bull crap! You are mooning over this man, whose raison d'etre is to track creatures that don't exist! Do you really want to get involved with this delusional man just because he's attractive and seems to dig you? Grow up, you Ninny! Snap out of it! Go get a shower and get out of that stupid rag bag outfit!

I wasn't, I'm just curious about what all they're setting up in the woods. I want to see it.

You're fooling no one!

I paused at the shed to breathe normally and redo my ponytail. I unlocked the shed and started up the four-wheeler. *Take your time, don't act too eager.* I got it turned around, hitched the cart to it. Something about leaning down and attaching the wagon brought Max to mind. Something he said once...what was it? He had been dogging me about being single.

"Woman, you need to get yo'sef hitched up to a man, and I got me a fine idea!" He had rubbed his hands together. And what was with pushing me to getting my hair done and buying a new dress? And he seemed to know that Buster was coming, and Buster was acting like we were set up for a blind date. I wished I had taken Max's advice about getting "gussied up."

Pondering this, I drove over to cabin one. Shane was carrying an oversized black duffle bag to the cabin.

That bag is big enough to haul a body, I thought.

Buster and Rebel were hefting a black cargo tote out of the Bengal Tiger. They shuffled the tote to the cart and set it down sideways with a thunk*!* Rebel pushed dials on the chunky padlock and opened the lid.

Holy moley. An assortment of camo and bark-colored wildlife cameras looked up at us.

"Wow." I said.

"Somethin' ain't they?" Buster said. "We've found that havin' an assortment helps. Some have better motion sensors; some take better pitchers."

I realized he meant "pictures", but he pronounced it just

like pitchers and my mind jammed up wondering how motion sensors and baseball pitchers or water pitchers were related.

He continued pointing and talking. "This one's great for clarity, but not distance. It won't trip even if a military tank rolls by sixty feet out, but it'll take a National Geographic quality pitcher of a butterfly landin' on a limb ten feet away." He pointed at another one. "That one's got great range but takes a grainy photo. And these will send a text to my phone to tell me somethin' just tripped. I can pull it up on m' phone as it's happenin' an' record it in the Bengal." He sighed. "It's hard to get it all in one package, that's why we cluster 'em." He pointed, "Let's save those three plus the 360 for Haint's property."

He turned back to me, "Nah this baby's somethin'." He patted one of the cameras. "A fixed camera can only shoot what's right in front of it, so you could have a bear picnic takin' place just a foot out of frame and miss the whole show…but this l'il honey shoots all 'round. It'll only miss if the bears climb into the trees. But we're not after bears, and the Skunk Ape don't climb trees." He patted the camera again like a faithful retriever.

Realizing he hadn't asked about access to my property, I got the uneasy feeling he already knew my property. There wasn't a fence between the retreat and my house, just dense foliage. I always drove around. There was no trail. But Buster wasn't asking me about fences or trails or property lines. He knew.

So…with all this camera stuff, night vision goggles…I wondered what all he had seen at my house. My back yard was all woods with the assumption of privacy. I had a hot tub and an outdoor shower.

Nervous butterflies broke free of their cocoons and flitted around in my stomach like agitated moths in a jar. I took a deep breath and became aware of the *yark! yark! yark*! coming from the office.

NB was throwing herself at the door and barking wildly.

"Okay! I'm coming" I called as I trotted over to let her out. She dashed out straight, then realized she'd shot past me, turned like an ocean liner and came back, stopping but bouncing in place. *Yark! Yark! Yark*!

"Yes, I'm sorry I left you. Let's go home. I think you must be feeling better, eh?"

We'd just reached the truck when I heard that sexy voice say, "What's all the ruckus about? Max told me you had an ol' dog. Aww. I love Bassets. Had one m'self, a while back. Named Boogieman."

NB leaped away from me to paw at Buster who bent down to meet her.

"Ain't you a sweet ol' thang."

She popped herself over, offering her belly.

"I'll get-cher belly. You like 'at?"

NB wagged her tail like she was making a dirt angel.

"Hmm. You wearin' Pink Stuff lipstick, little'un. Your mamma said you was havin' tummy trouble. Ya must be feelin' better now, I'm guessin'." He glanced up at me. "She's a heartbreaker, ain't she? How old is she now?"

"That's my little girl," I said. "Almost eleven. She was two when I got her. I can't stand that she's got a white muzzle. She's not allowed to get old on me."

"Whatsername?"

"Naughty Britches."

"That's a hoot."

NB stretched her hind legs out straight, pointing her toes.

"You look jus' like a little ol' ballerina with them toes," Buster cooed.

"She must like you," I said. "She saves the toe points for special occasions. She's frugal with her kisses too," I said, then felt myself blush. *Why was I talking about kisses? Shut up, shut up, shut up!*

He grinned up at me. "Hope her mamma isn't like that."

"Uh, we'll be back," I said, coaxing NB to get off the ground. "I've got to get cleaned up and see to some stuff back at the house..."

Buster's green swirl eyes fixed on mine as he stood up.

There was that awkward pause when a conversation dies and a new one hasn't hatched yet. I stood up. "Should I bring anything for dinner?"

"Nope, think it's all smothered and covered."

It took me a minute to catch on to the reference to Waffle House lingo. He meant it was all taken care of. "Surely I can bring something."

He shook his head.

"Oh, come on, beer? Wine? Dessert?"

"Y'don't have to brang a thang, but you do whatever...you...want."

Ooh. He made this sound like a proposition. I felt my face redden and my thoughts get melty. What should I wear? Were we just going to hang out on the porch of the cabin, or tailgate with the Bengal Tiger? Would they drag me off into the woods for surveillance after dinner?

"Ah, what about dress code? It's just dinner, right, or are we sitting in a tree stand later? Should I hunt up some camouflage cargo pants? Boots?"

His eyes twinkled. He got right up in my personal space with that yummy smell and said, "You can wear whatever you want." He made that sound provocative. He twirled a strand of my hair into a lazy curl around his index finger. It was intimate and, not that I wanted to, it also meant I couldn't pull away. He glanced at the top of my head. "Were you going to touch up the pink bits?"

"I was just going to wash it out."

He nodded and took his time twirling his finger back out of my hair.

"You're a be-yoo-ti-ful woman, Miz Haint Blue, pink bits or not. Fine as frog hair cut eight ways."

I know, I know, it sounds ridiculous, except that the way he said it was right in my ear, drawled out and sultry. I swear, if anyone else had said it, I'd have hurt myself laughing, but instead a hot flash came on just then, a bad one. An oven heat swept over me. I swear my hair follicles were sizzling. Time to go. "See you later, then," I said. We were by my truck. I boosting NB up to the passenger seat. I walked briskly around to the driver side, trying not to flap my arms like a chicken to get more air.

"Back in a bit," I said.

Buster hadn't moved. He was watching me with an expression that I couldn't quite make out. It reminded me of Ricky staring at Lucy, tongue-tied.

I waved and started the ignition. NB settled into coast mode, draping herself over the console. I turned the air conditioner to full arctic blast.

"I think your mamma's having a hot flash, Naughty Britches."

As we pulled away, I looked in the rearview mirror. Buster was waving.

I was halfway home when I remembered the edger.

"*Scheisse!*" I yelled and smacked the steering wheel. I was not going to embarrass myself by going back for it, no way.

"Your mother is a dingbat!"

NB turned her head and gave me the ever-suffering expression, "Whatever, Mommy."

"And I'm burning this damn shirt when we get home."

Chapter 14

No Big Deal, Piece o' Cake

What to make? I couldn't go empty handed. The guys hadn't even hinted at the dinner menu. What dessert does one serve after possum stew, anyway? It was too hot to leave NB in the truck, so I ran her home. Normally I'd call Lorraine and beg one of her to-die-for cakes, but with her foot wrapped up in that TV antenna, no way. The local Whatcha Need was good in a pinch for staples, but I wasn't going to find gourmet inspiration there…Ah! The Art of Tarts! Nina Nyugen (pronounced "Win"—her husband was part Vietnamese), the owner would fix me up. I roared into town, did a few laps around to find a parking space big enough for my truck and dashed into the shop.

"Well, hey, Haint? How'ya doin'? You need more breakfast goodies for your camp?" Nina asked from behind the counter.

"Hey, Nina, how're you? No, but I do need something desserty, something pretty." I eyed the offerings in the glass case.

"Sure, hon." She gave me a sideways, give-me-the-skinny look. "What's goin' on? You look kind of excited."

"Oh, do I?" I said, trying to steady my breathing. "I got invited to a thing," I flapped a hand like it was no big deal, "and don't really have time to fix something, so I thought I'd pop in."

She looked me up and down, her eyes sweeping me with the intensity of a bloodhound sniffing your pants.

"Well let's see what we have here. Chocolate cake with a layer of raspberry…or that one, it's a mocha cream with walnuts and pecans on top…"

"Hmm. Not sure about the nuts…don't know if they've got allergy issues." I pointed to a fruit concoction. "That's gorgeous. What is it?"

"Pear-cranberry cobbler. It's got a shortcake base to it. And it's made with pear brandy."

"Ooh! Sounds divine! That's the one."

I fidgeted while Nina made a cardboard box and set the cake in it, then tied it with a festive orange ribbon. *Breathe, you idiot. Calm down. It's just dinner! And no telling what that might turn out to be. Could be squirrel on toast points or roadkill casserole for all you know.*

I must have exhaled audibly, as Nina's head popped up and she gave me the hairy eyebrow, "Are you *sure* you're all right?"

I took a moment for a long inhale. "Yes. Ducky."

An annoying *tap-tap-tap* got my attention. Looking around I realized it was me tapping the debit card on the counter. Once Nina processed my purchase and handed me back my card and the box, I quick stepped out of the shop like a seabird scooting ahead of an incoming wave. My mind raced: quick dash home, SHOWER! Feed the animals, make lunch. Take NB for a walk.

Primp. Maybe even nail polish and a pedicure for sandals. Good grief. It'd been ages since I last used nail polish; I hoped it wasn't dried up. A*nd seriously! What the hell was I going to wear?* The afternoon was turning into a monkey-mind blur.

To calm down, I nudged Mischief off my meditation cushion and plopped myself down. I lit a few candles and some incense and watched the thin line of smoke trail upwards. *This is me breathing in…this is me breathing out…this is me breathing in…this is me breathing out.* I set my timer for fifteen minutes and by the seventh minute had managed to focus on my breath until my mind was calm. *Inhale. This is me being calm and clear minded. Exhale. Don't make an ass out of yourself, it's just dinner. Inhale. This is me being calm and clear-minded. Exhale all anticipation. Inhale. You are calm and strong. Exhale all doubt.*

NB sat on the bed watching me with a disheartened expression as I dressed in a dark lavender print tunic over plum silk pants. I had pulled my hair up into a Katherine Hepburn-style bun and popped in my lavender contacts. My efforts with nail polish had been successful, I thought, waggling my sparkly toes into my sandals.

I said goodbye to Naughty Britches, locked the door and strode to my truck.

Dang! I forgot the dessert. *Let's try that again.*

Back to house…Unlock door…cross kitchen…grab

box...Lock door...Truck...Seatbelt...Go.

Showtime.

It's Just Dinner

Out of habit, I parked my truck by my office. Getting out, I heard music and male voices off to my right. I unlocked the office momentarily to flip on the switches for the porch lights and orange string lights wrapped around the porch rails. The comforting glow highlighted the Indian corn wreath on the door. *Nice. Welcoming.* Walking toward the sounds of activity, I noticed that the lights were off in cabin six. My family of four was probably in town having dinner at Paco's or Guido's. Catfish Springs had only the two non-chain dining options, Mexican or Italian.

The rest of the camp was quiet. Annoyed at the increasing number of mosquitoes intent on tapping their fiendish feeding straws into me like a blood frappé, I windmilled my arms around wishing I'd left my hair down, to use it like a donkey tail. My neck felt exposed. As I walked along the front of the meditation hall I felt a little flutter of nerves, like a debutante about to walk on stage. *Don't be an ass. Be yourself.*

Passing the second bathroom pavilion, cabin one came into view. Earth Roamer and Benal Tiger were pulled up just behind the cabin, and a village of tents and cooking equipment was wedged between cabin one and cabin two, reminiscent of street vendor scenes from India or Thailand. Smoke and steam rose from various sources filling the air with an intoxicating, mouth-watering aroma of meats and spices. Rebel was in the center tent, tongs in hand, orchestrating the addition of ingredients, while Shane stirred a huge tureen of chunky something flecked with bits of bright red. *Hot peppers. Oh boy.* They had rigged up a wireless sound system that was playing Big and Rich's hit, "Save a Horse Ride a Cowboy." The men were bobbing to the beat, with Shane yelling a story to Rebel over the music.

Shane gesticulated with his ladle, "And dat *vieaux peeshwank* jumped outta his *patrack*♥ and ran for da woods fast as a jack rabbit!"

Rebel pointed the tongs at Shane, "Yeah, he did. Ran like a scalded Haint—Ah-ha-ha-ha!"

"Dat *Couillion*♥♥*!*"

I had no idea what they were talking about, and hearing my name gave me a flash of paranoia since they guffawed together. As the pounding song's refrain came around again, Shane leaned back and made a lasso motion with his arm, singing, "Cause I'll saddle up my horse…"

Oh my. Did I mention that this man was easy on the eyes? If they had Chippendale auditions for men over forty-five, he'd get hired just for walking in the door. He spotted me and his face lit up.

"*Cher belle*! *Mon Dieu, comme elle est belle!*♥" He put a hand

---

♥ *vieaux peeshwank* jumped outta his *patrack*♣ = old runt jumped out of his run-down truck

♥♥ idiot

♥ My God, she's beautiful

to his chest, his shoulders still rocking to the song.

He did have charm, yes indeedy. I waved him off and said, "I brought dessert," holding up the cake box. "Where shall I put it?"

"We'll take care o'that," Rebel said, taking it from me. "We've got a Jack Daniels' pumpkin pie and whipped cream, too."

I realized Rebel was wearing a mossy-green apron with a huge black Bigfoot covering most of the fabric. The Bigfoot had a turkey leg in one hand and a jar of barbecue sauce in the other.

"Love the apron!" I said.

"Thanks!" he said, looking down at it with pride, "me too."

A huge propane burner heated stew, a fish fryer was bubbling oysters to perfection, and in back, a mobile of cast iron pots was suspended over a bed of coals. One table was dedicated to ingredients, while another was dedicated to disposable plates, utensils, sauces and garnishes. A smaller table supported a huge colorful salad, a mosaic of lettuce, apple, blueberry, cucumber, carrot, peppers and sprouts. Probably more I couldn't see.

I raised my voice to be heard over the music, "This is a serious operation...how many are you having for dinner again?"

Chapter 15

Bunch of Buzzguts♥

A motion caught my attention behind Shane, as Buster came around from the porch, running a hand like a comb through his freshly washed hair. No longer in a ponytail, it fluffed in layers to the collar of his dark green Henley. The shirt managed to look loose and comfortable yet cling in all the right places to accentuate his T-frame and trim belly. He ducked his head to get under the tent.

"How's it comin'?" He asked Rebel, then spotted me. "Oh wow, you look..." His eyes scanned me up and down. "You sure look purty, Haint."

"You clean up nicely, too," I said.

He strode to me, brushed his lips on my forehead in a butterfly kiss, and put an arm around me, guiding me closer to the huge pot Shane was stirring. "Hope your hungry...we got fried oysters, or you can eat 'em raw, like I like 'em...and the boys are puttin' the magic on some rabbit stew here. Oh, Lordy,

---

♥ Arcane word of Cornish origin, a buzzgut is one who eats and drinks much.

don't that smell good?"

It did. Savory and spicy. I was salivating. In the back of my mind, I wondered where the poor rabbits came from. Probably best not to think about it. A quick flashback to Urliss and Hollis presenting me with a bag of dead squirrels the previous month gave me a shudder. I let that thought pass, overpowered by the fabulous smell.

Rebel moved to the coal kitchen, took a metal rod and lifted the lid off a cast iron pot. "Cornbread's ready."

Man did that smell fantastic.

Buster asked, "Can I getcha somethin' to drink? Beer? Wine?"

"Sure. If it's oysters, I'll have a beer."

"Perfect choice," he said, his arm sliding away from my shoulder as he moved away to the Bengal Tiger returning with two opened longnecks. He was just slightly bowlegged, adding a cowboy element to his lanky, sexy swagger.

A new song started up with a forceful beat that made you want to wear heavy boots and stomp your feet. I didn't recognize it, but Shane was singing along, his body swaying. The catchy refrain came around, "Somethin' bad about to happen…" New Orleans was mentioned, and Shane was sure to belt that out loud.

"Nice. Who sings it?"

"Miranda Lambert and Carrie Underwood. *Great* song!" Shane said.

Lights swept through the trees as a vehicle looped into the second parking lot, hitting us with high beams until they killed the engine.

"Expecting someone?" I asked.

"Invited a coupla people," Buster said with a mischievous grin. That familiar feeling of being left out of the know crept over me. Max made me feel that way. Lorraine's aunt Moira had called him The Trickster. At least I think she'd been referring to Max. I looked at Buster with suspicion.

Doors opened and closed, and once my eyes adjusted again, I realized it was Urliss, Hollis and…someone talking his time getting out of the back seat. I recognized those skinny legs and the shuffle: Max. I looked back at Buster.

"You don't mind, do you?"

"Of course not."

Max shuffled toward me and gave me a hug. "Hey, sweetie. Why you look like a fresh peach." He leaned closer and whispered, "Glad you took my advice about gussyin' up. He-he." He pulled back and squinted. "What'd you do to your nose, hon?"

I brushed my nose self-consciously. Guess the make-up hadn't covered the scratch after all. Oh well. I hugged him back, trying to hide the bittersweet feelings welling in my eyes. I was pleased to see Max. He looked better than usual. He'd made an extra effort to shave, comb his hair and put on a clean, collared shirt and wrinkle-free pants. Hugging him, watching him walk with tentative steps and looking at his sunken eyes, it was as if he was now living dog years, and each week he was thinner and smaller. His aftershave smelled good but did not completely mask the pervasive nursing home smell.

"Max, so glad to see you. They didn't tell me you were coming."

Max winked at me and whispered, "So, how's it going?"

I pulled back. "What? The camp? Well, I'm booked for Halloween—"

He grimaced, "No! Not that, *you know…*" His eyes flicked toward Buster.

I didn't know what to say. Meanwhile, the Oakey twins, as usual in matching overalls, lumbered toward the food tent and fell into conversation with Rebel. Buster took drink orders and whisked into to the Bengal coming out with three fresh beers for the newcomers.

Shane waved, "Where y'at!"

"Good to see you, man," Urliss proffered his arm and Shane grabbed his hand. They shook hands like wrestlers. This male bonding ritual continued as Hollis stepped up next and fist bumped Shane, while Urliss sidestepped to Rebel and shook hands. Max greeted the monster hunters with a modest nod and a light shoulder bump. When all males had punched, slapped or wrestled their greetings, we clinked beer bottles together. "Cheers!"

"You boys came *en bon temps*♥!" Shane announced. "*Allons, souper*♥♥*!*"

We loaded up our plates and were ushered to the cabin porch, where they'd set up a portable table with a red and white bistro tablecloth and camp lanterns. The volume of the music

---

♥ in good time

♥♥Let's eat

was turned down to a background level, and from country to instrumental zydeco. Tiki torches with citronella oil staked around the porch and mosquito coils in the corners kept the insects at bay.

We all ate with gusto. The oysters were the best I'd ever had: plump, crisp on the outside, soft inside. And oh, the cornbread. Great googly-moogly was that heaven! And the rabbit! Tender and succulent with potatoes, carrots, peas, peppers and okra with hints of chilies. It was close to my heat threshold, which sent me back to the beer and cornbread. I felt like I'd barely made a dent in my meal when Shane sopped up the moisture on his empty plate with a bit of cornbread, saying, "I'll be back. I need a *petit morceau*♥ 'o dat stew."

Buster skewered a carrot, "Right! Y'all watch. Shane's idee of a "putt-ee more-so" usually involves a u-tinsel the size of a backhoe bucket. He'll be back with another mounded plate. I don't know where he puts it, he don't seem to gain a pound."

Rebel put a hand on his rotund belly, "I know! I hate him. Don't know how he does it."

Hollis pushed his empty plate away and took a long drink of his beer. Something amusing came to mind; he almost spewed beer in his hurry to swallow and say what had tickled him. "Didja hear the story about poor Bubbha dyin' in the far?"

"Oh, here it comes," Shane called while ladling up more stew.

"Keep it clean, man, we got a lady present," Rebel advised.

♥ petit mourceau: French for little bit

Hollis nodded and waved, dismissing their concerns. "Poor ol' Bubba died in a fire. His body was burned up pretty bad. The morgue needed someone to identify the body, so they sent for his two best friends, Bo and Bill. Now, the three men had growed up together and always done everything together. Bo was called in. When the mortician pulled back the sheet, he grimaced and said, 'Oh, Lordy, I can't tell, his face is so bad. You better roll him over.' The mortician thought that was a little strange, but he rolled the body over. Bo looked puzzled. He shook his head, 'Nope, that ain't Bubba.' The mortician frowned. He turned to Bill. Bill looked at the body for just a second and said, 'Nope, it ain't Bubba.' The mortician asked the men, 'How can you tell?' Bill said, 'Well, Bubba had two buttholes.' '*What?* He had *two* buttholes?' asked the mortician. I've never heard of that.' 'Yup,' Bo said, 'I've never seen 'em, but everyone knew he had two buttholes. Every time we went into town, folks'd say, "Here comes Bubba with them two buttholes!"

Urliss fist-bumped Hollis, "Man, I love that joke."

Apparently, I was not the only one who thought that Urliss and Hollis could substitute for Bo and Bob. I fought not to choke on my cornbread. Buster pounded my back as tears came to my eyes.

Max slammed his hand down on the table and ba-ha-ha-ing with his mouth open, revealing his partially chewed oysters.

Shane, on his way back to the table, held his arms to his ribs as if his sides really were about to split. His heaping bowl of stew lurched, and I thought Max would end up wearing it.

Fortunately, he righted it in the nick of time, with only a dribble covering his thumb.

Buster's shoulders shook.

Hollis beamed, pleased that his joke had gone over so well.

And in that contagious way of laughter, we all ended up laughing at each other. We got ourselves under control and then Urliss repeated, "Them two buttholes!" which set us off again. I had to wipe tears from my eyes. My belly hurt.

I'd had a fleeting concern that the level of conversation was going to spiral downward toward dick jokes or some such but fortunately, it didn't.

Urliss and Hollis were not far behind Shane in getting up to get seconds, each returning with another overloaded plate. By the time they sat down and dug in, Shane was sopping the last juices off an empty plate again.

With the zippy music, the bounty of food and okay, yes, the beer, a warm, safe feeling of gratitude and peace settled over me. I basked in the proximity to Buster; I loved watching Max having a good time; the ease with which the three amigos palavered♥ lulled me into a deep state of contentment I hadn't felt in ages. This was a moment I wanted to hold onto forever.

Dinner plates were cleared making way for coffee and dessert. The pear-cranberry concoction from the Art of Tarts was a big hit with Rebel and Buster, while the Oakey twins decimated the pumpkin pie.

"I could eat this for breakfast," Urliss said, smacking his

♥ palaver: excessive, idle and possibly misleading speech.

lips.

"Sure could," Hollis agreed.

"Y'all can have it. Go on, we'll wrap it for ya," Rebel said.

Max patted his stomach. "I haven't eaten like that since I don't remember when. That was better'n Thanksgiving."

No wonder. I've seen the food at the Old Oaks. I leaned my head on Max's boney shoulder; he leaned his head on mine like a head hug.

"I should help clear," I said, and started to get up but was promptly blocked by Buster and Rebel.

"We got it, Moon Eyes," Buster said, outlining my jawline with his thumb. He managed to twang out these two monosyllabic words into something almost incomprehensible ending with "ahhs".

I pulled away, frowning. "Moon Eyes?"

"Your eyes. They call to mind the legend of the Moon Eyed People of Appalachia. Know about 'em?"

I shook my head.

"Oh, here he goes on dem," Shane said, rolling his eyes and whole upper body in exaggeration. "He's got a thang for dis ahtist who draws de Moon Eyed Princess."

"Well, don't she look like the Moon Eyed Princess?" Buster asked.

Rebel nodded, "Yup. She does. No question."

I'm sure I blushed.

Buster continued, "It seems there's this legend about a mysterious group associated with the Cherokee but differ'nt. They was shorter, but the most distinguishin' thang was their eyes, all silver blue and magical, shiny an' mysterious like the moon, an' as deep as lookin' into a kaleidoscope of stars. Now it seems likely, that if these people really did exist, they were albinos. Legend says that their eyes were extra sensitive to light, so much so, that they lived in caves an' only came out at night. I imagine them like you. Beautiful and mysterious. But yer taller."

I wasn't sure what to say. Fortunately, a fast, new song "Got a Rocket in my Pocket " began.

Shane jumped up and yelled, "Oh, *yeah*! Da Fabulous T'underbirds and Lou Ann Barton!" He grabbed my hand, hoisted me up and moved me to a sandy spot below the porch. "Come on, Princess!"

"No, I don't, I can't…" I began.

My Inner Critic said, *Thunderbirds again? You should pay attention –*

The pending advice was lost as Shane shot an arm around my waist, "Sure you can! It's easy. Follow me. Whoo!" And like that, I was up from my seat, down the steps and moving around the makeshift dance floor.

To his credit, Shane was an excellent leader and dancer. He rolled me in, pushed me out, spun me around, adding stylish foot flips and kicks. Zydeco, in theory, is not complicated. The basic footwork is step step-step step. Long short-short long. That should be easy, but I felt like a three-legged elephant: clumsy and plodding. And yet somehow, he moved me around as if we were in a proper dance hall and I knew how to dance.

"Whoo! "Let's go someplace where we can rock!" Shane sang, swinging me around.

I gave up on trying to think about the step count. My feet were stepping like I was dancing barefoot on hot coals, trying to keep from tripping Shane or stomping on him.

When the song ended, I was breathless and relieved. A slow song began, and I was moving towards my seat when Buster glided up to me and said, "May I have this dance?"

That's the last coherent thought I had for the next four minutes of the zydeco waltz. I'll say that there was nothing old hat or cliché about the "swept off my feet" experience that followed. Buster braced his arm on my back like a second spine, pressing my chest into his. You know the feeling of being strapped into a roller coaster that banks abruptly? You just hang on and go with it. Breathless. It was all my feet could do to keep touching the ground, I was swept up.

Buster pressed his cheek to mine, so I couldn't even move my head. Pressed together, I was aware that we were a good fit. Unlike other disastrous dance experiences I've had with partners too tall or too short, this felt really good. Secure. Right. And fortunately, I *can* count to three; with my Polish-Russian lineage embedded in polka, I felt my ancestors surrounding us in approval as we spun down the length of the porch and back. I was vaguely aware of Max yelling, "Yeah! That's it!" as we floated past him.

When the song ended, Buster's mesmerizing voice in my ear said, "Thanks, hon." And he kissed my temple before releasing me.

I staggered back up to the table and dropped into my seat like a dropped marionette. I poured myself a glass of water and drank the whole thing without stopping. In my head, a regal and barefoot Yul Brynner as the king of Siam was romping around Deborah Kerr's expansive silk dress to the tune of "Shall We Dance?".

"You make a great couple!" Max said with a chuckle and a bittersweet gleam in his eye.

"But we're not..."

"Sure, sure," he said dismissively, as if I'd just said that Cernunnos the Celtic god of the hunt was due to arrive any minute. His cheerful expression faded. I was sure he was thinking about Charlene. They'd been a great couple. I couldn't imagine the vacuum of her absence that he faced every day. I must have been lost in a reverie about the days when I first met Max and Charlene. The next thing I knew, the radio music was off, and Buster was tuning a dobro, Rebel was setting up a dulcimer and Shane was running his fingers up and down a fiddle.

I leaned into Max. "Do they perform as a band?"

"For fun."

"Have you heard them before?"

"Oh sure. They usually played evenings at the fish camp."

"You never told me that. In fact, there's a lot you haven't told me. I didn't know you were friends with these guys. I thought you said they were idiots."

"*Naaw.*" He waved a dismissive hand. "Never said no such thing."

The trio worked through a playlist of zippy zydeco tunes, ballads and love songs. Their voices blended well; their music was tight. I figured they must practice often. The music, the outstanding food and the easy camaraderie all made for a merry evening like a Norman Rockwell Thanksgiving scene, miraculously free of kitchen mishaps or family drama. Harmonious. Relaxing.

It was getting on towards eleven o'clock when Max stood up. "Guess I should visit the little boys' room. Seems like I gotta whiz all the damn time now, dammit. Then I've got to get back or they'll get worried about me and I'll get in trouble. I'm not really supposed to be out after dinner. They hate that. Means someone has to make sure I check back in."

Urliss stood, cradling the pumpkin pie. "I feel fat as a tick."

Hollis said, "That's 'cause y'are!"

I stood up too. We watched Max hold onto the porch rail then totter to the bathroom pavilion.

"Thanks for havin' us," Urliss said, and shook hands with Rebel.

"Glad you could come."

"Thanks for bringing Max," Buster said, shaking hands with the twins.

"Are you sure you don't need any help cleaning up?" I asked Buster.

"Nope. We got it. Do this all the time."

I made a sad clown face. "I hate to be a party pooper, but I'm going to head home too."

"Didja get enough to eat?" Rebel asked.

"Too much. I'm stuffed. That was amazing, thank you."

"Our pleasure, *chere bebe,*" Shane said.

As we all walked toward Urliss's truck, Buster asked, "Where's your vehicle?"

"Over by the office."

We waved as Urliss, Hollis and Max got in, backed up and drove off, the headlights backtracking through the trees.

"May I escort you?"

I was torn. I didn't want the night to end, but I was tired, a little drunk, and I didn't want to do anything stupid. Buster was close and smelled so good, his voice putting me into a pleasant trance. With great reluctance, I said, "No, no. I'll be fine. It was a wonderful night. Cinderella wants to run away before she turns into a pumpkin."

He raised an eyebrow, "I'm not rightly sure I'm familiar with that version o' the tale. Can't say as I recall Cindy bein' in jeopardy of becomin' a vegetable…" He'd managed to stretch "vegetable" out into a half-dozen syllables.

"Look, it's a mite dark 'atween here and over yonder. I'd just be walkin' you to yer car. Cinderella has to get to 'er coach, right?"

Yeeahh, so tempting. A friend once explained that she always left a party early, while it was at its apex. I got that now. I wanted to run away before anything could wreck this perfect evening. Like me saying or doing something I'd regret.

I brushed my hand down his arm. His muscular arm. *Damn.*

"I'll see you tomorrow," I said, turned my head and walked with determination toward the office.

"Sweet dreams, Ms. Haint Blue," he said, his accent drawing out each syllable like a Sugar Daddy caramel.

I rode home with those words repeating in my head, "Sweat dreams, Ms. Haint Blue." They had been said with tenderness and longing.

"You're a mess," my Inner Critic quipped.

I got home, turned the engine off and let myself out. I could hear Naughty Britches barking wildly in the house. Willie and Waylon were baying responses next door. I listened for a moment but, not hearing anything to indicate the cause for the commotion, unlocked the side door and let myself in. NB was wound up tight, bouncing and barking. She bounded around the living room then shot back into the bedroom and out the doggie door, still barking.

"Well, hello to you too," I said. *Please don't find anything in the yard,* I prayed, imagining her cornering an opossum or armadillo.

She barked her way to the Oakey side of the property. I'd probably have to go drag her back inside, but I had to pee like a donkey. I moved toward the bathroom and realized the door was open. I usually shut it to keep NB from peeing the rug. And there in the middle of the bathmat was a crooked yellow stain where the plush pile had been mashed down with urine.

"I was only gone a couple hours!" I yelled to no one. I stepped over the spot, went about my business, picked the mat up carefully and walked it to the washing machine. "Can't mommy have a little bit of a life? No. What was I thinking?"

Meanwhile, the barking outside had lost its oomph, and NB crashed through the doggy door, trotted up the steps to the bed and woofed at me. She stomped a foot like a two-year-old having a hissy fit.

"I got your message!" I said, rubbing her head.

She flopped over, put her paws in the air in the aren't-I-the-cutest-thing? pose. I patted her belly. There was a mysterious lump under the covers, too small for Mischief who was curled up on my meditation cushion. I poked it. It was hard and square. I pulled back the covers and discovered a box of votive candles. The corner of the box was chewed up, two candles were missing from the box and there were waxy chunks and bits strewn across the sheet.

"So, you were so hungry, because Mommy never ever feeds you, you had to eat *candles* to survive? Is that it?" I held up the remains of the box. "Not for you! Bad dog!" NB wagged her tail vigorously in agreement and threw up a paw in a wave.

"Really?"

She licked her lips, tail wagging, with a look that said, "Get on with the petting."

I complied.

I'd long since given up with any kind of discipline with this dog as she shows no remorse, guilt or shame. Putting her nose in her mess and spanking her only gets a wag and a look as if to say, "Yes, that's my work. I did that. Pretty good, huh? Sorry, but I was pissed. You'll get over it."

"Good thing your mommy loves you." I said.

The sumptuous food and beer put me to sleep almost immediately. My dream picked up at the dinner again, zydeco music, oysters, laughter. Then I was leaving and again Buster said, "Sweet dreams, Ms. Haint Blue." He kissed me on the cheek, then pulled away with a sad expression that tore at my heart. I got into my truck and drove home. As I got on the main road, my truck turned into a giant gourd and a crowd of people outside on the road were saying, "Cindy's going to turn into a vegetable!" I turned my head to see a huge prune sitting in the front passenger seat, and a life size potato and broccoli sat in the back seat, all with solemnity. My hands on the steering wheel felt waxy. I must have been having a hot flash, because I threw the covers off in a sudden sweat. In the dream, my body was turning into a human-shaped, angry red pepper. The last thing I remembered was thinking, "I don't want to be a vegetable, but at least Buster'll think I'm hot."

Chapter 16

Schweitzer's Sunday

Giving myself plenty of prep time, I got over to the dining hall a little before seven, not expecting my guests for at least forty-five minutes. The mighty myth chasers had advised that they wouldn't be conscious until well past eight, and I doubted the honeymoon couple in cabin three would leap out of bed early Sunday and demand breakfast, but one never knows. I'd hardly seen them since they arrived. The family in cabin five had moved like daydreaming sloths. I doubted they'd join us early either.

I put on an apron and turned on my little radio. Sunday mornings, it's hard to get anything much besides church broadcasts, but I finally found a friendly voice chatting about the sacredness of a Sunday. I poured some ground Sumatran Blend into the basket of my new fancy Machitechvorm coffee pot, hit the on button, and began pulling containers from the fridge. The pleasant voice said, "...and Albert Schweitzer once advised, "Don't let Sunday be taken from you. If your soul has no Sunday, it becomes an orphan."

I pondered that as I broke eggs into a mixing bowl. I'd

never considered my soul needing a Sunday, but it made sense. The orphan part confused me a little. If you don't have a day of rest, you become isolated yes, but also kind of edgy. I'd have tacked on an adjective like "demented" orphan. Of course, we need rest. The Buddhists speak of abiding in tranquility. One can only see clearly with a tranquil mind, and a tranquil mind must be rested. I was pleased that other than providing meals for the three myth chasers, my schedule was clear for the day.

Not that I'd gotten drunk the previous night, but too much food, too much stimulation—my mojo wasn't working, my groove wasn't groovy. I pulled out a container of rice pudding and stared at it. Yes. My thoughts were sluggish like lumpy rice pudding.

The Machitechvorm emitted a long end-of-cycle wheeze like the last breath of a heavy smoker. It seemed so wrong that like a Pavlovian dog, I was becoming conditioned to salivate at this horrible sound of an old man's death rattle.

I poured some milk into a serving pitcher and set it out, then poured some into my cup and added coffee. Oh, heaven. I put the milk back in the fridge and cradled the coffee cup with reverence. I turned the burner off and took a moment to savor the coffee and breathe.

I held the cup to my third eye and said out loud, "I am grateful for this moment of peace, and this delicious coffee. I wish that all sentient beings could enjoy this comfort. I offer up the merit of this wish to all sentient beings to find peace and happiness."

Having a dull mind kind of morning did have advantages: too dull for monkey mind. I finished prepping breakfast in a foggy bliss, able to focus on cooking eggs, setting out fruit and yogurt, arranging pastries on a plate, pouring orange juice into a large pitcher. Stirring a pot of grits half hypnotized me. I added butter and watched the melty swirls make a monochrome mandala.

I was jolted out of my bliss when the door swung open and the family of four came in, all talking loudly at once about what the plan of the day would be.

"But it's hot! I want to go to the springs!"

"I thought you said we were going to see the elephants in Williston!"

"Your father wants to go to the flea market in Waldo."

"Good morning," I said. They mumbled unintelligible sounds, not looking at me. The family swarmed the buffet line, piling their plates. I got the grits into a serving pan and out for them just in time.

"I wanted pancakes!"

"They don't seem to have pancakes, Jean. Have a Danish."

"Billy, stop touching all the pastries. Just take one."

"Oh man, I hate eggs. What's this?"

"Grits."

"Gross! Looks disgusting."

"Look, there's cereal over there in that dispenser. Have some cereal then."

"There's no Fruit Loops."

"Well, you'll have to make do with corn flakes."

"I don't like corn flakes."

Fruit went flying, yogurt was slopped; the used yogurt

serving spoon fell to the floor, sending a white splut up the side of the buffet. The group moved to a table by the back window. I winced. The previously perfect Danishes now featured finger-sized dimples and smeared fruit toppings. They struggled to breathe back into the former full shapes but did not succeed.

Lovely.

I fetched a damp cloth, dustpan and broom from the kitchen and set about wiping the counter, buffet and floor. I dropped the serving spoon in the sink, set out a new one and swept up the eggy bits from the floor. After washing my hands, I got a refill of coffee and waited, watching the family talk and eat with a combination of fascination and disgust. Mouths open, shoveling in more, food spinning, spilling out, all while talking, talking, talking. Forks clanked on plates. Billy set his juice glass down with a bang that sent a sharp parabolic wave up and out of his glass that fell back down on itself. Jean crammed a blueberry Danish into her mouth. Chomping while arguing with Billy, she wiped blueberry off her nose with her forearm.

I was losing my appetite. I stirred the untouched grits to keep them from getting that dried out look.

Fortunately, the family soon got up and moved to the door. As they passed me, the mother looked at me and said, "You *should* put pancakes on the menu."

I nodded. She was probably right. Or maybe I'd get one of those do-it-yourself waffle makers, so I didn't have to do the cooking. I wondered if there was a way to make pancakes in advance and refrigerate them. Wouldn't they taste dry? I'd look into it.

I went back to the kitchen for a tray, some disinfectant and a large cloth. They'd left me a sticky mess on the table, the chairs and the floor.

Unbelievable.

Well, there was merit in serving others, right? I reminded myself to keep my thoughts virtuous and joyful. No sense tarnishing my thoughts with complaints. My soul needed this Sunday.

Lovebirds

To my surprise, the honeymoon couple arrived, arm in arm, as one body wrapped in connubial harmony. Morning people, evidently. I assumed they'd sleep in and probably miss breakfast.

"Good morning," I greeted. "Please help yourselves to breakfast, and holler if you have any requests."

The dark-haired woman's lips burgeoned into a Buddha-serene countenance of appreciation as if I'd offered her a bowl of moonbeams.

Her husband said, "Great, will do."

I studied the couple as they appeared to glide from the coffee station to the buffet line then to a table by the window. They made an attractive couple. Similar in height, weight and coloring, they moved with the grace of two weeping willow branches brushing and touching in a gentle breeze. They talked in soft tones as if afraid to wake an invisible infant.

They broke contact to set down their mugs and plates, moving their chairs to sit side by side and look out the back window. To compensate for the disappointing view of the parking lot, I 'd attempted a small flower garden with a bird bath, bird feeder and a concrete female figure in meditation. The couple gazed out.

"Look at that cardinal."

"Mmm."

"The chickadee is so cute."

"Mmm."

Realizing that I was staring at the couple, I shifted my attention to contemplate an apricot pastry.

Behind me, the couple continued their soft chatter. The man asked, "Is that a hummingbird?"

"I don't think so, but it looks like one."

"Huh. The coloring isn't right."

"Look at how systematic it is…flower to flower…"

I had succumbed to the lure of the apricot pastry and was enjoying the taste when the woman's voice called, "Excuse me, could you tell us, is that a hummingbird?"

I set my plate down and walked across the dining hall to stand behind them and have a look. I finished chewing, swallowed, and ran my tongue over my sticky teeth.

"It's a hummingbird moth," I said.

"I've never heard of that before. It's a moth? Really?"

"Yes. If you look carefully, it has six legs like an insect, not two, like a bird. Also, a proboscis, not a beak." I had a flashback to an outdoor lunch a few years ago when Running Deer told Iggy, "I'm like that moth, Ig. I seek harmony with the Earth and delight in nature." She had flitted away from him like a moth seeking a new plant, too. It made me sad to be reminded of the terrible pain her leaving had put him through. But here, now, the moth seemed the perfect, delicate little sign of this couple's unity.

"Oh, yeah, look at that," the woman said.

The tranquil wildlife moment was broken by the sounds of boots, the door opening, and male voices laughing.

"Sure, you can pay me to go to Hawaii to hunt for the Mold Woman in the Wahiawa Botanical Garden!" Rebel bellowed.

"I don't know 'bout dat. If she likes me like Spotted Fawn does, could be bad." Shane said.

They laughed again.

Not in a mood for their boisterousness, I moved quickly across the room and spoke in a low tone hoping they'd catch on, "Good Morning, gentlemen. Didn't expect you so soon. Thought you'd be sleeping in yet." I made a keep-it-down gesture with my hands and rolled my eyes to the couple sitting serenely by the window. "Shh. Look. They're newlyweds. Aren't they sweet?"

The trio looked around with Three Stooges finesse. "So? Why we have to keep it down for?" Shane asked.

"They just looked so serene. They were watching a hummingbird moth."

Rebel looked at me like I was nuts, shrugged, and focused on piling his plate. I watched Shane load and reload the grits serving spoon. He put four huge heaps on his plate before starting on the eggs.

Grabbing a coffee mug, Buster tipped his chin toward Shane, "Shane here's sayin' he had a late-night visitor."

"Oh?" I raised an eyebrow. I had picked up a plate and started to spoon on some fruit but froze. I felt frost form along my spine replaying their banter. They'd mentioned Spotted Fawn.

Shane looked sheepish and waved a serving spoon. "What can I say. I'm irresistible to women…even dead ones."

"*What*?" I asked. Just a month ago, Lorraine's psychic aunt Moira had told me that the Lotus Lodge was haunted by a Native American woman, Spotted Fawn and her young sons. They had all died in a fever epidemic. She lost them one by one before she too fell ill and died. Max had deftly avoided telling me about Spotted Fawn when I bought the property, but when confronted about it, confessed that there had been numerous minor incidents attributed to paranormal activity.

Buster moved next to me and hip bumped me in a flirtatious way. "When I first started comin' here, I's by mese'f, don't recall any activity in pa'ticlar, but then when these two started to tag along, ol' Shane here had nightly visitations."

"What *kind* of…visitations?" I asked, looking at Shane.

"At fust, I felt a hand touch my face. Den, I'm lying on m' stomach and a hand carresses ma back…sweet, like Mama sayin' good night."

"Think she likes him more like a woman than like a Mama," Rebel said with a libidinous laugh. He took his plate and orange juice to a nearby table, turning sideways to allow the departing honeymooners to get by.

"Thanks for breakfast," the woman said to me in her gentle voice. Her eyes flitted to her husband and back to me. "When is checkout again?"

"Technically noon, but you can take your time," I said with a dismissive wave. "Don't have anyone booked there tonight.

Her eyes turned to her husband. "Oh, great. Thanks." They left as they had arrived, arms touching, moving like one being. The relaxed feeling they exuded left with them. Thoughts of Spotted Fawn and ghostly activities made me apprehensive. What had happened?

Shane ate with gusto. He smacked his lips. "Dat hits da spot." He leaned back in his chair and considered. "It's no big deal. Da woman likes me, dat's all."

"What did she do?" I asked, putting a spoonful of grits on my plate.

Rebel leaned forward, "I thought I saw her last night after you left. Just for a second, I saw a woman standing by the cast iron cook fire. Thought it was you 'til I remembered you'd gone. Outta the corner o'my eye, I saw a woman and two children lookin' at the cook fire. When I turned my head to look straight at 'em, they weren't there no more."

"I'll hunt that dog," Buster said, "The cook fire's probably familiar to 'er an' the boys."

"Yeah, well she's gettin' *too* familiar wid me!" Shane said with a laugh. "Las' night she has pulled the covers back and got *into* the bed with me. I felt da weight on da bed. But instead of bein' warm and snug, it's like lyin' next to a block 'o ice!" He shuddered, "Cold, cold!"

I sat down next to Rebel, who had put a napkin over his overalls like a bib. There was a fresh dribble streak down it.

"*Psiakrew!*♥ What did you *do*?" I asked.

"Whadyou say?" Buster asked, looking up from his plate.

"Sorry. Polish. I lapse sometimes," I answered. Looking back to Shane, I said, "I think I would have levitated to the door."

"I heard a voice. Not sure if it was real or in ma head, but it said, "Baby" real sweet. The first time, you bet, I jumped up and ran outside nekked. Got et up by *moustiques*♥♥ too, standin' out dare in de dark."

We laughed.

Shane jabbed his fork towards Rebel. "You see if you still laughin' when she gets in you bed, mon."

"This has happened more than once?" I asked, the ice formations spreading outward from my spine, imagining an icy ghost getting in bed with me.

"Oh yeah. She pat me back and pull da covers. The cold moves across de bed and she says, 'Baby, yes' and I feel it comin' and it's tough, mon. I feel dat she wants me…you know, dat's a powerful ting, that woman need. Mmm! But at da same time that I should be, you know…" Shane rotated his hands near his groin, "…aroused, I'm frozen with fear. It's like cold death comin' for me. Her hand movin', rat cheer." He looked down and moved his hand slowly across his chest to his heart.

I rubbed the goosebumps from my arms.

♥ Polish equivalent of "Oh, hell!"

♥♥ mosquitoes

"I feel a frozen arm move across me chest. And cold weight alongside ma body, movin', movin' like she's puttin' a leg ova me. I t'ought sure she was comin' for ma soul."

I put both hands over the back of my neck and hugged myself. Was he going to relate having sex with a ghost? How did we get here? Couldn't we just have a normal breakfast? My Schweitzer Sunday was slipping away.

"But I always have a gris-gris bag wit' me. Afta da las' time, I'd got it from da Roamer and put it around ma neck. Last night I felt da hand movin' across ma chest and da leg comin' ova and den it stopped. She musta felt da bag. She pulled away. Da whole bed was so cold, I coulda been at da morgue, you know? But scared as I was, I felt bad too. Like I hurt ha feelin's. Lettin' her down, and dat ain't like me ta disappoint a woman. I found meself sayin', "*Cher bebe,* don't be angry, its jus' dat you frighten me. You're no alive no mo'. You an' me can't be…together like dat."

"Oh, come on, man, you're makin' this shit right up," Rebel said.

"Swear!" Shane said, making a cross over his heart, then, palms together, kissing his thumbs. He pulled a black cord from under his shirt displaying a gray leather pouch about an inch long. I never take it off when I'm here."

"So, then what happened?" I asked.

"She still comes. I feel her. Sometimes I hear her or see sometin' in da mirror. But it's not bad. She just watchin' me now. I don't tink she's evil. I tink she's lonely."

I poked at my cold eggs. "What's in the bag?"

Shane put it back under his shirt. "Herbs and gemstones.

My grand makes dem for da family and friends. She won't say what she puts in dem. Sometimes dey stink but dis one's not too bad." He patted his chest where the bag rested.

I rubbed my hands down my thighs like an antsy child and asked, "So, what're you boys doing today?"

Buster said, "Gonna run us up t' Lake City. There's a park ranger in the Osceola National Forest who wants to talk to us, off record, 'o course. Says he thought he saw sumpin' the woods. Found odd tracks and tree marks he wants t' show us. Complains o' damage to some ol' metal trash bins got tossed about an' mangled."

"Probably just vandals, but we told him we'd come have a look," Rebel added.

"He don' sound like a *couillion*," Shane said. "I tink he's got himself scared."

"Then, dependin' on how much fartin' 'round that takes, we're off to Two Egg," Rebel said with a guttural sound somewhere between a smothered laugh and a cat puking up a hairball, "to talk to a little lady about the Stump Jumper."

Shane stretched his arms behind his back and exhaled a world-weary, "Lord, *Lord*, I hope dey ain't too chatty and we don't get stuck lookin' at dead trees an' stumps all day."

Buster groaned, "Me too."

"Stump Jumper? I've never heard of it," I said.

"That's 'cause it don't exist!" Shane said, thrusting his hand forward for emphasis.

"It's supposed ta be a miniature Bigfoot," Rebel said.

"Yeah, a hairy, hunched midget that crosses the road.

Supposedly ran right out in front of a school bus full of kiddies—" Buster said.

Shane smirked, "Most 'o de time, what day say is tracks is where wild pigs rooted in da mulch."

"Don't seem like no one's been able ta track down the bus driver--" Buster said.

"Or the school that the bus came supposedly came from—" Rebel said.

"*Mais,* da local TV's doin' a show for Halloween," Shane said. "Dey wan' to talk to us."

"Our part'll git edited out," Rebel said, shaking his head. "They want the publicity, not us debunking the local myth. Even so, tourism goes up no matter how far out the story."

"Locals report wild animal roarin' an' caterwaulin' at night," Buster said, "Most likely, it's a bobcat or lost panther."

Rebel and Shane nodded.

"They's plenty of folk with wild animals with shady licensing or no licensing for animals they ain't supposed ta have, so when the lion or the black panther escapes, they don't exac'ly call the cops like they should."

"A cute young ting's got a shine for Buster—she keeps comin' up with more 'evidence' she wants to show him—"

"Says she's doin' a documentary," Rebel said with a laugh. " 'Member how Blair Witch was ninety minutes of a girl runnin' 'round with a camera yellin, 'I'm so scared'? It's the same--this girl sees footprints in every pine shat depression."

"And *feels* the *presence* of Stump Jumper activity!" Rebel said, wiggling his fingers. "Oooh, scary!"

"It's just them ol' places where wil' pigs ha' been rootin' around." Buster said.

"And she's obsessed wit' Da Wild Man," Shane said.

I raised an eyebrow. "The Wild Man."

"Captured in Ocheesee Lake area in 1884— "

"What? Seriously? O-cheesy Lake? Come on! You made that up!" I said.

"*Non, beb,*" Shane said looking at me earnestly while crossing his heart with a finger.

"Most likely an escapee from an asylum," Rebel said. "At least, that was the theory. He was definitely human, but feral."

"An' covered in hair," Buster said.

"What happened to him is lost in history," Rebel said. "He was captured and on his way to Tallahassee. No tellin' after that."

"Prob'ly acted up and got hissef killed," Buster said.

I was cradling my coffee cup like I was holding onto the last shred of normal in my world. I took a sip of comfort.

Buster touched my arm with a finger. "What're you doin' with yo'self today?"

"Haven't decided yet. Busy week ahead. Think I'll spend some time cooking. Then relax. Maybe read a book."

"Wanna see inside o' the Tiger? See what all we do?" He cocked an eye at me with a hopeful expression. "We got a little time yet afore we got to run off."

His finger brushed lightly down my arm again. He was well inside my safe space body bubble, and I thought of the honeymoon couple brushing arms as they walked.

"Sure," I said, feeling swayed by his magnetism. "I just need to wipe down a couple tables and clean up the kitchen. Won't take too long."

He winked at me and brushed a hand over my shoulder as he stood up. "Come on over, then." The men bussed their empty dishware to the kitchen and left, wrapped up in a conversation about Astor, Florida being a hotbed for ghosts, Pinky sightings, strange lights, and Skunk Ape sightings. Yikes! I'd driven through Astor and thought it was a sleepy cluster of mobile homes with a jiffy store and a fish camp.

As I wrapped up the leftovers and loaded the dishwasher, my thoughts bounced from ghosts and monsters to Buster's scent and proprietary attentions to me. Was he like that with all women? A player? A habitual flirt like Shane? My spidey-sense--as Iggy used to say, Spiderman being his childhood hero--was all out of whack, like a compass surrounded by magnets. Why did I have the persistent notion that he assumed we were dating?

I had an image in my head of Max sitting in his chair at the Old Oaks. Max had asked how we were doing, as if we were on a date. What exactly had Max told Buster about me?

Chapter 17

The Bat Cave

Stepping inside the Bengal Tiger, I felt like Vicky Vale wandering into Bruce Wayne's secret bat cave: low voices crackled from a radio up by the driver's console; computer screens glowed from every wall not covered by maps freckled with push pins; an organized bookshelf full of labeled three-inch binders; camera equipment and binoculars were secured on a wood rack for easy access. The floor looked like real wood, maybe bamboo; there were custom drawers and cubbies, and highlighted with wood trim. Gorgeous. The ultimate man-cave. Mounted on the ceiling were several huge footprints I assumed were plaster casts or plastic replicas of footprints wider than my face. A detailed Bigfoot doll two feet tall glowered from the top of a video monitor. I leaned closer to study the remarkable detail of it, the tiny lines in the forehead, the beady eyes and flared ape nose. I caught a whiff of something unpleasant and noted uncomfortably that the matted brown hair on it looked real. I pulled back.

Buster gestured toward a leather chair with all the debonair of Errol Flynn as Robin Hood welcoming me to Sherwood.

"Please, make y'self comfortable. Can I fix you an iced tea, lemonade or water?" He opened the chrome refrigerator and waved a hand across the bottled drinks in the door like a game show model displaying the prizes. "Let's see here...in the tea department, I've got mi-yint, peach and green tea with pom'granate...oh, or an Arnold Palmer, it's a mix o'tea and lem'nade, for the folks who just can't decide one or th'other. I kind'o like'em m'self."

"Mint sounds grand, thanks," I said.

"Want a glass, or are you a straight-from-the-bottle kind of gal?"

"Bottle's fine." I glanced down at an open magazine on the table. A sketch of an ape with a pompadour covering a cone-head skull filled the page. The caption read, "Female Sasquatch by Ivan T. Sanderson."

I picked it up and waved it at Buster. "You can't possibly take this stuff seriously. I mean," I tapped the drawing, "this looks like Fonzie's Neanderthal girlfriend. Yet you don't seem like a nut job. Tell me, with your money and experience, you could do anything you want. Why this?" I pointed at the computers and maps.

He passed me the mint tea bottle. He twisted the top off his Arnold Palmer, took a swig and sat down opposite me. "Why anythang? Why'd'ya buy an ol' fish camp?"

I shrugged. "Several things. Since I live next door, I couldn't stand the notion of someone coming in and changing everything. The Elks club was eyeing it, so were the Boy Scouts. There was also talk of tearing it down and building a restaurant. It was empty for a year and a half and drug dealers and other night crawlers crept in. Since I live just next door, I felt it was an opportunity to control my surroundings."

I paused for a sip of the mint tea. It was refreshing.

Buster said, "Well, I know Max is pleased that you bought it and fixed it up."

I nodded. "I look at those dreamy ads in the magazines about retreats in Colorado and Canada…but I won't get there. I've got pets and responsibilities here. Building a meditation retreat was a way to save the Stinkin' Skunk Ape and myself; enhance my practice by teaching. Invite other instructors to come. Only that hasn't happened at all. I haven't sat on the cushion much at all since the retreat opened."

He tilted his head sideways, studying me. After a few beats of silence, he said, "Maybe you don't want it bad enough."

My head snapped back, "What? What makes you say that?"

"Whoa…just talkin' now. Don't go gettin' your hair up, now."

I tapped the Pompadour. "So seriously, how'd you become a Bigfoot hunter?"

"Researcher, if ya please." He sipped his drink and leaned back in his chair. "It all started with 'Momo,' the Missouri Monster. A famous case at the time but lost in obscurity now. I'as first raised up in a little ol' town o' Louisiana, Missouri—"

"Wait, Louisiana, Missouri? For real?"

"That's somethin', ain't it? Well, it was named after the founder, Mr. Bayse's daughter, not the state, like yer thinkin'. Anyways, it's right on the Mississippi River with Illinois just over the bridge. Anways, I 'as best friends with Timmy—same age as me and in my second-grade class, but I had a *huge* ol' crush on his older sister, Dana. She tolerated me okay but teased me. Called me 'The Twerp'." His face relaxed as he travelled back in time.

"I'as just glad she took any notice o' me a-tawl. It was the summer o' 1972. I'd gotten m'self in trouble for somethin' or other and had to do chores at home else I'd a bin thar. Timmy and his younger brother were outside playin' when they heard a faint jinglin' sound and a grunt that'd put the hair up on y'neck. Timmy looked up and saw this hairy monster lope behind the wood pile carryin' a bloody animal. The creature growled at him and pawed the ground. Timmy and his younger brother ran screamin' inside like the Devil was after'um. Dana was in the kitchen washin' dishes when she heard the ruckus and saw 'em fly in the house and up the stairs. She ran outside to see what they were carryin' on about and like t'ave run right into the thang. The beast'd been right close to catchin' Jimmy, the little'un, and was right up there on the porch."

"Oh, Geez!" I said.

"Dana said it was so tawl, her eyes were about level with its 'nekkidness'. It roared at her and lunged for her, 'bout scaring her half to death on the spot. But she screamed, and I reckon the high pitch and volume spooked it good. It backed off and took off for the woods. Turned out, the jinglin' sound Timmy'd heard was the dawg collar; the thing had kilt a neighbor's dawg."

Oh yuck. Not wanting to appear gullible, I said, "But come on, it was probably a bear or a big dog."

"Nope, though that's what everyone said at first," he said, tapping my knee ever so gently with a finger. "The story mighta got disregarded as you know, kids makin' stuff up. But here's the part where the cheese *really* binds: their pa found footprints far bigger and wider than his own by the wood pile. And later that week, there was a prayer meetin' at their home, and as people were leavin' they heard strange howls comin' from the re-ser-vo-er. Like nothin' nobody'd ever heard before. Momo was spotted by adults too. A farmer caught sight o'somethin' runnin' off leavin' behind a mutilated baby goat. Even closer to town, a jogger, a mailman, even a cop reported seein' somethin' odd. They all described it as a dark, hairy thang walking upright like a man."

It must've been the air conditioning, but I got goosebumps all of the sudden and rubbed my arms.

Buster continued, "Dana had nightmares so bad she had to get on sleepin' pi-yills on account o' she kept wakin' the house with screamin'. Timmy's family was so freaked, they even moved away for a while, went to live with the grandparents."

"Okay…but we're talking about the seventies, right? How about a hippie guy with a big beard acting weird on drugs, eh?"

He shook his head. "That was proposed too. Or a hobo. But the footprints weren't like no human footprints or shoe prints. They were too wide, with a big space separatin' the big toe from the rest." He leaned back in his chair. "I thought Dana was so brave runnin' out there like that. I must have made a right fool o'meself moonin' after her, but she didn't seem to care."

"So *that's* the reason you got into all this?" I waved at the equipment. "Wow! What a romantic you are! Are you trying to prove something over a grade school crush? You've dedicated everything to proving Bigfoot or whatever exists—so what? You can prove it to her?"

He looked at me with a sad, tired expression. "Not at all. She saw it. She knew it was real. I don't gotta prove nothin' to her. No…to tell you the truth, my family moved away, and I forgot all about Momo. When I 'as in high school, I thought I wanted to get into makin' movies. The process o' tellin' a story on film fascinated me; instead of words it was all camera angles, lightin', special lenses and such. I made some pretty crude nature shorts usin' time lapse. Thought I'd travel the world and make doc-ya-mentries. But then in college I discovered Alan Watts and Alan Ginsburg. My Dad and I never got on too good, so when my mom died shortly after I graduated, I took off. Decided to bum around for a while. Heard about an amazin' ashram in India, so I worked any odd job I could get to scrape together the money, and off I went. Did a spur-rit quest in India, Nepal and Bhutan."

"Wait, a *what*?"I asked. *Spurt quest? Huh?* Then it hit me: he meant 'spirit'. I caught up again realizing he'd just rattled off a list of countries on my bucket list. "Holy Bob Hope and the U.S.O., you've been to Bhutan? That's number one on my bucket list."

He leaned back, closing his eyes. His sigh suggested a yearning that he could not put into words. There was a serenity about him that reminded me of a dying person eager to cross over to be reunited with a loved one. Finally, he opened his eyes and said, "It's an amazin' country. Jus' like Eden. Y'oughta go. It sure was hard to leave, believe me." His eyes were focused on something back in time. After a moment he added, "That's where I saw it."

"What?"

"A *migo*."

I thought he was calling me *amigo* and blinked. "Yes, *amigo*?"

"Sorry, not *amigo*, a *migo*... it's what the Bhutanese call a Yeti."

"Oh, right."

"The temple monks where I was studyin' told me that the *migo* are mystical guardians of Shambhala that only appear to believers."

"Okay, so...like a Tibetan unicorn. Got it." This was all a bit much. I took a swig of my mint tea hoping it would clear my head. As my eyes floated over the scene around me, hairy monsters seemed to stare back at me from the walls, the computer screens, the top of the refrigerator. I felt like Alice down the rabbit hole. This was a whole different world. I felt like a pacifist in a gun show, or an un-crafty person at a craft fair. I once went to a knitting convention with a friend. Aisles and aisles of knitting paraphernalia I didn't know existed, and women talking excitedly in a weird language of needle gauges, patterns, stitches...when I heard someone say "double knitting in the round" I pictured English country dancers knitting and dancing in a complex circle and was looking for a stage and people in costumes.

That prickly unease was building. I was drawn to Buster, this engaging, magnetic man with perfect dimples but repelled by his cryptozoological obsession. He was eyeing me, and I could feel his disappointment and frustration.

"Haven't cha ever," he began, "haven't cha ever had an experience that was so outside the realm of normal tha'cher whole reality shifted-like? Even just for a moment?"

My word of the day the other day had been "numinous" meaning magical, other-worldly. Yes, I've had a few numinous moments, but felt vulnerable about sharing. "Sure, watching the X-Files. I used to be addicted to that show." I hoped that being flippant would amuse him, but it fell flat.

The hopeful look in his eyes dulled.

I capitulated. "Okay, okay. Yes. I was living in Weirsdale, down near Lady Lake. It makes Catfish Springs look like a metropolis. There was a flashing light at THE intersection with THE corner jiffy store. There was a post office and I think a Laundromat. Dead orange groves. I refer to my time there as 'my Pastoral Period.'"

Buster nodded encouraging me. I loved the way he was listening to me as if what I was saying was amazing. Oh, those dimples. Mmm!

"Anyway, I was driving back from watching an episode of the *X-Files* at a friend's house. It was around 10:30 p.m. Country dark. The sky was clear and full of stars just like at the planetarium. I was put-putting along in my ancient Volvo when the googly headlights—one went off to the left, the other was aimed at the ground—picked out three white creatures hopping across the road *boink boink boink* gone into a hay field. I saw them for about a second and a half : albino wallabies."

He raised a skeptical eyebrow.

I pointed my finger at him, "No, I wasn't doing drugs nor

was I drunk. I still get gooseflesh about how very eerie it was to be out there in dark nowhere with a head full of *X-Files* and see that. My explanation was this: about ten or fifteen minutes away by car, there was a place called Fausner's Exotics. It was a wild animal rescue that reportedly had a menagerie of tigers, lions and who knows what else. It was next to a dairy; it was hinted that perhaps old dairy cows went next door to be dinner for the big cats. I never got a tour, never saw any of the animals, but the place was sprawling with massive, high fences. The Weirsdale Wallabies must have been escapees from Fausner's."

"Ah-ha. Reasonable conclusion. Anythin' else? Y'ever seen a ghost?"

I had a flash to an early childhood memory of someone in my bedroom hovering over me. I shuddered. Then there was Spotted Fawn. Had I seen her out in the meditation circle? I'd felt a presence in the meditation hall several times. I hedged the question. "Maybe…but what about your *amigo* and Bhutan?"

"Oh yeah. A spur-rit guide told me that I needed to purify myself by makin' a pi-yilgrimage to a temple way, way up in the mountains." He pushed a hand in slow motion through the air indicating distance. "To be perfectly honest, I'm not real sure if it was in Bhutan or Tibet. It took a long spell to locate a guide and there was waitin' around for the weather to cooperate, but finally we could go. The guide took us to a village about halfway to the temple, where we stayed with a family—"

"Wait, wait, wait…a spirit guide? Like in a dream?"

"No, a shaman I stayed with."

"Oh." I'd always dreamed of a connection with a spirit

guide. I wanted the cool adventure in the Himalayas. I took a deep breath and let that useless wistfulness pass by.

"It was into evenin', and we were fixin' to have supper when the animals outside--goats and ox and all--got all agitated, stompin' and carryin' on. The husband went out to check on them, and came back all excited, wavin' us to come look, which we did. Not far away up the mountain, three hairy bipedal figures was movin' across an open area. Two were full size, one was juvenile. They stopped and looked at us, then hurried on towards the tree line. And, my Sweet Moon Eyes, I did feel like I was seein' unicorns. I couldn't believe it. The guide explained that they were *migo* and hadn't been seen for some time and were a very auspicious sign. The family was very excited to see the juvenile. For them the sighting had huge significance for spur-ritual blessings and growth. They believed that my presence had drawn the *migo*. After that, they were eager to help me on my pi-yilgrimage to the temple." As if he were seeing a resplendent angel, a luminous serenity seemed to smooth out the lines in Buster's face.

"So, then what happened?"

"Oh, the trip was spectac'lar. I regretted not speakin' Bhutanese or Tibetan 'cause the sightin' of the migo energized the group. They were sharin' stories and laughin' the whole time. About wore out the guide translatin' for me."

"But what about the purification?"

"It was indescribable, right like outta a pitcher book o' mystical places. The temple was real modest in size, but magnificent and ancient. The monks greeted us warmly, surprised o'course to have visitors. The guide explained to the monks that I was called to be purified, so they put me through this process of washin' me, making me fast, then drinkin' herbal concoctions, keepin' me isolated for a time, then chantin' around me for hours. It was intense. I felt like I had a darkness in me that they could release, but it wasn't going to just go peaceful-like. I cried a lot. It called up a lot of anger…I mean, throw myself off the cliff kind o'anger." He paused for a moment, eyeing me to see how I was taking this in.

"I've heard that even Vipassana meditation can be intense, this sounds pretty rough," I said.

He nodded. "It was. But I felt safe there, like they'd catch me before I lost it completely. The head monk was an exceptional sort, a little bitty man with happy apple-doll wrinkles all over his cheeks an' a kind of aura 'bout 'im like he wasn't quite real. He bonked me on the head with a sacred wand kind o' thang, and he put a hand to my heart and chanted. Got right up in my face with all them wrinkles, the wrinkles kind of shrouded his eyes, but there they were, snake eyes borin' right into mine. In a commandin' voice, he said somethin' like '*nying kha chhe pa*!' My guide said it meant 'open wide heart.'"

I was so engrossed in his story, I wasn't paying attention to the basic coordination required to sip my tea and managed to dribble some down my chin and onto my shirt. "Just wanted to be minty fresh," I said pulling the shirt away from my skin. In a smooth move, Buster got up, pulled a couple of tissues from a box nearby, handed them to me and sat down again. He moved with the control and dexterity of a panther, no wasted motion.

"Then what happened?" I asked, wiping at my shirt.

"The next mornin', I 'as alone drinkin' tea and watchin' this ant crawl across the floor. It stopped, waved its antennae at me, then moved on. This'll sound crazier'n a rabid 'coon, but I felt like the ant had dismissed me to go back to my life again. I'll tell y' what, a different man walked down that mountain."

I didn't know what to say. What an extraordinary and beautiful story. Envy sniffed around me to get my attention, but I focused on reveling in his experience, not the lack of the mystical in my own life. To disarm the creeping negative thoughts, I exposed them.

"That was beautiful. Thank you for sharing that with me. I have been yearning for some guiding force in the world to help me along like that, and the closest I've come is in dreams. But in the dreams, there is always something lost in translation--the spirit guide's mouth moves, but no sound comes out. Or, I am handed a sacred object, but there is no instruction manual. I don't know what I'm supposed to do with it. It didn't come with the secret decoder. I am not usually prone to *invidiousness*♥," I said, as the Word of the Day from last week came to mind, "that is, the old green-eyed monster, but I must say, it's working me right now."

"Aw, I'm sure you've had y'own magical moments," he said with a quick wink and a hint of mirth around his mouth. "Reckon you must be blessed with good karma to have this place. Max is so pleased you took it on."

♥ jealousy

Uh-huh. Max again. Trickster? Matchmaker? Just what was he up to?

While looking for a trash bin to put my damp tissues, my eyes roamed to the front window, taking in air-freshener dangling from the rearview mirror, an oversized Bigfoot. "What does a Bigfoot air freshener smell like?" I asked, wincing. "Can't be good."

Buster grinned. "Aw, it's a joke. People see'em in stores and give'em to us. They're supposed to smell like pine."

"Well that's a relief. I was thinking they'd be somewhere between skunk and wet dog smell."

He nodded and took the paper mess from me, moving closer.

"So, uh, can I ask you something?" Buster's closeness made it difficult to breath properly and still think. I took a step back and lightly touched a plaster footprint.

"You can ask," Buster said with a provocative nudge. "Might not answer. Depends."

"You and Max," I started. That wasn't the right tack. I tried again. "I get this feeling that Max has…talked to you about me. What…what did he say?" Well, shit, that sounded like I was fishing for a compliment. That wasn't the point. I bit my lip. "I mean, I get this feeling like…you both know something I don't." That didn't sound quite right either, just made me sound paranoid. "Did he suggest that we?" I pointed a finger between him and me, still tongue-tied. "See each other?" I finished.

His dimples found their groove. He tucked a stray strand of hair behind his ear. Now it was his turn to search for words.

"Well, Max did say that uh, ...well, he thinks the world o' you, and that we oughta meet. Thought we might make an innerestin' couple."

I felt my face flush.

"He showed me a pitcher o' you once, an' after that, I jus' kinda knew."

"Knew *what*?"

He pursed his lips and took me by surprise by changing the subject. "Y'ever been in samadhi?"

"Huh?"

"You know, deep meditation? The mind source?"

I remembered seeing him for the first time on Saturday, sitting on a cushion in my meditation hall, totally absorbed in his meditation.

"Honestly? I'm not sure. Maybe for a few seconds."

He looked disappointed, and moved to a trash can, dumping my used napkin. Something in the way he tossed the trash made me think he was giving up on something else.

"Why?" I asked, feeling like I'd said the wrong thing, blew the moment.

"Well, maybe we could meditate together sometime."

The words sounded promising, but the tone was not hope-filled.

The door opened, and Rebel and Shane came in. "Oh, sorry. You 'bout ready, Buster?" Rebel asked.

"Yup. Let's do it," he said, clapping his hands together decisively. Turning to me, he said, "Don't worry about dinner for us. Not sure when we'll be getting' back tonight." The intimacy in the air was gone, the spell broken.

"Oh? I was hoping to have you all for dinner tonight. Kind of pay back for the feast last night. My Polish specialty."

"Aw, we'd love to, Hon, but no tellin' how long we'll be. Most folks are talkers. Even if there's nothin' we might be there a while."

"It sure sounds good though," Rebel said patting his belly, "hope we can try it sometime soon."

With a quick pat to my back and an intimate butterfly kiss to my forehead, I found myself back outside the bat cave, feeling disoriented. Why had he gotten moody all of a sudden and changed the subject? What did samadhi have to do with anything?

I stood in the parking lot and watched the Bengal Tiger tow the camouflage-tarped boat out of my retreat.

Gowno!♥ *You gonna stand there like the village idiot?* The Inner Critic chastised.

Even without them, I was in the mood to cook. Bigos is great Polish comfort food made with kielbasa and sauerkraut. I could make it and freeze it. Take some to Lorraine. I made my feet move, retrieved the cooker and locked the dining hall. Did I have all the ingredients at home? I was pretty sure I did, maybe even a hunk of venison in the freezer.

When I got home, NB and Mischief greeted me as if I'd been gone for a month, rather than a few hours. I held the door open for NB to dash out and do her business. When she came

---

♥ Polish word for shit

charging back in, we had a terrific cuddle on the bed.

Avoiding thinking about Buster, samadhi, Pinky, the St. John's river salamander, or sleeping with frigid soul-stealing ghosts, I took NB for a long walk then put on an apron and got to it.

Bigos, or Hunter's Stew

My mother had been a limited but capable cook. One of her favorite meals was *bigos*, or hunter's stew. Iggy lapped it up as soon as he cut teeth, but I recoiled from sauerkraut, and could not be cajoled or spanked into eating it.

Decades later, my palate broadened to embrace the mighty cabbage, including it in my seasonal cooking repertoire with bratwurst, corned beef, and *bigos*. Perhaps hunter's stew is a posh name for what may have been more like poacher's stew. At any rate, the recipe calls for any combination of rabbit, venison, *keilbasa* (Polish sausage) or lamb, shredded cabbage, mushrooms and prunes, primarily. Perfect for a slow cooker, it has climbed to top of my list of comfort foods, just below garlic-mashed potatoes.

I moved to my bedroom, turned on the computer, and streamed a Polish rock song station. Soon I was rocking out and chunking cabbage to Hazel's pop song, *I Love Poland, Kurwa Mach* and swaying while washing mushrooms with Breakout's groovy blues. I had no idea what the song was about. I never learned much Polish or Russian; our mother felt her Old-World Polish was pointless for us to learn as we moved a lot and English worked everywhere. Iggy and I absorbed bits and phrases, most of them not intended for polite society.

I called Iggy to see if he and Louise would come over but hung up when it bounced to voicemail.

That evening I had a big helping of stew with a glass of white wine and distracted myself by binge watched episodes of *George Gently*.

Chapter 18

Monday October 27: What's Samadhi Got to Do with It?

Just before waking up, I was involved in a vivid dream. I was cooking at the retreat dining hall. There were bowls of ingredients in front of me to make Skunk Ape salad—it looked like chicken salad, but with twigs, nuts and leaves. This was my first attempt at making it, and something was wrong: too thick, hard to stir, and it smelled awful. The radio was playing, and I was singing along with Tina Turner, "What's samadhi got to do with it?"

Buster said, "You used skunk cabbage, right?"

I nodded. "But it's so...*yucky*." I held up a spoon of glop and made a face.

Buster was gone. I felt disappointed and confused. Had I hurt his feelings somehow? There seemed to be something essential about the skunk cabbage. I stared at the stinky green leaves...piles of leaves that resembled dirty money.

Tina's song was rationalizing confused behaviors. Looking down at the mess in the bowl, I frowned and said, "I'll have to clarify this with butter."

I came to consciousness with the words "clarify this with butter" repeating in my head. The repeated sensation of someone pricking my lower back with needles brought me fully awake. "OW!" Rolling the irritated spot into some covers, I disrupted Mischief who'd been using me to sharpen his claws: flex and insert, relax and release. Flex and insert, relax and release. He jumped off the bed.

NB stretched, stiffening her entire body, stretching her head back, legs extended. Since a Basset has such short legs, the stretching looks a bit pointless. The extremities just can't go very far.

"Out you go, little girl. I've got to shower."

I let her outside noting a bit of autumn crispness in the morning air and got into the shower.

While lathering my hair, my mind took me to a fantasy land where Buster and I were the perfect couple wallowing in mutual attraction and fascination…and in my fantasy world all was *sympatico* until I had to introduce him socially. I pictured a small group gathered, wine glasses in hand. I introduced Buster.

"And this is Buster Shadetree, my boyfriend." I gaze at him, doe-eyed. I look back with pride to a group of women who transform from ordinary women into sinister, judgmental creatures with blood-red nail polish, perfect hair, noses angled high so they can look down on us—a feat since we're both tall.

"So nice to meet you," one woman greets him with an artificial smile that could crack a mirror.

"Pleasure to meet you, Ma'am," Buster responds with a slight bow.

"And what *is it* that you *do,* Buster?" One of the women asks, her eyes like laser beams narrowing for a psychic blast, nails clicking like talons.

"Why, I'm a cryptozoologist."

Blank faces await further details.

One woman titters, "Is that like a zookeeper?"

"Naw, ma'am, That's the study of all the critters that as yet are somewhere between fact and legend, such as Bigfoot, the Loch Ness monster, Chessie, the Chesapeake Bay monster, the rougarou, chupacabra, various sea monsters—"

The women toss back their heads and howl with laughter.

One can barely get the words, "You are a Bigfoot researcher?" out because she is laughing so hard.

Another one hisses, "Bigfoot hunter."

Then they turn on me, needle-sharp teeth exposed like those freaky angler fish in the Mariana trench, and laugh like deranged sea gulls, "*Ya, yuh yuh yuh!* Your boyfriend is a… *Ya, yuh yuh yuh,* Bigfoot! Oh, it's so rich! Bigfoot *hunter! Yam yuh yuh yuh!"*

The vision disturbed me back to the present. My high school crush feelings swirled toward the drain with the shampoo, washed away by a conditioner of fear and embarrassment.

Who Wants to Go to Lettuce Lake?

All the doubts and fears about Buster evaporated when he walked into the dining hall for breakfast. He brushed a tanned hand through his hair and our eyes met. This ordinary gesture pulled his T-shirt just a little closer to his defined abs and flat stomach and flexed his bicep…and I was distracted enough to drop the wooden spoon sticky with pancake batter on the floor.

"Good mornin', Haint," he drawled.

I flushed, "Hey, good morning" and bent to pick up the spoon, toss it in the sink and grab a clean one. "Sleep well?"

"Yeah, I did," he said with a voice layered with inuendo like I'd missed out on sleeping really well with him.

I bit my lip and stirred. "Sweet potato pancakes sound good?"

"Mm-mm," he nodded, pouring himself a coffee.

And as easy as that, I was a giddy schoolgirl again. It was almost a relief that Shane and Rebel came in, so we weren't alone together.

"*Quoi de neuf*?"Shane asked.

I looked around not sure what that meant or how to answer.

Rebel elbowed Shane and rolled his eyes. "He means, what's up?"

"Oh, good morning," I answered with relief.

"Good mornin', *cher Beb*," Shane said eyeing the pancake mix. "What you devilin' up for us dis mornin'?"

"I'm no devil. They're sweet potato pancakes," I said. "Hope that's okay."

With a wink he replied, "A bit o' heaven, Angel."

"What are you boys up to today?" I asked.

"Road trippin', as usual," Rebel said without enthusiasm. In fact, stifling a yawn, he looked like he'd rather sit on a porch rocker and count cars driving by.

I flipped some pancakes on his plate. "Oh? Somewhere near here?"

"Nah, I wish," he said.

"Yeah, when we go, mon?" Shane asked. His plate was loaded to capacity, but he was eyeing the baked goods.

"I thought you were staying through the weekend," I said, mentally wincing at how pouty that sounded but they hadn't said anything about leaving. My inner voice reprimanded me about sticky attachments as I set out breakfast on the buffet.

"Well, ain't no rush, but sometime after breakfast," Buster drawled. "We wanna get down an' back afore the Tampa traffic gets all snarly."

And there it was. Just as I was getting more comfortable with having Buster around, I caught on that they were talking about driving to Tampa.

Shane caught my eye and waggled a warning finger at me. "Don't *boude*, Beb. We'll be back before you have time to miss us."

So, the Three Investigators†♥ were leaving. I set a platter of eggs down with a heavy thunk. Oops.

"Dig in, don't be shy, there's plenty."

Once the trio had loaded up their plates with pancakes,

♥ When Iggy and I were young, he got the complete set of *Alfred Hitchcock and the Three Investigators*. Similar to *The Hardy Boys*, but featuring three boys: Jupiter Jones, Peter Crenshaw and Bob Andrews. I preferred these books over *Nancy Drew*, but still read her too.

sausage, grits, and eggs, I followed, my plate looking like a child's plate in comparison with theirs.

I sat down across from Buster. As soon as I had set down my plate and coffee, he patted my hand and spoke through a mouthful of grits. "We'w be back."

"Well how was your trip to Two Eggs and Lake Cheesy?" I asked.

Rebel grunted, "Lame as usual. Pictures of mulch piles."

Shane added, "Dat woman got her pictcha wid Buster, an' dats all she really wanted."

"So kinda boring then?"

Buster patted my knee. "Kinda borin'."

"What's in Tampa?" I asked, jabbing at my grits.

"Lettuce Lake Park." Rebel said. "Two guys just released a video purporting to show a Skunk Ape stomping around and taking a bath. The footage is total crap, and this isn't the first time these two have claimed to have 'proof.'"

Shane added, "Oh, it's a hoax, for sure. We're gonna play along though. We've arranged a meet up with dem, but dey don't know who we really are. We'll let dem talk and take us to the location of da 'sighting.'"

Buster said, "We're gonna see about a water monster in Astor called 'Pinky' and stop in on some friends in the Ocala National Park on the way back." He patted my hand. "We'll be back Thursdee."

"*Pinky*? Is that like Barnie?" I asked.

"More like a giant salamander," Rebel said. "Been seen in the St. John's River too."

"Oh, right. Dopey me." I said. Dismissing Pinky as another ridiculous myth, I wondered if I should offer a small refund since they wouldn't be using the cabin for two days. "Do you guys want a dis--"

Buster must have read my mind. He shook his head and swallowed, "Don't worry none 'bout the rate. We're leavin' stuff we don't need in the cabin."

Rebel began a technical conversation about the frames of the footage they had reviewed. I drank my orange juice and gnawed on a biscuit. Usually I love biscuits, but somehow this one seemed like Play-Doh: a tasteless gob, hard to swallow. I gave up and removed myself to the kitchen.

Why was I so out of sorts? They'd be back. I had a camp full of people coming for the weekend. There was plenty to do to get ready. I needed to visit Lorraine, go grocery shopping, mop the meditation hall. Yeah. That sounded fun.

The wise part of me knew I should play it cool with Buster. The part of me with the butterflies-in-my-gut crush wanted to take the kind of dangerous risks Bob Seger was singing about. I wanted to go to Lettuce Lake. ♥

With Buster.

It didn't take too long for them to wolf through their first round of food and go back for seconds. And soon they were pushing back their chairs and bringing me their empty plates.

♥ "Who Wants To Go to Fire Lake" is a song by Bob Seger. The lyrics imply that going to Fire Lake is akin to letting your hair down, doing something potentially risky or dangerous.

"That was a mighty fine boo-fay," Buster said, handing over his plate. Our fingers touched. He didn't fully release the plate. It was not my imagination that he'd ever so subtly pulled me toward him. And connected by this zen round white circle of china, he said, "Say, 'afore we shove off, howdja like ta come hang out for a tick in the Tiger? Rebel still needs ta take a shar… and that could be a spell."

The Inner Critic chided, *"Say no. He's shifty. He's leaving. He's not your type. Be smart. Clean the kitchen. Let him go."*

Yes, that's what I should do.

And I heard myself say, "Okay, sure. Let me finish up here. Won't be long." I hoped he couldn't hear my heartbeat quickening. Internally, it was distracting and loud.

"A 'right," he said, tilting his head and smiling. He released the plate.

And then I was alone in the kitchen trying to get my heart to calm down.

And where had I left my brains?

Chapter 19

Just 'Cause It Snarls, It's Not Necessarily a Monster

"I just have to pack a few thangs…have a seat an' git comfortable," Buster said, gesturing to the leather chair. We were back in the Bengal Tiger where once again, I found myself feeling as out of place as a nun in a hookah lounge.

I looked around at the plaster footprint casts, the matted hair samples, the carefully cataloged binders and that damn doll. Despite my attraction to this man, I had no place in this bizarre world, even if he really had seen a Yeti and was an enlightened world trekker who could meditate rings around me. He was easy on the eyes; I didn't mind watching him bend over to pick up a messenger bag or reach up to grab a book off a shelf; watching him move about was like watching a leopard: smooth and mesmerizing. But he was distracted by packing and I didn't trust myself to generate idle conversation; I babble when I'm nervous.

"Well, hey, I'll let you get ready. I should get out of your way," I said, getting up to leave.

"Hey, Sweet Moon Eyes, what's the matter? You ain't

leavin' are ya?" He put his hands on my shoulders. Uh oh. He was between me and the door. Close. In my space looking like he was going to kiss me. That woodsy musky Buster smell was enveloping me.

"You guys have a, uh, good trip," I said, moving to step around Buster.

His hands moved ever so gently down my arms. He leaned in to kiss me.

Oh, scheisse, no no no.

It was gentle and wonderful, and I couldn't help kissing back while my mind went haywire. I pulled away from him and my mouth opened. I wanted to stop myself, but the cage door was open. The frightened pigeons of doubt and fear flew out in all directions as I blurted, "I can't. Oh shit. Look, with all respect, you are a *really* intriguing and attractive man and the last thing I'd want to do is hurt your feelings," I faltered, looking around. "How can you believe in *this*? I mean, sure, I wanted to believe in Bigfoot when I was *twelve*, but has there been one shred of true evidence? All these plaster casts of bogus footprints—look at them!"

I gestured wildly towards his wall display. "You can tell they are cookie cutter, made from plywood…there's no depth to them…and…and you know, when Max told me about you, I didn't know much about Bigfoot, so did some poking about. Got a couple books out of the library and watched videos online."

He regarded me with a mix of wariness and surprise as if I'd just pulled a boa constrictor out of my handbag.

I wiped some saliva off my lower lip. "Look, Buster, I tried,

I really did. I spent some time online watching videos with supposed 'proof.' " I was shaking, my hands flapped wildly. "*Wasted* time I will never get back, watching people point to broken tree limbs claiming it's Bigfoot damage, or, or a few sticks is a 'shelter,' a random hoot is a 'call,' a limb falling from a tree is a Bigfoot 'knock'. It's CRAP! Buster, it's all delirium, wishful thinking and BULLSHIT! The videos that were supposed to be ultimate proof were hoaxes. The hair samples were dogs or bears. After decades there just is no evidence. How, how can you invest your money, your time, your *passion*—"

He looked at me with the patience of the ages and that damned dimple popped out. He cocked his head and quietly said, "Shh,shh,shh."

He put his hands over my ears and kissed me. A long, sweet, gentle kiss that short-circuited all my energy. I heard a whimpering sound and realized it had come from me. The last pigeon flew out. The cage was empty.

And then I was kissing back. Mmm. After a long moment he pulled back.

"Sweetheart, sit you'self down an' listen. Don't interrupt, hear me out. When I'm done, if you still wanna bolt out that door like an ol' bull outuvva a chute, ya can. Deal?"

I nodded. I felt like I was five years old about to be cheered up after skinning my knees.

He patted the sofa. I sat down; he eased down next to me. In one smooth move, his arm was around me and we were huddled together as if taking shelter in a storm. Once again, his welcomed scent settled around me like an old friend.

"I reckon you've got things about me a little contrariwise. I do believe I saw something in the Himalayas like I told you. And yes, I've clocked a lot of road time, travelled to just 'bout every state we've got, and passed many moons followin' up on stories of alleged sightin's of various beasties. Yes, I'd like to have absolute proof that a Bigfoot, Sasquatch, Yeti or whatever you wanna call it exists."

He touched me very gently on my breastbone with his finger. "Did *you* know that the giant panda was considered a myth for somethin' like sixty years afore one was finally found?"

"No."

"And the giant squid was thought to be an ol' whalin' legend, but now with global warmin', sightings are getting frequent enough that the wonder of it is gone and now it's ho-hum, another dead squid, and who's-gonna-get-this-stanky-thing-off-the-beach?"

I interrupted, shaking my head, "I watched one of those old A&E specials about Bigfoot. You know, the one narrated by Leonard Nimoy. You think, 'Oh, well, if Dr. Spock is on board with this, and they've got video, maybe there's something to it.' But no, since then, it's been debunked. All of it. In fact, the guy who wore the gorilla suit admitted that it was a hoax." I sounded like a whiny kid arguing about Santa Claus, but I couldn't stop. "Even worse, the show ends with some Native American guy claiming that Bigfoot is a spirit animal and can 'dematerialize'. Seriously? How can you stand going to seminars and visiting people who perpetuate these hoaxes and believe this garbage?"

"'Cause a big part of my job is *exposin'* the hoaxes."

"What? Really? But…you came here and set up video cameras and stuff…like you expect to see something."

He tilted his head, "Well, we got to get proof one way or t'other, don't we? We could get lucky and spot a real one, or we might also get video tape of Billy Bob Bogus walking around in the woods plantin' 'evidence'. Get it? We gotta act like it's real, and, 'til we prove it is a hoax, there's always the chance that this one *is* the real deal. Most o' the time, I'm writin' blogs exposin' fraudsters. Trust me, I'm *not* a real popular guy. He put a hand on his chest in false modesty, "I know that's a hard one ta swallow."

It sure was. I was getting very distracted sitting this close.

"It's all swell to tell the local newspaper that a Bigfoot ate your cat to get some attention, but trust me, most folks ain't so happy to see my Siberian Tiger pulls up to their house. They get kinda unfriendly."

I pictured a door slamming in his face and bit my lip.

He chuckled. "By the way, that Native American was debunked as well. He weren't even marginally Indian; he was from Germany! The Hopi Nation had him high on their most annoyin' fraudster list."

"Good to know," I said. "So why have you kept coming back here? You haven't actually found anything *here,* have you?"

Buster shifted position to rest his chin in his palm. He massaged his face with his fingers a moment, as if thinking of how to answer. Finally, he said, "The short answer is, I like Max. I liked Charlene a lot too, and I know he must miss her somethin' awful. We like to check in on him." There was a gleam in his eye that reminded me of Max, damn it. There was something he wasn't saying.

"*What?*" I pressed.

I could tell he was considering telling me but shook it off.

"Besides, Catfish Springs, it's central t'everythin'. Have you looked at a map of North Florida lately? Between the Okefenokee Wildlife Refuge up north a' here connected with the Osceola National Forest, the Steinhatchee wildlife and conservation areas. Go a little south you've got the Ocala National Forest, Goethe State Forest, Chassahowitzka Refuge and the whole o' the Green Swamp Preserve. Next to Canada and Oregon, Georgia and Florida's got the best habitats for Bigfoot or Skunk Apes you can get. I got reports comin' in awwlll the time."

"Do you have a shred of anything tangible?"

He gave me that an almost pitiable look like a math teacher losing hope that the failing student will ever find the value of x. "You seem to think that it's all about proving that a large hairy beastie exists, call it whatcha want. That'd be a huge disappointment. Lemme tell ya a little story 'bout a werewolf in France."

I rolled my eyes and sighed, but immediately regretted it. That was rude. I nodded. "Go ahead. Let's hear it."

"Between 1764 and 1767 'round a hunderd women and children were killed in a region of France—throats slashed, some even decapitated, and their guts ripped open. Descriptions all purty consistent of a hairy beast with a long neck, fierce eyes longish body. Everyone comes to believe it's a wolfman. Hunters kill every wolf around, including one super-sized one. Killing keeps on. The king of France gets involved, wants the monster killed. A man is caught tryin' to rape a woman while he's dressed up in furs. But even with him caught, the killin's keep steady."

"Is this for real? I've never heard of this before."

"It is. The Beast of Gee-voo-dan."

"Right."

"Well, here's th'interestin' part. Along comes this crusty, dark horse guy name Jean Chast-al. Now he ain't well liked, lives on the fringe. Kept to hisself. But then one day he marches into town, prob'ly the local pub, an' he makes a big ol' show of these special bullets he's made from melted down Christian coins of th'Virgin Mary or some such. Claims he got these bullets blessed by a *Catholic* priest—now right there that's kinda questionable, on account o' the fact that he's a Protestant...a Protestant whose been grumblin' about the Catholic church, see? So, he gets his bullets blessed and the next day he goes out in the woods. Not long after, he comes out with an animal that don't look like nothin' they've ever seen before...it's hairy with a long neck and huge teeth. He shot it with *one shot* straight to the heart, becomes an instant hero. Gets a special reward from the Catholic church, sets him up good. Meanwhile, statues and plaques honoring him can't go up fast enough, and he's gettin' free drinks and meals at the pub."

"So, what was the animal?" I asked. "A wolf?"

"Nope." He shook his head with conviction. "There's a scanty record that the carcass was on display for some fifty years, and it weren't no wolf. Back in the nineties, the History

Channel sent a cryptozoologist and a cop to France to do some diggin' about. They rooted aroun' and interviewed a bunch of folks in museums an' all. It was a cheesy show, but here's the thang."

Buster tented his fingers then made an arrow with his index fingers, pointed it toward me, tapping my knee with it. "The men came to this conclusion: seems ol' Jean's story was mighty fishy on account 'o the gun he supposedly used. It was real unlikely that he coulda hit the target as far away as he claimed, 'cause it just warn't that ac'rate of a gun, and even *more* unlikely that after the king had sent marksmen out for *months*, that this guy would catch it in one afternoon." He paused to let that sink in. And no, it didn't make any sense. How would he know where to even begin looking for it?

Buster's eyes flared. "On toppa *that*, the big ol' show about the special bullets, even if they were silver, it wouldn'a made him shoot *better*. It just warn't that acc'rate a gun. A runnin' target way off in the woods? Between trees? No way." He paused again, touching my knee with the finger point arrow. "But it were surefire if the target was a lot closer and not movin'. Like a trained *pet*."

"A dog? Surely all the townspeople would have recognized--"

"Nope. A long-haired hyena. A hyena has a bite strength almost double of a dog; they're smart. Trainable. Perfect killing machines."

"Right. Well, last time I checked, hyenas weren't really native to France, or Europe."

"No. But the very well-to-do often kept exotic animals in

private zoos. It's not such a stretch to guess that old Jean got a hold of a pup somehow—maybe he was an estate zookeeper or friends with one...hyena has pups, one goes missing...who'd notice? The region was very rural with forests. He could have hidden his animal no problem. Trained it to kill...maybe with a whistle. A serial killer who uses an animal to do his killin' for him."

"And he gets a heaping reward and becomes a hero?"

"Sick, ain't it?" There was a glimmer in his eyes. "So, no monster. But what an investigation." He studied my face. "Get me now?"

"Yeah." I had a cold shiver spreading across my back. "You said that was in the 1760s? Sounds kind of like *The Hound of the Baskervilles*. You think Arthur Conan Doyle got the idea from this legend?"

"Reckon so."

So maybe Buster wasn't as crazy as I thought. And he was so close. And smelling so good. And talking to me like he'd never had an intimate conversation before he'd met me. And then the door opened, and Shane and Rebel came in loud and joking, until they about knocked into us.

"Oh, sorry to walk in on you." Rebel said, looking like he might go back out the door. "We're ready to roll when you are."

"Well ain't you purty?" Buster teased.

Rebel exhaled a disagreeing, "Hyehh."

"He cleans up good, don't he," Shane said with a laugh from behind Rebel.

Rebel's hair was combed with a neat part, he was wearing a short sleeve plaid shirt and a pair of clean, dark jeans. He'd even shaped his beard.

"Ya look like you're goin' on a date, there, handsome," Buster teased.

"You do!" I agreed, stepping back to let them in. The magic moment was broken as we parted, and Rebel and Shane lumbered in between us.

I turned to go but Buster caught my hand as I reached for the door handle. He pulled me to him, kissed my forehead in that feathery light way and said, "We'll see ya when we git back."

"Yeah," I said as he hugged me.

And then he was holding the door open for me.

Chapter 20

Lorraine and Seven Psychopaths

The departure of The Three Investigators left me feeling adrift and conflicted. What was wrong with me? With no other guests due until Wednesday and guilt that I'd neglected poor Lorraine, I called her hoping to make a dinner date.

"Howdy, stranger," she answered.

"Hey, how's the ankle?"

"Same. A tripping hazard that hurts a lot and snags on the edges of dust ruffle. I'm beyond stir-crazy, but I can't really go anywhere, can I? I asked the doctor if they could just put me on cold storage like Walt Disney and thaw me out when I'm all healed, but they said no, the cheap bastards."

"Want some company?"

"You bet. Dinner and movie and a bottle of red sound good?"

"Yeah, but you aren't cooking, are you?"

"No. Figured you wouldn't mind picking up something seeing as I'm not much in the kitchen. If I call in an order to

Paco's, do you mind picking up? I've got a craving."

"You bet! I've got some *bigos* for you too. I need to run into G'ville for dog food anyway, and I saw a tempting display of peach pies at Fresh Fresh Foods the other day, I'll pick one up. You get to pick the movie."

"Old or new?"

"Don't care, your choice."

"I'm feeling feisty. How about *Seven Psychopaths*? I'm in love with Sam Rockwell."

"Uh…sounds…creepy."

"I know, but you'll love it. Promise. It's got Christopher Walken in it."

"That's not stepping away from creepy, that's walking right up and inviting it in, Lorraine."

"Trust me."

I wasn't at all sure about the movie, but she was the invalid, she got to pick.

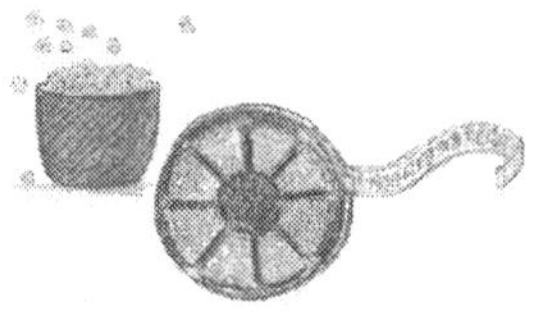

Towards evening, as NB and I were heading towards Lorriane's house, my phone chirped. I didn't recognize the number, and the caller ID said G B SHAD--didn't know anyone named Shad. I let it roll to voicemail, assuming it was a phishing gimmick. But then my phone blipped that I had a message. A creeping traffic situation allowed me to punch the message button.

"Oh…it's just me," Buster said in a low, sleepy voice. I had a moment to call. No p'ticlar reason, just that there's a purty pink sunset settin' up over Lettuce Lake. Made me wish you were here…remind me to tell you about Loon Lake, Washington sometime…" There was a silence, then a breath. "Hope you have yo'self a good night, Haint." Click.

My heart raced a bit.

I patted NB's head absently. "Oh, little girl, your mama's fixin' to hitch her wagon to one wacky-ass, monster hunting star. *Schiesse*."

We arrived at Lorraine's around 7:15 p.m. N.B. scampered to the kitchen door with me following close behind.

Opening the door, I called out, "We're here!"

"In the living room!" Lorraine answered.

NB ran to greet her while I set down the Paco's take-out bag, the Fresh Fresh Foods pie and the Tupperware of *bigos* in her fridge.

"Well hello, how's my girl?" I heard Lorraine coo to the dog. "Here wait…" she groaned, "no, leave that alone. Ow. Don't touch that. Yeah, big owy mess. Here, come sit here."

I knew she wasn't talking to me, but I called out, "Oh, I'm okay, I guess."

"Good girl," I heard her say.

"Thanks!" I called, feeling a bit snarky.

"You're a good girl, too, Haint!"Lorraine yelled.

Lorraine called out, "Do you mind getting plates and

setting us up? My foot is killing me. It's propped up. I'm impatiently waiting for the Lortab to kick in."

"I'm on it. Hey, I put some bigos in your fridge. I was going to have the cryptozoologists over, but they were on a mission."

"Haint? You haven't had company over besides me and Iggy since Bill Clinton was in the White House. Now you've got some oddball monster hunters coming over?"

"Well, I was, but--"

"Are these the nut jobs that Max jokes about?"

"Well, yes, but—"

"Ah-ha…"

"What ah ha?"

She didn't respond.

I rounded up plates, napkins, and utensils. I was reaching for wine glasses, when it occurred to me, alcohol probably clashed with her medications.

"What are you drinking?" I hollered.

"I've got a huge water in here. Help yourself to whatever you can find. There should be some beer in the door."

I found an IPA for me, and pulled two TV trays out from her pantry, and arranged our meals on the trays. I soon had us settled in the living room ready to eat dinner, but unsure if I was ready for something called *Seven Psychopaths*. The rig around Lorraine's ankle still freaked me out, I could hardly look at it. NB had settled on the couch next to Lorraine in a spot with a close view of our plates.

Lorraine was wearing a faded nightgown and robe. She was slumped in the sofa with her leg propped carefully on an ottoman. Her eyes were puffy and red.

"Hey, sweetie," I said, adjusting her TV tray, "you look like you've been crying. Are you okay? Can I get you anything?"

"Oh, it's nothing," she said, sniffing, "I've just been really emotional lately. I think it's the painkillers. They said mood swings was a side effect along with dizziness. Just sitting, I'm fine but if I stand up or move too fast--*whooey.*"

"When do you get out of that?" I asked, sitting down and adjusting my tray.

"Not soon enough. Oh, hey. Belinda Wheeler stopped over with a carrot, soybean and cabbage salad. It's in the fridge. It's pretty good. Want some?"

"I'll pass." I looked down at my massive burrito. "I'm happy to get you some if you want, but I've got plenty here."

She shook her head. "I'm good. They said nausea was a possible side effect. Don't have that, but my appetite is hiding somewhere around here." She looked around as if her appetite had fallen on the floor or fallen between cushions. "But this looks good. I'm so grateful to have you as a friend. Thanks so much for bringing all this." Her voice had a sentimental whimper to it and sure enough, she had puppy eyes like she was going to get weepy on me.

"Well, I feel guilty I haven't been over more."

Lorraine took a tiny bite of her food. "Oh!" She exclaimed and paused to chew. "Belinda said to tell you that she and Cog are going to want a small cabin—he's going to be in the prepper meeting, and she's in with the Take It Off ladies, but they want their own time, if you get me."

"Okay. No problem."

"You look edgy…what's up?" Lorraine asked, putting down her fork, eyeing me.

I had just taken a huge bite of the burrito, which gave me time to avoid the question. When I could speak, I said, "I'm kicking myself. This Buster guy…talks like Andy Griffith with a twang that makes most hicks around here sound erudite…he's got this tidy metrosexual beard thing that sets off his jaw line…dimples…and marble, green-brown eyes that just bore right into me…Uh! He acts like we're already dating and gets all up in my body bubble with his crazy magnetism. Crap, I act like a complete ninny when I'm around him. It's ridiculous. He's like Fox-freakin' Mulder, he travels all over the country hunting mythical beings like Bigfoot and sea monsters. He's a complete loony-toon…and maybe even a drug dealer, but he's really sexy. I can't stop thinking about him."

"Sounds like you're falling hard for this guy."

"Yeah. It sucks."

"Got pictures?"

"No, haven't really had the chance."

"Is he on All-About-Me-Book?"

"How would I know? You know I don't do social media."

Lorraine shot me an annoyed look and reached for her phone. "I can see it now…Mrs. Buster…what'd you say his last name is again? Crabtree?"

"Shadetree," I said, putting my hands over my face.

"Oh, like a shade-tree mechanic? Ha! Well, let's see if Mr. Shadetree..."she fiddled, "is out there, 'cause I want to see this Man of Mystery. Hmm. Not there. Let me try CandidLife."

I waited wondering whether it was a good thing or a bad thing that she didn't seem to find him. Was he just private or was he hiding something? "Forget it. Eat your dinner."

She frowned. "I will in a minute. Not finding a Buster Shadetree here. I'll try NoLickaPrivacy…" she trailed off, engrossed in her hunt.

I worked on my burrito.

"Huh. Nothing. Well, Mrs. Buster Shadetree…hmm. Or Mrs. Haint Blue Shadetree--you know, I kinda like that! Buster may not be his given name."

"True. I don't know. Haven't found a way to ask yet."

"You aren't very helpful."

"Shut up or you'll be wearing your dinner!"

"Girlfriend, you're a hot mess!"

"I know. My head and my heart are not on the same page by a long stretch."

"What's about the drug dealer business?" she asked waving a forkful of salad in the air.

"No. Well, maybe. I don't know. I don't think so, but he seems to have a lot of money."

Lorraine gave me the stink eye. "Last time I checked, that wasn't a bad thing."

"I'm sure he's not. But can he really make megabucks as a Bigfoot hunter? He's got vehicles and a boat and gadgets…"

She shrugged. "Ask him."

"Mmm!" I said, covering my full mouth. After a bit of chewing I asked, "And just how do I bring that up in conversation? 'By the way, how'd you get so loaded?' It's none of my business."

Lorraine waved her hand, "You'll figure it out. And how is Iggy? Did he sort out his love triangle?"

I sighed. "He's working through it, yeah. I'd feel better if Running Deer weren't hanging around. As long as she's in town, his heart'll be fragile as a hummingbird."

"Why is she back, anyway? Does she hope to get back together?"

"It looks that way, but Iggy said her mother is dying in Hospice, so she came back to be with her."

Lorraine shook her head. "Of all the nerve. After she dropped him like that." She took a big sip of water and swallowed. "Kind of cycle of life stuff going on, uh? Mom's punching her timecard and the baby is coming soon?" She took a fork full of refried beans.

"Yeah. Must be a lot to take in," I said, thinking of the loss of my parents. "Losing a parent while getting ready to be a new mother--especially as a single one."

Lorraine said a muffled "yeah" as she chewed. She swallowed. "Thanks again for picking this up, Haint. I was in the mood for Mexican. This is perfect."

"My pleasure," I answered, saluting her with my beer.

"Did you see Yolanda?"

"I did. Told her I was picking up food for you, in fact. She said to tell you she hoped you recovered quickly." Yolanda was the manager at Paco's; her hunky brother Pedro was a guest during my disastrous retreat opening. Lorraine called him "Mr. Delicious." He'd been flirtatious and dropped a hint that he'd see her around. My intuition reasoned that Lorraine was hoping that Yolanda would get word to Pedro about her broken foot, and perhaps he'd contact her out of sympathy.

My phone rang. "Sorry, I should have turned it off. Probably a robo-call."

Lorraine shrugged.

I pulled my phone out of my pocket. "Oh. It's Nicole. Uh-oh. Hope she's not backing out of doing the yoga classes for me."

Lorraine frowned.

"Hello? This is Haint."

"Hey, Haint. Nicole. You know, the yoga sub?"

"Yes, of course," I said, waiting for the bad news.

"Hey, listen, I know we talked about doing morning yoga sessions, but—"

"That's a problem?"

"Oh, no! Not at all. But I talked to Boo and she said that maybe evening sessions would be good too since some people aren't morning people."

"Oh."

"So, I was wondering if it would be okay, like, what would you think if I did morning and evening classes? Like, before breakfast and before dinner? Get more people?"

That sounded good, but I'd have to pay her double. It did make sense, though.

"Um, and since it's for my friends and I'm kind of new at teaching, I could give you a really good deal—honestly, the references would be more golden than the extra money."

"That's not taking on too much? Two a day?"

"Nope. I've done back to back classes before. It won't be a problem. I can do it."

"Well, okay, that'd be terrific." We negotiated a price. I hung up and looked at Lorraine, dumbfounded. "Well, if you ever hear me besmirch a Millennial for being unmotivated, slap me hard."

"She's highly motivated. I'm telling you, she's going to put me right out of a job."

"Well, she *is* cheaper," I said, raising an eyebrow.

She chucked a magazine at me, then said, "Oh. Hey. That reminds me. Check your calendar. You have a booking for Wednesday for three Kerry May wannabes on their way to a training in Miami, and a retired couple on their way to Atlanta for an art show. They've paid already. I emailed confirmations."

I'm resistant to technology; without Lorraine's help, I'd be lost. I prefer looking at a big computer screen to hovering over my phone and jabbing at buttons. I keep forgetting to look at our online booking page unless I'm in my office. Fortunately, she's patient as my booking backup.

I leaned back in my seat. "Cool! It's going to be a busy week. Glad I have tomorrow to get ready."

Lorraine waved her huge water glass at me. "Oh, Did I tell you? Lerlene was here earlier to help me make some cakes for *Guido's*...she's been contacted by *Our Town* magazine." She paused to take a long drink. "I've been so thirsty, you can't imagine!" She set the glass down hard. "They're doing an article on Lerlene's artwork. They should be contacting you about taking pictures of your Lotus Lodge sign. They love her colors, apparently."

My Blue's Lotus Lodge sign was the pearl in my oyster. Lerlene offered to paint it for me but ignored my vision of a soft, tranquil lavender lotus flower and a flowing font. The installation went up just days before my soft opening, and voila. My guests are greeted by an aggressive slashing black font surrounded by a psychedelic artichoke. Andy Warhol meets Audrey II, the vampire plant from *Little Shop of Horrors*. Yet there *was* something about it, the bright colors, the weird sixties vibe, the shouting font. It was *so* outrageous it was almost cool. In the month that it had been up, it had become a local landmark. It hadn't lured in guests but it was getting talked about. Despite being conflicted about the kaleidoscopic sign, I was happy for Lerlene that she was getting the publicity. "That's exciting. Good for her."

"Well. Ready for some zany fun?" Lorraine pushed the remote buttons.

"I guess," I said, taking a full sip of beer.

Seven Psychopaths turned out to be a perfect distraction. Just what I needed. Sam Rockwell was utterly charming as the primary psychopath and Christopher Walken was hilarious. We went right to the special features.

"You know, Buster looks a bit like Sam Rockwell," I said.

"Oh? He *must* be cute then. Is he a psychopath?"

"I don't think so. He has friends."

"Sam Rockwell's character has friends."

"Yes, but they're all nuts, too." I said.

Lorraine swung her head around to glare at me. "Exactly my point. Just proceed with caution, sweetie." She blew an air kiss at me. "I love you." Her eyes were watery again. She looked tired.

"Can I help you to bed?" I asked.

"Oh, please. I have to pee like a racehorse and I'm not sure I can get up."

I stayed and helped her to bed, put away her leftovers and took out her trash. She was snoring by the time NB and I left.

Driving home, listening to the radio, Buster's beguiling smile came to mind. The Beach Boys song "Kokomo" was playing. In my mind, Buster and I were holding hands on a dock watching a sunset at Lettuce Lake.

Creatures of the Night

I was deep in a dream about a shootout in the desert when a shrill scream woke me up. NB's head snapped up, she let out a tentative woof, a what-the-hell woof, more air than voice. I reached for my glasses as her head swung around to face me. Had I heard it too? Her ears were up. We listened.

"Ai-yiii! Ai-ya-yi!"

I've never heard a banshee before, but this high scream was close, and agonized. I felt that crystalizing feeling of adrenaline flooding my body.

NB looked to the window and leapt to her feet. This time her bark was an all systems on high alert, a full, from the chest, WOOF! WOOF!

"Ai-yiiiaaah!"

The wailing was moving deeper into the woods away from the house. I heard frenzied howling coming from Urliss's house; I hoped Willie and Waylon were securely confined, imagining them climbing a chain link fence to get at whatever that thing was. NB ran to the back door and threw herself against it. I got up turning lights on as I moved through the house to join her at the door. I flipped the outside lights on. Half-expecting some hairy monster staring back at me, I was relieved to see nothing out of the ordinary. NB looked up at me as if to say, *Come on! Let me at 'em!*

"No way, Short Stuff. I don't want you tangling with whatever that was."

She looked at me wild-eyed and slammed against the door again.

"Nope. Come with me, sweetheart." I bent down to pick her up, but she wriggled away from me.

I stood up and listened. Whatever it was had stopped vocalizing.

"I think it's gone. Want a treat?" I asked, moving back to the kitchen. It wasn't until I crinkled the treat bag that she broke her concentration. Still woofing, she trotted into the kitchen. Her tail wagged, the barking stopped, she accepted the dog cookie.

I put the kettle on for a small cup of tea. By the time I added honey and a blup of milk, all was quiet. No baying sounds from next door. No doubt Willie and Waylon were disappointed, but safe. NB followed me back to the bedroom, climbed the steps, circled and pawed herself a little nest and flopped down. After a few sips of soothing chamomile and a few paragraphs of a pretentious magazine article on karma, I fell back asleep.

I had uneasy scattered dreams doing wildlife research

comparing odd characteristics to known nighttime animals and coming up empty. Book after book, checklist after checklist, the results were the same, nope, didn't sound like that, nope didn't run like that. What was it?

Chapter 21

Tuesday the 28th : Saudade

There is something about mist and rain that makes me introspective, fills me with a yearning for something I can't quite remember, a chronic unfulfillment. It was fitting that Tuesday morning began with fog, a gray drizzle, and the word of the day on my calendar : **saudade** –noun: a feeling of melancholia, nostalgia. Characterized in much Brazilian music. Acute sense of the untenable, also as in Portuguese Fado music, expressing loss.

In no hurry to slough off the saudade, I dug a Brendan Perry CD out of my bookshelf and turned it up. This solo album has a haunting quality, as if recorded in an ancient castle, his voice calling out from a not-so-earthly realm with the loss of the last dinosaur calling across vast distances for a mate and hearing back silence, yet not able to give up. As if the ancient castle air, the echoing empty space becomes his silent singing partner with the clarity and mystery of Gregorian chants.

I made breakfast for myself, NB and Mischief while Brendan sang of being trapped in time and living a lie. I stepped outside with my cup of Molten Mocha and let the rain gently fall on my face like fairy hands attempting Swedish massage, polka-dotting my pajamas and disappearing in my morning elixir like snow.

Behind me, Brendan advised showing true feelings. Where to start? This mid-life business was an adjustment. I never thought I'd be alone at almost fifty, living in Catfish Springs, Florida running a floundering retreat. I'd lived in New York City, Kyoto, Japan, London, England, Bern, Switzerland and Kaiserslautern, Germany and never imagined I'd settle in a tiny town, barely a spec on the map. Were my travelling years over? What had I accomplished?

My pajamas were getting a bit too damp, I moved back inside.

I was learning to shuck off the poisons of samsara: need for stuff, need for status, need for approval from others. I had abundant gratitude for all my blessings, excellent health, solid friends, my quirky house.

I missed Dillon.

What would Dillon think of Buster? Ha! Did it matter? What did *I* think of Buster? I hardly knew him, yet I felt the heart-tug of the left behind. The crazy bow-legged cowboy rode out of Dodge without me.

A long hot shower helped. I took my time combing my hair, putting on make-up. Overdue for a haircut, I trimmed my bangs and put the rest up in a Katherine Hepburn-style bun.

"Need to make a grocery list, little girl. Come help." After the grocery run, the plan was to cook and clean all day. Clear my space and get a jump on the meals required for later in the week when the retreat was filled with preppers, Wiccans, partiers, the weight loss team and the three amigos.

I located a pad and pen, sat down on my fainting couch. Naughty Britches popped up next to me, flipped over, threw her right paw up in a wave and wiggled. *I'm so cute!Pet my belly, Mom!*

I obliged while scribbling out ingredients for black bean burgers, salad fixings, spinach and scallop salad, that fabulous pomegranate chicken recipe, and various quiches. If I paused for any reason, she would grumble and lurch at me. *Hey! You stopped! Focus!* Eventually, petting wasn't enough. Woofed at me and gave me the evil eye.

"Walkies?" I asked.

She leaped off the couch and ran to the front door, woofing. My cell phone rang just as I caught up with her. I trotted back to the kitchen to pick it up.

"Cat's out of the bag," Lorraine whimpered. "I'm doomed. Saint Eleanor is coming tomorrow."

"Tomorrow?" Cradling the phone awkwardly in my neck, I leashed NB and got her outside. "What happened? How did she find out about your ankle? Did you tell her accidentally?"

"Are you being punny? No, *of course* I didn't tell her about my accident. God no! She called Lerlene last night, kicking up a fuss about Thanksgiving, as usual."

"But that's a month away."

"I know. She starts worrying about it just after Labor Day. She's meal planning, place setting and wants to know who's coming so she can plan bedding arrangements, as if we need place cards. It's ridiculous. We always find room no matter how many show up, but she agonizes anyway. So Lerlene the Babble Queen let slip that I probably wouldn't make it because of my foot. She called me to tell me she's coming tomorrow afternoon."

"You couldn't talk her out of it?"

"Did the Native Americans talk the white man out of 'manifest destiny'?"

"Oh dear," I chuckled.

"I need a miracle," Lorraine moaned. "She even asked if Thanksgiving should be at my house this year, so I didn't need to travel, and everyone could come to me!"

"Oh. Would that be so bad?"

"Are you kidding? No way."

"How long is she likely to stay?"

"Until I'm fully healed and ready to train for a marathon. At least a couple weeks. I'm doomed. I need a blizzard to shut down the roads and the airports, so she can't come."

"Hmm. Don't recall the weather report predicting snow in Florida. Tomorrow."

"She's in Blue Ridge, Georgia. That's a different climate zone. I could get lucky."

"Tell her you're on your way to California to see a specialist," I offered.

"Then she'd fly out to California to confer with the doctor," Lorraine said.

"Hmm. Can't you spin it to your advantage? Sit back and binge watch *Downton Abbey* while she cleans your house?"

"It doesn't work like that. She'll want to talk with me the

entire time. Imitating her mother's voice, she said, "Oh, you don't want *this* do you? I'll throw it out and get you a new one. Sweetheart? You've got *milk* in the fridge. You aren't drinking *milk,* are you? Adult humans aren't meant to drink milk. I'll get you some almond milk. Where do you keep your sugar substitute packets? I'm making a cup of tea and it's *not in here.* Don't you have stevia at least? And I *wish* you had an electric stove. Gas makes me so *nervous.* Your tea kettle looks ancient. I'll get you a new one in a *festive* color. How about *orange*?"

I felt my shoulders slumping with defeat, "Was your mother the role model for Gladys Kravitz by any chance?"

"Who?"

"Busybody neighbor on Bewitched?"

"Probably."

"Well, good luck."

"You *will* visit me in prison, won't you?"

"Yes, but the cake I bring will be store-bought. I can't compete with yours. And I doubt the file will get through the metal detector."

"Well that sucks." There was a pause. "Think I could get on an airplane with this foot?"

"Not a chance."

Pause. "If we leave now for Miami, maybe we could catch one of those Caribbean cruise ships. By the time she tracked us down, we'd be at sea! Perfect! I'll start packing."

"I can't get all Thelma and Louise until after this weekend. I'm booked through Sunday."

Lorraine sighed. "*Crap.*" Pause. "Well, since I can't drive, maybe I can keep her busy running errands for me. Oh! Hey! Seriously, I'll tell her we want spiced and pickled peaches. She's going to drive right past Lann's on her way down here."

Lann Southern Orchards is a tourist landmark off of I-75 outside of Byron, Georgia. The fried fruit pies and canned peaches are well-worth the detour.

"Please! I'll happily pay her back. I'm good for six jars. And peach syrup! I can put it out for guests for their waffles. Peach jam, too. Lots. "

"You're making waffles now, too?"

"Possibly. A guest informed me that I need pancakes. I'm not doing that, pancakes are too fussy, but one of those do-it-yourself waffle makers, like they have in motels sometimes. That'd be fun. Then I don't have to cook. Everyone likes waffles."

"Except the gluten-free folks."

"Oh, *scheisse*. There must be gluten-free batter."

"Must be. We'll send Saint Eleanor to find it!"

"Yes!" I laughed. "You'll be fine. Remember, she loves you. And allowing someone to help you increases your merit."

"So does not killing her, I guess, huh?"

"Well, that just keeps your karma neutral, I think. And keeps you out of prison. They don't have toilet seats in prison, you know. The toothbrushes fall apart, and the beds aren't very comfy. They sure don't have pretty quilts on them."

"All right, all right, I won't kill her."

"Good. If she drives you nuts, send her over here. I'm sure I can put her to work somehow."

"Right. Gotta go."

"Bye. Good luck."

I hung up.

Grocery list in hand, I said goodbye to a pouty NB and a napping Mischief and headed to the Whatcha Need Mart in Catfish. They had an aisle for small appliances. I might get lucky and find an inexpensive waffle maker. I hit it at the right time, it wasn't very busy and I found a parking space close to the entrance.

Mashing a collection of reusable shopping bags into the child seat of the buggy, I set out for the appliance section. Tada! They had a flip-style maker that promised to be easy to clean with old school technology: you pushed a start button, and a light would come on to tell you when it was done. Perfect.

Despite the ambient music emitting from discrete speakers in the ceiling, "What's Love Got to Do with It" was playing in my head as images of Buster's killer-dimple smile kept popping up in my mind's eye.

Focus on the food. Make the shopping a meditation. Be mindful.

It took over an hour to work my way around the store selecting items for the retreat and my house. The cart was ridiculous. Overloaded like the Grinch's sleigh in Dr. Seuss's *The Grinch Who Stole Christmas.* I steered it with difficulty into a checkout lane. With the final turn and push, I exhaled, "*Uffda.*"

The little old lady in front of me turned with a stiff neck to look at me. "Are you Danish? Oh! You're an albino, aren't you? I've seen pictures. Never seen a real one before. Interesting. You're pretty. Do you *feel* different?"

Och naja!♥ "*Excuse* me?"

"Different from…oh, I don't guess you'd know what normal felt like, would you? No, of course not. But *are* you Danish? You said *uffda*."

The woman had a beige leather handbag over one arm that held a toy dog. Both creatures looked at me expectantly: the woman over a pair of glasses, the dog with a profound underbite and a tongue that hung limp to one side as if too large for its mouth.

Unsure if the woman was being rude on purpose or was naturally oblivious, I answered, "No. Polish-Russian. Albino, too. And I'm *fine*. Just fine."

"So how do you know *uffda*?"

What a question. Does one need to be Japanese to eat sushi or French to know what a crepe is? Good grief. I stopped myself before blurting a snarky response and answered honestly. "I heard someone say it once and loved the definition: putting ten pounds of sh…crap in a five-pound box. I should have made two trips, but…" I stopped myself with a shrug. Why was I apologizing to this woman about my shopping habits? I changed the subject. "Who's your friend here?"

The dog had a pale blue, faux-diamond collar. From my angle, I saw POOP embroidered on it in purple, and thought with dismay *that just can't be right.*

"Poopsie." The woman said with pride while patting its

♥German for "Good grief, or gee whiz"

head with a discolored and arthritic hand. The touch cut off a snarl that was building momentum as more teeth had become visible. The collar jingled and shifted as the full POOPSIE became visible along with a rabies tag and bone shaped ID tag. "He's a Shichi, cross between a Shitzu and Chihuahua."

"Ah. Cute," I said.

"Hello, Mrs. Bunderbridge, how are you today?" asked Lynne, the checkout girl, like a seasoned bedside nurse.

"Well, I haven't been sleeping too well lately, and I've got to see the doctor about my lumbago—"

"And how is little Poopsie doing?" Lynne interjected smoothly before Mrs. Bunderbridge could disclose her medical history.

"Poopsie has had some dietary issues but is doing better." This induced another clumsy pat. Poopsie's head ducked trying to avoid the inevitable hand before disappearing under it. "Aren't you, Poopsie?"

Mrs. Bunderbridge pivoted to swing the handbag closer to the girl. "See?" She presented pitiful Poopsie as evidence. Poopsie squirmed and snarled.

"That's great. So good to see you, Mrs. Bunderbridge. Please say hello to your husband, will you?"

"Thank you dear."

Sean, the bag boy, eased Mrs. B's cart forward and offered to help her out to her car. She nodded and followed with a slight limp. As they moved away, I heard a snarl and saw Sean jump away from the handbag.

Lynne glanced behind me, there was no one. She leaned

forward and whispered, "She lives down the street from me. Her husband is the sweetest man, but she's a battleax. And that damn dog terrorizes the neighborhood. *She* lets it roam. Swears it's an angel. It shits in everyone's yard and chases small kids on bikes. I *hate* that dog. Bit my nephew last Christmas. She swears it never goes out of her sight. *Uuuughh*!"

Lynne leaned back and began swiping my canned goods. "Sorry. I shouldn't have said that. She just makes me bonkers."

"No worries." I said, handing her my pile of shopping bags.

Another bag boy, Jamal, appeared and helped to reload my cart. We were pulling away from the register when Sean came in the door, holding his thumb in front of him.

Jamal asked, "What's up, dude?"

"That dog bit me! I'll be back in a sec. It's bleeding. Cover for me, will ya?"

Lynne muttered behind us, "I h*ate* that dog."

Chapter 22

Wednesday October 29: Oh, Deer

Menu planning in the retreat kitchen Wednesday afternoon, I was snacking on carrot sticks, sliced apples and smoked Gouda cheese chunks when I heard voices outside. I whipped off my apron and trotted out front.

Three women were wandering toward the picnic pavilion.

"This is nice."

"Wonder which one is ours?"

"I'm not getting any answer to my text."

"Hello!" I called, waving a hand.

"Oh, hello," one of them said. "I texted and didn't get an answer." They waited for me to catch up. They were all slender, pretty and very young. One didn't even look old enough to drive.

"Hi, I'm Haint Blue, the owner. Are you the Kerry May ladies?" I asked.

"Yes, that's right," answered a sunny woman stepping forward to shake my hand. "I'm Kayla."

"I'm Amber," said a green-eyed woman with a smile that animated the few freckles on her cheeks.

"And I'm Meghan," the last woman said, offering a hand. She had short dark hair, a heart-shaped face and wide, dark eyes.

NB had begun barking in the office. "Sorry, I was lost in meal planning. I'll show you around. Would you mind if I brought my basset hound? She's in the office and loves meeting people."

"Aww! A Basset hound!"

"Of course!"

"I love dogs."

"There's a pretty view from the dock over by the other pavilion. How about I meet you there?"

"Sure," they agreed.

I jogged over to the office, ducked in, leashed up NB and let her out to greet our guests. She took off, front-wheel drive digging into the dirt, pulling me along.

"Oh, look!"

"Aw, she's so sweet!"

"Look at that! She's rolling over! Awww!"

After the essential meet-and-pet, allowing them a chance to look up and down the river, I led them toward cabin two.

"This should be nice and quiet. There's a couple in cabin three, and a group in cabin seven and that's it."

NB tried to tug me down the trail. "Wait, we have to show them the cabin," I said, coaxing her up on the porch. "My friend, Lorraine made all the quilts."

The girls swept passed me.

"So pretty!" Meghan cooed.

Amber threw herself on one of the beds. "Oh, this is great! I get this one!"

"Can I ask a nosy question?" I asked.

"Sure," Meghan said.

"I'm just curious. What all do you do in a Kerry May boot camp? I mean, do you get drilled on make-up colors, or practice doing make-up on each other?"

Kayla simpered. Her blonde hair swept forward like a shampoo commercial. "No! It's so much more than make-up. I mean, that's the *product*. But we're learning a *business*. My cousin is a rep; she's the one who talked me into doing it. She said the training is life changing. She said this with underlining emphasis. You learn how to get organized, how to make goals, implement a sales plan, run a business. She's been very successful. She says it looks really good on a resume, too."

Maybe you ought to go through Kerry May boot camp, my Inner Critic whispered.

Maybe.

"Wow. That sounds really good," I said, noting the hollow quality in my voice. These girls looked like they were on the fast track to success whereas I felt like I was floundering in the slow lane with a couple low tires.

"Feel free to explore the grounds. There's a loop trail oft that way that leads to a meditation circle. Just don't walk and text…this is the woods… we do have spiders, snakes, poison ivy and the occasional alligator. All avoidable if you watch where you're going."

"Snakes?"

"Alligators! I want to see one!"

"The rest room and bath house are here," I gestured.

NB dragged me over to a tree to check her pee mail. She left a message and we moved on to the dining room.

"I was going to do a scallop and spinach salad tonight with mango, bacon and pine nuts…any allergies, or issues with the bacon? Are you vegetarians?"

"Nope! All good," Amber said.

"Sounds delicious!" Kayla said.

Meghan nodded. "All good!"

I tied NB to the porch and led the ladies into the dining hall.

"Oh, wow. This is so relaxing! And look out the window!"

The group wandered over to peer out the window at my little flower garden. A blue-tailed skink padded across the window. A cardinal perched in the edge of the bird bath and took a drink. Two squirrels chased each other round and round a young oak tree making figure eights.

"If you're lucky, you'll see some deer at breakfast."

"Aw!" Meghan and Amber cooed.

"Oh, I hope so," said Kayla.

They chit-chatted a bit then said they'd go unpack and get settled. I followed them out where they said goodbyes to NB and headed to the parking lot. I took NB for a walk along the woods trail. We watched a hawk swoop ahead of us. I so loved it here in the woods with the wildlife. Dynamite couldn't get me to Miami for a Kerry May boot camp.

Towards dusk, three non-descript medium-sized vehicles

showed up. Eight men gathered and moved together like a herd of deer into my office.

"Hi, I'm Haint Blue. Can I help you?" I asked.

A clean-shaven pudgy man in a tan T-shirt and faded blue jeans held out a hand and said, "Hi, I'm Jim Calhoun."

I stood to shake his hand. My brain was slow to make the connection. Jim Calhoun. Party of eight. But these weren't students. "Ah, yes," I stammered, "I've been expecting you."

"And this is my wife, Julie."

Dressed as she was in cargo pants with a utility vest over a T-shirt, I had mistaken her for a teenage boy. Her pageboy bob bounced as she stepped forward and offered her hand. She had a strong, boney grip.

Jim introduced the rest of the group by first names, which I forgot before he got to the third man. They all had basic names like Joe, John, Harry, Jerry. They were mostly men in their sixties, although one, perhaps Jerry, was clearly a son. Second generation. All wore clean but plain T-shirts and pants. They all seemed moderately athletic, or at least had been at one time before the belt had to go under the stout gut. They weren't the college preppers or some corporate group, not by a long shot.

I've heard that the actress Marilu Henner has a videotape memory of everything she has ever experienced and can haul up any detail like a computer. Name, date, time, weather for any day in her past.

Bill Clinton is credited with a name-face-detail memory such that if he meets someone at a cocktail party and chats for a few minutes, he can recognize and remember the conversation indefinitely. Run into him in a hallway years later, and he can remember your name, and will likely have follow-ups like, "Hi, Kala, looks like your knee surgery was a success," or "Ralph, good to see you again. Say, did your daughter get accepted to Brown?"

My memory is so spotty…I tell myself I'm just so good at living in the moment, I don't recall the past, but seriously large chunks of my life have just gone fizzy-poof. I have retained moments from grade school, but honestly, they are either moments of elation or humiliation with not much in between. If I don't make a name connection right after the person says his or her name, it's gone. I've tried name tricks like saying them out loud.

"Carlton? Hi Carlton. Nice to meet you, Carlton." This sometimes works but I feel like a moron--not that that ever stops me.

I had a wee panic attack looking at these men who, at a glance, had an unnatural same-ness to them. Lacking a poker face, my welcome must have seemed half-hearted. In return, I received oblique glances and awkward gawks. Between my albino features and colored contacts, I'm used to slack mouths and double takes.

"Welcome!" I said, forcing conviction and moving toward the door. "I'm so glad you chose the Lotus Lodge. Let me give you a quick tour. If you want to follow me." I ushered them outside and over to the dining hall. "As promised, you'll have exclusive use of the dining hall for your, uh, meetings. At present you are the only ones here, but with Halloween coming at the end of the week, we should be pretty full. I doubt this will interfere with your agenda, although we will have to use the dining hall for meals."

The men looked around nodding.

"Speaking of meals, you've only signed up for breakfast, is that correct?"

More nodding.

"Well, that's fine. I can give you some recommendations for restaurants in the area, and if you change your mind and want to take meals here, just let me know the day before so I can adjust—"

Jim coughed. "Ma'am, we'd like to practice making cook fires. Do you have somewhere where we could do that?"

I must have looked blank. "Sorry?"

"You, know, cooking over coals with cast iron? We just need a place to set up," he said glancing around. "Like, by one of the covered picnic tables. If that's okay."

Huh? Somehow in my mind, lectures had meant office people in corporate casual, white collared shirts and khaki pants. Wow. Were they going to cook all their meals outside? Ambitious. I thought a moment. Where would they be out of the way all week? "Sure. There's a space between the picnic pavilion and the river by your bunk house. I'll show you."

We crossed the parking lot, and I pointed to the picnic pavilion, a covered structure with an old concrete picnic table and charcoal grill. "And here's number seven, your bunk house. You should have the place to yourselves until the 31st. Then there's going to be a party in number nine, but you should be far enough away, and they've promised to keep it down after midnight." We clomped up the porch and I opened the door and held it as they entered. "I know it's a bunk house design, but I tried to make it homey. There's a kitchenette at the back there with all the amenities. Unfortunately, these cabins were not built with bathrooms, but you have a shower and bathroom pavilion just across the driveway, there."

More nodding and some odd looks between themselves.

Julie Calhoun made an approving assessment motion with her mouth and chin. Again, she looked so much like a boy, I'd forgotten she was Jim's wife.

"Uh, you know," I began, wondering how comfortable she was going to be in a cabin with a bunch of men, "I do have a small cabin available if you and your husband would prefer some privacy…"

"Oh, that's kind of you but not necessary. I'll be going back home in the evenings. You see, my mother lives with us and we've got dogs and two horses. Mother does okay by herself for a couple of hours, but I'll go home to fix her some supper and take care of the animals. It's not very far."

"Oh, I see. Well, if you have any other questions, or need anything, just holler."

Some of them stayed inside and some followed me back to the parking lot to get their belongings. We were all distracted by a Nissan pickup truck pulling in. As it pulled alongside the cabin, the side window rolled down and the man inside called out, "Hey, sorry I'm late. Had a bit of trouble loading the, er, cargo." He thumbed the bed of the truck, which had something wrapped in a gray tarp. "Where should I park?"

Julie looked nervous. Jim was shuffling his feet; two others were eyeing him. Jim studied his boots. I was about to point to the other vehicles in the parking lot, wondering why this was even a question, when I was interrupted by a man with thinning hair in a ponytail.

"The thing is, we will be dressing a deer. It's...part of the class. So, yeah, that's a deer in the back of the bed there. Jim didn't mention that I guess... hope that doesn't freak you out or anything."

Dress a deer? Here in the camp? Bless me, Carmen Miranda and the fruit in her hat!

"No, he didn't mention it. Um, what is your group again? I'm sorry, I was expecting some kind of college preppers or a corporate event...you aren't salesmen, I'm guessing..."

Julie put a hand to her mouth and murmured, "uh-oh," shooting a look at Jim.

I glared at Jim, but he was still deep in study of his boot laces.

"We're preppers," Julie said.

"Oh," I said, searching my memory for a link but coming up short. They didn't look pre*ppy*. Prepp*ing*? For what?

"Preparedness for any catastrophe. Social collapse. Meteorite strike. Plague. Flood. End of day," said Jim, or John.

I thought of the disaster movies from the 70s. In my mind Pierce Brosnan was carrying a child, running from flowing lava. How did you prepare for that? I must have looked clueless.

"It's like a survival skill thing," added Jim (or was it Jerry?) "Like the reality shows. What would you do if you were dumped on an island with a knife, kind of thing."

"Oh," I'd heard of *Survivor*, but hadn't seen an episode. I took a breath. Were they going to be running around my retreat like Rambo? Surely not. "Well, no matter, you have the place to yourselves. There is a hose over by the dock, it used to be for cleaning boats. Do what you need to, all I ask is that you don't leave me a crime scene, and please don't feed the bits to the gators. I don't need them getting any friendlier than they are already."

I heard myself saying this, but was picturing half-naked, mud-covered people running carrying a deer carcass across my parking lot. The carcass thing made me uneasy. They could just throw the remains deep into the woods, but there was the chance that a predator might drag something out for a guest to find. I thought about the meditation circle, but no, that wouldn't work since the Wiccans were coming, and would not appreciate that kind of mess one bit. I have a mini-meditation circle at home, and often leave bones, or refrigerator purges in the center of the circle for wildlife. Hawks, possums, coyotes, owls—something always took my offerings. I didn't really want to offer this up but dumping it in the dumpster would attract flies and would be just gross.

"What were you planning on doing with the, uh, innards, hooves and whatnot?" I asked.

"Ma'am, usually we dig a hole under the deer and all that falls in, then we cover it up," one of the older men said.

"Or dump it in the river."

I cringed. "No, that's not a good idea. I don't want to encourage the alligators."

Why hadn't they asked me about this first? Had they intended to just process the deer and hope I wouldn't find out?

I was annoyed, but what could I do? The deer was in the back of the truck. I couldn't very well tell them to find somewhere else to do this, I couldn't think of a place, for starters.

I pictured a guest walking out to the bathroom at night and surprising a bear digging up deer guts. Or some kids seeing the fresh dig sight and fantasizing about buried treasure. Yuck. I wasn't comfortable with this at all. I realized I would also always associate that spot with buried body parts. *Aw, Look. There is a nice family picnicking in the pavilion… right next to where a deer head and hooves are buried.* I closed my eyes and took a deep breath. The image of a fox I've seen periodically in my back yard came to mind. That would be a satisfying meal for him.

"Tell you what…I don't want to attract predators here at the camp. If you can contain the remains in something covered and portable…" I couldn't believe I was saying this. "I'll take it home with me and dump it in my woods."

The men's expressions vacillated between surprise and relief.

"Seriously? You don't mind? That would be great."

Hmm. No, the situation is not great, at all, but let's move on. "I have a meditation circle I put offerings in--old leftovers, dead chickens, back when I had chickens--it's like an offering back to nature. Something always comes."

"Bet so," Thinning Ponytail said.

"Uh, you don't have any other little surprises for me, do you? You aren't planning on… snaring rabbits, for example, are you? I really don't want you killing anything here. No shooting, no trapping, please. While I won't pretend total piety, I'm not even a vegetarian, although I am moving slowly in that direction, I am a Buddhist. You know, do no harm?"

I got some empty stares back and uneasy shifting.

"Thou shalt not *kill*?"

This time, I got a couple of nods.

A tan Nissan pick-up rolled in and a stout couple got out and headed toward us.

Julie called out, "Hey Belinda, Hey Cog."

"Hey y'all," Cog answered.

The Wheelers were dressed in jeans and plain T-shirts. Belinda had straight brown hair loosely braided down to her butt and the posture and tan of a horsewoman. They both stared at me.

"Hi, I'm Haint. You must be Mr. and Mrs. Wheeler. I was just showing the rest of your group their cabin, number seven and they were telling me about the…uh…meal plan."

"You have the most amazing eyes," Belinda said. "Such a pretty blue…and I always thought that albi--" A look of horror swelled in her eyes before she looked away.

"Relax, you're quite right. They're contacts. I'm legally blind and my eyes are a white-blue. It's my little bit of vanity, the colored lenses, but they help with glare and bright lights."

"Oh," she said. "I'm so sorry, I didn't mean—"

"No worries," I said with a quick pat to her shoulder. "Let me show you to your cabin—you'll be in number three, over there, just left of the pavilion. You might want to move your truck closer, over to the second parking lot."

Cog nodded, got back in the truck and started it up while Belinda and I walked to their cabin.

"You know, long as I've lived out here in Catfish, and I've known Max and Charlene, bless her heart, but I never came out here before…never before," Belinda said looking around. "This is nice. I heard it was kinda run down before you got it and fixed it up. Cog used to come fish here a long time ago with his buddies. Said Max had really kind of let it go…let it go."

Belinda seemed to have a built-in echo for the last few words of a sentence. I wondered if she was aware of it.

"I hate to say it, but that's true. Max tried, but he just didn't have his heart in it after Charlene got sick. He seems to be doing all right at the Old Oaks, but he looks a little lost. I try to visit regularly."

"I know you do. Cog says Urliss and Hollis visit him a lot too and take him out for meals and such. That's good."

We arrived at the porch. I ushered Belinda in as Cog caught up with us, carrying two tidy tan duffel bags.

Cog followed Belinda into the cabin and said, "Haint, you've done a super job fixin' the old place up."

"Thank you. Please let me know if you need anything."

"Do we get a key?"

"Ah, no. There's a dead bolt to lock yourselves in, but we're on the honor system, just like Max had it."

"Hrrmph. Should get locks. Can't be too careful." Cog said.

"It has come up. I'm looking into options," I said. "The rest room and showers are just across the parking lot there. I think you'll find a bit of improvement from the old days—all renovated."

Cog grunted. "You need to get some locks."

"Right," I said.

I liked these people well enough, but lately I keep hearing that our thoughts become things and what we focus on, where we put our attention is what we attract. I couldn't embrace a culture of fear, assuming a doomsday and waiting for it all to come crashing down. I didn't want to have locks against zombies. I wanted to go home and put birdseed out, make a cup of tea and listen to the birds. Abide in tranquility and envision a peaceful world.

I'd arranged with my five dinner guests to arrive by six o'clock, so I could leave for my monthly meditation class in Gainesville. The Kerry May trio arrived and oohed and ahhed over the spinach-scallop salad I'd prepared.

"Man, I wish I could make salads like this," Amber said.

"Oh, I can't wait to try it," Meghan said.

"My secret ingredient is a chocolate infused balsamic vinegar," I said.

"Oh, wow!"

"Really? Chocolate vinegar?"

Their bubbly chatter faded as they tucked into their meal. I'd paired the entrée with a biscuity white wine that they all accepted.

The thirty-something couple, Mr. and Mrs. Gularte, from cabin three came in. They'd hardly said anything to me when they'd checked in earlier. Both attractive in a plain way, they had mousy brown hair, clean cut and all, with no bright colors or striking styles of haircut or clothing. The kind of people your eye wouldn't linger on, and yet, there was something peculiar in their demeanor that fascinated me. They shared an energetic aura of soulless sloths.

"Good evening," I began. Getting no response from the odd couple, I spoke loudly enough that the Kerry May ladies could hear me as well, "As I said earlier, I'm afraid I need to go to a meeting tonight. As you can see, dinner tonight is a scallop, spinach, mango and bacon salad mixed with a chocolate infused vinaigrette. With optional walnuts on the side. My recommendation would be to pair it with the white wine there in the chiller, but you can, of course, help yourself to soft drinks or beer in the door of the fridge. For dessert, there is a key lime pie in the refrigerator, or if you prefer, sorbet in the freezer. I trust you to help yourselves. I apologize that it's self-serve. Please leave your dishes, I'll be back after the meeting to clean up. So, unless there are any questions, I'll leave you to enjoy your dinner."

The couple began to tong salad onto their plates.

Had I even heard them speak? I couldn't remember. Were they deaf? Surely not. I thought back to their reservation. They had booked online. Maybe they didn't speak English! Crap. I didn't have time to delve into that mystery, I had to hit the road. I walked to the refrigerator and opened the door. "Mr. and Mrs. Gularte? Dessert—pie here, okay? Beer here, Okay? Please," I gestured.

They looked at each other then back at me.

"Okay," she said.

"Thanks," he said.

Well, sorry to bother you, I thought, then immediately felt guilty. So, they didn't talk, either to me or, apparently, to each other. They didn't rave about my dinner. My ego was bruised. Big deal. Maybe they weren't expressive people. Why was I getting huffy? Why did I care?

I coerced my mouth into my best 50's homemaker, nothing-gives-me-as-much-pleasure-as-being-at-your-service, smile and closed the fridge.

My phone rang, a welcomed rescue.

"How do you kill someone and dispose of the body when you are chairbound?" Lorraine asked in a stage whisper. "She's like Amy Vanderbilt on amphetamines: mopping, cleaning, doing laundry and plumping my pillows, force-feeding me soup and sandwiches. I've got a broken ankle, for Pete's sake, I'm not a starving refugee! But the worst thing is, she won't stop talking. She's giving me tinnitus."

I waved a final goodbye to the stony couple and headed outside. I could hear NB woofing in the office. I lingered on the porch so I could hear Lorraine.

"Well, at least you don't have preppers gutting a deer on your front lawn."

"What?"

"Turns out the group I thought was a bunch of college preppers are end-of-days preppers."

"Oh. Must be Jim Calhoun and Cog Wheeler."

"Yes! You win! Would you like to go on to the bonus round?"

"No. I just want Saint Eleanor to disappear. I think Lerlene is going to take her shopping tomorrow so I can get some rest."

"Good plan."

"What's new with the Incredible Hunk?"

"Oh, I don't know. They won't be back until tomorrow."

"Oh, you *are* hooked. I can hear the puppy love in your voice."

"Speaking of puppy love, I've gotta run NB home so I can get to meditation. She's howling the office down. Gotta run. Kiss kiss. And don't kill Saint Eleanor. Extra bad karma for killing a saint."

Wednesday Night Meditation

As our *sangha* or meditation group got settled, my mind strayed to thoughts of Buster—the warmth and caring in his eyes, his smell, those dang dimples, his voice that strummed my core. *This is me breathing in…this is me breathing out.*

Both the meditation and the potential relationship seemed impossible. Buster chased the bogeyman for Pete's sake. And travelled a lot. I had moored myself in Catfish Springs…no, not just anchored, I'd *run aground* in Catfish. I just wasn't a fling kind of girl. I wasn't going to linger in a relationship that had no future. I've never been a one-night stand type.

Assuming we became a couple, wasn't I too old and too tired to gallivant around the country with a crazy man, albeit a sexy one with money who behaved like my long-lost soul mate. Maybe not. If business picked up, I could hire a manager, couldn't I? I liked to travel, but I liked a home base. How would NB do? Or Mischief? What the heck would Buster do in Catfish? It wasn't a fishing hotspot. I couldn't think of a thing. This was a biggie. But then again, wowzers and Warren

William♥, it sure felt right.

Nope, best to cut bait and run. *Breath in…and breath out. Focus on the cool sensation on my nose.* I remembered how I had found Buster too, deep in meditation in my own meditation hall! So gorgeous and serene… *Breath in…and breath out.*

"What with Halloween around the corner, not to be morbid or anything, but I thought we could meditate on Death," our lay teacher, Walter said, jarring my thoughts. My eyes popped open.

Walter is a retired pharmacist. He is Filipino with a cherubic face and a ready smile. His eyes glimmered, as if eager to begin his teaching. "It is traditional in Tibet for novice monks to have to meditate with a dead body over a period of days, watching the slow decay, watching as the body that was once recognizable becomes food for insects and loses all resemblance to one once cherished. The purpose is to know and understand death and not fear it." His face was radiant, as if instead of talking about death, he'd said we all just won a free dinner.

"It will come for each of us. We do not know when or how, but it will come. We tend to put off things for later…oh, I'll call my sister next week, I'll read that, fix that, go there, next month, next year. We think we have infinite time for all those things we want to accomplish. But one day we won't have tomorrow."

Again, the beatific smile, as if not having a tomorrow was a bonus.

♥ Warren William is a favorite actor of mine from the 30s. Photos on haintsretreat.com 😊

"So, in this next meditation, I'd like you to think about two things. One, is the awareness of your state of mind. If you die peacefully with prayers in your mind, you will go to a pure land. If you die with confusion and anxiety, *that* is what you will carry into the next realm. You may be reborn in a lower birth as an animal or you may return in a war-torn country without the benefit of a safe place to meet. No spiritual guide to help you." This time he pouted like a comical spoiled child. "Very sad."

The group laughed.

Familiar as I was with this teaching, to the point of having a crystal skull on my altar, I was still far from comfortable with it.

"We think our death is a long day away. We can worry about it later. But in reality, today might be our last day. I encourage you to live as if you may die at any moment. Each time you leave a place, close a door, imagine you are leaving for the last time. When you say goodbye to someone, say goodbye with heart. Maybe this is the last goodbye."

Wow. That was a heavy thought, scary and freeing at the same time. No more to do list. No more fix-it jobs. But so many things left unfinished. Naughty Britches, my grand attachment appeared in my mind, barking and stomping for dinner. Then Buster appeared, smiling. I felt another pang.

"So, living in this mindful way, how does this change the way you relate to your family? Your friends?" Again, the chubby cheeks and infectious beam.

I thought of Max. Max who looked more and more like an old man in a nursing home.

Walter leaned forward and lowered his eyebrows. "On a more practical level…what are you avoiding? What are you cluttering your time with that you could do without? Maybe you should call your mother. Plan that trip. Write that article. Make up with your friend. Go on that blind date!"

Ugh! Not what I wanted to hear! Buster was practically a blind date, wasn't he? Would I regret that we hadn't made a go of it? It'd gotten me all twisted around the axle that he'd left abruptly to go to Lettuce Lake for a couple days. Would I be okay if he just up and took off for Montana or Wyoming? Should I cut bait or haul him in as the prize catch?

Breath in…and breath out.

Walter continued in a soft voice, "In this meditation, we think, 'I might die today,' 'I might die today.' There is no point in attachments to this world because we might die today, and it will all be gone. And so, we should dedicate our minds to practicing the Dharma wholeheartedly."

Right. Cut bait. Focus. Meditate. I might die today. Breath in…breath out. But I really like this guy…

To Be in the Picture, or Not in the Picture —That is the Question.

I was in my pajamas about to watch a *George Gently* episode on Netflix when I thought to check messages. I must have been at the meditation when the message went to voice mail.

"Hi, this is Winter with *Alachua Chatter* magazine?" She made it sound like a question. "This is a courtesy call…we were planning to come out to the Lotus Lodge to do an interview and get a photo of the artist, Lerlene Watts in front of your sign? We'll be out there around ten tomorrow morning. If you'd like to be in a photo, you're welcome to come out. Sorry for the short notice, we've had to shuffle a few things. Looks like this article might squeak into the November issue?"

Great googly-moogly. I had to serve breakfast to my preppers first thing, but I could do it. Support Lerlene. *That damned sign.* I muddled and fidgeted. Did I want to be in the magazine associated with the Lerlene's depiction of a lotus flower that looked like a tie-dyed bunch of spinach? Not really, but then again, negative publicity is still publicity, and my business could use a boost. Like it or not, it was my sign and already getting some attention. Besides, they were going to take a picture of the sign regardless. I sighed. I'd do it.

Trying to put it out of my mind, I picked up NB, set her in my lap like a baby and clicked on the DVD player. Normally, *George Gently* detective shows comfort me. This BBC series features George, played by Martin Shaw, portraying a conscientious detective in North East England in the mid-sixties. A knight-in-shining armor, wise and thoughtful with a sturdy frame and thoughtful voice. A man who could stand his ground despite his gray hair. A man with at least one last battle in him to make the world a better place.

This episode was high on the melancholy scale. Not comforting. A heart-friend of George's got killed, almost discarded for being in the wrong place at the wrong time.

Well that was a bummer. My shining knight was not able to save the day. So much for comfort.

Walter's voice came to mind, "I might die today. I might die today."

True. But if I don't, I have a photo shoot first thing in the morning.

Better figure out what to wear. I picked out a simple outfit and hung it out for the next morning.

Wanting a distraction to get the *George Gently* episode out of my head, I sat down at my computer and Googled "preppers" to learn more about their agenda. It seemed they took the Boy Scout motto, "Be Prepared" to an extreme that made me queasy. Their underlying assumption is that an apocalyptic event is unavoidable and imminent. To survive, one must prepare for a post-apocalyptic world. The disaster may come as an asteroid, earthquake, war, or act of terrorism. Oh wait, there's more! An EMP, or Electro-Magnetic Pulse that is, a huge burst of energy from solar flares or nuclear attack that would obliterate all computer-operated devices: heavy machinery, hospital equipment, modern vehicles, power grids and phone service. Remember the hysteria over Y2K? That was just practice. One way or another, life as we know it will end. No more grocery stores, banks or technology; we'll be back to caveman days. We'll all be guest stars on *Survivor*. Soon. Like maybe next week. TEOTWAWKI is nigh: The End of The World As We Know It.

The news is bleak and discouraging enough. I don't want to focus my life on the end of days. Nor was I compelled to stockpile my house and barn with bags of dried beans, cans of soup, bags of rice and boxes of corn flakes, guns and ammo. This unpreparedness, I read, apparently made me a "zombie": one of the unprepared masses who will descend on the preppers and be aggressively locked out, unless of course I can demonstrate valuable survival skills. I pondered this. Medical skills? Nope. Skinning animal skills? Nope. Map skills? Yes. I'm good with maps and directions. Probably not enough to make me an asset. Self-defense? Yes. Ability to cook? Check. Weapons? Well, I did know how to shoot a gun and could hit an archery target. Phew! What a relief! They might take me in, after all.

Chapter 23

Thursday, October 30 TEOTWAWKI

The Machitechvorm was sending out heavenly French roast smells and I was stirring waffle mix when Jim and Julie Calhoun tromped into the dining hall, each burdened with a full backpack.

"Good morning," Julie said. "Wow. Like your outfit."

"Good morning. Good grief, do you need help with that?"

"No, I've got it," Julie said, breathing hard. She had some serious muscle definition in her arms. "Do you think you'll need all the tables this morning, or could we move one to the wall?"

"That should be fine." I answered.

They set down their packs in chairs and moved a table to the wall then walked back out, presumably for more stuff.

I followed the directions pouring the batter into the waffle maker just so. I closed it and waited. No dribbles or leaking. All good so far. I gnawed a fingernail until the green light came on. As promised, it released easily. To my surprise, the waffle was absolute perfection. *Subarashi*!♥ If I could do this, anyone could. I double checked that my new waffle station had waffle mix, butter, syrup and a little sign with directions for the machine's use. I set out a cold tray with single serving yogurt containers and a fruit salad.

The door opened. The couple shuffled in supporting a classroom-worthy whiteboard. They propped it on the table and began unpacking their backpacks. As I set out juice pitchers, they hauled out wire bound notebooks, hardbound books and pens.

I occupied myself making a big batch of scrambled eggs. As I gently pushed the spatula around the pan, I looked up to see Jim, marker in hand, standing back from the board, eyeing his work:

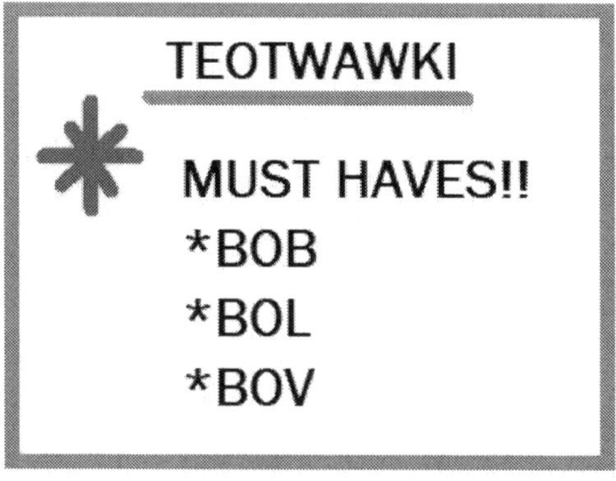

Curious, and to be conversational, I asked, "what's TEOTWAWKI?"

♥ Japanese for super or cool

Julie was arranging an assortment of books on the table, mini bookstore display style. She answered without looking up, "The end of the world as we know it."

"Ah." I stirred the eggs. I transferred them from the pan into a serving dish and covered them.

"And BOB, BOL and BOV?" I had no idea what these were and was curious to know if I needed them or not.

"Bug out bag, bug out location, bug out vehicle."

"Oh, yeah. Right," I said nodding, as if I had a clue. Actually, I had no idea at all. I contemplated the notion of bugging out while I arranged pastries from The Art of Tarts on a serving plate. Where would I go? Why? How would it be better than here? If the worst-case scenarios came to pass, mega meteorite, massive terrorism, economic collapse, catastrophic weather…how could you know where the best place to go would be? Wouldn't it depend on the circumstances? I could flee temporarily if I had to, just grab the dog, cat, my contact lens case and a toothbrush…and go where?

"I have a question," I asked filling the skillet with sausage patties. I set the burner on low and walked about halfway to the whiteboard, so we didn't have to shout at each other across the room.

Jim stopped writing and looked over to me. "Shoot."

"So, I want to bug out. In the worst scenario, I can't depend on gas stations to remain open, right?"

"Right."

"So…to be smart, I'd have to keep a vehicle tanked at all times..."

"Correct."

"So, my Bug Out Location has to be within a tank of gas."

"Exactly."

I frowned. "In my F-150, that's not far."

Jim chuckled. "Good truck though."

"Well, okay, I get that south is a bad idea," I continued, "and I'd barely make it to Atlanta. What does South Georgia have that we don't have here? Can't I stay put?"

They looked at each other then back at me.

Jim answered. "You're screwed."

Julie nodded.

As if to corroborate how screwed I was, the sausages hissed as they hit the skillet. *Ksss! Ksss! Ksss*!

Jim said, "Florida is second only to Hawaii for the worst state to be in."

"Oh." *Really?* I asked, backing up to push the sausages around with the spatula. Should I reveal my stupidity by asking why?

Turned out, I didn't have to, Jim was more than happy to educate me. He came closer to me, held up a hand and started counting off the negatives: "Obviously, you can't go south, there's nothing there except the golden horde and the ill-equipped Polyannas trying to hold off against them..."

"Wait, who? Golden horde?"

"The riff-raff, looters, thieves...Miami, Lauderdale, Orlando...it'll be the Super Dome on an epic scale. Then you'll have the other kind, the hopelessly ill-equipped people trying to escape the chaos. The kind that will use up your resources and suck you dry with neediness. They'll be trying to make it north, and they'll pound on every door along the way, taking food, medicine, water. You think zombie apocalypse is a joke. No. It's real. They won't be the undead, but they'll be just as needy. Suck you dry, they will. Kill you for a carrot or a Band-Aid just as look at you."

"Oh."

Buddhists have a saying that if you think you have a problem and you can fix it, it's not a problem, and if there's nothing you can do, then there's nothing you can do. Either way, it's useless to worry. But this picture made me uneasy. A feeling of doom floated around me like a swarm of mosquitoes. I took a breath and pushed the sausages around.

"Well, can't neighbors band together?" I asked. "You know, round up the wagons, pool resources, shore up borders, that kind of thing? Share? Barter? I give you eggs, you make me bread? I take night watch and like that?" I flipped the sausages.

He ticked off another finger. "First off, no one in their right mind wants to be in Florida without air conditioning."

Absolutely true. I still think Henry Flagler was a madman for coercing the rich to vacation in Florida, pre-air-conditioning. In Victorian clothes? Whale-bone corsets, high collars and full-length dresses? Hell, no! They had a hard time keeping ice.

"When the power goes, you're gonna slow roast." He ticked another finger. "If you do hunker in, you've got a laundry list of creatures to contend with, especially with your doors and windows open for air. Even *with* screens, stuff wriggles in. Mosquitoes, chiggers, ticks, snakes, lizards, frogs, horse flies…" He made a welcoming sweep with his arms.

"They'll move right in with you. Yellow flies alone can make you crazier than ants in a stomped ant mound. And speakin' of those damn ants, those regular ones welt me right up somethin' awful. You git bit by enough fire ants, they can kill you 'fore you can git to a hospital."

Cog and Belinda Wheeler walked into the hall. The two couples greeted each other; I waved.

"Please help yourself to coffee and juice," I said, gesturing to the coffee pot. "Breakfast'll be up in a jiff." Who could have an appetite with this doomsday mindset?

Cog turned his head with a wince, his neck tight as if he had fused vertebrae. "Hope it's strong. Didn't sleep so good last night...shoulder's botherin' me from fixin' the fence." He wore a moss green T-shirt that strained over his paunch to reach the waistline of his jeans. He picked up a mug and poured some coffee. Belinda followed him. She wore a filmy pink and gray top over a gray camisole with pale gray capris pants and matching gray flats. The look was becoming on her but made me think of urban camouflage.

Belinda said, "But we love the cabin. Love the cabin."

My mind was still stuck in Jim's apocalyptic world, imagining lying in bed at night, covered in sweat, listening to an insect marching band coming in to kill me. Remember the beetles in the Brandon Frasier version of *The Mummy*?

He ticked again. "And *if* you survive the oppressive heat of summers, hurricanes, tornadoes, then you still have limited resources. The soil is sand. Even if you're expert at composting, you're still gonna have to water your crops, and that'll be tricky. You better have a hand pump and a well."

I turned off the skillet and transferred the sausages to a paper-toweled plate to soak out the excess grease while considering my preparedness. I had a well. No hand pump. Rabbits, deer, moles, aphids and scale have annihilated my gardening efforts. By a miracle, a Cubanelle pepper plant has thrived and provided steady little offerings, and a few scraggly basil plants have hung in there, but that's about it. My thumbs aren't green, they're white: blight white.

"We're lucky we've got the aquifer, but we're going to be in water wars in about a decade. We'll be fighting to keep our own water, that's a fact. There'll be companies re-routing it or bottling it for dry states and we'll sell it, 'cause money always wins."

Well that was depressing.

He ticked. "Plus, you got major military targets in Jacksonville, Pensacola, Panama City not to mention a nuclear power plant in Crystal River that'd make a tasty target for an attack.

"Oh."

That glum feeling returned, hovering like a massive drone. Do I have any friends in Idaho? Montana? I moved the sausages to a serving platter and set them out on the buffet line next to the eggs. I frowned. "I thought Crystal River was shut down a while back."

"Sure. But do you think it got all cleaned up? You think those are empty concrete towers over there? Yeah right."

"Oh." I pictured the huge concrete silos just sitting there, full of contaminated waste just waiting for the right moment to leach out into the St. John's river. Not good.

The three Kerry May trainees arrived talking and laughing all at the same time, almost slaphappy. I had expected them to be wearing stiff pink suits with exaggerated makeup. To the contrary, they were dressed in business casual with clean faces with tasteful suggestions of mascara and lipstick. I'd caught myself stereotyping and kicked myself. I admired their comradery and pre-coffee energy. These ladies were morning people. They gravitated toward the Machitechvorm.

"Good morning, ladies," I said.

"Good morning," they chorused.

"How was your cabin? Did you sleep well?" I asked.

"Yes. Fine. Great," they answered.

Amber looked at the coffee maker in dismay and said, "Oh. I was so looking forward to a latte. You know, I went on a Caribbean cruise last year and there was this machine--so cool--it ground the beans and you just pushed a button for whatever you wanted: latte, mocha, espresso, plain coffee, coffee with milk…"

I felt my upper body slump with disappointment. Here I was so pleased with my Machitechvorm--a couple hundred dollars for a coffee maker. Amber was talking about La Cimbali M1, a truly magnificent machine an Italian monster with all the bells and whistles. "I know the one you mean," I said. "They run close to twelve-thousand dollars. I asked Santa for one, but I guess he didn't get my letter. I could heat some milk for you, like a café au lait, if you'd like."

"No," Amber said with a sigh, "never mind."

"You sure? It'll just take a sec. I'll have it for you before you can finish getting your breakfast."

She poured herself some coffee and added milk. "No, it's fine."

They moved on toward the buffet line. I felt like I'd let her down somehow. Had my Santa comment sounded snarky? I'd meant it to be light. Oh, well.

Let it go, my Inner Critic said. *You can't please everyone.*

More of the prepper group arrived and greetings were exchanged as they got coffee and hovered near the buffet. As with Belinda and Cog, they were dressed in shades of mulch and moss and wore similar expressions of solemnity and resignation. Their collective energy weighed on me. The drone of glumness was making another pass, but disappeared a moment later, lost to laughter as Shane and Rebel walked in together, laughing.

Rebel clapped Shane on the shoulder, "Right! That was the best! That guy swore that the Sasquatch was gonna 'kill him dead' until he handed over the bottle of Jim Beam… then they got drunk together!"

And then Buster walked in right behind them, saying, "And that's why the pictures were so hopelessly out of focus…'cause he was too drunk to take a proper selfie of him and Sasquatch!" They all laughed again.

"Blurry picture of a 'hairy foot' and the ground!" More laughter.

"It was probably the family dog's ass!" More laughter.

"Good morning, gentlemen," I said, my heart all twitterpated. "You're back early."

The men regained their composures and nodded. "Good Morning."

Buster winked at me, "Got an early start. Weren't no reason to stay."

Shane bumped Buster's shoulder, "He had a notion ta git back. Wanted to be here for his—"

"Halloween," Buster interrupted. "Ma favoreet hollyday." He winked at me again and poured himself some coffee. He eyed me up and down. "You look great. Goin' somewheres?"

"Not really. A photo thing for the local paper out in front of the Lotus Lodge sign. It's for Lerlene, not for me. She painted the sign."

Turn off the babble, you idiot. No more caffeine for you, my Inner Critic sneered.

Glancing over at the prepper group and the codes on the board, he asked, "What's goin' on here? Oh, hey, Jim? Izat you?"

"Oh? You know them?" I asked dumbly. "Julie and Jim Calhoun, Belinda and Cog Wheeler?" For the life of me, I couldn't remember the other names of the prepper folks. I was saved by Buster putting out a hand to greet Jim, Well, heck yeah."

The two groups merged, introducing themselves and I tried to catch and retain more names this time, but after pulling a bowl of yogurt out of the fridge, setting out granola and a squirt bottle of orange blossom honey, I'd lost them again.

"Breakfast is ready," I announced. "Have at it."

My memory might be crap, and we might all be going to hell in a handbasket, but at least we'd have a hearty breakfast.

And the boys were back. Buster was back.

Chapter 24

Paranoia or Systematic Infiltration?

My hopes for a restorative conversation over breakfast were blasted as the youngest man, I was pretty sure was named Jerry, began a conversation about extremists getting into our prison system and converting our most volatile criminals as a thinly veiled way of recruiting them for service once they got out of prison.

"While the media is trying to mainstream them and make us all politically correct, they're getting in position to take us over," Cog said.

"Yup. Take away our guns so we'll be like sheep to the slaughter." Jim said.

"They are sneaking into society actin' all concerned and moderate when secretly they're settin' the stage."

"They're in politics, in the media…they're everywhere."

"Hell, they have key positions in the White House and the Pentagon!"

"Mm-hmm."

Jerry stopped chewing and pointed a fork, "I got me a semi-trailer buried in the back o' my B.O.L. Been stockpiling it. Food stuffs on one side, ammo on the other. Got hidden ventilation pipes going up the surface..."

"Yeah? Where'd ya get the semi-trailer? I been lookin' for one."

"I was lookin' online and got lucky. This guy..."

Looking around the tables as the conversation continued, my guests nodded in agreement, I felt like Neo in "The Matrix" resistant to the "truth" that was being revealed to him. Rebel and Shane tracked this conversation as if in agreement. I wondered if either of them had a bug out location or a trailer buried somewhere.

Unaware that I was reverting to my Slavic heritage or reptile brain, looking for the man to be the head of the household and the voice of reason, I looked at Buster hoping he would bust out laughing at this insanity, but no, he was polishing off his eggs and nodding like the others.

Pity's sake and Peter Lorre, you idiot! Are you looking for logic and reason from a man who spends his days travelling the country in search of a big hairy monster?

I kept to the kitchen as much as possible during the meal as their conversation made me uncomfortable. How much of it was true? Did I even want to know? This sounded crazy but possible.

I was putting a carton of eggs in the refrigerator when I caught a fragment of conversation just out of my view. It was two female voices. Must have been Belinda Wheeler and Julie Calhoun. They were by the coffee machine and I was behind the fridge door.

"Where do you *think* he gets the money for the fancy vehicles and the boat?"

"You mean he's a drug dealer? A *drug dealer*?"

Were they talking about Buster? I froze hoping they wouldn't realize I was there and could hear them.

"Well, all I know is, I heard him on the phone with someone. He was talking about a 'new shipment' and saying, 'these are a sure thing, man' then he was saying stuff like 'bedazzler', 'psychedelic polliwog', 'crystal creeper' or something like that, and 'silver doctors'. Then he said something about 'they'll blow your mind' and 'get 'em hooked'! He gave me the stink eye when he realized I'd heard him. He walked away."

"Gosh, I had no idea. Wonder if Cog knows…if Cog knows."

The voices moved toward the dining hall.

You sure know how to pick them don't you? The Inner Critic leered. *You were wondering about where the money came from, weren't you? Makes sense, doesn't it? Tell us what she's won, Monty! A drug dealing love interest! It would explain the fancy vehicles and all the travel, wouldn't it?*

You don't know that for a fact, I argued back. There are any number of perfectly good explanations. But as I returned to the dining hall to check on my guests, I couldn't think of any.

I gravitated to the prepper table where Buster, Shane and Rebel were conversing with Jim, Julie and Cog. Easing into the conversation, I noted the books on display. Titles popped out at me:

Five Essential Knots

BOB's Your Uncle

Live off the Grid

Thrive in the P.A.W. (Post-Apocalyptic World)

and WTSHTF YOYO

(When the Shit Hits the Fan, You're on Your Own).

They were swapping stories of prepper mistakes like preparing for only one type of disaster or depending on cheap gadgets that fall apart when you really need them.

Jim had just added more topics to the whiteboard:

*EDC

*INCH Bag

"EDC? INCH?" I whispered to Buster and shrugged.

"Everyday Carry and I'm Not Coming Home Bag."

"And what's an Everyday Carry?"

"The weapons you'd have on your person at all times."

"Weapons, plural?"

"Sure. You need a survival knife, a smaller knife, a handgun that'll do the job but isn't too bulky, like a Kahr PM9."

"I have no idea what that is."

Buster glanced around, nodded at Jim and pulled out a small black pistol, muzzle down, and turned it over.

"Cheezit the cops!" I said between my teeth. "You're carrying a *gun*? Is that loaded?"

"Sure is."

"But it's got a safety on, right?"

"No."

"What?"

"Doesn't need one. It has a long trigger pull and a striker block."

"Oh, well. Thank goodness." I threw up my hands in a there-you-go gesture. "So glad to hear it. What's a striker block?"

"The only way the gun can fire is if the trigger is pulled."

"Ah." I found myself stepping away from Buster. I glanced nervously over at the Kerry May group expecting hysterical screams at any moment. Buster had the gun close to his body, his back to them. They were oblivious, thank heaven.

Forget the doom drone, I felt like Alice in Prepperland staring at the Mad Hatter. Was this my dining hall? I thought I'd opened a meditation retreat, a place for peace and serenity. I was looking at a gun.

"There are some nutty people out there. You never know."

"Yeah," I said. "You never know! Could you put that *away* now?" My mind was scrabbling about like a fish on the deck of a boat. I could feel the gears in my head grinding against a blockage. I looked around. The room looked familiar, and yet there were doomsdayers talking about bug out bags and the end of days while this super-handsome man and his cronies planned mythical monster chases. Might as well chase the wind while they were at it.

His hand moved back to his hip and the gun disappeared.

"How do you *know* this stuff?"

Buster waggled his eyebrows in a quick and subtle

wouldn't-you-like-to-know way. He turned to Jim, "How was Prepper Camp this year?"

"Oh, man, it was awesome. There were more vendors this year than ever before, and some really terrific speakers came. Rick Austin and Survivor Jane, man. Great. Just great."

I blinked. Was Buster a prepper too? *Oh, please no.* I glanced back at Amber, Meghan and Kayla, happily chatting away. I thought, *I wonder if I can be a stowaway in their car… they could drop me off at a beach on the way to Miami…I've heard Cocoa is nice…*

They'd never let you take NB with you, the Inner Critic said.

Oh, yeah. Nuts.

"Prepper Camp?" I asked, coming back to the moment. "Like summer camp?" The old commercial for Dr. Pepper popped into my head *I'm a prepper, he's a prepper…*

The three turned to me with incredulous looks as if I'd just announced that I'd never heard of Christmas.

"Yes. It's an annual event in North Carolina. It's *huge*." Julie said. "You have to register, it's not like a fair where you just show up. There are classes. Bet you never thought about all the things you can do with a tampon, for example."

I blanched, I'm sure, which is quite a trick for an albino. "No, probably not."

"Unfortunately, the plastic applicators are more versatile than the cardboard ones, so environmentally it's a downer, but the tube can be used as a straw, the tampon cotton can filter water or pack a wound, the string can be a candle wick."

"So…you make your own candles with tampon strings?" I asked, thinking I really hoped she did NOT answer yes.

"Not yet, no, but there was a woman teaching classes on candle making at the camp. I had a schedule conflict this year, but I'm going to take it next year for sure."

TMI and time to leave Prepperland. I had to go. Monsters, end of the world, gun-toting hotties and to boot, I even had the wrong tampons in my closet. And here I'd been looking forward to menopause and not having to use them anymore.

And I had a photo op with Lerlene, the cosmic thistle artist.

"I've got to go," I said, "but I won't be long."

Buster reached for my hand in passing. Our fingers touched. He stopped my momentum by squeezing my hand. *Zing*. I kept moving before he could tell I was twitterpated. I joined the Kerry May trio to say goodbye.

"You'll probably be gone before I get back," I began. "I wish you the best of luck and success with your boot camp and careers and all." They were so young, bright, hopeful. I'll confess I felt pale shades of green envy slither over me like Virginia creeper. A less secure version of myself might have worked up a resentment towards them. I brushed it aside, wishing them well. There was nothing for it. My salad days were behind me. "You're all going to be amazing; I just know it."

"Aw, thanks! And thanks for having us."

"I hope you'll come back sometime," I said, waving. *If I still have a business*, I thought. I left quickly as if trying to outrun my jumbled emotions.

I slowed my truck by the entrance to the retreat and had to park dangerously close to the ditch to avoid the cameraman checking his gear. I glanced over to the sign gratified that I'd made the effort to decorate it. Lerlene was mid-interview with an attractive young woman with that kind of clean look—the look that says, 'I was born beautiful. I live on a steady diet of bean sprouts and almond milk lattes. I have thousands of friends on social media—please follow me to see just how perfect my life is and how color coordinated my bedroom suite is. I read about dirt in an ebook once and demanded a refund." She didn't look old enough to drive.

You're just in a twist because she's so young, it makes you realize you're getting older, the Inner Critic sneered.

Yes. Sadly, that was true. But also, she looked so pampered. I didn't think I ever looked like that when I was her age. My mother had me cleaning the house when I was in first grade. She even had me polishing silver when I stayed home from school with a cold.

"That's the story you want to tell yourself?" the Inner Critic chided.

Okay, okay, she just has that pampered *look.*

"Hey, she's got a job, she's a go-getter. That's a good thing."

Yes, it is.

As I walked closer to join them, I heard part of the conversation.

"...influenced by a show at MoMa in Queens called "Humble Masterpieces" Lerlene gushed, "about how ordinary objects that we take for granted, still had to be designed by someone. Did you know the paper bag was invented by a woman in the 1870s? Amazing! So yeah, ordinary objects as art. I dig it. Warhol, of course, I'm a *huge* Warhol fan. Love color. Love, love, love psychedelic art. It's so *lit* that psychedelic is having a resurgence." Lerlene tucked a curl behind her ear.

Lit? Literature? Oh, no. I remembered. This was one of Lerlene's pet expressions that meant lit, as in lit on fire. Hot.

The cameraman said, "Winter? Sorry, I need to change lenses. It'll just take a minute."

Her name was Winter? An odd name for a Florida native. It was practically Halloween and already a sheen of sweat was forming on my skin as I stepped into the sun to join them. If Winter was a native Floridian, I'd bet her mother was a homesick transplant from Michigan.

Winter nodded, "Go ahead, Bill," and stepped back and perused her phone.

"Hey, Haint," Lerlene said. She gestured to Winter who punched buttons on her phone, "This is Winter, from the *Chatter*."

Winter turned to me and blanched a moment. Her hands fell. She almost dropped her phone. "Oh. You're…Ms. Blue?"

"I am."

She offered a wilty hand and grasped my fingers with a suggested squeeze. "Bill, take some with both of them and the sign, okay?"

Bill nodded, gesturing for me and Lerlene to pose beside the sign. After a few faint clicks he reviewed his camera. "Great. Okay. You--go to the other side of the sign and mirror what she's doing."

I stepped forward, put my right hand casually on the

supporting beam and attempted the perfect, confident, photo-op look. Unfortunately, the sun was in my eyes. I couldn't even see Bill. I blinked and squinted as if caught in a UFO ray gun beam.

Click, click, click.

"Heard that Saint Eleanor is coming," I said.

Lerlene winced, "Yeah. She's here. I really screwed up. Lorraine's kinda pissed at me."

"Say 'sunshine'," Bill directed.

My eyes still managed to tear up even while closed to slits. Masacara seeped into my left eye. "Ah, crap!" I seethed, my eyes tightened and widened seeking relief.

Click, click, click.

"Okay," Bill said. "Got 'em."

I ran my fingers under my eyes and blinked. "Nah, she understands. Your mom would have ferreted the story out sooner or later."

"She knows how to work me, that's for sure," Lerlene said.

"Thank you for your time, Ms. Blue," Winter said with a momentary glance in my direction. "Let's get back to the interview, Ms. Watts. Tell me about your childhood influences."

So much for further conversation with Lerlene. I felt my ego flare up at this dismissal. But wait…I hadn't really wanted to do the photo shoot to begin with. I'd spent over an hour deciding what to wear, fussed with my hair and make-up and it was over like that. Now I was hot and sweaty and raccoon eyes.

Get over yourself and move on, my Inner Critic urged.

Right. More guests coming. Dinner to prep.

I waved to Lerlene. She really looked great. Accomplished. Perhaps one day this photo would be on display in a famous gallery. She beamed back at me. I was truly happy for her.

Appee Coo-king

Jacques Pepin and Julia Child did a charming, one-season cooking show together in 1999. Jacques tackled the heavy work of hacking up chickens and toting heavy roasting pans while Julia provided a matronly authority, banter and a sense of playfulness. Each episode concluded with her saying, "Bon Appetit!" and Jacques saying in his heavy French accent, "Appee Coo-king."

I donned my apron, ready for a culinary adventure.

I love prunes. Imagine my joy to discover a Moroccan tagine♥ recipe with prunes and sweet potatoes. It came with an intimidating laundry list of ingredients including saffron threads (my first time using it) and celeriac (had to look that up, it's also known as celery root). The ingredients didn't sound

---

♥ A tagine "ta-zheen" is an earthenware cookpot with a tornado-looking lid that apparently does magical things with heat and blending flavors: Recipes will still work if you don't have a tagine. I use a Lodge cast iron/enameled cook pot.

like they would be complimentary. I wouldn't have thought to combine tangerines, onions, prunes, garlic, cinnamon, black olives, sweet potatoes, chickpeas and parsnips, would you? But I promise, the result is not just tasty, it *transports*. Served with rice, this healthy, vegetarian, gluten-free meal would be my offering for dinner for the Take It Off ladies, the Wiccans and the Cryptozoologists. Served with a side salad just in case.

It was shortly after lunchtime, and I was in the kitchen at the dining hall getting all the ingredients ready in separate bowls just like on the cooking shows. I was making the herbal salt when I heard a female voice calling, "Hello? Yoo-hoo! Anyone here?"

Wiping my hands on my apron, I went outside.

I rounded the corner of the office and almost ran into Nicole.

"Hey, Haint! Is it okay if I'm a little early? I wondered if I could check in and wander around? I was curious to see the meditation hall to get an idea of my teaching space. Do you mind?"

"No, of course not. You might want to drive around to the second lot. You'll be in cabin four over there. The other lot's closer."

"Oh. Gotcha."

She trotted back to her Element and parked in front of the bathroom pavilion. I met her and waited as she pulled out a suitcase and soft bag.

"Need any help?" I offered.

"Nope. Got it. I try to pack light," she said, following me to cabin four.

"This cabin has a great view up and down the river," I said as we got to the porch.

"This porch is super! I brought little pumpkins—we can carve our jack o'lanterns out here tonight!" She wore a different pair of fancy flip-flops. These had large white flowers over the arch in a Hawaiian theme.

"I've put bug spray here on the porch," I said, holding the door for her. "They'll carry you off if you don't use something."

"Oh, that's thoughtful. Oh, how cozy!" she said, walking into the cabin. She ran a hand over the nearest bed and sat down with a bounce. "Gorgeous quilt!" She fell back and spread her arms. "The bed is great. This is so much better than I was expecting. YMCA camp when I was a teen was rustic. Our cabin smelled like dirty laundry."

"Yup. Sounds like my camp memories as well. Glad you like it. Shall we check out the meditation hall?"

"Sure," she said, springing up from the bed. I envied her energy. The tender spikes of hair on her head evoked an urge I often get around men with military buzz cuts to rub my hand over the top. I resisted.

We crossed the parking lot, and I opened the door to the meditation hall. Sunlight slanted in the windows hitting the center of the room like spotlights. "I have a CD player over there if you want to play music," I said.

Nicole looked at me as if I'd said something ridiculous. "I've got my own player."

I realized she meant she had one of those remote gadgets--Bluetooth, android, something or other. I haven't kept up with technology. I still have CDs. Someone gave me an MP3 player, but I never figured out how to make it play music in a room, I could only listen to it with earplugs, and couldn't figure out how to select individual songs. Seemed like it always started through the play list from the beginning. "Great," I said.

"Where is the dining hall?" Nicole asked.

"Next door. Want to see it? I was prepping dinner when you arrived."

"What's for dinner?" she asked.

I described the tagine recipe to her as we walked and the next thing I knew, she was donning an apron and helping me.

"Don't guess I need a hair net, do I?" she asked with a wink, passing a hand over her almost-bald head.

"No," I said, reminded that I should put my hair up.

As we chatted about ingredients and favorite recipes, she said, "My mother's a good cook, but she isn't very adventurous. She sticks to basic foods she knows: steak and potatoes, casseroles, fish and rice, that kind of thing. I love trying foods from different countries. I've always really liked fish. I love corn too. Anything made with corn: corn on the cob, cornbread, corn nuggets, and succotash. Makes me wonder where I'm *really* from. I was adopted when I was a baby. Never knew my real parents. I have no idea what my heritage really is."

I ground dried orange peel, lemon peel, cumin seeds, coriander seeds, fennel seeds, chili peppers and sea salt in a mortar, contemplating what it must feel like to be adopted.

"That must be strange, not knowing. Perhaps it's better not to know, that way, you have no family baggage," I said, thinking about my mother's crooked family tree, populated with people on both sides of the law and both sides of the sheets. We could not claim anyone famous in our lineage, and rarely mentioned the great-uncle with grabby hands who had been systematically kept apart from small children or the wild cousin who disappeared in Las Vegas with a guy twice her age named Alejandro.

Nicole rinsed and cut the stem nubs off of the Brussel sprouts. "Yeah, but do I have siblings? Do I have a genetic history I should know about? Was my mother an actress or a junkie? Was my father a car salesman or a congressman? I'd kind of like to know."

"Well, either way, I'd say you've turned out well. You're healthy, attractive, smart, motivated. You make your own destiny, regardless of who your parents were. Don't you think?" I asked.

The mixture had achieved a consistent coarse texture that I spread out on a baking paper on a cookie sheet and shoved in the oven.

With Nicole's help, the separate stages of the tagine were combined into the slow cooker. It was a pleasure to share a kitchen with Nicole. We worked together well. I enjoyed her company and her jaunty energy was uplifting. I came into cooking late in life, as my mother made partnering in a kitchen with her absolute drudgery. I couldn't slice a tomato to her satisfaction, and she had a gift for waiting until I was doing something irreversible, like adding eggs to the flour, before yelling that I wasn't to do that yet. Suffice it to say, I didn't learn to cook from my mother.

"Thanks so much for your help, Nicole. That was fun," I said, hanging up my apron.

"Yes, it was," she agreed, taking off her apron. "You know, I had a premonition earlier that we'd be cooking together. I was looking forward to it."

"Oh? Do you have premonitions often?"

"Yeah. Nothing scary or weird, just quick pictures or impressions. Like sometimes I pick up the phone just as it starts ringing because I saw a vision in my mind of my friend picking up the phone to call me, or I'll drive more carefully because I know deer will run out in front of me."

"Must be handy," I said.

"My best friend Boo is gifted. Not surprising, really, so is her mom. I've had a strange feeling that something is coming. I can't explain it, but I keep dreaming about open doorways and newspapers. Boo says she feels something new coming for me too. Do you know her? She should be here soon."

"No," I answered, distracted by a prickle down my neck like a phantom beetle sprinting for my belt line. "You know, I almost got run off the road the other day by this black Thunderbird. I had the strange feeling something was coming too, come to think of it." I thought of the Bengal Tiger and finding Buster sitting in my meditation hall.

"Yeah?" She asked, washing her hands.

"Well, when it happened, it scared me…but now I think I know what it meant. It wasn't something bad coming, just something unexpected."

"Cool!"

"Hey listen, I've got to run home to get my dog. You are welcome to explore—there are trails around to the meditation circle in the woods. Don't' forget the bug spray."

"I might do that. I'd like to see the circle."

"It's not finished yet, I want to get more rocks and build it up, but the pattern is laid out. You get the idea."

We were heading toward the door when it was opened by a tall, dark-haired girl with freckles. She wore a colorful T-shirt with two large-mouthed fish facing each other. The logo said **PISCES: BIG MOUTH BIG HEART.**

"Boo-boo!" Nicole squealed.

"Hey, hon!" Boo answered as they hugged. "Thought I might find you here." She had her mother's stature and smooth voice. There was no doubt she was Theadora's child.

"Yeah, we were cooking! Dinner is going to be amazing. Have you seen the cabin yet? It's super cozy."

"No. Great! Show me." She turned to me. "Hi, I'm Boo Nutterberg. You must be Ms. Blue?"

"Haint, please," I said, shaking her hand. "Welcome."

"I was just going to go for a walk," Nicole said, eyes wide with eagerness. "Let's get you settled, and we can go together, eh?"

"Sure!"

They headed towards what I assumed was Boo's car. I called after them, "If you go near the water, watch out for gators."

"Okay!" they called, bounding away arm in arm.

Watching them, so chummy, I thought I needed more girl time with Lorraine. I'd have to go see her when the weekend was over.

Chapter 25

Prudence—Cardinal Virtue in a Cat Sweater

Mid-day Thursday, Naughty Britches was lying on my office couch staring at me with a look of utter boredom, her face evoked memories I had of first grade staring at the clock on the wall wondering if the day would ever end. Remember the lined paper and the tedium of practicing letters?

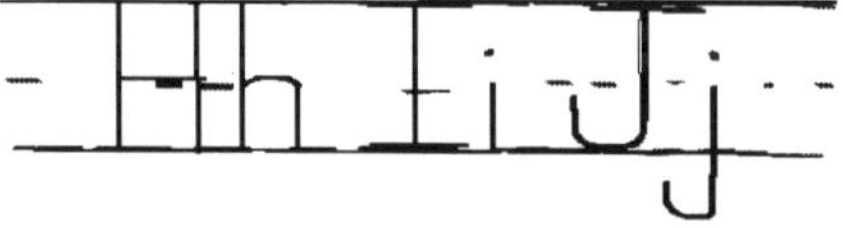

Those days seemed to stretch for an eternity, a mire of boredom. They don't even teach cursive in schools anymore, do they? Sad to think future generations won't be able to read historical documents or letters from elders. I never imagined that I'd feel like a dinosaur in mid-life. I hated having to read *Death of a Salesman* in school, but now I felt a kinship for Willy Loman feeling useless, the culmination of his life's efforts a vacuum bag filled with dust.

"I'm sorry this is so boring, little girl," I said. "As soon as I finish checking the schedule and paying some bills, we'll go for a walk, okay?"

Her ears moved forward. This was promising news, but she'd believe it when she saw me get the leash.

I scrolled through the bookings. While Halloween weekend was full, aside from a few couples booked for the economy cabins, there was virtually nothing for November. Even if this weekend was a complete success, word of mouth couldn't travel fast enough to drum up the business I needed.

Naughty Britches lifted her head and looked toward the window. An underdeveloped woof--a cross between a burp and a bark--escaped her lips as we heard tires rolling across the parking lot. I glanced out to see Prudence Blackwell's red compact car pull in. Most compact cars look alike to me but entering a parking lot dominated by the preppers' drab vehicles, her car resembled a ladybug tiptoeing around rocks. As if seeking comfort in another brightly colored creature, the ladybug pulled in beside Nicole's purple Honda Element.

As Prudence was tall and plump, her attempts to disembark from a vehicle low to the ground involved a series of rocking motions to dislodge herself from the steering wheel, swing her legs around to get the momentum to stand up. Her husband, Skeeter, sported a beer paunch and had a dodgy hip. He drove a fairly new, roomy, pickup truck which he had no trouble getting in and out of.

I hoped there was a more suitable vehicle in Prudence's near future. I bet scrunching into that car was doing a number on her back as well.

She slung an oversized bag over her shoulder, slammed the door shut and beeped the door locks. She paused behind the

Element and when I could see her face again, she was frowning.

Naughty Britches bounded off the couch for the door with a steady stream of high C barks. I grabbed her collar and pulled her away from the door just before it swung open and Prudence freewheeled in, face set in a grimace.

"Hello, Pru, what's wrong?" I asked, crabbing around her to close the door while still holding NB's collar.

"I heard you had some pagans staying here. I'm not sure I'd have booked us if I'd known you had that sort staying here. *Really*, Haint. I thought you'd have more...*sense*." She clucked. "Will you let just *anyone* stay here?"

I wasn't sure how to answer or if I should at all. Where would I draw the line? What if the KKK decided to do a rally here, would I book them? That was a sticky question I hoped I would never have to address other than as a hypothetical one. Now that I thought about it, wasn't there some not-so-nebulous, white-sheet connection in Skeeter's gnarly family tree? It was tempting to point that out to Prudence, but it wouldn't be...prudent. I realized she must have seen Nicole's bumper stickers about the brooms and flying monkeys. Surely, she couldn't find that threatening, could she?

I changed the subject. "I think you're the first one here from Take It Off. Let me leash up Naughty Britches and we'll show you your cabin. Did you have any trouble finding the retreat?"

"No. Your directions were perfect. Thanks for reminding me about the detour. I knew where this was. That sign is kind of an eyeso—uh, eye- catching. Couldn't miss that, could I?" She clucked.

"Lerlene painted it for me as a gift," I said. "It inspired her to do a whole series of vegetable paintings. Lorraine tells me she's finished a psychedelic broccoli and she just got a commission from a vegan grocery in Gainesville for a cosmic cornucopia in time for Thanksgiving."

Prudence sniffed. NB pawed at my leg but then wagged patiently as I hooked her leash to her collar. As I opened the door, her nose caught a whiff of something in the air, she took a careful reading and about pulled me right off the porch.

"Wait up, little girl, we have to show Miss Prudence over to cabin six." NB canted her body, walking almost sideways as I tugged her in the opposite direction. After a few yards she gave up and trotted along with me.

"I take it Belinda Wheeler's here already," Prudence said. "She and Cog are good people, even if, well, this prepper stuff. I think they take it a bit too far, but that's just my opinion."

I responded with a non-committal expression that some call neutral bitch face, I call Polish face. I wasn't going to rise to her bait.

As we walked up the steps to the porch of cabin six, Prudence slowed her pace and turned to look at the river. The water flowed steadily carrying a few colored leaves. We heard the woodpecker hammering into his tree not far away*: dtt-dtttt-dttt-dttt-dttttdttt.* Prudence's demeanor relaxed as she exhaled loudly, shoulders dropping, face slackening.

"It's pretty here," she said.

"Yes," I said, glad to see she approved of the view.

Here we were at the end of October, and it was still in the low eighties, although blessedly not as humid as it had been a month ago. The recent rain had washed the dust from the parking lot and refreshed the foliage; the grounds looked vibrant, the fresh paint on the cabins gleamed in the sunlight. Remembering how run down the camp looked when I bought it, I was struck with how terrific it looked now. Well-tended. Inviting. I glanced back at the office and the pumpkin planters. Next year, I'd have to put pumpkin planters in front of each cabin.

Opening the door so she could look in, I said, "There's a fridge, a coffee pot and a microwave in the kitchen area." I pointed under the bench outside. "Oh, and bug spray and a flashlight. It gets dark out here at night."

"Mmm. Yes, I expect it does."

NB's tail wagged at the same time we heard crunching gravel. I said, "Oh, might be someone else from Take It Off. We'll go see." As I turned NB to go down the steps, Prudence sat down on the bench.

"It's really peaceful here."

"Yes, usually," I agreed, pleased that she was taking to the place.

Belinda Wheeler strolled toward the cabin. When she got close, she said, "Thought I'd see who had arrived. Hello, Pru."

"Belinda."

Prudence acknowledged Belinda with an assessing, barely tolerating nod that reminded me of Dame Maggie Smith. "How's your meeting going?" she asked in a way that implied she felt a compulsion to say something but not that she was invested in the reply.

"Oh, just fine. Very informative. Thought I'd take a break, though. My head's kind of swimming. Kind of swimming."

Prudence gave a haughty nod. "I brought the scale for the weigh-in. It's still out in the car. We'll need to get all signed in before dinner."

Belinda made a face. "I know. Need any help? Got more stuff?"

"That would be helpful, thank you," Prudence said with surprise.

Poor Prudence, I thought. She means well, but always seems to have a pessimistic, suspicious nature, opposite to Belinda who seemed friendly and good-natured.

We were walking back toward the parking lot when a vibrant green Mazda rolled to a stop in front of Arnie. Prudence and Belinda headed towards Pru's car.

"See you at dinner in a bit," I called after them.

Belinda turned back to wave. Prudence did not acknowledge me.

This Take It Off group was such an odd mix of people! I would never have put slinky Serena Hot-to-Trot and Prudence the prim, cat-shirt woman and Belinda Wheeler the boyish prepper in the same club! I was dying to know how they got together and whether they really got along and helped each other reach their weight loss goals. Perhaps it was their differences that held them together.

The Odd Couple: Sonny and Theadora

As NB and I crossed the parking lot, we heard a squawk and a trilling sound emanating from the car. A tall woman with straight gray hair flowing down to her waist emerged from the car, turned, retrieving something whitish-gray that she put on her shoulder. It flapped and cooed.

"Here we are, Sonny," she said in a motherly voice.

"Hello," I said. "I'm Haint Blue. Welcome to Blue's Lotus Lodge."

"Hello, Theadora Nutterberg. I'm with Vida's group of ladies."

The bird puffed its feathers and growled, looking down at NB. She wagged her tail and flared her ears out at the strange sound.

"This is Naughty Britches," I said. "She's very friendly. She won't hurt your bird."

"This is Sonny. I'm sorry, I should have asked if I could bring him, but I was tying up loose ends and forgot."

"Hello, Sonny," I said, getting a little closer to get a better look at him. He was a beautiful bird. Healthy looking.

"Hello, Sweet Cakes," he said in a sultry woman's voice. "Don't damage the merchandise."

I laughed. "I won't."

Theadora's composure faltered, her face projecting a slide show of emotions embarrassment, amusement and adoration. "He's a rescue. He's an ancient Congo African Grey. My friend died a few weeks ago—cancer, poor thing, it was dreadful--and I took Sonny. He's quite a character. Often talks in a woman's voice." She cocked her head to look at him. "Don't you, Sonny?"

"Whatever you say, lover," Sonny said and shook his head.

"June, that was my friend who passed, said she was pretty

sure he belonged to a lady of the night a long time ago…his vocabulary certainly suggests it."

I laughed again. "That must be entertaining."

"Let's get this party started," Sonny said.

Theadora had a long face with a well-defined jawline. When she smiled, her perfect teeth were offset with a lustrous shade of candy pink lipstick. She was tall with the posture of full-figured ballet dancer. A maternal aura of earthy sensuality and magnetism surrounded her. I liked her immediately.

"Let me grab my overnight bag. Here, would you mind taking Sonny's cage? I promise he won't be a bother. He'll be with me most of the time, and he sleeps in his cage at night."

"Sure, of course," I answered, taking the cage from her. Colorful toys dangled and rattled inside. The cage was bulky but light for its size. Theadora pulled an overnight bag out of the Miata, pulled a slim purse over her free shoulder and slammed the door shut.

"Right then. Which cabin are we in?" She clicked her remote and the car beeped, locking.

"This way. Cabin four, the one to the right of the picnic pagoda. You'll be just across the way from the bathroom and showers there," I pointed.

The cabins all face the river. As we rounded the back side of the cabin and approached the porch, a Carolina wren chittered at us from the railing before hopping up into an oak branch.

"Hey, Toots!" Sonny called out.

The wren danced side to side, chittered and flew off.

"Sonny, were you flirting?" I asked, bemused.

Theadora's candy pink lips upturned with delight, "I love those little wrens."

"I guess Sonny does too," I said, opening the cabin door for her, feeling a little hinky about setting his cage down on the table without a towel.

Theadora picked up on my hesitation, "Oh, just set it on the floor for now. I'll get him settled in a minute."

"Just relax, Beefcake, take your time," Sonny said in a sultry woman's voice.

I laughed.

"Did Vida ask you if we might use the kitchen this evening after dinner?"

"No, but you can, I guess. What are you cooking?"

"I'd like to do a mini class on making dream tea. I could do it here, but it'd be easier to have a bit of space, you know."

"Dream tea?"

"Yes, it's a blend of herbs like chamomile, peppermint, nutmeg and ginger that helps encourage sleep and incubate dreams. Creating the tea with intention and a blessing helps."

"Huh. Interesting. Sure. That's fine. There's a teapot and mugs. I'll be sure it's unlocked tonight, if you'd make sure to lock it when you leave."

"You're welcome to join us, if you like, there's nothing secret about it."

"Hmm. I might. Although, I dream all the time anyway…not sure I need more encouragement."

"Do you? Dream language is fascinating, isn't it?. Dreams

sometimes frighten people because they don't understand them...for example, if you dream of a baby dying--that sounds awful, doesn't it? But unless there really is an ill baby in the dreamer's life, more likely the 'baby' is some project, hope or effort in its infancy. The death of the baby is the death of that project or hope. See?"

"That makes sense."

"There are many common themes that people have—being naked at work or at school—feeling exposed or vulnerable; teeth falling out—lack of control: travelling in circles or strange places—not having good bearings or direction, being trapped in a closet or box—literally feeling trapped, probably in a job, and so on."

"I've had flying dreams, only I don't seem to go very fast or get very far off the ground."

"Flying is very common and has several meanings like freedom, ease about something. Flying beats walking, covers more ground, it's higher, and faster. See? It might relate to a relationship, a job or an internal issue."

"Huh."

Naughty Britches had been eyeing Sonny as he preened and moved about. She dropped into play position and offered an airy *woof.*

"Back off, sister," Sonny said in a gangster voice.

Encouraged, Naughty Britches barked with more conviction and lunged forward.

"Cheese it, the cops!" Sonny yelled.

"Hush, Sonny," Theadora said, pulling a treat from her pocket and offering it to him. Turning to me, she added, "Think about it. The group meetings are very useful. Plus, it's lovely girlfriend time."

I nodded. Hmm. Girlfriend time. Other than Lorraine, I had acquaintances, but not close friends. Besides, getting the retreat fixed up had filled most of my time for the last year. I wasn't much of a joiner, but I could give it a try. How hard could once a month be? Might do me some good, I thought.

I turned to leave. "Dinner will be at 6:30. Feel free to wander around before. The trail loops back here, you can't get lost."

"Thanks. Think I might get settled then just stand on the dock a while."

"Don't feed the gators," I said.

"You have alligators? For real?" She said, her voice edging into a higher octave.

"A couple. Not big ones, but still, we don't want to encourage them."

"Oh, I won't!"

"Big?" Sonny asked in a husky woman's voice. "Baby, size doesn't matter."

"He's incorrigible," Theadora said.

"So I see!" I said. "Well, I'll let you get settled. Holler if you need anything."

"Just whistle," Sonny said, doing an exaggerated wolf whistle.

I took NB back at the office and was getting her settled with water and some kibbles when I glanced out the window. A pudgy woman who appeared to be about sixty standing in the parking lot with an air of uncertainty. I waved to her and stepped outside.

"Hi, I'm Haint Blue, welcome to Blue's Lotus Lodge," I said, offering my hand.

The woman fidgeted with the strap of her oversized quilted bag to shake hands. "Oh, good. I wasn't sure where I was supposed to go. I'm Annie Woddell, with the Take It Off group. I saw Pru's car, but I wasn't sure which cabin…" She trailed off, and I gestured for her to follow me.

Annie had a soft, friendly face with warm brown eyes, short dark hair and no make-up. As if her head had been stuck in elevator doors, her facial features protruded forward like a trout, her eyes were far apart, and I couldn't help wondering if she was able to see straight ahead. A further contribution to her oddly compacted look was the fact that she was knock-kneed; her knees rubbed against each other audibly as she walked. Round in the middle and pinched top and bottom.

"I understand that you and the others have just started this Take It Off group."

"Yes, this is our kick-starter meeting. We wanted to do something really fun to get going," she said, readjusting her quilted bag.

"Here we are. Cabin six," I said, trotting up the porch steps to open the door for her.

She leaned on the rail and huffed up the short steps. "My knees are shot. Stairs are tough." She turned to look at the river. "Oh, what a pretty view! This is lovely! I'll look forward to having my coffee out here in the morning," she exclaimed.

I held the door for her.

"Oh, how darling! This is so cozy." She let her bag slide off her shoulder onto a chair with a thud. "I overpacked. I always do. Oh, I love these quilts! My grandma was a quilter. I never had the patience, myself. I love to look at them and use them, but not to make them."

I smiled. "My best friend made these."

"Really? Wow. Very talented."

"What all are you doing this weekend?" I asked. "I heard you had a weigh-in."

"Yes," Annie said, her voice dragging like a teenager's being told to empty the dishwasher. "But it'll be fun. We each get a workbook with checklists of stuff we can get credit for and there's credits in different categories. Like, diet. We keep track of our diet, and the person who gets closest to the diet guidelines gets the most points, and the person who does the most physical stuff gets more points."

"Points for what?"

"Well, we all put in some money at the beginning. If we win best of goals, we get a gift card towards a new wardrobe! We're planning a dinner in six months to celebrate our success and we can show off our new clothes."

"That's a cool idea," I said. I didn't want to ask what happened if you gained weight instead or didn't lose any significant weight. Stay positive, right?

"This weekend, we have talks about reasonable diets, not those fad things. We're following the Paleo diet. It's sensible. And food habits--not binging, like I do! Meal planning, good snack habits. Exercise. Yoga! We're taking the yoga classes. I've never done yoga before. It's supposed to be good for you."

"Yes, it is. I've been doing it for years. You have to be patient," I advised. "It takes a while to get used to it. Don't worry about what others are doing, just do what you can do. You'll get better over time. It can be daunting at first. Don't be hard on yourself. And keep breathing. That's the main thing. Do what you can and keep breathing."

She laughed. "Good advice! I'll try to remember that. I'm looking forward to all of it. Prudence says there's lots of gimmicks to keep us motivated. And we'll have exercise outings twice a month. Like hikes and kayaking and stuff."

"Sounds great. How did you all meet?"

"Oh, it was Prudence and Serena, believe it or not. Serena was at the library checking out diet books and they got to talking. Serena said something about wanting to fit into a dress for a friend's wedding. That's what started it. Then let's see…Prudence and her husband go to the same church as the Calhouns and…"

Not for the first time, I found myself listening to a small town, everyone-knows-everyone, six degrees of Kevin Bacon kind of explanation. I couldn't follow the threads but did have my answer.

We heard voices coming toward the porch and stepped out as Prudence and Belinda walked up.

"Hey, Miss Annie, how're you?" Prudence said, giving her a quick hug.

"Glad to be here," Annie said with exuberance.

"We just took a little stroll down to the dock," Belinda said. "The cypress knees on the other side of the river look like little people huddled together. We saw two turtles, too. Two turtles."

I smiled. "The cypress knees look like meerkats to me. The ones on this side look like Asian sages. The sages and meerkats have a perpetual staring contest."

"They do!" Belinda said with a light laugh, repeating, "they do!"

I started down the steps. "I've got to get back. Holler if you need anything. Dinner is at 6:30," I said.

Crossing back to my office, I heard Naughty Britches barking and saw a large back-sided woman backing out of the office, saying, "You stay. Be good. Stay."

She closed the door, and I heard the heavy thump of Naughty Britches throwing herself at the door.

"Here I am, sorry about that," I said as the woman turned around. It was Maggie Beth Burgess, protectively hugging a colorful thirty-two once cup of something rattling with ice cubes to her chest, looking relieved.

"Oh, there you are," she said with a smile revealing a significant gap between her front teeth. Maggie Beth has an infectious jolly aura that makes Santa Claus look like an old grumpus. She was wearing capris jeans with embroidered flowers on the outside of the legs and a bright orange blouse with pumpkin earrings. "Sorry, thought I'd find you in the office."

"Let me leash her up and we'll show you your cabin," I said. "Prudence, Belinda and Annie are there now."

"Great," she shouted.

Having heard my voice, Naughty Britches had cranked up the volume and speed of her barks.

"She'll keep barking until I get her…hang on," I yelled. I

popped inside, leashed NB and brought her back out. She swirled around and bounced in place a few times before sniffing Maggie Beth's extended hand.

Maggie Beth bent down to pet her, holding her drink up high. NB rolled over offering her belly.

"She's adorable!" Maggie Beth exclaimed in her gap-toothed, spumante way.

"When she's not driving me nuts barking," I said. "Come on, little girl, let's go for a walk."

NB gave me a quizzical look as if to say, "Not now, Mommy, I'm getting petted!" With a bit of coaxing, she soon had her nose to the ground, sniffing intently.

Maggie Beth glanced at the surrounding buildings. "Haint, this place is amazing. I've never been out here. I heard that when it was the fish camp, it was kind of run down. Don't take this the wrong way, but I wasn't sure what to expect. You must have worked your butt off to do this."

"Thanks," I said.

Maggie Beth leaned closer to me and lowered her voice, "Has HTT made her grand entrance yet?"

"Who?"

"You know, Serena Hot-to-trot. Oh, she'll probably come later. Always makes sure to make an entrance."

"Nope. Not here yet," I said. "Like I said, Annie and Prudence are here. And Belinda Wheeler—guess she's doing double duty between your group and the preppers."

Maggie rolled her eyes. "She's okay, but they're off the chain. Like I'm gonna sleep on bags of rice and stack cans of tuna fish in my pantry. Please!" She laughed with gusto then lowered her voice to a stage whisper, "And I heard you have some Wiccans staying this weekend. Prudence is a bit bent out of shape about that, I can tell you. I say, 'live and let live,' you know?" She got louder again. "As long as they aren't harming anyone, hey, it's none of my business what they do." She shrugged.

I bit my lip, not sure what to say.

Maggie Beth's eyes got wide. "Is that Nutterberg woman coming? The one with the bird?"

"Yes, do you know—"

She brayed and pawed my arm, "Ha! I was at Blondene's Beauty Barn. She had Sonny with her. Oh, *that bird!* He's so *naughty*!" She pawed me again. "*So* embarrassing. Who would have thought she would put up with that, eh? She's so classy and regal-like. Well, this'll be entertaining." She waved and hand, then looked hopeful. "Who all else have you got this weekend? Any attractive single men?" She asked, eager-eyed.

"Maybe...there are the preppers—"

Maggie groaned and took a big sip of her drink. "Aah. My diet drink fix for the day."

I was so tempted to tell her that diet drinks are a misnomer, but figured it was none of my business. Listening to the ice swilling around in the cup was making me thirsty.

"There's a big Halloween party tomorrow night in cabin eight. The guy who called sounded kind of young over the phone."

"Ooh! That sounds fun! Might just have to crash that." She gave a mischievous wink.

The sun was making its way toward the horizon with that mellow yellow light that signals the end of the day is approaching.

"Golly, I can't get used to the fact that it gets dark so early," I said. "This summer was so hot and long…sometimes I think with the threat of global warming that we'll never have cooler weather. July-August-September will be deadly, and the rest will be barely tolerable. But I do miss having light so late into evening. Reminds me, I've got to get dinner going here soon."

An orange Fiat rolled in and whipped into a parking spot. "Cute as a bug" as my husband Dillon used to say. The car lurched to a stop revealing two bumper stickers. The first, **I accessorize with an athame!** was underlined by an ornamental knife, centered by two pentagrams. The second featured a cartoon witch riding a broom across a half moon and proclaimed, "Whoo-hoo! Momma's got a new broom!"

"In-teresting," Maggie Beth commented.

We watched a tall, skinny girl with wild red hair get out wearing a skimpy camisole. Her uncovered body was a canvas exhibiting a colorful tattoo collection of Chinese characters, koi fish and writhing mythical beast. A fox face peered out from her tummy, its nose covering her belly button.

"Hi!" She pointed to the office. "Is this where I need to check in?"

"Hi, I'm Haint, the owner. Welcome to Blue's Lotus Lodge."

She flipped the driver seat forward and wrestled a paisley overnight bag from the back seat. "Yeah, that's right. I'm Rose

Water. I think Boo said we're in cabin four?"

"Yes, need any help?"

"Nope! This is it, thanks." She flipped the seat back and hooked the door with her foot, kicking it shut.

Maggie Beth thrust her hand out. "Maggie Beth. Love your car. And your hair. Gotta ask, what's an ath-aim?"

She looked puzzled, then followed Maggie Beth's eyes to her bumper sticker. "Oh! It's pronounced ath-a-may. It's a ceremonial dagger. My brother made me one. It's awesome. Want to see it?"

We nodded dumbly. Why not?

She dropped her bag, turned back to her car, clicked a button and rooted around in the back seat, pulling out another bag. She reached in and retrieved a velvety purple bag. Unwrapping this, she held up a short silver blade studded with gemstones and an ornately carved hilt. "Killer, isn't it?" She held it out for us briefly, then in a flourish it was back in the wrapping, the bag, the car, and she clicked the door lock.

"Nice!" Maggie Beth nodded, but shot me a quizzical look.

"It's for Wiccan ceremonies," Rose said.

I wondered if Rose had chosen the fox tattoo because she had a similarly narrow face and small nose. I also thought about Buster brandishing a gun and Rose carrying a knife. Was I the only one not armed here?

"Oh. That sounds more interesting than my diet group. This is the official start weekend for Take It Off." She sighed. "We officially start with a weigh in. That'll be depressing, but got to start somewhere, right? Still, it's so unfair to do before dinner!" Her shoulders slumped. "But the new diet we're trying isn't one of those you-can-eat-all-the-Brussel-sprouts-you-want kind. It's supposed to be flexible. Sure hope so," she said, tipping her head back for the last bit of her drink, "Nice to meet you. I'm sure I'll see you around."

"You too," Rose said.

Maggie Beth wandered away as I walked Rose to cabin four.

"Will I be able to drive to the circle tomorrow? I've got a lot of stuff for the ceremony. How far away is it?"

While the path to the meditation circle was meant to be a walking path only, it was certainly wide enough for her little Fiat.

"You won't be able to get to the center, but you can get pretty close."

"Great. I brought some little pumpkins to carve. I think we're doing that tomorrow. Do you know where the Cellon Oak park is? Is it far from here? I think we're going there for sunset."

"Oh, it's over in LaCrosse. Not much of a park—it's really just a field with a couple of pecan trees and the one massive oak tree. No facilities or trails or anything, just the tree. It's supposed to be the oldest tree in Florida."

"Yes, that's what we heard. And Mill Preserve? I think Theadora said we were doing a little hike in Mill something."

"Mill Creek Preserve. Take water and a compass! I got lost in there once—missed the turn and went round and round. A good part of it is planted pines. But it's shady, and like Cellon, it doesn't draw people. You'll probably have the place to yourself."

"Perfect!" Rose beamed.

We arrived at the cabin. I held the door for her as she walked in. She paused at the threshold, looking up at the corner. I followed her gaze to a purple smudge where the trim joined. "I see Theadora's been here." The mark was fresh and deliberate. I was about to touch it when Rose stopped me. "Oh, it's a sigil in chalk. Won't do any harm. It's a blessing."

I pulled my hand back. "Oh." As long as it wasn't permanent or damaging, I didn't mind, I supposed.

Rose had entered the cabin and set her bags down. She was admiring the décor. "Oh, look at those quilts! Just gorgeous. Oh, this is so homey!"

"Hey, sexy!" Said a male voice that made both of us jump until we realized it was Sonny in his cage on the far end of the cabin.

"Hey yourself, you troublemaker!" Rose replied with a little bounce. "Well, aside from his crazy antics, this'll be great."

"Glad you like it. You should be comfortable but let me know if you need anything. I've got to get back to start dinner. See you in a bit."

Scaturient: adjective: gushing or overflowing

I'd left NB in the office and was fixing dinner in the dining hall, eavesdropping on the prepper presentation. The whiteboard had new bullet points about BOL:

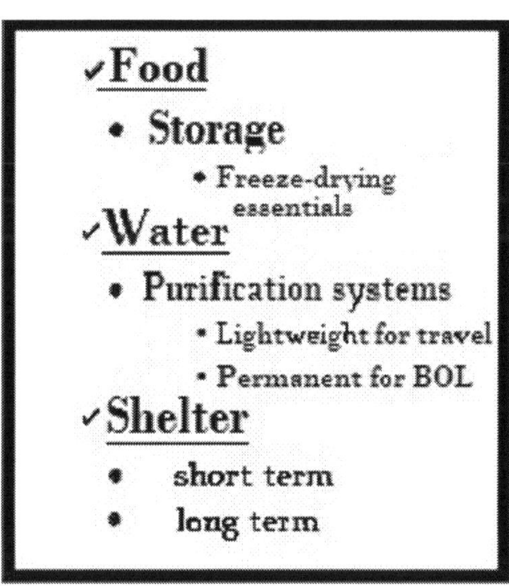

As their last session was wrapping up, I overheard a proposal for a group event that night, "The GOOD game."

Belinda Wheeler was close by. I crooked a finger and whispered, "I know I'll regret this, but what's the GOOD game?"

She flashed a rueful smile, "Remember the classic game Life? Get Out of Dodge is kind of like that, only the prepper version. It's a strategy game where players have to make their way to their B.O.L. (Bug Out Location) while dodging apocalyptic hazards. You start with your I.N.C.H. (I'm Never Coming Home) bag, not forgetting your "ballistic wampum" trade items to barter with other survivalists, work your way past the "Pollyannas"—the people in total denial that it is TEOTWAWKI (The End of The World As We Know It) and it's all WROL Without Rule of Law. First player to make it to their B.O.L. and get all their required tasks accomplished wins."

"Wow. Sounds like a gas," I said.

"Oh, it is, especially if you get a lot of people playing. A *lot* of people playing."

To each his own. I used to love board games as a kid, but this one sounded depressing. I just didn't want to think about living in an apocalyptic world.

The door flew open with a burst of conversation. The Take It Off ladies entered all talking at once with Serena Lippincott as queen bee in the lead. She talked to the others over her shoulder, "I don't think that scale is correct and besides, it's always best to do a weigh in first thing in the morning not at the end of the day like this," she declared in her thick smoker's voice. She was an autumnal vision in shades of orange and brown—burnt orange long sleeve blouse with a thin, stylish pumpkin and black cape clipped around her shoulders with a gold pin in the shape of a chrysanthemum. Her platinum blonde hair framed her face well, with tendrils curled inward towards her bright red lips. While everyone else dressed in covered shoes, sweaters and jackets for a chilly late-October night, Serena wore sparkly sandals with three-inch heels that click-clicked across the floor. Her toenail color, fingernail color and lipstick all matched coral orange.

What was the word of the day recently? Oh, yes: **scaturient**: *adj.*, gushing or overflowing; see Serena Lippincott.

I didn't know that much about Serena, but she had the look and deportment of someone accustomed to pageantry. Still attractive and eye-catching, there was something artificial and strained about her presentation. I suspected that she was struggling to maintain her former glory days by way of supportive undergarments, too much makeup and some minor plastic-surgery enhancements.

Belinda Wheeler broke away from the prepper group to join Serena, Prudence, Maggie Beth and Annie.

"Belinda, there you are," exclaimed Serena, giving her the once over as they moved closer to the buffet line.

"I'll have everything out in a jiffy," I said.

Prudence directed steely eyes at Serena and asked, "So, when is Javiar, our trainer coming?"

It was brief, but Serena's habitual I'm-above-it-all,-little-people mask cracked as a flash of anger, possibly hurt flared in her eyes. "He…couldn't make it after all," She said with a dismissive flip of her head. "It's all good. I don't, I mean, *we* don't need him anyway."

Prudence's eyes flared as her lips formed a wicked, satisfied pucker.

Serena's mouth twitched as if she was going to hiss at Pru but thought better of it.

Oh dear. Was this diet club or cat fight club? First rules of cat fight club, there are no rules, right? *Reoowr!* I prayed they could behave themselves for the weekend.

MONKEY HEART

Chapter 26

October 31 KEEP THE GOBLINS OUT

Bleary-eyed, I wandered into the camp dining hall at around 6:30 a.m. The words KEEP THE GOBLINS OUT jumped out at me from the whiteboard.

Jim Calhoun turned, whiteboard pen in hand, "Oh, good morning."

"Good morning. You sure get up early."

"Lots to cover today. Busy day."

"Goblins?" I chuckled. "Shouldn't you have a game plan for zombie attacks, too?"

His face was blank. Guess I wasn't as amusing as I thought. "You know, today is Halloween? You've got goblins up there," I pointed.

"Oh, right! Didn't realize today was Halloween. No, goblins are real, I mean, that's one of the terms we use for the cretins who take advantage--the looters and rapists--the lowest denominator. You have to have a plan for when they show up. 'Cause they will."

"Ah," I nodded. *I can't deal with this stuff right now,* I

thought.

The Take It Off ladies had requested smoothies for breakfast. I've worked spinach into fruit smoothies before and thought it was okay, but since it was autumn, preferred working with the season and craved pumpkin. Adding coconut milk and coconut yogurt to an online pumpkin smoothie recipe had turned out well. With lots of cardamom, allspice and cinnamon, it tasted like a pumpkin pie. I'd made two batches the day before. I set out the huge glass pitcher and a bowl of out chopped filberts to float on top if anyone desired.

Shane was the first of the "three amigos" to arrive for breakfast.

"Morning, Shane." I greeted.

"Morning, *Belle.*" Shane poured himself a mug of coffee, glanced around and slid up next to me. "We got dinna and da cake covered. Reb is pickin' it up. You comin', yes?"

I stared at him. "Cake for what?"

He looked surprised. "For Buster's birthday! We got some gag gifts, too, and a tas-tee bottle o' Nicholas Feuillatte champagne."

"His birthday? *Today*? *Halloween*?"

"You din't know?"

I shook my head and frowned. "Dinner? But I—" I'd planned on sweet potato and buffalo chili for my guests. I scratched my head. I could serve dinner and leave. Or even bring some chili as my contribution to dinner. I'd figure something out. But what about a gift? I couldn't show up empty handed.

I leaned against the counter and folded my arms. "I should

get him something. I have no idea what—crap. Wish I'd known earlier."

"He won't care about a *ting*. He don' need tings. He'll just be glad you dare."

"Right. But I can't be empty-handed."

"Den open your heart. You'll tink o'sometin'."

"Well, what about the menu? I'm doing bison and sweet potato chili for my guests. Can I bring some?"

"You bring you sweet seff, dat's all," Shane said, gently raising my chin with his forefinger. His fingertip gently traced my jaw as he .

No gift, no food offering? Easy for him to say. Well, maybe I could run out after lunch. Where? For what? Fishing gear? What does one get a cryptozoologist for a gift? Sounds like a joke. Bottle of wine? Something for dessert again? Crap and Christopher Walken, why did I always feel behind the eight ball?

Shane busied himself with the waffle maker. I hovered, fingers crossed, until he popped out a perfect waffle.

Yes! I said to myself. The thing works. Yay!

Mentally I was driving all over town hunting for a gift for Buster and coming up empty. *What to get him?* I glanced at the prepper table. Prepper tools?

A mob of preppers entered, deep in discussion.

"See, that's part of the N.W.O....they *want* us to give up paper money and go all electronic. In the short term, they can tap our accounts. They've already done it in Australia with the 'shave and a haircut'..."

"Really?"

"Yup. The government just sucked a percentage out of your account. Figured you had enough."

"Holy shit! Is that legal?"

"Does it matter? Then the banks will close for a long weekend and swoop! Day after the holiday, where's your account? Gone! Hope you enjoyed the barbecue, 'cause you've been wiped out. It's YOYO time (You're On Your Own). Can't even stuff your mattress 'cause paper money will have no value. It'll all go to the big wigs in charge and for us it'll be *Hunger Games* time, baby."

Julie Calhoun lagged behind the argument, spooning grits onto her plate.

"What's N.W.O.?" I asked, not sure I wanted to know the answer.

"New World Order," she said.

"Oh, right."

My financial situation was tenuous enough without worrying about any mysterious New World Order leaching my checking account. On the bright side, if TEOTWAWKI were to happen, maybe my retreat could be like the commune camp, and the preppers could help me in return for shelter. I could house a small village in "The Crunch".

The younger prepper—Jimmy? Jerry?—wiped at his temples, "It this is October, when does the temperature get cooler? I can't believe it's this hot already."

"This IS cooler. May through August, you can pull a baked potato right outta the ground around here!" One of the men said, adjusting his brown suspenders.

The men laughed. This was an exaggeration, but not by much.

A man with a white mustache nodded, "If you sit at one o'them long lights like they got down in Gainesville, around Archer Road, by the time the green light comes, the road has melted into your tire treads."

John or Jack, the guy who had the same body type and face shape as Jimmy/Jerry and must be his dad said, "Oh, give him a break, he's not used to it. He's been living in Pennsylvania for the last 18 years." He puffed out his chest, "He came down here to be closer to his mother and me and we're glad to have him home."

This generated another round of good-hearted teasing, "Aww. That's sweet."

Jimmy/Jerry looked momentarily embarrassed, but it was clear that the others were happy for John/Jack. Possibly envious.

Jim stood back from the whiteboard and set down the marker. He' written:

Somehow security hit a tender chord with me. What kind of security did I have? I had none. I'd worked too many jobs in too many places to have any retirement plan to speak of; I had some savings, but most of it had been poured into the retreat. I had no security at my house, no real financial security…

I was relieved when Vida and Theadora came in; their grounded and bright energies made me forget the end-of-days-are-coming thoughts immediately.

"Good morning, ladies!"

"Good morning, Haint," they answered in unison.

"What have you all got planned for today?" I asked.

Vida's eyes sparkled with excitement. "Well, we're just going to do a light breakfast here. We're supposed to meet some other folks in Gainesville for brunch at the East End Eatery, I think it's called."

"Great place!" I said. "Super nice folks and a great menu. Don't miss the smoked Gouda grits. Serious comfort food. They serve breakfast all day, but also have terrific paninis, soups and sandwiches. The waffles are so fluffy—with fresh fruit—excellent. I also love the Moroccan chicken salad."

"Oh, yum! Sounds divine," Theadora purred.

"And then a kind of a field trip to various shops in the area. We've got a list—an herbal shop, a crystal shop, a repurpose place and a pizza place with killer salads."

"Sounds great!" I said.

Theadora glanced at the whiteboard. "Goblins?"

"Don't ask," I said.

All this talk about food made me hungry. I poured myself a pumpkin smoothie, adding the nuts on top. Quite tasty. As the allspice and cinnamon excited my taste buds, I forgot all about how I'd cope in The Crunch. I normally avoid waffles, but thinking of East End waffles, and having watched Shane make his, I had a sudden craving. I busied myself with pouring the batter out onto the griddle.

What to do about Buster's birthday.

So, Buster was a Scorpio. Hmm. Didn't know much about Scorpios, but thought they had a reputation for being uppity or testy and hot tempered. Looking around the dining hall, I spotted an empty seat next to Vida. Buster was absorbed in a conversation with Cog Wheeler about purifying water. Under the premise of checking in with my guests, I wandered from table to table making small talk, asking how everyone was, and was the food satisfactory? I got complimentary feedback. I made my way to the Wiccan table with my waffle and smoothie and took the vacant seat by Vida. Feeling sheepish, I asked quietly, "What can you tell me about Scorpios?"

In that swanlike, unhurried way of hers, her eyes passed

from mine across to Buster and Cog and back. She pursed her lips and rolled her eyes towards them.

"Male Scorpio, I take it?" She asked, raising an eyebrow.

I nodded. "Shh. I don't want him to know I'm asking about him."

"Of course. What sign are you, dear?"

"Virgo."

"Hmm. Well, you'd be compatible. Water and Earth." Vida shifted in her chair and dropped a hand to her shoe as if adjusting something. She took a long look at Buster then straightened. "Good looking man, that one. Good energy." She took a deep breath and looked me in the eyes. "Scorpios are very self-assured and goal-oriented. They like to be in charge and get their own way. They are driven and won't yield or give up. They see things in black and white, no gray, and make decisions accordingly."

I slumped in my chair in disappointment. Sounded like an arrogant *zho-pa.*♥

"Oh, Darling, it's not so bad as it sounds. Your man is likely to be very perceptive, intuitive and intelligent." Her eyes darted to him and back to me. "Is your man a journalist or a researcher by chance? A detective?"

I almost choked on a mouthful of waffle, "Uh, sort of, yes."

"Well, he'll be good at it. Scorpios *love* investigating puzzles." She brushed my shoulder with her hand. "But you

---

♥ Russian for bastard

want to know what kind of lover and partner. Mmm? Well, Scorpios, like their scorpion animal friends, are very tactile, very sensitive to touch, and often very, shall we say, dynamic lovers? They like to...uh...investigate and explore in that department too, if you see what I mean."

I felt my face flush. Oh my.

"On the downside, if they think they've been wronged, whoo! That stinger will come flipping right out! They can be suspicious and possessive, a little on the controlling side. Best not to try to hide anything from a Scorpio; they'll ferret out your secrets. Pick you apart like a Swiss watch repairman. You'll have to be very honest with a Scorpio. And what'll aggravate you is that they aren't always up front about themselves. Keep to themselves until they feel safe. They can be complicated."

I frowned, imagining a stubborn control freak with secrets and claw hands.

"Oh, don't fret. A Scorpio man in love is attentive and uh, zesty in the boudoir, shall we say?" She eyed me as if sizing up my potential for X-rating potential in a porn film. "You sure won't be bored! The only thing that might be a bone of contention is that they spread themselves kind of thin. If his goal is time consuming, you won't see a lot of him. He'll be wrapped up in his work or his quest, whatever it is."

Hmm. Wasn't that just bang on, as the Brits say? Yes. Off chasing monsters.

"What is the actual birthdate?" Vida asked.

"Today. Halloween."

"Really?" She pursed her lips again. "Well, that's auspicious. End of the month, a bit mellower than the others.

Very sensitive. Perceptive. Strong spirit. Very successful."

Cog eased away from Buster and got into another conversation with two other preppers. Buster shifted and looked around the dining hall. *Possessive. Suspicious.* He spotted me and tipped his head in an oh-there-you-are way.

"Thanks Vida."

She patted my hand. "Don't sweat it, Darling. You'll figure it out. Speaking of sweating, either your man is getting me all hot or I'm having a hot flash."

Vida pulled a handkerchief out of a pocket and dabbed at her forehead and throat. "Wonder if they'll ever go away. It's been going on for ages."

"Oh, don't say that! I just started getting them!" I moaned.

"Just think of it as a power surge, Darling."

Talking to Vida was so easy, as if we'd known each other for years. Still, what she'd said about Buster was a bit intimidating and risky, like playing with a skunk. Suddenly I remembered the bold, black Thunderbird roaring up the road at me, careening off the curb. What had Vida said? Indomitable spirit and determination wasn't it? Hmm.

What to get Mr. Indomitable Spirit for his birthday? A gag gift? No, he was too intense for that, although if I'd had the time, a Bigfoot air freshener for the Roamer would have been a must. I couldn't even get a fantastic cake, 'cause Shane said they had that covered. I had a little window to run into Gainesville, but I'd have to know what I was hunting for. None of the usual male gifts seemed right. Father's-day gifts flitted through my mind. Soap? Ridiculous. Cufflinks? Don't be silly. Pen set?

Please. Shaving stuff? No, with his manicured little beard, he had very particular shaving equipment.

Don't panic. It will come to you. Think about something else and it will arise.

I bumped into Rose on her way to join the Wiccan table, and nearly dumped her plate. Nicole stuck out a quick hand and caught it just in time.

"Sorry!" I exclaimed.

"No prob. Got it," Nicole said.

Rose regained control of the plate. "Thanks!" Turning to me she asked, "Oh, hey. The guys were wondering if they could come over for dinner—they won't stay the night, but they want to come for dinner."

"The guys?"

"Yeah, Buckshot and Jonah. They're Wiccans," Nicole said.

"They work at the Whatcha Need," Rose added, "They couldn't come for the weekend, but they're off tonight and coming for the Samhain ceremony. Can they just pay you for dinner?"

I guess I knew men could be Wiccans, but I was surprised, and pondered how someone came to be named Buckshot. "Sure. No problem."

Both women looked pleased. "Thanks!" They moved past me to join Vida at the table.

Serena Lippincott undulated toward me, cradling her smoothie and licking her lips like a sex kitten. She wore a low-cut short sleeve top that revealed vast territory of cleavage. "This is *de-licious,*"she cooed. "You *must* give me the recipe."

"I'll be happy to. Glad you like it."

"Like it? Haint, this is *fab*-ulous. Any chance you'll be making more? There's almost none left." She moved to the side and pointed to Maggie Beth Burgess, emptying the pitcher.

"Wow! I thought I'd made plenty. Sure, I can do another batch." I'd been just about to sit down and tuck into my own smoothie and the much-anticipated waffle. I hustled toward the kitchen, praying I had another can of pumpkin. Perplexed about how I had underestimated the smoothie supply, my eyes darted around to see who had taken smoothies.

Does it matter? The Inner Critic asked. *They want more. That's good.*

Yes, but how had I screwed up the math? Who cared. They wanted more. I scooped up the empty pitcher and empty nut bowl and happened to see Maggie Beth tip her head back and guzzle her drink in one go and lick her lips. She regarded her empty cup like a toddler who dropped her ice cream cone on the playground.

Ah.

Chuckling to myself, I whipped up another batch of pumpkin smoothie, emptied the remainder of the chopped filberts into the bowl and returned bowl and pitcher to the smoothie station, where Maggie Beth and Serena waited.

"Here you are, ladies."

"Oh, yum!" Maggie Beth said, wrapping a meaty fist around the pitcher.

Nicole suddenly stood up on a chair and tapped her juice glass with a spoon. Her brisk action reminded me again of a circus performer taking charge, moving with ease. The chatter tapered as people looked toward her, confused by the interruption.

"Hi all, my name is Nicole…Happy Samhain, or Happy Halloween! If anyone is interested, we will be carving pumpkin lanterns tonight after dinner in the kitchen and, as it turns out, we've got extras. I will be teaching a short class on carving techniques. If anyone is interested in stopping by to have a look, or joining us, please do."

There was a moment of silence as her audience reacted, some with approval, some without, but the murmur of conversation began again.

This was my window before lunch to run home and take Naughty Britches for a short walk and try to come up with a gift for Buster. What? Desk stuff? Did he have a desk? Some kind of knife? A multi-tool set? The guy had over a thousand dollars of surveillance equipment alone, he couldn't possibly need a stupid knife. I was barely aware of driving home. Mentally I was picking up and discarding useless presents: tobacco, pens, pocket protectors, a drone—no doubt he had a fancy one of those, too.

NB set up a steady bark while I unlocked the house and let her out of her crate. As I turned around, a stream of sunlight hit something shiny on my bedpost. Curious, I walked over and pawed the collection of amulets, scarves and talismans that have accumulated over the years.

"Eureka!" I shrieked.

NB wagged her tail. Mischief swiveled his head around, looking for danger.

Shane had said "tings don't matter". Well, this "ting"

wasn't valuable in a monetary way but would make a perfect little heart-gift. I'd bought the *dvarapala,* or guardian talisman for Dillon in Chatuchak market in Bangkok, Thailand. Unfortunately, Dillon's cancer was diagnosed not long after we returned from that vacation. Wearing the charm in the hospital had not been practical. I'd hung it on the bedpost on his side of the bed.

A *dvarapala* is a fierce fangy warrior-giant holding a staff. Massive *dvarapalas* guard doorways at the royal palace in Bangkok. This one was encased in a custom-sized silver box with a glass window and hung from a black woven necklace. Exotic and masculine, I felt sure the *dvarapala* would appeal to Buster.

"This is it, kids! Problem solved!"

I trotted to the linen/gift-stuff closet and dug out a small box and some tissue paper. Naughty Britches and Mischief followed me: NB bouncing and fussing to go outside, Mischief hoping I'd open the closet door.

The closet is a scary place; the top part with the sheets and towels stays fairly orderly, but below is a rat's dream: bags of recycled bows, a plastic tub filled with all-occasions of wrapping paper, surrounded with salvaged boxes of various sizes. Mischief jumped behind the wrapping paper and disappeared into the ribbons and bows bag. He re-emerged, a bit of metallic ribbon trailing out of his mouth.

"Give me that! I know they're shiny, but they're not for you!" I said, yanking the ribbon out of his jaws and coaxing him out of the closet. He shot me a lofty glare as I slid the door shut.

"Merrr!" He argued.

"Do you want to have stomach surgery to remove that?" I asked.

He rubbed against the wall, back arched. "Merr."

"Yeah, I don't think so."

He strutted away with the aloofness of a model on a runway.

I leashed up NB and took her for a quick walk. When we returned, I wrapped Buster's gift and found a comical orangutan birthday card in my desk. It wasn't quite a skunk ape, but I'd think of something to scribble relating the two.

When Cultures Collide

With the Wiccan group out shopping and Belinda Wheeler joining the preppers with whatever their meal foraging plan was, we were a party of eight for lunch. I had lots of tagine leftover. Some sautéed chicken and a salad to stretch it out. Coconut chocolate bars for dessert.

At first, The Take It Off group sat at one table and the

crypto cronies sat at another. Rebel, Shane and Buster had their usual boisterous banter going on. Conversation was stilted at the Take It Off table. Serena and Prudence avoided eye contact. A frosty invisible barrier seemed to divide the two groups.

I was taking empty plates from the buffet line when I overheard Prudence say in a stage voice I'm sure she intended me to hear all the way in the kitchen, "I'm not at all comfortable that those heathens are here doing Lord only knows what…"

I moved to the dining hall side of the buffet line to hear better.

"Oh, they're fine," Maggie Beth said. "Leave 'em alone."

"And that woman with the bird…Honestly, you wouldn't *believe* the vile things I heard it say. I ask you, who would have a bird like that?"

"I would. I think it's funny," Serena answered with a laugh.

I knew I liked her for some reason. I turned to glance at them in time to see Serena roll her eyes. She stood up and threw her napkin down. I retreated toward the kitchen as I thought she was coming back to the buffet line for dessert. Instead, she wiggled her way over to Shane.

"So, what are you handsome men doing here?" I heard her coo.

Annie Woddell soon broke ranks too and hovered by Rebel. Then Maggie Beth abandoned Prudence to join the others. Serena had a hand on Shane's shoulder. I couldn't quite hear the conversation, but Serena leaned forward as if she couldn't hear either. This meant that one ample boob replaced her hand on Shane's shoulder. Meanwhile, Shane had an arm around Maggie Beth's waist.

Prudence jabbed at her food with her fork.

Serena swayed over to Buster.

I set my plates down.

Prudence dropped her fork on her plate making a jarring clattering.

I felt my jaw tighten as she leaned back to bray in laughter over something Buster'd said. Her hip pressed up against his arm.

Shane and Rebel laughed.

Prudence checked her watch.

I looked away, mad at myself for being possessive.

"We'd best be going," Prudence announced like a grade-school teacher addressing an assembly.

Serena brayed again.

I busied myself rinsing a serving tray with the vegetable sprayer.

"That was a mighty good meal, Ms. Haint," a sexy voice said behind me.

I jumped. The redirected spray nozzle spritzed the counter. Releasing it, I spun around. Buster was standing behind me carrying a stack of plates. I'm sure I turned a few shades of embarrassed as I recovered. At least I hadn't sprayed him. "Oh, thank you. Glad you enjoyed it."

"Between you and Rebel," he began, stretching his hands across his taut stomach, "if I git much bigger, It'll be easier to go over me than git around."

Yeah, right! Looking at his body the way he was displaying himself, getting on top of him sure did come to mind.

"Hardly! What are you and the boys doing today? Do cryptozoologist have a special thing to do for Halloween?" I asked.

He passed a hand over his eye, "Uh, cryptids don't know about Halloween...it's just another day, you know? Now Wiccans and horror fans, that's sumpin' differ'nt."

I cringed. "Guess so. Sorry."

"One o' the cameras picked up sumpin' last night. We're gonna check that and then we got a video confer'nce about skinwalkers."

"Skinwalkers," I repeated, not hiding the skepticism in my voice.

"You prob'ly don't wanna know 'bout them."

"Why, what do they do?"

"They can take on any form, run faster than a cheetah, they can mimic anything or anyone and they can steal your soul."

"R-r-right. Okay. Well, I'll let you get back to your thing," I said, half turning to the sink.

"See you tonight, 'right?" He asked, touching my arm.

"Yes. Of course," I said wishing I could think of something else to say, but what do you say after the skinwalker steals your soul explanation?

"Good," he said, letting his hand graze my arm ever so gently as he left me to join Rebel and Shane who were extricating themselves from conversation with Serena and Annie.

Prudence had collected some abandoned plates and silverware; she brought them to me.

"I'll take those," I said. "What are you ladies doing this afternoon?"

"We've had to change things up a bit since Javiar bailed on us," she explained in a disparaging tone, "but we've got weights and straps. We'll do a strengthening exercise routine, take a trail walk, then the yoga class. We're going to Lake City to go bowling tonight after dinner."

"Sounds like a full day. Don't forget bug spray when you go walking."

She flipped me a tight thumbs up.

I was relieved to have the place to myself again. I cleaned up the dining hall and the kitchen as a kind of meditation, being mindful as I wiped down the surfaces and put dishes in the dishwasher. This was welcomed down time before the next wave of activity that evening.

Chapter 27

Lefty's Licks and Cockies

The tomatoes, sweet potatoes and bison chili was beginning to bubble. I was washing the cutting board when I heard voices outside.

"I don't know, maybe in here?" One voice said.

I wiped my hands on my apron and called out, "Hello? I'm in here."

The door opened and two men entered. The younger one, in his twenties I guessed, was blonde with a square face, a heavy jaw and large blue eyes. The older one wore glasses and had thick russet hair and a matching beard.

"Hello, can I help you?" I asked.

"Hi, Jonah Water," the bearded one said, offering a hand. We shook. "This is my friend Buckshot. My sister, Rose is here with a Wiccan group. She said it was okay if we came just for dinner and the Samhain ceremony."

Jonah's hair was a deeper rust color than Rose's red, but they shared the same general narrow fox face, small nose and watchful eyes.

"Nice to meet you. I'm Haint Blue."

Buckshot blushed, "I'm sorry to stare, but you really are the palest person I've ever seen. I can see your veins."

Jonah punched him. "Shut up!"

"Hey!" Buckshot said, flinching. "I didn't mean nothin' by it."

"No, it's fine," I said, "I am pale. It's true." How many times had I had moments like this? Best to change the subject. "I know that they went out. I'm not sure if they are back yet but let me show you where their cabin is."

"Something smells amazing. Is that dinner?" Jonah asked.

"Sure is. Sweet potato bison chili," I said.

"Wow. Are you open for dinner all the time?"

"So far, only for guests. I'm not a public restaurant."

"Dang," he said, looking heart-broken.

"Let me point you in the right direction to find them," I said, guiding them back outside. Parked askew in front of the office was a bright red Chevy Blazer with a sign on the door.

"Lefty's Licks, eh?" I asked.

"It's a blues band. I play strings," said Jonah.

"I think I've seen you—have you played at It's All Love, that outdoor café in Gainesville in Wisteria Parke?"

He nodded with obvious pleasure at the recognition.

"What do you play?" I asked Buckshot.

"Oh, I'm not in the band," Buckshot said. "No musical ability, sadly."

"He's a blacksmith. He makes awesome knives and axes."

Buckshot brightened. "If you ever need a dagger, a battle axe or a mace, let me know."

"I will do that," I promised, hoping that the need would not arise.

Rose's bright orange Fiat zoomed around the corner of the meditation hall and came to a stop in front of the rest rooms.

"Here's Rose now," Jonah said.

Rose got out and hollered a quick "Hey, guys!" before partially diving into the backseat. We heard a muffled "guess what I got?" and as before more tattoos were exposed as she leaned in.

I heard another car engine and looked around to see a metallic green PT Cruiser with the top down creeping towards the first parking lot. As I didn't' recognize the car and the driver seemed unsure of his bearings, I left the Wiccan reunion to see who this was. Two well-groomed metrosexual-looking young men got out. The taller one waved.

"Hi, you must be Haint. Whoo! You are farther out than we thought, and that detour got us a bit lost, but here we are." He offered his hand and we shook. "I'm Aubrey Sinclair, and this is my partner, Chet Lewis."

"Hello and welcome," I said. "I was wondering…I figured you'd have arrived by now to set up for your party. Is everything all right?"

Chet waved an imaginary wand, "No worries, we've got a crew coming. It'll be like Tinkerbell waving a wand, it'll be transformed into party central before you can say RuPaul is a nasty bee-otch."

Aubrey winked, "Can you say fairy dust?"

They both laughed.

"So which cabins are ours? Those over there at the end, I presume?" Chet pointed.

"Yes. That's correct, and the shower and bathroom are just over there," I pointed to the building by the parking lot.

A candy apple red Jeep Cherokee pulled in and braked just in front of Chet. Three men hopped out, all in their twenties, two looking remarkably similar to Chet and Aubrey, while the one from the back seat was heavier and sported a Teddy Roosevelt moustache. He struck a dramatic super-hero pose and said in a deep voice, "Did someone call for the Burlie Boys?"

I assumed he meant "burly", but Aubrey nudged me and said, "we spell it with an 'i-e', like girlie, isn't that fun?"

"Clever," I said.

One of the men, a young Tom Cruise lookalike, clasped his hands together and said, "I just love glamping."

"Sorry, what?" I asked, no doubt looking clueless.

Aubrey touched my arm, "It's glamourous camping, hon.

We don't rough it. We don't sleep on the ground, and we *don't* cook with Sterno." Aubrey and Chet shared a smirk.

Chet said,"We like fine dining, silk sheets and fresh cockies."

"Mm-hmm." Aubrey agreed.

I couldn't help it, I'm sure my eyes bugged. I don't have anything close to a poker face.

"Cockies—cocktails, dear." Aubrey said with a you-poor-dear expression."

Aubrey and Chet pointed out the cabins, and soon there was a flurry of unpacking; the parking lot was quickly strewn with boxes, bags, speakers, lights and electronics I couldn't readily identify.

A periwinkle Prius arrived with more men and more bags and heavy-duty coolers on wheels. Most of these men were young and buff, reminding me of the finale of a Chippendales show. With ant-like organization, there was soon a stream of athletic bodies hauling stuff the way leaf ants carry leaves in the forest.

You Better Get This Party Started

Once again, I found myself repeating, 'it's just dinner' like a mantra to ward off nervousness. My fingers twitched so much that getting my earrings hooked into the ear holes was turning into an event. I changed my outfit three times. Put my hair up, pulled it down. Green contacts or blue? Would he like the *dvarapala* pendant? They told me not to bring anything food-wise and wouldn't even hint at the menu. Should I bring wine?

Beer? Dessert again? Why was I so nervous?

Hair down, purple contacts in, and wearing my favorite black jeans and a long black tunic top, I was finally ready.

"What do you think, little girl?" I asked Naughty Britches. I jiggled my head so the skeleton earrings would shimmy and jingle. "I get to wear my favorite Halloween earrings," I sing-songed.

She could tell I was going out and was giving me the stink eye. After a long hard stare, she let out a sulky *woof.*

"Don't get your leash in a twist. You can come."

She wagged her tail.

I scooped up the wrapped gift and the orangutan card and made room for them in my purse. Remember Let's Make a Deal? I often think I could have made a few easy hundred bucks pulling random stuff out of my bag. I grabbed my keys.

"Let's do it, sister."

NB leapt up and scampered to the door, throwing her front feet at it as if she could push the door open.

As usual, I did a quick safety sweep through the kitchen to make sure I'd turned off the stove, unplugged the toaster and coffee maker. Washer and dryer were off. I zipped past the liquor cabinet then backtracked.

Hmm. Anything interesting here?

The label of an unopened bottle of a favorite Czech herbal aperitif seemed to sparkle for attention. The taste is similar to Chartreuse or Benedictine in that alcoholic-version-of-a-cough-drop kind of way. *Well, that might work as an after-dinner wind down thing… it's not like one drinks that every day, is it?* I pulled the bottle out, tucked it under my arm and joined NB at the door.

It was about eight o'clock when I drove into the retreat. No signs of life at cabin eight or nine. Though strings of lights had been hung around and between the porch cabins, the cabins were dark.

I pulled my truck into a parking space in the second parking lot and helped NB out. A feeling of déjà vu hit me seeing the cook tents and lights, hearing the blaring zydeco music and getting the first whiffs of the delectable, spirited aromas that encompassed cabin one. The three amigos had a good-natured banter going, each involved in cooking, stirring, or chopping. As before, Shane was moving to the beat of the music coming from a discreet speaker on the porch rail.

Naughty Britches whimpered and tugged at the leash. I'd been juggling my purse, the leash and the stuff I'd brought--I almost dropped the bottle I was carrying.

"Well, hey you, pretty girl." I heard Max say. NB half-barked, half yowled in joyful response and yanked me around backward.

I looked up to see Max getting out of the back seat of Urliss's truck.

"Oh, hey, guys," I said, pulling on the leash.

Hollis came around from the passenger side of the truck. "Damn, woman! You look hot as a June bride on a feather bed!"

I blinked. Pretty sure that was a compliment, I mumbled

"thanks"—appreciative but also self-conscious that I was the only female in this little party.

Max gave me the once over and harrumphed. "Thought you promised to get a dress."

Hollis chuckled. "Ain't never seen her in a dress."

"I know!" Max bellowed.

Urliss looked confused. "Who said anything about go-to-meetin' clothes?"

Hollis shook his head, "Nobody."

Naughty Britches pawed at Max's legs until he stooped to pet her.

"*Max*! I didn't think this was a dressy kind of affair. We're eating on the porch of a cabin; it's not exactly black tie at the Carlyle."

He muttered something incoherent, too involved with petting NB's belly.

"Hey, Haint!" Rebel called, moving away from the huge steaming pot on the camp burner to come greet me. He crouched down to pet NB, "Hello, Slobber Chops! Ain't you somethin'?"

Shane, flipping some kind of patties on a grill, called out, "*Cher bebe*! Welcome! Hope you got an *ahnvee*♥ for some crab cakes today, 'cause I am fixin' da best you evah gonna hang your beautiful lips aroun' !"

"Okay then, can't wait!" I said, unable to move closer as NB

♥ perhaps derived from envy but means hunger.

was still getting petted. Max stood up and gave me a quick side hug, eyeing the bottle.

"What the hell is that? Becher-what?" He pulled the bottle from me and squinted.

"Thought I'd bring something a little unusual."

"Oh?" Buster said, sidling up to us from nowhere like a magician. He must have been in the cooking tent with Shane. He seemed to move so quietly, with, well, stealth was perhaps too strong a word. "Whatcha got thar?" he asked with a raised eyebrow. "Is 'at mouthwash?" He flashed a mischievous grin.

In his defense, the flattened green bottle did resemble a sinister mouthwash.

"It's a Czech herbal aperitif I like," I said, showing him the label and pronouncing it.

"Gesundheit," he said, eyes lingered on mine before moving to the bottle for a moment then back to me. "Nice. Lookin' fo'ward to givin' a try, Purple Moon Eyes. Fun earrings, the skeletons. You look magical."

"And this is for you," I said, handing over the little wrapped bundle and card.

His face lit up. "Aw, you didn' have to go an' do that." He felt the present, squeezing it gently up and down.

NB must have sensed she was no longer the center of attention. She rolled herself upright, pawed Buster's leg and woofed.

"No, sweet girl, this is for me," Buster said, leaning down to pet her on the head. Still feeling the package with the other hand, he looked sideways at me. "Is it a lighter?"

"Nope."

"It's so small. Wonder what it is?" he said, with an intrigued expression that made it sound like a question.

NB was not going to be dismissed with a simple head pat. She barked and pawed again.

"Yes, I know," Buster said, bending further to pet her back while holding the present out of her reach, "I'm happy to see you."

Rebel came out of the tent, eyeing my bottle. "Hey, Haint, whatcha got there? Let me get that from you. What is it?"

"Oh, I thought we could have a sip before dinner, or after dessert. It's just an herbal liqueur I like. It's from the Czech Republic."

"Well, now, I am intrigued. Let's save it 'til after. Dinner's ready. Come on."

As we moved past the tent toward the porch, I paused to inhale, savoring the spicy aromas. "What's on the menu?" I asked.

"Da birthday boy's favorite," Shane said, "Rebel's special etouffee, beet salad, roasted corn and buttermilk biscuits."

"Wow! Smells fantastic." There was a tantalizing, earthy smell that took me back to my childhood. "This reminds me of my mother's *solyanka*--a meaty stew with carrots and potatoes. I used to just love that."

"Well then, Missy, you're gonna just love this," Rebel said, carrying a cast-iron stew pot to the table, setting it down on a tea towel. "It's got the holy trinity and the pope."

"What?"

"Celery, onions, bell pepper and gah-lic, *Bebe*," Shane said.

NB's nose swiveled, tracking the pot. She licked her lips and whimpered.

"Mmm, I'm so hungry, I've been fartin' cobwebs," Max said. "What they serve at the Oaks is the worst slop. Oughtta to be illegal. Naughty Britches won't even eat the 'food' at the Oaks, I know! I tried to sneak her some as a test. She gave me the stink eye and turned up her nose."

"Well, reckon she approves of this meal here," Buster said, tipping his head to NB, who was straining to get closer to the tabletop. I tied her up and made her settle under the table.

Buster pointed to a full carafe on the table. The liquid I assumed was wine was a peculiar color somewhere between a pale rose and pale lavender. "Issat what I hope it is?" he asked, eyebrows raised toward Rebel.

"Indeed, it is! The special nectar for your birthday, ma friend, compliments of my sweet sister."

"Oh, I've heard you talk o' this, but never got to try it," Max said, leaning forward, rubbing his hands together.

Buster turned to me, pointing to the carafe as Rebel picked it up, "Rebel's sister makes this limited edition, kudzu rosé every summer. It's quite something."

"Yup. Fresh batch from the end of September."

Rebel beamed, "she calls it, 'Evangeline's Truth Serum' – "not because it makes you *tell* the truth…" He chuckled and poured me a glass, "but because if you get to the bottom of the jug, you *find* your own truth. Go easy… it's stronger than you think."

Rebel continued around the table until everyone had a

glass. He set the carafe down and raised his own glass, "Happy Birthday, Mr. Shadetree."

We all raised our glasses and clinked to the toast. I took a tentative sip. Then another. As the liquid moved around my palette, I got light notes of fruit, something floral and a bit of pepper. I couldn't decide if I liked it or not. Maybe it would grow on me.

In short order, we were tucking into a meal to rival Thanksgiving. The corn was succulent, the etouffee was even better than my mother's *solyanka*, especially when you could sop up the juices with a perfect biscuit. The beet salad had carrots, nuts and spinach and a tangy dressing. Fantastic.

"I'd love the recipe for this," I said, pointing my fork at the stew on my plate.

Hollis said, "Well, I can getcha the squirrels, no problem."

"Yeah," Urliss agreed. "We got more squirrels than sense around our place, ah-ha-ha!"

"Seriously?" I asked, "This is squirrel?"

"Squirrel, sausage, rabbit and venison," Shane said, nodding. "And carrots, onions, peppers, tarragon, sage, file', bay leaves, cayenne pepper, garlic, and salt."

"I put some pearled barley in for extra thickness," Rebel said.

I've eaten some strange things in my life, so the squirrel wasn't a complete surprise, but it did stop me in my tracks for a moment. Not long ago, Urliss and Hollis had tried to gift me a bag of squirrels and I'd made excuses to let them keep the bag. I stuck a biscuit into the etouffee. No denying, it was positively delicious. But I did have a few flashes of cute cartoon animals of my youth getting killed and tossed in a pot.

Max asked, "So, Buster, what birthday is this? A big one?"

Buster finished chewing a bit of crab cake, swallowed and said, "It's just a day, really. I mean, is there really a differ'nce between fifty and fifty-one, or fifty-five? It's a number. Ya know, some cultures don't even recognize birthdays."

"How old?" Max pushed. "Ya can't be older than me, ha-ha!"

A Cheshire cat smile stretched across Buster's face, "old enough."

"He's fifty-five," Rebel said, winking at me.

Buster shot Rebel an I'll-get-you-back look.

"What's the mystery?" Rebel said, voice all innocence. "Ya said yourself it's just a number."

Buster shrugged it off, but I could tell he was disappointed that the mystery was solved. But why? Did he not want me to know his age? Vanity?

"Well, I just turned forty-nine last month. Can't say I'm excited about fifty, but I hope I get to turn fifty," I said.

Buster's face relaxed. "There you go. Elvis didn't make it to fifty. Think o' that." He seemed to study my face. " I was thinkin' you was more like forty, if that."

Ah. Was *that* it? He thought I was too young for him? Interesting.

Conversation remained light and intermittent as we enjoyed the bountiful feast. As before, Shane had a steady stream of music playing that ranged from country to zydeco, blues to hip hop and southern rock.

I couldn't help myself. I split a second crab cake with Max and had another helping of the etouffee.

"Don't forget, *chere bebe,* there's birthday cake, too," Shane said.

"Oh, I'll have to wait. I'm stuffed. That was fantastic," I said, slightly appalled by my clean plate.

A new song started up with a stomping beat. *"Let's turn the redneck up!"* the singer encouraged. Buster wiped his mouth with a napkin, "Oh, come on, I love this song." I was pretty sure he got three syllables out of "song". He stood up and swooped me up to dance.

"No, I couldn't. I'm so full," I protested as he lifted me up.

"Shh. Shush now," he said low and close to my ear. His hand was on my back, pressing me up against him. He had me two-stepping, gliding across the small open space on the porch. Turning. Following. A little to this side, a little to that and all the while, he sang along, his deep voice words going directly to my brain, leaving no doubt that he would be an attentive and confident lover with experienced, talented and amazing hands.

Whoo.

Party On

I hadn't planned on having a late night out, honest. I was going to enjoy Buster's party then go home. NB was yawning on the porch—it was way past her bedtime and approaching mine. But just as I was getting the momentum to make my excuses and leave, there were hints of activity up toward cabin nine.

"What's goin' on over dere?" Shane asked.

"A bunch of guys having a party," I said.

It seemed that in almost no time, things were getting downright raucous over there.

"That's some party," Urliss grumbled.

"Did I just see a mostly naked cowboy?" Max asked.

"There's some beautiful women over there," Hollis said, sucking in his ample gut.

"Let's go have a lil ol' look see," Buster said, pulling my elbow.

"Looks like dey got ever-y-ting 'cept da parade and da throws," Shane said, stepping forward. "Come on."

I untied my bored Basset and we all wandered toward the front entrance where cars were parked all along the road and up any available grass. Parking lot one was full to capacity.

Above the parking lot, in the window to the night sky framed by cypress, oak and palm leaves, the half-moon hung in a clear sky. Electronic music pounded from bunk house nine; white dots from a disco ball escaped through the curtains teasing the ground and nearby foliage. Like Bourbon Street during Mardi Gras, there were costumed people everywhere singing, dancing, strutting. Just in front of us, a muscular Beyoncé look-alike in a butt-cheek short gold lamé dress and a black leather S&M Madonna were helping a Cher look-alike with a wardrobe malfunction involving her massive head gear.

NB perked up as if the party was for her. She wagged and woo—wooed demanding attention.

Beyoncé said, "Bitch, this is a crime scene. It don't want to do right. It keeps sliding off."

Cher said, "It'll work, it has to. Use that big clip like I told you."

Beyoncé said, "You know, if you can't fix it with duct tape or a martini, it ain't worth fixin.' And I for one, need another drink."

Cher whimpered. "Come on, I can't go in there like this. You've got to make it work."

Madonna screwed up her face and made an adjustment. She stood back in admiration. "Applause, applause. You may thank your fairy godmother Miss Thing, I *am* a miracle worker. You may now go to the ball, Cinderella."

Cher cooed and clapped. "Oh, thank God and stand back, 'cause Herself is here. Mmm!" The trio moved arm-in-arm toward the porch where a packed group was strutting and waving to the lyrics, "fly, fly fly, fly, now sissy that walk."♥

They caught sight of us and stopped dead to ogle Shane and Buster. NB felt slighted and woo-wooed with more vehemence.

"Well hello, sweet thang," Cher cooed.

The costume angst reminded me of the first Thanksgiving after my husband, Dillon died. Unable to cope with social pleasantries, even with Iggy, I disappeared to a rented cabin in North Georgia with thoughts of long walks around a lake, exploring little shops in town, drinking cocoa by a fire, crying a lot, and melting in a hot tub before bed. The temperature

---

♥ RuPaul's "Sissy That Walk"

plummeted and a determined wind bearing flurries made me change plans. I woke that Thursday in an eerily silent world with frost-covered windows. I drank cocoa and watched the Macy's Thanksgiving Day Parade then binge-watched season one of RuPaul's Drag Race. It was on all day. I wanted to stop but kept getting sucked back by the fabulous costumes and the tension.

I blinked. Aubrey Sinclair had brought the drag race here. I was torn between dazzled and mortified. When Aubrey had said a party, I had stupidly assumed maybe thirty people tops. After all, they had booked bed space for a maximum of sixteen. I was looking at upwards of eighty people. I shot a nervous glance towards cabin seven, wondering why the preppers weren't pitching a fit at the noise and mayhem. I walked past cabin eight where a cowboy wearing only a hat, a thong, chaps and boots was having his butt cheeks fondled by a swarm of schoolgirls in multi-colored pigtails. All were laughing and waving champagne flutes.

"Hey *Brokeback Mountain,* you can love me, I won't tell nobody!" one of the girls petting him cooed. The cowboy vogued with pleasure for his fawning, egging admirers.

"Ms. Haint!" a voice called. I turned to see a green fairy skipping toward me waving a tulle-wrapped wand speckled with glitter. The fairy's hair and face were green. She clutched a bottle of Lucid absinthe. A woodland elf with a super-sized droopy felt hat that would have made Pee-Wee Herman envious followed her.

"It's me," the elf said, "Aubrey."

"The name Aubrey means elf king. Isn't he perfect?" the

fairy asked, and I realized the fairy was Chet.

"Well, this is some party," I began, not sure how to continue, my eyes following party lights strung between the buildings, in the trees and out toward the dock. The words "fire hazard" came to mind as I wondered how many stringed lights constituted a serious problem. *Dear God, please protect my property and these party animals. Don't let anyone fall off the dock tonight. I don't need a lawsuit.* Where were the preppers? Why hadn't they complained? I was surprised. "Earlier it was completely dead here. I kinda thought you'd be here earlier."

"Well, we had a disco nap before the show." Chet and Aubrey eyed each other, and I suspected more than napping took place.

"Show?" I asked. "Disco nap?"

"It's like a short power nap when you know you're in for a long-haul party," Aubrey said with a loving look at Chet. "Chet's family owns the Produce Co-Op, you know, on the other side of the tracks in Catfish. His parents went to an RV show in Ocala for the weekend, so Chet staged a mob drag show for our anniversary. BYOE. Bring your own everything! We weren't sure how many people would show, but it was *packed*! Boo-coos of people. We would have just had the party over there, but it backs up to a residential neighborhood and they've called the cops on us before."

I cringed. This was turning into the exact nightmare I had dreaded. Why did they assume I wouldn't call the cops? I had made it clear that they had to keep the party tame, hadn't I?

Reading my face, Aubrey said, "Don't worry, the locusts will move on when we've run out of food and drinks."

The mostly naked cowboy galloped away leaving the giggling swarm of pleats, bangles and knee socks in search of a new target. The zeroed in on the elf and fairy. We were soon surrounded by them, pawing, laughing and slopping champagne. They had taken great care with their colorful outfits, featuring layers of clothes with added buttons, ribbons and plastic hair accessories. There was something Asian about their look, but I didn't know who they were imitating.

"What are they?" I whispered to Chet.

"Harijuku. It's huge in Japan. Tacky plastic is the ticket: bracelets, hair accessories. These girls have *nailed* it."

Hmm. A distinct look to be sure, but it sounded like something that needed a medicinal remedy. I imagined a bad voice-over in an anthropological documentary: *He was diagnosed to be suffering from a severe case of Harijuku, but after fasting for three days and drinking the witch doctor's potion, the victim was cured of his affliction.*

Someone yelled, "Where are the rice queens?"

The Harijuku giggled.

"Rice queen?" I muttered.

Chet heard me, leaned close and said, "A queen who prefers Asians."

The music paused and a shrill voice trilled, "Make way! This is my song!"

Chet grabbed my arm and tugged me toward the porch. "You can't miss this. Cookie just rocks Christina Aguilera."

"She's a glamazon!" Aubrey shouted.

A leggy platinum blonde emerged wearing a forties-style

black girdle, skimpy white top, gold suspenders and a cute pill box strutted out on impossibly high, red sequined heels. Horns blared five times, she boomed out one long "Heeeyyayy" then launched into a high energy routine, throwing a leg over a railing here, dropping into a backbend there, and disappearing out of view followed by a mob to a refrain of "Ain't No Other Man." The lip-sync was perfect.

"Yes! You go, girl!" Chet yelled, passing me to follow the crowd reminiscent of the swirl following Dorothy as they followed the yellow brick road.

I looked over at cabin seven again.

A handsome creature in a white leather duster with a wide brimmed hat approached me from the parking lot. I recognized him as the Tom Cruise lookalike I'd met earlier.

"Great outfit," I cooed, still taking it all in.

He bowed with a flourish. "My homage to Falco. 'Spirit Never Dies.' "

"Falco? As in "Rock Me Amadeus"? Isn't he before your time?"

"He's a legend, like Elvis. He'll never truly die." He put a hand on his heart and added, "may he rest in peace."

"Oh? I didn't know he died."

He looked stricken. "Car crash. 1998."

"I had no idea."

He smirked and put a hand to his forehead. "He's probably partying with all the greats. Freddie Mercury, Michael Jackson, Whitney Houston...and who is *this*?" He bent down to pet Naughty Britches.

"Right. Well, you look terrific. This is Naughty Britches."

Falco cackled. "Oh, darling, that's so wrong! You couldn't possibly be naughty, could you?"

NB's tail spun like a propeller. She bounced with delight at the attention.

I was more concerned about the preppers in cabin seven, surprised that they weren't complaining about the noise.

Falco must have noticed my nervous glances toward the silent cabin. "Oh, like, if you're worried about those uptight guys, they aren't there. They kind of figured we were having a party and said they were going to rough it in the woods tonight."

"*What*?" Had they chased away my guests?

"No, it's cool. They said it was part of their training, whatever that means." Falco floated away like a luminous dream.

So, where were the preppers? I hoped they weren't bothering the Wiccans in the meditation circle; I had promised them privacy.

Motion to my right caught my attention and I did a double take. Mostly-naked cowboy had an arm around Shane. They were swaying to the music, Shane steadying a long neck beer steady in his free hand.

As if on ice, in a smooth James Brown or Sam Rockwell glissade, Buster slid behind me and wrapped his arms around me. He spoke in my ear, "Great party, eh?"

"Uh, yeah." I agreed with reluctance.

He jiggled me. "Relax. This is great! Enjoy it."

I wanted to, but it was all so…out of my control and out of my comfort zone. I watched Shane and almost-naked cowboy, their shoulders undulating in unison.

"Is Shane gay? Does he know cowboy-guy?"

"Naw. He's Creole. Got party in 'is chromosomes. If a parade passes by, even a funeral, so long as there's music, he'll get in on it."

I did a double take. Belinda Wheeler was wearing a feather boa and dancing with Jonah, Maggie Beth Burgess, Serena Hot-to-Trot and two Harijuku girls.

"Well I'll be," I said.

"I've seen a lot of things in my day, but this is sure somethin'," Max said, rubbing his chin. "Here. Let me take Naughty Britches. You go dance."

"Oh, I think I'll just go home—" I began.

Shane yelled, "Come on! Get over here!" He waved the beer.

And the next thing I knew, we were caught up in a dance party that went until a ballad called "Outlaw of Love" paired up couples and paired me with Buster in a sexy slow dance. And then we were kissing in the parking lot and the shank of the evening was passing.

"Somebody's got to get me back to the slammer," Max said.

Urliss nodded. "Ready when you are."

"I'm beat," I said, rattling my keys. "I'll see you tomorrow. Thanks so much for a terrific night." I said as we walked back towards our vehicles. Naughty Britches walked as if each step was sheer torture.

"Y'ever see the Norwegian film, *Troll Hunter*?" Buster asked.

"Nope."

"Okay, that's it, then! Let's go t'yer place."

We'd arrived at the second parking lot. I unlocked my truck. "It's way past my bedtime."

"Wait right cher, I got the DVD and the popcorn in th' Roamer."

"No, really, I'll just call it a night--"

"Don't move from this spot," he said, then sprinted away in a comical fashion, elbows and knees high.

I helped Naughty Britches into the truck.

Buster returned from the Roamer rustling a super-sized bag of popcorn and waving a DVD box.

"Maybe another time?" I said half-heartedly.

"Start 'er up. You got to see this 'un." He waved the DVD again. "Ya know yer too keyed up to sleep right off, an' you're gonna love this. It's about a crew of troll hunters in Norway. Promise I'll leave when ya want me to. Course, you'll have ta drive me back, less ya want me to walk…"

Though watching a movie about trolls was *nowhere* on my bucket list, I couldn't turn him down. It seemed surreal that after years of avoiding unwanted attention, this kooky, urban-cowboy-sexy, backwater-drawling, man could show up and dismantle my defenses with his disarming persuasion… and a movie about Norwegian monsters.

"Fine. Get in," I said.

Chapter 28

Trolling

The party was in full swing as we drove past cabin nine. Music hammered as costumed bodies danced and writhed to a new beat on the porch, in the yard, even out in the parking lot like it was a mini Mardi Gras. I stopped to let a fine Scottish lad dash in front of the truck, heading for the rest room pavilion. The costume was perfect: hat, kilt, sporran, fancy dress socks with flashes, fancy jacket…only the jacket was missing sleeves, revealing smooth buff arms, there was bare chest under the jacket, and the kilt was the shortest kilt I've ever seen, shimmying just below his butt cheeks.

"I got some Scots blood," Buster said shaking his head. "Don't reckon my forefathers dressed quite like 'at though."

I gave him the once over and said, "You could pull it off."

"Ya thank?" He asked with a devilish grin.

When we got out to the main road, I steeled myself and asked, "So, remember when I asked you about Max trying to play matchmaker with us, and you asked me about samadhi? Why'd you change the subject?"

"Just figured what with yer retreat, that you'd be good at meditatin', 'at's all."

"But…what's that got to do with…you and me?"

He shifted in his seat. "I'd rather not say 'xactly. Don't want ta jinx it."

"Jinx what? Look. I'm no spring chicken, but I'm no one-night stand either," I said.

"Issat what you thinks goin' on?" He asked, straightening himself.

We arrived at my house. I put the truck in park, turned off the ignition and faced him. "Maybe this is a mistake. Look. I find you *really* attractive. You've been acting like we're a predestined couple. Max asked me how it was going, like we were dating. And he's always keeping stuff from me. Just tell me. Did I miss a memo or accidentally delete a text? What's going on here? Do you two have some kind of bet going or something?"

"Good Lord, no, Moon Eyes. Damn, I'm sorry if you've been thankin' that. An' I don' mean to be squirrely." He sighed. "It's just…a while back Max was talkin' about you, tol' me he was real happy 'bout you buyin' the place. He showed me a pitcher 'o you, and… soon as I saw you, I recognized you."

"We've met before?"

"No…but I've seen you in visions and in meditations. Soon as I saw you, I'as sure we'd get together again."

"Again?"

"Hope ya don't think I'm crazy as a two-peckered billy goat, but I think we've been together in many past lives. I kinda hoped you'd recognized me an' just know we're supposed to be together." He looked down. "But it don't matter none…it'll be what it is. Let's go watch a movie and chow down some popcorn."

He opened his door and got out. Reaching for my door latch, my mind reeled. The Virgo, practical side of me was running around like a Nascar pit crew team with panic disorder:

We've known each other before? Is he nuts?

Do I want him in my house? Stop. Think. Holy shit. What are you doing? I don't know anything about him really. He *remembers* me? Does this mean he's my soul mate or a slick move to get in my house and my bed? What if it's true? Is this why I feel a magnetic *swwack!* when I'm near him and he feels so…familiar? Naughty Britches liked him too. She was sparing with her allotment of kisses to me, yet she'd given Buster several since she'd met him. That had to count for something.

Meanwhile, my Inner Critic was giddy with laughter. *You're a complete mess! If you could just see yourself!*

My intuition overpowered my doubts. I opened the door, got out and helped NB down. She dragged herself to the door, half-asleep. I turned on some lights and directed Buster to the living room. NB staggered to the bedroom.

"An' who's this?" Buster asked as Mischief meowed and head-butted his leg.

"Mischief. He's NB's cat, not mine."

"Oh?" Buster asked.

"You're not allergic to cats, are you? I can put him in the bedroom..."

"Naw, naw, I'm fine. Love animals."

Whew. Good. Check that box:

√ Okay with dogs and cats.

The Inner Critic said, *Brilliant. He could be a drug dealing, date-rapist, but at least he likes your pets. You've got your priorities in order.*

"Want something to drink? Wine? Beer? Tea? Lemonade?" I asked, moving toward the kitchen.

"I'd love a hot tea. Somethin' herbal? Mebbe some honey, if ya got it?"

Huh. Wasn't expecting that, but perfect. I was in the mood for hot tea, too. While waiting for the water to boil, I rejoined Buster, watching him snoop around my house like a cat burglar who knows the occupants are overseas. He took his time, touching the book spines, studying the artwork, poking his head into closed rooms.

"You have a pool room?"

"Apparently."

"You shoot pool, I take it?"

"Sometimes. It was a mid-life crisis purchase. Kind of like the retreat. Thought I'd have more time to perfect my game. That hasn't happened."

"The time don't make itself. You gotta make the time," Buster said, closing the door again. "Nice room."

"Thanks."

The kettle whistled; I ducked back into the kitchen. When I returned with a tea tray and a packet of Girl Scout Thin Mints, Mischief was curled on Buster's lap. *Troll Hunter* was cued up on the television, ready to go.

√ Good with electronics

"You've got a right welcomin' home, Haint. Feels good. Safe. Very homey."

"Thanks. Hope so," I said with pleasure setting the tray down on the old trunk that serves as coffee table.

The three of us snuggled on the couch and watched a film crew and a troll hunter drive all over Norway, tracking trolls.

As the credit began to roll, I said, "Well, I gotta give it to you, that was great. Engaging. Clever. Very well thought out. The first troll—the woodland troll was it? That was cheesy, but from that point—" I laughed, quoting the film " 'Did he say *trolls*?' I got sucked in. Thanks. I would never have picked that movie, but I really liked it."

Buster patted my knee. "I enjoyed watchin' it with you. Can't thank when I've had a better birthday."

I was leaning against Buster's shoulder, nervous as hell about what was going to happen next.

Just be in the moment, The Inner Critic said.

Right. Buster is here in my house. I want him. I can't want him. He travels all the time. He's a boogyman chaser for heaven's sakes. What am I doing?

Just... be in the moment, The Inner Critic whispered. *You're not getting engaged or anything. Lighten up.*

He might be a prepper, too. What do I really know about him? He could be an axe murderer, right? How do I know his handsome face isn't on a wanted poster in Idaho or something?

"I've been meaning to ask you..." I began, kind of kicking myself for breaking the comfortable silence.

"Shoot."

"Uh, about the preppers... you seem to know a lot about them. Do you have a Bug Out Location? Bags of rice under your bed? A bunker somewhere stocked with boxes of corn flakes and cans of beans?"

I felt his chest move as he laughed softly. "Would that bother you?"

Merde alors♥, *he does!* I thought. Oh sister, you're falling for a Bigfoot hunter AND a doomsdayer. Well done! I straighten myself, pulling away from him so I could look him in the eyes. "Are we talking a few canned goods and a full tank of gas or...a lifestyle? Do you go off on these retreats? How far down the rabbit hole are you?"

He raked his top teeth over his bottom lip and squinted at me. "Do you have homeowner's insurance on your house?"

"What? Yeah, of course."

"And car insurance?"

"You have to have car insurance."

"Why's that?"

"Well, in case anything happens."

He nodded. "Phil Burns, owner of the American Prepper's Network puts it like this: you get you'self some insurance so you're protected-like in case somethin' happens, dontcha?"

"Oh, I see," I said.

"And preppers are just doin' the same thing... getting

♥ French for "shit"

prepared in case something catastrophic happens."

"So… you *do* have a Bug Out Location and all that."

He grinned. "Let's just say, if something happens, you'll be glad to have me around. I mean, I'd hope you'd be glad in any event, but—I'm more prepared than the average guy."

Put like that, it didn't sound so crazy. And the way he said it sounded sexy, too. He rearranged his position and kissed me. Supporting my head gently with his hands, the kissing moved from tentative and sweet to impassioned. I felt that magnetic click between us. The Inner Critic and the Nascar team withdrew for the evening.

I thought it would feel strange to be in someone else's arms, to align my body with someone not-Dillon. Perhaps Buster was right, and we had known each other in a previous life. Kissing and hugging gave way to undressing and exploring each other's bodies. The usual monkey chatter in my head were silenced by low sexy moans close to my ear, kisses went down by neck and firm fingers caressing my hips. Our lovemaking was like cosmic slipstreaming, relinquishing all sense of self, time and space.

Chapter 29

Saturday Morning, or, What You Need to Know About Filing A Missing Persons Report

I came into consciousness with a pounding sinus headache accompanied by a familiar high-C barking, *Yark! Yark! Yark!* Naughty Britches ran up and down the hall; her toenails click-clicking on the tile. The pounding in my head was echoing a pounding on my front door. I moved to get up only to find my body pinned by Buster's leg. He threw an arm around me and murmured, "Hey, gorgeous."

I'd forgotten to take out my contacts the night before. Normally I can't see much first thing. It was a pleasant shock to take in Buster's naked body in the mess of sheets. *Whew!* Vida had sure been right about Scorpio: he had been unhurried, attentive and intuitive last night. Distracted by his shapely buttocks, I pulled my robe out of the closet. How does a man who sits in a van monitoring phantom monsters on a computer screen keep that kind of muscle tone? Surely not fly-fishing, right? *Wowee.*

Careful not to trip over the bouncing Basset, I bumped

down the hall toward the noise.

Yark! Yark!Yark!

Bang! Bang! Bang!

"Okay! I'm coming! Shh!"

NB squeezed her muzzle through the gap when I opened the door an inch and looked out. Our local Sheriff, Dave Marshall was standing on my doorstep, shifting his belt under his broad torso. He could win a look-alike contest for Hoss on *Bonanza.*

Yark! Yark!Yark!

"You didn't answer your phone," he said.

I unlatched the chain and opened the door a little wider, trapping NB in my legs. Fortunately, she knows Dave and traded barking for wagging. She slithered past me and threw herself at him, then rolled and waited for him to pet her. He bent down and dutifully ran a hand over her belly.

"Who's a good girl, eh? Okay. That's good. Okay, I have to talk with your Mommy."

He was taking in my mess of hair, the robe, my bare feet. After taking the visual tour of my body, his eyes returned to my face.

"Had a night, did you?"

One night a long time ago, I got drunk and kissed Dave. Long sloppy kisses. It was a mistake. But Dave has never forgotten it and gets puppy-eyed over me. I've done nothing to encourage him, yet he remains optimistic. It's awkward. If his hip-cocking was a sign, he was already sliding out of officer-of-the-law mode into player mode.

"Was there something you wanted to see me about?" I asked.

"Well, it's probably nothing, but I tried you on your phone and figured you had it turned off, so I came over."

How convenient.

I heard movement behind me as Buster sidled up like my shadow catching up, his hand casually brushing over my ass. Glancing back, I was relieved he'd pulled on his jeans. Naughty Britches, switching allegiance, stood up and darted past me to jump on Buster.

"Sher-uff? Is there a problem?" Buster asked, putting a hard drawl on the title. He petted NB with a bare foot.

Dave's mouth opened and closed. He glanced from me to Buster and back, his jaw tightening, his expression anvil hard. I imagined a spaghetti western standoff in the middle of town with the whoo-eee-ooo-eee-ooo wah wah wah from *The Good the Bad and the Ugly* as the two men faced each other. Buster leaned into me with a casual familiarity while Dave straightened to drill-training stiffness.

Dave snarled. "Yes. The department received a call that one of your guests may be missing. Unfortunately, a missing person report cannot be filed unless the conditions fall under the guidelines—"

My stomach felt sour. "Who's missing?"

"Fawn..." He pulled out a little notebook and glanced at it.

I didn't recognize the name. *Who was that?*

"Fawn... Nicole Janus. Described as small with a super short hair."

What? Oh. Buzz cut. Nicole. Right. *Missing*? I rubbed my eyes as if it'd help clear my confusion.

Dave continued, his face tight, "A missing person report can only be filed in suspicious circumstances, such as evidence of foul play, suicidal threats, a history of emotional instability, or mental incompetence."

I shook my head. "No, no. She's a bright girl. No mental issues that I know of. I don't understand. Who called you?"

Buster's hand moved up to my shoulder.

Dave referred to his notes again. "A Mrs. Vida Glossimer. She reports that Ms. Janus was last seen late last night. She excused herself and never came back."

"Is her car still there?" I asked. "Maybe she just went home?"

"Her car is still in the parking lot. And one of her friends found her...ah…bag in the woods."

"Her *bag*?" My head was pounding something awful.

He cleared his throat. His eyes lingered on Buster's arm around my shoulder before he referred to his little book again. "They called it a 'mojo bag'. It's what she was carrying the…er…stuff for whatever it is they were doing in the woods."

"So, are you organizing a search party or, what are you doing?" I asked.

"Well, No, not just yet. We'll be interviewing your guests. I'm waiting on Anson to get back. We had some vandalism in town last night and a coupla home invasions."

"At the Lotus Lodge?"

"No, in town. Usual teen stuff, bashing mailboxes and

driving through flower beds. Someone tried to break into a couple houses including one full of Chihuahuas."

I covered my mouth to stop the erupting laugh.

"The owners were away, but the dogs went berserk, the neighbors heard the commotion and the robber limped away to the getaway car. There were small blood stains on the porch. They dropped the bag of jewelry and stuff they'd stolen. Anyway, Anson's over there now taking statements, so I don't have the resources for a search." He glared at me. "Something funny?"

A giggle escaped my covered mouth as I tried to clear the image of the Chihuahua attack from my mind. "Are the dogs okay? Is Lulabelle okay?"

"Who?"

"The mommy Chihuahua. Last time I saw her, she looked like she had a watermelon implant. But she had eight puppies."

"How do you...? On second thought, I don't want to know."

Concern for Nicole and visions of a police presence at Blue's Lotus Lodge again sobered me. "What does that mean, you don't have time to find Nicole?"

"I didn't say that. I'm on this."

"So, what's the plan?"

"Well, I'll have to interview your guests, get a timeline, contact her family. She'll probably turn up. Halloween party or something. Like as not she just slunk off with someone." The ghost of a smirk floated across his mouth.

I narrowed my eyes. "Or she may be in danger."

He clenched his teeth again. "Right."

Buster's hand squeezed my shoulder, "I'm sure she's jus' fine, hon."

He didn't know the horror of the double murder I'd been through the previous month. I had seen both bodies, the images were vividly branded in my mind. I couldn't be so cavalier. I hugged myself and pressed into Buster's warm body.

Buster said, "We've got surveillance equipment all 'round the prop'ty, includin' a camera aimed right at the entrance. It's likely somethin'll show up when we run through it."

I swear I saw Dave lips quiver in the barely controlled snarl. He looked at me then back to Buster. "And why would you be spying on Haint's guests?"

"Spyin'?" He snickered and shook his head "We're not *spyin'* on guests. We're here on a crypto-zoo-lodge-cal investigation." Of course, he got about fifty syllables out of cryptozoological.

"A *what*?"

"In this case, a Skunk Ape sighting."

Dave whooped, "Skunk Ape! Yeah right! And I'm a monkey's uncle." His face reddened in a quizzical look. *You passed me over to shack up with this wingnut?*

Buster muttered in my ear, "Monkey see monkey do."

Judging by the way Dave lowered his head like an angry bull, I guessed that he resented this "wingnut" offering technology that might be helpful, putting him at a disadvantage. "Of all the— " He blew out a breath. I expected him to paw the ground next. "I'll need to see the footage."

I pressed my lips together hard. This was the dreaded moment, the one where I stood next to Buster waiting for the smirks and laughter as he explained his career choice. Here it was, only I wasn't feeling embarrassed the way I'd expected. Knowing that Dave was jealous and irked was oddly…gratifying. My concern for Nicole, the feeling of dread and desperate wish that she wouldn't turn up dead was vying for attention against that naughty sense of pleasure at Dave's jealousy. The little red ego flag in my head began waving. It was wrong to relish someone else's anguish. I imagined his position and wanted to feel some compassion, but it didn't come easily.

Dave had ignored my ongoing subtle signals that I wasn't interested. He'd asked me out, I'd made excuses. He'd move in close; I'd step away. When he got familiar, I got formal. And yet none of it had seemed to register with him. Part of me was delighted that maybe he'd finally get the hint and stop thinking of me as a potential lover who just needed more time. It was never going to happen.

He grumbled, "I'm going over to the Lotus now to interview your campers. I'll need a guest list. Will you be…?" His eyes moved from me to Buster and back. He flicked a thumb toward the driveway.

"Yes. Of course. I'll be over in a tick."

Dave nodded and stepped back. I was swinging the door closed when he said, "Oh, almost forgot to mention it. Seems a drunk driver took out your sign last night. Plowed right into it, blew it to shit, then backed up and kept going. Left huge ruts in the grass where he musta spun tires gettin' out."

I opened the door wider. "*What?*"

The corners of his mouth were turned up. "Your sign out by the road," he waved his hands. "Kerblooey."

"*Motka Bosca*!" I closed the door and leaned against it. Missing persons and on top of it, the gaudy, controversial sign that was becoming a local landmark, possibly the work of a soon to be "discovered" artist was splinters and my entryway was torn up. I'd hated it at first, but I'd been getting used to it. Fan-freaking-tastic. I knew we needed to get going but I couldn't get my body to move.

Buster ran a finger down my cheek. "Hon, was 'ere somethin' between you an' him I should know about? He was workin' up a lather over me bein' here with you—"

An embarrassing, involuntary snort erupted; it actually hurt the back of my throat. "Oh, dear God and Alan Rickman, no. I got drunk at a party once and kissed him. He's been hopeful ever since."

"Poor guy, no wonder. Ah, how does Alan Rickman come into it?"

"Sorry. My brain makes weird connections. Rickman was a perfectly evil Sheriff of Nottingham."

"Ah." He looked relieved and kissed my nose.

As we walked toward the kitchen and the life-giving coffee pot, my head pounded. "Guess I overdid it yesterday or I've got a sinus headache. Maybe I'm dehydrated? I feel like I was dragged behind a wagon on a bumpy road."

"After last night, I'd say dehydrated's a good guess."

The rest of the evening came back to me. Buster and I left his buddies, watched the wild party for a bit, oh yes, came to my house for *Troll Hunter*. Then the kissing session migrated into my bedroom. Oh my. My, my, my. We went to bed, but sleep didn't happen for a long time.

Buster slid his arms around me and pulled me close, "Moon Eyes, I hope you feel better than that...you were in fine form last night..."

Naughty Britches trailed in behind us looking annoyed. Why were we up again?

"What? We didn't keep you up. You were snoring z's, little girl."

With a bored glance at us, she waddled over to the water bowl and drank. *Slurp, slurp, slurp.*

"She does have personality, doesn't she?" Buster asked.

Slurp, slurp, slurp.

"Wow. She sure drinks a lot."

I nodded.

Slurp, slurp, slurp.

"Gosh, you sure she doesn't have kidney issues or somethin'?

Slurp, slurp.

"No, she's fine. She's just tanking up like a camel so she can leave pee-mail messages and have plenty of ammo to pee a carpet if I piss her off or neglect her in any way."

NB waddled back to us with a non-plussed expression on her face, as if to say, "It's just scandalous how she besmirches my character like this." She sighed heavily and plopped down in front of Buster, rolling over to offer her belly.

"Aren't you the sweetest li'l ol' dog," he cooed, dutifully

scratching.

Her tail swished; she lolled her head over and gazed at me with a look that said, "I've got him right where I want him now."

"Let's go get you some breakfast, little girl."

As I popped a filter into the coffee maker and poured in my favorite Cuban coffee, Buster pulled out his phone and punched buttons. "Rebel. Get Shane up. We've got a little situation and…what?" His jaw hardened showing off his perfect pencil line beard. "Shane's missing? Well, *find* him. I need you to start pullin' the feeds from the cameras and see if we got anythin' last night. Someone went missin'. What? Yeah. A guest." He looked at me. "The yoga teacher, Nicole. I'll be there shortly."

"Shane's missing too?"

He shook his head. "I doubt it."

"You don't think he and Nicole…" I began.

He shook his head. His expression was of annoyance, not concern, so I left it alone. I handed him a mug. "Milk? Sugar?"

He shook his head and poured himself a coffee. "Smells amazing."

I got the milk from the fridge and made myself a cup. "Oh, great googly-moogly!" I blurted, almost slopping my cup. "Nicole was supposed to teach a yoga class this morning. Guess I'll have to do her class. Nuts! I wanted to see all the video feeds. I wonder if Iggy would mind doing me a favor…"

I retrieved my phone and called Ig. He answered after a few rings. Sunday. Probably woke him up. And he was probably with Louise. I felt guilty and was about to disconnect when he answered. I took a swig of the elixir. It was perfect. Helped calm and focus me.

"Sis? What's up?"

"Sorry…I shouldn't have called…but I have a situation. Is Louise with you?"

"Yeah. Why?"

"Oh, I'm sorry. Any chance you both want to do some yoga this morning?" I explained that Nicole and Shane were missing, and I was hoping to be in on looking a surveillance footage, so would he cover the ten-thirty class? As I talked, I poured kibbles in NB's bowl and dumped a can of "salmon soufflé" into Mischief's bowl. There was a muffled pause as Iggy relayed this to Louise. After a moment he came back.

"No problem. Louise'll tag along. Breakfast and lunch are on you."

"Absolutely! Love you, *Brat*, and I owe you big-time. See you soon." I hung up.

"Reckon I need me a shar," Buster said running a hand through his hair. It took me a second to translate that he'd said "shower". "It'd save water if we shared…" he added, looping a finger around my pajama strap and pulling me towards him.

"I've got people missing and breakfast for an army to prep. I don't have time--"

"I know, I get it. Wholesome and ex-pee-dited. I kin shar quicker'n a duck on a June bug, but I'd like the comp'ny anyway."

True to his word, we had a lovely intimate shower together, but we didn't dilly-dally. We dressed and hustled over to the Lotus Lodge.

Making the turn down the retreat road, we spotted the wreckage of the Lotus Lodge sign. It pained me to see the tire ruts and the remains of Lerlene's psychedelic artichoke, but at least the driver was able to drive away.

"Sorry 'bout yer sign," Buster said, patting my knee. "It's just a temporary setback. Easy fix."

"Yeah." I said, trying to keep the dejection from my voice. "You know, I hated it before. Now I kind of miss it."

"Don't miss what you got 'til its' gone, right?" he drawled.

And somehow, I knew I'd miss him terribly when he was gone too.

Chapter 30

Alibis please!

Dave was standing in the first parking lot when we arrived, talking to Vida and Boo. I guessed they had been waiting for him. The sea of cars from the previous night were gone; the magical and potentially hazardous party lights were off. The only signs of the wild party were a few marabou feathers and beer cans between bunkhouse eight and nine. All was quiet over there.

I parked, we got out and joined the Wiccans and Dave.

"Have you heard anything?" I asked.

Boo was typing rapidly on her phone. She said, "nope" without looking up. She sounded worried and annoyed.

"And when did you see her last?" Dave asked Vida.

"It was too buggy to have our feast outdoors, as we would have liked, so we had it in our cabin. That was around seven o'clock. Then we went to the cemetery for our honoring the dead ritual…"

"And Nicole was there for that?" Dave asked. visibly

uncomfortable with the notion of Wiccans, rituals and visiting cemeteries.

"Yes."

"Which cemetery? Most cemeteries are closed after dark. I hope you weren't trespassing."

I suspected that he was being contrary on purpose to get at me.

"It's a private cemetery. We had permission," Vida said.

Dave's left nostril twitched. "Go on."

Buster interrupted, "I'm going to find Rebel and hunt down Shane. He's got to be here somewhere."

Dave asked, "He's missing too?"

"Not on my watch," Buster said, looking grim. He walked off towards the Roamer.

"We came back, put on bug spray, and went out to the meditation circle," Vida answered.

"What time was that?"

"Somewhere between eight and eight-thirty. We had a fire and made offerings, let's see, that would have been around nine thirty or so. We did a banishing spell, a vision quest…we invoked the Goddess. Nicole left somewhere after that. I thought maybe she was going to the rest room, but she never came back."

Dave smirked and scribbled in his notepad, talking aloud, "In-voked the God-dess. Right. Did she say where she was going?"

"Not to me."

"What time was that?"

"Oh, we finished up about 12:30 a.m. so, she must have left about 12:15 or so, I imagine."

Boo put away her phone and added, "Rose and I found her mojo bag on the trail. Not like her to drop it like that." She chewed on a non-existent fingernail. I noticed that she had the kind of frog toe fingers, more pad than nail, and the nails were bitten down to nothing.

"Did she say anything to anyone?"

"No. But it would have been rude to interrupt the invocation. We all thought she would come back." Boo said. "We thought we'd run into her on the way out, but we didn't. We heard weird noises in the bushes though. Kind of freaked us out. Like some animal was following us."

Dave seemed to dismiss this. "Armadillos love palmettos and can sound much bigger than they are. You didn't see her when you left. How about during the…invoking? What was her demeanor? Did she seem different at all?"

Vida answered, "Not that I noticed, but we were focusing on the ceremony. You have to keep the intention and focus for it to work."

Dave raised an eyebrow, "Were you, ah, dressed or, uh—"

There was a playful look in Vida's eyes. She moved closer to Dave and put her hands on her hips, "Were we skyclad you mean? Nude? As a matter of fact, we were not. Sorry to disappoint you."

Dave made a guttural noise. "Who else was with you?"

"There were just the seven of us, me, Nicole, Boo and her mother, Theadora, Rose Water, Jonah and Buckshot."

Vida pulled out a handkerchief and mopped at her throat.

Dave watched her with a suspicious eye. I imagined he thought she was patting herself because she was nervous, possibly guilty. I was sure a hot flash wouldn't have crossed his mind.

Boo closed her eyes. "You know, I feel like she's okay, she just can't communicate right now."

I remembered what Nicole had said about a premonition of something coming. What? Why didn't she tell anyone if she left on her own? I remembered that Nicole had said Boo and her mom had psychic gifts. I sure hoped Boo was right.

Dave shifted his weight, "And where are…Theadora and Rose now?"

"They're in the cabin. They're both heavy sleepers."

"Were you all in a cabin together?"

"We womenfolk were. Jonah and Buckshot just came for the ceremony. I think they went home after. At any rate, they didn't stay with us, so you can stop with that suspicious look."

"Did she leave with them then?" I asked.

"No, I checked," Boo said, waving her phone. They didn't see her leave."

Dave tugged at his belt. "You have men in your, uh, group? I thought witches were all female."

"We're Eclectic Wiccans, officer," she said, her eyes moving slowly from his feet to his face. "We welcome male energy in our circle."

I pressed my lips together, determined not to giggle. She was amazing. Just the hint of suspicion of anything in my direction makes me nervous. She was relaxed and enjoying this interview.

Dave rubbed a hand on his neck. "Rii-ight. And…and what about the woman with the two children? Who is she?"

"Woman with two children…" I pondered. "I don't have a guest with two—"

Vida winked at me.

"You've seen them?" I asked her, ignoring Dave. I wasn't up for explaining an American Indian ghost family.

Vida's mouth twitched. "I've seen them a few times. Meant to ask you about them."

"Well?" Dave demanded, hands on his hips.

I felt my upper body sag under the weight of not wanting to go there.

Vida jumped in, surprising me. "They're ghosts. A mother and her two children. I don't think you'll be able to question them, though she probably does have answers."

"Who saw them?" I asked.

Dave pointed towards the dock. "I saw them when I drove in this morning." He glared at me. "You've got to be shi—"

"Max must have mentioned Spotted Fawn before, Dave. I'm not making this up. Ask him. Anyway, um, listen. I've got a camp full of people expecting breakfast. May I be excused to get that rolling and maybe you can interview people in my office…again?" My office had become interview central during the last incident at Blue's Lotus Lodge. "I'll make you coffee."

Dave looked even more uncomfortable. "Anson is in there now interviewing some of the men from cabin nine."

"I thought he was dealing with burglars and Chihuahuas," I said.

"He's efficient. He got here just before you did."

Anson was a young and naïve deputy. Nice guy but clueless. The picture of him interviewing the Burlie Boys was like a bush baby asking a tiger a few questions.

Without looking at me, he jutted his chin toward the dining hall. Mercifully, I was excused. I winked at Vida as I moved away.

Jim and Julie Calhoun were already in the dining hall setting out pamphlets when I arrived. Belinda and Cog Wheeler were eyeing the whiteboard agenda for the day:

- ✓ **SHELTER**
  - o Temporary Structure
  - o Permanent Structure
  - ✓ **SECURITY WROL (Without Rule of Law):**
  - o Secure your dwelling
  - • Safe alarm systems

- ✓ **PERSONAL SECURITY**
  - ▪ Best bang for your buck: guns, knives,
  - ▪ Makeshift self-protection

- ✓ **STORAGE**
  - o Survival storage
  - o Food storage
- ✓ **SUPPLIES**
  - o FOOD
  - o CLOTHING
  - o MEDICINE
    - ▪ Ditch medicine essentials

"Good Morning!" I greeted them. "Sorry for the delay. Coffee coming right up." I turned the cold water on and held the coffee carafe while it filled.

Julie asked, "We saw the sheriff's car out there. What's up?"

Feeling like an actress testing out a character, I hoped my voice masked my concern, "One of the guests seems to be missing. Hopefully, it's nothing--false alarm."

And where was Shane?

The carafe full, I turned off the water and poured the water into the coffee maker and hit the on button.

Prudence and Annie arrived, prompting a round of morning greetings. Prudence was her usual overmodest self while Annie's soft face and warm eyes were shrouded with worry.

"Have you seen Maggie Beth this morning?" Annie asked with a hollow voice, "I was hoping she'd be here."

"No, I haven't," I said.

"Her bed wasn't slept in," Prudence said with an arch expression.

Annie massaged her temples, "I can't remember everything from last night. I need some water. I don't feel so good."

"I'll fix you right up," I said, turning away to prepare a pitcher of ice water.

"Oh, thank you," Annie said closing her eyes. "I overdid last night. I wish I could remember when I saw Maggie Beth last. We were up…uh, talking, and I think she walked with me back to the cabin. I don't remember much after that."

The ice cubes clinked as I set the pitcher out. She poured herself a large glass of water as I pulled pitchers of milk, juice, and the premade smoothies out of the refrigerator.

"Well, I'm no help. I went to bed early and slept soundly," Prudence said. There was something about the way she stated this that implied she slept well due to a clear conscience, or at least that was the impression I got from her slightly upturned nose.

"Maybe she got up early, made her bed and went for a walk?" I suggested.

Annie cradled her glass. "I doubt that somehow."

"What's Dave doing here?" Prudence asked. "There isn't another mur—" She stopped herself and shivered. "He started asking me a bunch of questions but wouldn't tell me anything." Prudence was wearing an almost-sheer cream-colored blouse with short black sleeves. The entire front was a Siamese cat's face; the black sleeves were the peaks of the cat's ears. She looked about, clearly ruffled.

I had to be supremely careful about my answer. Prudence

could get the rumor mill cranking and destroy me by lunchtime without meaning to. "He's helping us look for a guest who seems to be, uh, missing. Probably was out partying last night and passed out somewhere or something. Just a precaution. He's doing me a favor."

Yes, I lied. My intention was good. I'd worry about redeeming my karma later.

"Well, Maggie Beth is missing too," Prudence said with severity.

I was saved from further scrutiny by Serena Lippincott's dramatic entrance, calling out "I'm not sure that a caffeine infusion will be enough! Someone get the jumper cables!" She wore flowered cotton pants and sparkly sandals. Her breasts were barely confined in a red-carpet-red top with exposed shoulders. Her lipstick was the same shade as her blouse. Despite her pretense of barely dragging in, she'd obviously spent significant time on her hair, makeup and wardrobe. As she approached us, I caught a whiff of smoke and perfume.

"Oh, merciful heaven. The coffee smells fantastic," she groaned in her deep voice as she reached for a cup. "That idiot sheriff wanted to talk to me. I told him he would just have to wait."

I set out a plate of pastries from the Art of Tarts. Cog had snagged a pastry before the plate had settled on the counter. Belinda helped herself to a smoothie.

Annie asked, "Have you seen Maggie Beth this morning, Serena?"

"No, why?" Serena answered, her attention on Cog's chewing then to the plate of assorted Danishes. She seemed intent on consuming one with her eyes.

"Her bed wasn't slept in and her bag is just the way it was yesterday."

Belinda said, "That yoga teacher is missing too."

Serena sipped her coffee and closed her eyes, moving away from the plate of temptations. "I'm sure they're fine."

"Maggie Beth was dancing with us last night," Belinda said. "But I think she was still there when I left."

I wondered if Serena knew something or just didn't want to be bothered pre-caffeine. I tipped scrambled eggs into a serving bowl and set it out. "This is crazy. They've got to be here somewhere."

"Maybe it was a UFO abduction," Cog said through a mouthful of pastry.

"Oh, stop, it's not funny," Belinda said, bumping his shoulder. Looking at me she said, "I'm sure it's something simple and everyone is fine."

The door swung open. Buster and Dave did the awkward dance of two people moving to get through the door at the same time, pausing, moving, shifting, moving. Buster stepped aside and Dave lumbered forward, his face tight.

Buster eyes met mine. I'd known him less than a week, and yet there was a comforting familiarity, a shared something that passed between us that was warming and assuring. It contrasted sharply with Dave who approached me like a charging rhinoceros.

"We need to talk," Dave said between gritted teeth. "You've got big problems."

I stuck a serving spoon into the fruit bowl and ushered him to the back of the kitchen. When we seemed to be out of earshot I asked, "What now?"

"It seems that not only is Nicole missing, but a Maggie Beth, one of your fatties is also unaccounted for."

"*Excuse me*?" I said.

He waved it off. "You know, that fat women's weight loss group. Prudence says one of them is missing. You know Haint, I don't know what kind of a place you run here, but two murders a month ago and now missing people. What the *hell*, Haint? You're a disaster magnet."

I was feeling too defensive to add that Shane was missing as well. He lowered his eyes as if he knew he'd gone too far and already regretted it, but I let him have it anyway. I gripped the counter for support, took a breath and spoke in a crisp tone. "Listen to me very carefully, Dave Marshall. You're being ugly to me because you're jealous. Jealous because I slipped and kissed you once in a sloppy drunk and you've held this hope that you might get lucky with me again. Now Buster has come along and cut in on your little fantasy-fest. Well it was never going to happen, Dave, so stop holding your breath. You think your reputable family background makes you a prince among men so you can look down on the rest of us. You have your princely moments, I'll grant, and I'm glad that we're friends, but you aren't better than everyone else. I'll thank you to not belittle any of my guests ever again. How dare you? Prudence has put more than one meal on your plate, I'd bet."

I hoped he couldn't see that I was trembling. I poked a shaky finger toward his belly and hissed, "You could stand to lose a few pounds yourself, mister. Maybe you should join the ladies. Your belt buckle looks like it's disappearing into your gut."

Dave stepped back as if I had struck him.

Unfortunately, I *had* been worried that my camp was a disaster magnet, like in the murder mysteries where the caterer always finds a body at the banquet, or the gardeners always find a body in the begonias. Terrified at the prospect of another murder or even two or three, my fear hacked up another ball of verbal bile and threw it at Dave. "And as for the disaster magnet crack, If you can honestly lay your hand upon that badge of yours and say you believe that I put all my savings into this camp with the intention of attracting dead bodies and missing persons because I need more mayhem in my life to bankrupt me, then consider our friendship ripped up like a bad check and get the hell out of my kitchen." My finger visibly trembling, I pointed to the door.

Buster was watching from the other side of the kitchen. Though I hoped he was too far away to have heard me, he could see my face, my rage. He must have felt compelled to come to my rescue. In a few paces, he closed the distance to Dave.

"Excuse me, uh, Officer, I don' mean to interrupt, but, like I said before, me and the boys 'a got cameras in the woods. We can review the footage with you, mebbee it'd shed some light on—"

Dave grimaced, his face red. "You need to give me that equipment. I expect you to dismantle it and have it available for me to—"

Buster shook his head slowly and chuckled. "We can get

'round to it direc'ly, but I'm thinkin'it'd be a better plan to—"

"Excuse me? Are you telling me how to do my job?" Dave asked.

"Naw...naw sir. I'm not meanin' to get your dander up, it's just all the cameras are connected to video screens in the Tiger. We can run 'em all at the same time, see, to see what was happenin' all over? They're synced up, like. If we dismantle 'em like you said, one, it'd take a while, two, it'd be a reg'lar pain in the patoot, and three, you could jus' as easily watch it in the Tiger...see everythin' at once."

Dave's jaw was clenched. I could see in his eyes he hated conceding to Buster.

Hoping to soften the moment, I said, "Dave, you won't believe the Tiger. It's amazing, like a portable Bat Cave."

Dave didn't see the humor. Without looking at me, he answered in a snide tone, "Must be nice having expensive toys to chase the boogie man."

Serena had gone through the breakfast line and was walking by the prepper board. She cackled, "Booby traps?" and put a hand to her cleavage. She cast a come-hither spell over Cog, saying, "Sugar, now why is that crossed out? You got something against booby traps?" She cackled and sashayed to a table not waiting for an answer.

On the other side of the room, Iggy opened the door and held it for Louise. Oh thank goodness!

Without a glance at Dave, I crossed the kitchen to meet them. "Oh, yay, I'm so glad you're here."

"What's the word?" Iggy asked, as I hugged him. "What's up?" he asked, nodding to Dave. "Hey, man, big game today.

Gators are going to muzzle Uga."

Dave's jaw clenched. "Yes they are and I'd like to see it but unfortunately, Haint here — "

"I've got *three* people missing!" I interrupted, fighting to sound calm despite the frantic feeling creeping over me.

Iggy put a calming hand on my shoulder. "I'm sure it'll be fine."

"Thanks for taking the yoga class. I owe you one," I said.

"She roped you into this circus?" Dave asked Iggy with a scowl.

Iggy's face slackened in indifference, "*Nie mój cyrk, nie moje małpy*♥, dude. Not my circus, not my monkeys. I'm just teaching the yoga class." Iggy raised an eyebrow to me as if to ask, "what's with him?"

I glanced at Louise and said, "Hope this doesn't wreck your plans for today."

"Not at all. I could use the stretch out."

"Please help yourselves to breakfast," I said, gesturing to the buffet table.

The door swung open again. Shane and Maggie Beth entered, followed by Rebel looking like their truant officer. It was quite the tableau: Rebel herding them like two naughty children, Shane looked relaxed and satisfied with himself, Maggie Beth's hair was abnormally poofy, her lips looked swollen--a splotchy red ring outlined her lip line like a child

---

♥ Polish phrase "Not my circus, not my monkeys"

had crayoned outside the lines, and her shirt wasn't buttoned correctly. She noticed eyes on her shirt, looked down and rebuttoned.

There was a clattering noise as Annie dropped her spoon and got up from the table to hug Maggie Beth, "Oh, there you are! What a relief! I'd feel so guilty if I was the last person to see you and didn't know what happened." Her tone of urgency and relief turned protective then as she added in a lower voice, "Land's sakes! You need a hairbrush and a mirror, Sweet Girl."

Maggie Beth rubbed at her face. "What's going on? What do you mean last person to see me?"

"Am I glad to see you!" I said, giving her a huge hug.

"Uh, good morning to you, too," she said. "What's going on? Why is everyone so weird?" She asked, attempting to smooth out her hair.

Stepping back, I pressed my lips together. I was so relieved to see Maggie Beth it had taken a moment to put the pieces together. It sure looked like Maggie Beth and Shane had gotten snuggly together. Where? The Earth Roamer? It probably had a bed tucked in somewhere, but surely Rebel would have checked the vehicles.

Rebel handed me the unopened aperitif bottle from the previous night. "Sorry we never got into this. Thought you might want it back."

"Thanks," I said, accepting it. "Maybe next time." Who cared. Maggie Beth and Shane were found.

"We got into somethin' else instead," Buster said with a mischievous grin.

I blushed.

Dave tugged at his strained belt and said, "I'm Sheriff David Marshall. Ma'am, are you Magnolia Beth Burgess?"

"I am, why?"

"Some of your friends reported you missing."

"*What?* No! I…uh, we just…I didn't think to tell someone where I was. It was so late--" She looked at Annie, face like a lost puppy in the rain. "Sorry."

"No worries, dear, just glad you're in one piece."

"You really called the *cops?* For *me*?" Maggie Beth asked.

"Ma'am," Dave asked, "Do you know a Fawn Nicole Janus?"

"Fawn who? Oh. Nicole. Is she the one who was doing the yoga classes?"

I nodded.

"Well, I took the yoga class with her yesterday, but I don't really know her," Maggie Beth said. "I need some orange juice and some grits or something. My stomach is growling and I've got a mother of a headache."

Shane, Maggie Beth and Annie moved toward the buffet while Buster pulled me aside and whispered in my ear, "You really need to get locks on your cabins, Haint, if you know what's good for you."

"What? I decided not to. Max went by the honor system for years. I thought— "

Buster stage whispered, "Well, if you don't mind your guests sneaking off and shacking up in an empty cabin, that's yer business, butchyera fool if so."

"*What?*"

Shane, who was getting coffee just behind Buster, said "Sorry about dat," he took a sip and moaned, moving closer to us. "Not bad. Almost as good as home. There is dis place called Da Lab in Lafayette, dey make the most amazing—"

I interrupted, "What is he talking about?"

Shane flashed a con artist smile. "We, ah, kind of ended up in cabin two las' night. Oh. I should mention—tell your *bricoleur* dat blow was wigglin' an' makin' noise."

"*What?*" I asked, thinking "blow" usually meant cocaine, and I didn't know a brick-o-ler.

Rebel said, "He's askin' if you've got a handyman. Your ceiling fan needs lookin' at. It's makin' noise."

Shane glanced at Maggie Beth with amorous eyes. "Dat is some woman." He sighed. "I was checking on de cameras and she was in de woods with the *frissons*—"

"The free-what?" I interrupted.

Shane snapped his fingers looking for a synonym. "I guess you'd say...spooks, chills. She taut she heard someone in da woods besides me and was frightened."

"What was she doing in the woods?" I asked.

"Not for me to say. But we got to talking. Den we heard da music over at da party cabin. What a party! We crashed it. Dat woman can dance! We rocked it 'til she said she was gonna drop. Den we took a walk by da river—"

Rebel joined us with a cup of coffee and a tart. "And ended up in an empty cabin, 'comforting' each other. You are such a player, man."

Buster shook his head. "He likes 'em sturdy."

With Shane's toffee skin tone, it was hard to tell if he were blushing. "I do like some *avoirdupois*," making a gesture suggesting heft. "But I play wid no one. I listen to my heart." He turned to me. "You should get your doors fixed. I can set you up wid touch locks, any style you wan'. I'll show you some options, you jus' pick out *queque chose,*♥ I'll get dem installed, no problem."

Buster said, "You really should. He'll fix you up."

"How? What, you happen to have some locks in your truck? For what, locking up a Sasquatch?"

"Dat'd be a special order, *assez sur,*♥" Shane roared with laughter and looked at Buster.

Buster's snickered, "No, hon, he's got his own company, Security Acadien. Alarm systems, surveillance, gates, door locks. You want locks, he's your man."

Shane roared again, "If you want locks on doors, I am da man. But I'm not lockin' up no Sasquatch, no how!"

Buster wiped a hand over his eyes, looking bemused.

Shane took a moment, pressing his beefy hands to his rib cage. Composing himself, he said, "But yes, *cher,* I can get you all square."

"I'm confused," I said, feeling the gears in my mind grinding like they needed more grease. "You're on the road chasing Skunk Apes and Chupacabras. How do you have time to install burglar alarms?"

♥ from the French, quelque chose. Means "something"

♥ *assez sur*: French = sure enough

They laughed again.

Buster touched my shoulder. "We have other jobs, you know. We don't do this all the time."

"*What*?" This was news to me. I felt some gears in my mind slipping.

"*Non, beb*," Shane said, "I have employees back home dat run my shop while I'm gone, and I keep up with dem." He tapped his phone. "I can run de business from anywhere. I order supplies and monitor installations. I'll be back home next week."

"Oh. I thought you guys did this Bigfoot stuff fulltime. You mean this is just a hobby? A moonlighting gig?"

"Yeah, sort of." Buster said. "Rebel is a re-tarred architect." He dragged the word retired out so long I'd thought he'd said retarded or re-tarred, like tarred and feathered. It took me a second to catch back up to the conversation. "Now he does woodworkin' and commissioned high-end antique repairs. He did all that cool custom work in the Siberian Tiger, all them extra drawers and storage cubbies, the sexy trim stuff."

"Oh!" I said. "I had no idea. I thought you just paid through the nose for that."

"More like bartered."

"Oh?"

"I had an excessive amount of fly-fishing gear. He helped me part with it."

"You fly fish?"

He looked hurt. "I guess Max didn't tell you, did he?"

"Tell me *what*?" I asked with a hint of dread, now worried

that Buster was a bigamist, on a most-wanted list, or a pedophile. But surely Max wouldn't have told me to get my hair done to impress a pedophile or an ex-convict.

"My *main* gig is fly-fishin'. I've got a coupla books published and pop'lar social media channels. Got signature flies for sale online: Buster Luster, Buster BeDazzler and The Buster Beatle, the Disco Dropper, the Cryptid Creeper—I got oodles of 'em."

"Disco Dropper?"

"Hey, it works. Shiny as a disco ball."

"I bet," I said.

"My channels are the real money maker besides fly-fishin' which conveniently, often coincides with my research, especially out west in Oregon or Montana. See, I can set up surveillance equipment, take a group out fishin', come back and check on the monitors, go to supper, give a presentation, then spend an hour or two sittin' in a tree stand watchin' a feed lot. Or go interview witnesses. Doin' stuff I love an' getting' paid for it! Best of all worlds!"

I was flooded with relief. It must have shown.

He squinted at me, "Why? Whadyou *think* I was gonna say?"

"I had no idea. I knew you weren't wearing an ankle bracelet, but that didn't rule out the possibility of a police record, a parole officer on speed dial, or a most-wanted poster with your face on it. And someone overheard you talking on the phone about blue-meanies or some such." I winced. "I was nervous that you might be, um, a drug dealer."

He busted out laughing. "*Drug dealer*? Ha ha! Now that's

nuttier than a squirrel turd. Naw, none o' that! You can even meet my Maw-maw if y'ant-to. You can climb around in the family tree; it goes on and on."

"So long as it keeps forking," I said. "You play the dobro. That's almost a banjo." I did a quick imitation of the beginnings of "Dueling Banjos."♥

Rebel hooted, "She's got ya there!"

Buster jerked in a silent chuckle.

I turned back to Shane. "I've debated about door locks, but then wasn't sure how to deal with keys…if I have a cabin full of people--"

"Easy, *Belle*. No keys. Touch pad." He waggled his fingers. "Combinations you can change any time."

"But isn't that crazy expensive? I've got nine cabins. At three to four hundred dollars a pop, I'm looking at like, $3000, right?"

"Ga-lee non, Beb! You leave it to me. We'll look in da catalog. You pick whad you want, I get you a deal. Fix you right away." He said this in that perpetually flirty voice. I wondered what exactly the deal might entail; he made it sound naughty.

Rose Water staggered into the dining hall wearing pink jammies and sunglasses, looking like the living dead. She paused in the doorway and yawned.

Vida got up to meet her.

♥ Banjo tune made famous in the movie *Deliverance*, associated with backwoods, inbred and scary men.

"Oo-ee! Dat woman don't like da mornin'!" Shane laughed.

"Flyblown by sundown," Rebel chuckled.

"*What*?" I asked.

"It's just an expression," Buster said. "Like she won't live to sundown. He's just joshin'."

"Please, no jokes about people dying, okay?" I asked.

Buster patted my arm.

I walked over to join Vida and Rose. I hoped maybe she knew something about Nicole.

"I don't know," she said. "She was in a hurry to leave the circle last night. I'm not sure why. I think she got a phone call."

"Any idea who from?" I asked.

Rose yawned again. She scrunched her eyes shut as if straining to remember. "No, sorry. I was tired and focused on walking out of the woods. It was a little spooky."

"Did she sound upset?" Vida asked.

Rose scrunched her face again and sighed. "Not upset exactly. Focused? Sorry. Wish I could help more. I wasn't really paying attention."

Buster, Shane and Rebel were bussing their table and heading towards us for the door.

Buster touched my shoulder. "Comin'?"

"Yeah, just a sec."

"I sure hope she shows up," Vida was saying. "We have to be at the Emporium at one o'clock."

"Where are you going?" I asked.

"There's a special class today just for us at the Emporium on soul contracts. We've signed up for readings, too. I don't know what to do if Nicole doesn't show up. And where is Theodora? Please tell me, she's not still sleeping."

"No," Rose said, "She's just feeding Sonny. She's coming."

"Oh, that *bird,*" Vida said. "Well, glad to hear it. Maybe she knows something helpful."

I interrupted, "I'll be back in a few minutes. I'm just going to go—"

To the bat cave? Is that what you were going to say? My Inner Critic sneered.

I let my mouth stumble for words it couldn't find, and my fingers spin like mini-hamster wheels toward the door. "I won't be long. We'll be in the Roamer. If Theodora has any info, or if anyone needs me, please come get me." I said this last loud enough so that most of the group in the dining hall could hear me. Forcing my shoulders to relax, I took a deep breath as I walked out. Iggy's got the yoga class covered. *We'll look at video and it'll reveal what happened. Keep calm.*

I hoped to see Nicole walking toward the dining hall when I stepped outside, but of course that didn't happen. Buster and I were turning toward the Tiger when I noticed Aubrey and Chet coming from cabin eight loosely holding hands. They looked like they'd been up for hours. They were talking softly.

I waited for them. "Good morning, Didn't expect to see you up so early. That was some party last night."

"Morning," they answered in unison.

"Hope we didn't bother anyone," said Chet.

"Don't think so. I know for a fact you had some crashers who had a great time. Great music."

"Thanks!" Chet said.

"What's with the sheriff's car?" Aubrey asked, looking at the squad car parked by my office. "We didn't do any damage last night that I know of." He ran a hand through his hair. "Did we?" He shot a nervous look to Chet.

Chet shook his head. "Don't think so. I know we have to clean up before we leave, but we were going to have breakfast first. I need about a gallon of coffee."

"No, no, it's not about you. Uh, one of the guests is, uh, missing."

"Oh, he just partied too hard last night and is sleeping it off in the bushes somewhere." Chet said with a wink and a wiggle.

"Or maybe got lucky and went home with someone," said Aubrey with a naughty lip curl.

"Yeah, I hope it's nothing. But Nicole was supposed to teach a yoga class this morning. She just disappeared last night. No one's seen her since around midnight."

"Oh, it was Halloween, Girlfriend! She got her witchy goin' on, that's all. Know what I mean?" Chet said.

Lucky guess? I doubted that he knew that she really was a witch.

Chapter 31

Candid Camera in the Bat Cave

Rebel, Shane, Buster, Dave and I were crammed into the command deck of the Bengal Tiger. Ten video screens of various sizes were arranged in a curve in front of us.

Rebel said, "Okay, I've run through it once. At a little after eight, cameras three and four picked up the Wiccan folks movin' into the woods toward the circle. Cameras one and ten picked up intermittent activity of men in the woods but nothing strange. Around ten-thirty camera three, up in the tree by cabin three got nudged by somethin' dark and furry. Think it was a 'coon headin' to the picnic table area there. The camera *was* aimed over cabin three toward the river but won't be much help now; it's aimed at the bathroom and parking lot."

Shane harrumphed. "*Merde, alors!* I had dat ting up dere good."

Rebel said, "Oh, don't go *bahbin* now, Shane. It don't matter. You'll see."

Shane sniffed and crossed his big arms, reminding me of Mr. Clean.

Looking at the cameras, I was amazed at the quality. I had expected grainy, hard to decipher pictures; instead, each view looked crisp and bright as if it was daytime.

Rebel continued, "Really not much to see of interest before about 11 p.m., so I'm gonna start it from there. We've got it set up like a panorama, with the driveway camera one on the far left going around the property counter-clockwise and ending up with camera ten back on the trail almost to the driveway again."

Rebel reminded me of a flight attendant demonstrating the safety features of the plane as he gestured to the images on the cameras.

"Camera two here is on the roof of the first picnic pavilion—it has a great view of the river and the shallow, sandy area on the other side. If anything was goin' to cross the river, that'd be the mos' likely spot. These cameras here are scattered through the central part of the camp, while these two here, cameras eight and nine, are deeper in the woods, over to Ms. Haint's house."

"Someone say, 'roll 'em'," Buster said.

Shane, Rebel and I complied in unison. Dave scowled and reviewed his notes.

"No popcorn?" Shane asked. "*tant pis.*"♥

Dave growled, "Let's get on with it."

Rebel narrated, "Okay, like I said, not much activity 'cept for a couple runs to the john by the group camping off the trail

---

♥ pronounced "tahn-pee" means too bad.

behind the first bathroom facility. But then, a bit after 11 p.m., things pick up. Vehicles start arriving in a steady stream and…well, you'll see."

Rebel shot a quizzical look at me as if to say, "Do you have any idea what goes on at your property?"

Uh-oh. I chewed my lower lip.

A PT Cruiser zipped past camera one. Instead of turning into the parking lot, it turned right, alongside cabin nine.

"Oh!" I said, "That would be Chet and Aubrey coming back from their party at the Co-Op."

Three more cars followed in quick succession and parked in the parking lot.

Motion on camera four got my attention. Two women emerged unsteadily from the laundry shed area heading toward the second parking lot.

I leaned in for a better look. "What the—who—?" My brain was not making sense of what I was seeing.

Rebel chuckled. "Don't think they were doin' laundry." He laughed again. "Unless they were washing clothes with Wild Turkey!"

Annie Woddell overextended her steps in a peculiar crisscross, often turning and bending her torso in laughter. Maggie Beth was an impressive vision. Her filmy, sleeveless floral shirt suggested feminine whimsy while her short denim shorts revealed massive muscular thighs tapering to modest calves before disappearing into heavy socks and clunky sneakers. She wore a thick watchband on one wrist, and several charm bracelets on the other. Her fist was firm on a large clear bottle, mostly empty. Her body language said, "I can lift you from a crushed vehicle like hydraulic rescue machinery and then party like a rock star."

We watched as Maggie moved forward with the determination of a river barge, yet with the special care of the inebriated, wary of a gravity flux. Annie bumped into Maggie Beth and bounced back on course. Maggie Beth did not appear to notice.

Shane leaned in for a closer view. "Dat's Maggie Beth. Mm-mm." His eyes twinkled.

Annie lurched forward, laughing, then righted herself in a corrective twist. She raised a hand to slap Maggie's shoulder, but hesitated as if she couldn't track her target. The hand feinted a hit, hovered, feinted, then wilted and fell to her side. Maggie Beth trod forward hugging the large bottle like a recovered treasure. Maggie Beth put a finger to her mouth in a shushing gesture as she moved off-camera. Annie threw her head back in laughter and lurched out of view behind the bathroom pavilion.

"Which group are they with?" Buster asked.

"They're in the weight-watching group."

"Don't look like they been stickin' to their diet."

Rebel laughed, "Wild Turkey's not on any diet plan I've heard of, but if it is, then that's the diet for me!" He patted his belly.

"No wonder Annie looked a bit rough this morning," I said.

"Oh, dey jus' lettin' off steam, mon," Shane said waving a dismissive hand. "Ain't no big deal." He pointed to the screen. "Besides, dat woman danced her *ass* off when I caught up wid her."

The screens got streaky with fast-forwarded static for a moment.

"This is where it gets interestin'," Rebel said, turning around to look at us for a moment before turning back to the monitors. "Right about…here."

I couldn't believe what I was seeing. As the digital timer on one of the screens flipped to 12:14:46 a.m., two lumbering figures appeared on camera one. Hairy, upright, ape-like creatures. They were the same size and walked with the same stride although both staggered as if tipsy. In two strides they were out of the frame.

I felt as if a long thin icicle had slid down the back of my shirt. "No…way." I managed to say.

Buster crowed, "Hoo-doggie!"

Shane hollered, "Whoo!"

Dave scowled. "You gotta be shitting me. Play that back."

Rebel reversed the frames and the figures strode into view again. Two Bigfoots…or is it Bigfeet? Two cryptids strolling down the driveway, doo-dee-doo-dee-doo.

I grabbed the back of Rebel's chair to steady myself. It couldn't be. I thought about the deer carcass that had disappeared and all the weird noises in the woods lately. No. Not possible.

Go ahead, Moon Eyes! Explain that! my Inner Critic whispered.

Buster ran a hand through his fluffy hair and asked, "Do we see them again?"

Rebel glanced at his logbook and answered, "Wait for

it…wait for it…now!"

Camera ten, located beyond the first pavilion, was apparently equipped with sound recording capability. Muffled sounds like footsteps through dry leaves grew louder followed by rising yips.

"Wookie! Yii!" the one on the left called out.

"What the hell?" Dave asked.

The view of the trail was momentarily obscured by hairy midsections that passed out of frame followed by more noises, *"Yiii! Yiii! Mo-mo! Mo-mo!"*

Buster eyebrows rose in amusement. "Vocalizations. Nice! Any knocking?"

Rebel answered, "Yeah. Later on."

Buster nodded.

Shane shook his head, "Ga-lee."

They seemed so ho-hum about this, like it was no big deal, just another day with big hairy creatures stomping around in my retreat. Before I could ask, camera nine picked up a conversation.

"D'you hear that?"

"Sounded like it was right here."

"That weren't no night bird I've heard of."

"Nope. Cain't say I've heard that neither."

The camera was obscured again by a body in jeans and a camouflage pattern shirt, hands on hips just above a loaded utility belt. I couldn't tell what all the pouches and snapped leather sheaves were for, but the large knife and small axe were eye-catchers.

The man moved; we were once again looking at the trail. A flashlight beam tracked across the ground and the trees.

"Huh. Weird."

"Yeah. I gotta take a piss. Back in a sec."

"Yeah, okay."

The flashlight beam wobbled out of view as footsteps receded.

"Wait! Stop! You can't be serious!" I said. "You're telling me two Bigfoot or Bigfeet or whatever wandered into the camp and just missed getting seen by the preppers by the bathroom? Right past a huge party going on in cabin nine? No way!"

"Hang on, *bebe,*" Shane said, "keep watchin'."

Dave's face was twisted in disbelief. He shifted his weight back and forth.

We watched a parade of vehicles enter the retreat. The first parking lot filled up and drivers began parking near camera one, along the road and wherever they could find a spot.

A two-tone silver and gray Subaru Baja drove in, slowed and moved out of view.

"Wait. Back that up, can you?" I asked.

"Sure."

Rebel re-ran the feed and the Baja drove by again.

An uncomfortable feeling settled on me as if an invisible enemy had draped a shawl over my shoulders. "I know that car," I said. "Come on brain, think. Who drives that car?"

Dave and Buster looked at me expectantly.

I struggled but couldn't remember. "Keep going, I guess, it'll come to me."

Rebel hit the fast-forward button. In a moment, there was a flash of movement on camera six.

"What was that?" Buster asked.

"Dogs," Rebel said.

There was a blip of movement on camera eight.

Before we could ask, Rebel said, "Three deer heading to Haint's property."

"Runnin' from de dogs," Shane said.

"What kind of dogs? Hounds?" I asked.

"Yep. Bloodhounds. Two of 'em." Rebel nodded.

"Ah. That would be the Oakeys' new dogs, Waylon and Willie," I said.

Buster , "I like it."

Rebel asked, "They got new dogs?"

Dave shifted his weight again and flipped through his notes. He looked at the time on the video. "Twelve-thirty-five. Ha. Right around this time Mrs. Vida Glossimer reports they were packing it in. Magic time over. Claims she saw a tall man 'to the north' watching her from the trail entrance over there near camera six. Claims she thought it was the spirit of the 'Horned God'." He chuckled and rolled his eyes. "Wonder what they were smokin'."

Two hairy forms moved left to right along the path in front of camera seven. One stopped to pick up a thick branch. He thwacked it into his other hand like a baseball player checking the feel of the bat. He even swung it like a bat, hitting a small hickory tree. The other creature jumped up, grabbed a low branch, yanked it down and broke it at the base, leaving it dangling. The first creature hit the tree again.

"What the hell?" asked Dave.

Buster nodded.

Shane laughed, "That's great."

"What are they *doing*?" I asked.

Buster chuckled. "Oh, Bigfoot are known for making marks, breaking limbs, pushing down saplings--leaving a trail for fellow Bigfoot to follow."

"Yeah, right. And the batting practice?" Dave asked.

"Like a-ohls hollerin' to each other. Bigfoot can communicate by 'knockin' on trees," Buster explained.

I got lost in his vowely accent. It took me a sec to realize he'd said "owls". Something was off. Why weren't they reacting as if they had sacred footage of a "sighting"? "You guys don't seem excited about this 'evidence'," I said.

"Oh, no, this is great," Shane said with the excitement of a redneck about to say, "Y'all watch this".

"Something is up. Spill," I said.

"Hang on, let's see what else happens," Buster said, patting my shoulder.

Distracted by his warm hand, still struggling to make the Baja connection, I played the alphabet game. This often works for me, where a name or word will pop up with the sound of the first letter. I began, "A…Adam, Art, Arnold, Alan, Alvin, Abe, Agnes, Abigail, Anne, Asa…nope. B…Bob," I shuddered recalling the moment I found Bob my yard man dead in the shrubbery the previous month. "Bart, Betty, Brad, Ben, Bill, Bo, Bubba, Barbara, Barney, Burt, Benson, Baxter…Badger! It's

Badger!"

I must have resembled an excited game show contestant, the way I bounced out of my seat and flapped my arms. The men all looked mightily amused and oblivious to my dread. They did not seem to understand that Badger had no business being on the property. Granted, my trepidation regarding him was all based on a gut feeling. A bad one.

"But he wasn't a guest. He shouldn't be there," I said, pointing to the video screen.

Dave asked, "You're sure it's Badger?"

"Yes. Badger drives a two-tone Baja." I didn't want to confess that I knew this because Badger, of all people, drove a car that I coveted. Sadly, Subaru stopped making this half-truck half beach buggy model in 2006. I'd love to have one.

Dave's whole demeanor shifted from agitated and concerned to elation, like a poker player who just pulled four aces and can't wait for his turn. "Interesting," he said, shifting his weight side to side.

"Why?" Buster and I asked in unison.

"Oh, nothing," he said to the back of Buster's chair. "I was just thinking."

A boisterous group of women came into view from beyond cabin seven and boogied toward the dock. They seemed to be in high spirits, dancing, laughing, swaying, pawing at each other, some getting their high heels caught in the soft ground. Some waved flashlights, some twirled glow sticks.

"Who are they?" Dave asked. "The woman in front there looks familiar-- she's beautiful."

"Well, they aren't really women…" I said. "They're some

of the group from the party in cabin nine."

"Not women? Of course they're women." Dave leaned forward to study the screen.

"Well, that's not Beyoncé," I said. "That's a man in drag."

Dave recoiled from the screen and glared at me.

"God, they better not try to go jumping off the dock," I said, "It's too shallow."

"Nope," Rebel said.

"Oh, thank goodness and Greta Garbo," I said.

Dave continued to scowl.

A similar wave of partiers followed the first group, also dancing, swinging flashlights, beer, and champagne bottles. Soon, the dock was full; the overflow crowded along the bank.

There was a flash on camera three. Rebel backed it up and slowed it down.

"Hard to tell, but someone was jogging toward the circle. Can't see the whole body, but that's definitely a male."

There was a flash on camera six, something blurred left to right.

"It's the dogs again, but watch what happens next," Rebel said.

We watched as two hairy figures lumbered left to right.

"The Bigfoots are hunting the dogs?" I asked.

"Not exactly," Rebel said.

Two figures emerged on the trail in front of camera four, moving quickly along the path. One was very slight with almost no hair.

"That's Nicole!" I said. "I think that's Badger with her!"

Dave stiffened, "Rewind."

Rebel said, "No need—they get picked up on camera three."

"Is he kidnapping her?" I asked, looking for any signs of coercion. They were walking side by side. Badger did not seem to be threatening her, touching her or holding a weapon.

A few seconds after they disappeared from camera four, camera three picked them up moving toward the parking lot.

"She's walking of her own free will," Dave said.

They were moving quickly but there was no indication of reluctance or stress in Nicole's body language. Eagerness, in fact. She was keeping pace with Badger.

"Do they know each other?" I asked, my brain struggling with perky Nicole and shady Badger having any kind of relationship.

A moment later, the Baja drove passed camera one, leaving the camp. Meanwhile camera two revealed fireworks being launched from the dock.

"Okay, well, now we know how she left." Dave said, exhaling and shifting towards the door. "I'll track Badger down. Uh, thanks. This was…helpful."

"You might want to see the rest of this," Rebel said. "Won't take much longer."

Chapter 32

Evidence

Boo Nutterberg and Rose Water appeared on camera three, Boo wearing a backpack and carrying a small duffel bag, and Rose carrying a large woven basket. Moments later they passed camera three heading toward their cabin. A dog sped past camera three but circled back again.

And then the two Bigfoots lumbered into view, each hunched, holding a dog by its collar. One of the Bigfoots was limping.

"Wait a minute, that's Urliss and Hollis!" I exclaimed. "What in the world?"

"*Urliss and Hollis*?" Dave asked.

I looked at the three amigos and they regarded me with amusement.

"You knew all along, didn't you?" I asked.

"*Bien sûr,*" Shane said.

"Why didn't you tell me?"

"I thought you already got that biscuit," Buster said.

"I don't get it. What's going on?"

Buster patted my knee, "The short answer's this. When we came here to Catfish the first time, ol' Max and Charlene got to be like kin, just like our me-maw and paw-paw. We took to each other. But ol' Max had some fun with us, settin' up 'evidence' in the woods for us to find like a big ol' Easter egg hunt." He paused, clearly going back in his mind to that time. The way he'd drawled out "egg" rhymed with "plague". He turned his palms up as if revealing evidence, "It got to be a game-like, we'd pretend to get all excited 'bout his "evidence" and he could hardly contain hisself for thinkin' he was pullin' one on us."

"You knew the whole time," I said.

"Yup."

Rebel added, "We come every year 'cause it's centrally located, and it's fun to play him along."

"So, Urliss and Hollis are in on it with him."

"Oh, yeah. If you look, you'll find bits of hair, dog poop disguised as Bigfoot scat, and obvious tree damage all over your retreat. "

"What?" I remembered the other day when I thought I'd seen Max in their truck recently coming out of the retreat. They'd been planting evidence. Now that I let that sink in for a minute, it all made sense. Max reveled in talking about Buster and his team with the same kind of childish delight that kids get telling fart jokes. I thought it was because he thought they were nuts. I had no idea he and the Oakey twins were pranking them. "They're like a bunch of kids! And you all play along! But wait…what about the deer carcass? They didn't take that

away too. They didn't know about that."

"Coulda been a coyote or a bobcat," Buster said.

"I guess..."

Rebel fast forwarded again. "This is interesting. Right about... here." He released the fast forward and pointed to camera five. "Listen. Kinda sounds like that white screamer from Tennesssee or somethin'."

There was a slow, rising cry ending in an eerie cackle. Then silence, then it repeated. *MooooooOOOAAHH -ha-ha-ha*!

I looked at the others in disbelief. "What was *that*?"

"Dat's too moany for da screamer," Shane said.

"No skunk ape, neither," Buster said.

"That sounded like a ghost from a bad movie," I said. "The laugh at the end. Super creepy."

"We can come back to that later," Buster said. "What else?"

There was a burst of light as a more elaborate firework showered down in camera two. Sparklers and glow sticks bobbed in the crowd along the river's edge. Two entwined people moved away from the others toward the camera. I did not recognize the lovers who revolved around each other in a slow dance of passionate kissing. They disappeared from view under the camera.

Vida and Theadora appeared on camera four, walking slowly out of the woods. Vida had a large beach bag over her shoulder; Theadora carried a large box. Within moments they were on camera three heading toward cabin four.

"What am I seeing on that woman's shoulder?" Dave asked, pointing.

Sonny was tucked up next to Theadora's ear; it looked like he'd tucked his head into his plumage. Maybe he was asleep. "It's her bird, an African grey."

Dave rolled his eyes and moved to the door. "I've seen quite enough." He left, letting the door bang shut.

The loud noise made me jump.

"You're welcome," Rebel nodded to the vacated space. "Glad we could help."

I felt like apologizing for Dave's unfriendly behavior but reminded myself that I had no control over his actions.

"So, Bigfoot mystery solved," I said. "Badger and Nicole...I don't like it. He's twice her age. They *can't* be dating."

"Sher-uff Dave'll sort it out, hon," Buster said, pulling me into a hug.

"There they go," Rebel said, pointing to camera one. "The dogs got loose and followed them over here."

I watched with disbelief as two ape men walked out of the Lotus Lodge Retreat, each hunched over with a hairy paw holding a dog by the collar. I pulled myself out of my thoughts and looked at the digital clock showing real time. "Yikes! I've got to get lunch ready."

Just as I was getting up to leave, there was motion on camera nine.

"What was that?" I asked, pointing.

Rebel hit rewind. Something bulky and hairy crossed in front of the camera, so close it was just a hairy blur. Hard to know whether it was a leg and hip or a midsection.

Shane and Buster leaned forward.

"Again," Buster gestured.

"Well ain't that som'in'," Rebel said. "How high up didja mount that camera, Shane?"

Shane held a hand level to his chest. "'Bout like dis."

"That sure weren't no deer," Buster said. "Do it again, slow."

We watched as once again, a mass of fur moved right to left.

"Way too high for skunk," Shane said. "Bear?"

"Oh, come on, we don't have bears around here in Alachua County," I said trying to sound more confident than I felt.

Rebel swung around to look at me, "The hell you don't! With all due respect, I don't think you keep up with local news, or you'da heard that there are black bears from Payne's Prairie gettin' into Barr Preserve...that's just south of Gainesville. There's even been a bear spotted in oh...what's the name of that place? Somethin' Plantation?"

"Haile?" I asked. "That's a very restrictive community. They wouldn't allow bears in there. They don't even allow pick-up trucks."

Shane raised his head like a snake readying a strike. "Dare was da report right north of Gainesville in Turkey Creek too. Bear walkin' da golf course."

"Ha! Wonder what his handicap was. What hole was he playin'?" Rebel asked.

I felt stupid. I'd not heard these reports, but then again, I'd been caught up in renovation world for a while.

There was a gleam in Buster's eyes as he said, "I think we

need to have a look at the area around camera nine."

"You think it was a bear?" I asked.

Buster raised an eyebrow. "Won't know what I think 'til I have a look-see."

I shook my head in disbelief. "Wa—wa--wait. *Hell-o,* boys. We just saw Urliss and Hollis walking out of the camp. You said you've known for years that Max is in on planting evidence. So, isn't that probably Max?"

Buster leaned back and closed one eye, as if looking at me through a telescope. "How tall you reckon ol' Max is?"

"Oh, I dunno. Five foot ten or five-eleven, tops."

"Right," Buster said, "I'm six-one. If the camera is mounted about here on me, what'dya reckon you'd see on Max?"

"Well, that would depend on how close or far away he was…it was really hard to see."

"It was close an' blurry. Judgin' by the width on it, I'd say we saw the top of a leg, possibly a hip, not chest or shoulders," Buster said with authority.

I had to admit I couldn't quite picture Max romping around the woods in the wee hours, in the dark, in a big hairy suit. He *was* too short and too frail.

Shane asked, "Have you been hearin' any-ting strange at night?"

Mid-shrug I remembered the banshee sounds. "Actually, yeah. The other night. Something was in the back yard, scared the hell out of me. Sounded like a giant cat in heat or Scottish banshee…that is, what I'd guess a banshee would sound like."

All three men were looking at me now.

"What direction d'it travel in?" Buster asked.

Closing my eyes for recall, the image of NB and me at the door facing the back yard came back.

"Away from the house, away from Urliss's…into the woods, towards the river."

"Reb," Buster said, "You got that recording from last summer in Arkansas handy?"

"Sure, just a sec."

Rebel tapped on a computer keyboard, clicked a few times and suddenly a loud call reverberated in the Tiger. *"Aiyaah! Aiii-ahh!"*

The same adrenaline shimmy moved around my body. "That's it! That's what it sounded like," I said, hugging myself.

"Cho Co!" Shane exclaimed.

Rebel began talk singing, "No one knows where the Skunk Ape goes…"

I felt a ripple of energy pass between the men as Rebel stood up and Shane and Buster began gathering gear.

"Is that a real song?" I asked.

"Oh yes, a classic by a feller name o' Lenny Green," replied Rebel. "Darn it, I've forgot most o' the words."

Buster touched my elbow, guiding me to the door. "Go on and get lunch goin' for your guests. We'll be along in a while, but don't wait on us or nothin'."

The recordings were still running behind Buster's head. Movement on camera three distracted me.

"What was that?" I asked.

Rebel chuckled and punched Shane. "Oh, a beast alright. A

horny one!"

Rebel moved back to sit down and punched a button. The scene on camera three revealed two pairs of legs walking together. One set was bare legs like tree trunks stuffed into clunky sneakers, the other was black pants and black boots, both moving with purpose around the corner of the bathroom pavilion. They separated briefly as bare legs ducked in to use the facilities. Black boots waited, dancing.

"The boy's got moves," Buster said.

"Could still hear da party, mon." Shane said. "Couldn't hep mesef."

Bare legs joined dancing feet and they moved out of view by cabin three.

I glanced down at Shane's footwear. Black boots.

"We'll talk about locks, you bet," Shane said, patting my shoulder. "If I order 'em today, I can install 'em by Tuesday."

Buster shook his head. "Great salesman, ain't he? Shows ya how he breaks in then sells ya the locks."

They really had snuck into cabin two. Holy cow.

Buster's lips brushed mine. "We're gonna check this out. A'right?" I leaned forward to kiss him back but kissed air. He had already turned and grabbed a clipboard thick with paper, Shane and Rebel pushed past him, grabbing gear.

I let myself out and walked across the parking lot in a state of bewilderment. So much sneaking around last night! Shane running off with Maggie Beth. Good grief! What on earth was going on between Nicole and Badger? And what was that thing the camera had picked up? Surely not a Skunk Ape. Ridiculous. A bear then? In my back yard? Great.

Chapter 33

Closure

Lunch was ready to go by the time Iggy, Louise and the ladies from the Wiccan group and Take It Off stormed the dining hall after the yoga class like a hungry, conquering horde.

"How'd it go?" I asked Iggy.

"Great!" Iggy said. "A fun bunch. Mostly beginners, but they did well."

"Iggy was terrific," cooed Serena, "he's a great teacher," she said picking up a plate. Holding it vertically with one hand, she absently traced the plate rim with a forefinger as her eyes moved over Iggy.

Louise stepped closer to Iggy, "Yes, he's very patient and careful to make sure the students don't get themselves hurt." She picked up a fork and clenched it as if considering driving it into Serena's slippery face.

Boo said, "It was great. I've never had a male yoga teacher before." Her face sagged, "Sure wish we knew where Nicole is."

Theadora said, "He was terrific. I've had some young teachers who just move to fast for an old lady like me. He was very understanding."

"Thank you, ma'am," Iggy said.

"Theadora, please," she said.

"Wow. Lunch looks great, Sis," Iggy said, eyeing the black bean burgers and Brussel sprout salad.

"Optional bacon bits and cashews are there on the side," I said pointing to the small bowls next to the salad.

"It sure does," Maggie Beth said, coming up behind her. "I'm starving. You haven't heard anything about Nicole yet?"

"Not yet," I said.

Just then the door opened, and Dave barreled in, followed by Nicole, Badger and a very pregnant Running Deer. And Badger was holding Nicole's hand.

I gasped. He was almost twice her age!

Louise dropped her plate. Plate shards, salad and bean burger went flying.

Looking up from the mess on the floor and Maggie Beth's shoes, I saw all the blood drain from Iggy's face.

"Running Deer?" he said.

Nicole rushed toward me, "I'm so sorry I couldn't call you; we were out in the country with no phone reception and—"

"Running Deer?" Louise asked, gaping at the slight woman's huge belly.

In a moment straight from a French farce, we stood in a wobbly circle staring at each other, avoiding a big mess on the floor.

Nicole was still babbling apologies about not showing up for the yoga class.

Dave's deputy Anson entered followed by some of the Burlie Boys. The dining hall was getting crowded with people standing around looking on.

Dave, with his arms crossed over his burly chest and looking like a caricature of a country sheriff, gave Iggy the stink-eye and muttered, "Looks like someone ate before saying grace." His eyes rolled to Running Deer's stomach.

Badger scowled, "No, you've got it all wrong—"

Louise looked like she wanted to disappear into the floor. "I..." she faltered, "I'll just leave..."

"No," Iggy said, putting a hand on her arm.

Vida stepped into the fray, "Nicole, where have you been? We were worried sick—you just left like that without—"

Theadora added, "I'm just relieved you are safe, Honey."

"I know! I'm so sorry. It was—" she looked to Running Deer and then to Badger. "My mom, I mean, our mom."

Running Deer looked at her with a melancholy smile.

Meanwhile, a Greek chorus of murmuring from the preppers, Take It Off and Burlie Boys echoed around the room.

"What's going on?"

"Who are they?"

"Who's the pregnant lady?"

"Whoa, is someone getting arrested?"

"Is that Badger with that young girl?"

"Okay, okay! Hold it!" I blurted. "I need to clean this mess off the floor before someone slides through it and busts a hip.

Why don't you all go find a table and we'll hash this out. I for one, want to know everything."

A few calmer moments later, the story unfolded. We were all gathered around a table. Maggie Beth had cleaned off her shoes and sat at the next table, working over her bean burger.

"Badger found me at the circle last night," Nicole began.

"As you know, Iggy," Running Deer interrupted, "Mother was dying. Badger was with her when she got fitful and agitated."

Badger interrupted, "She confessed to me that she'd had a secret child that she gave up for adoption about twenty years ago. She'd always felt guilty about giving her up, but at the time, it seemed like the only choice. As she was dying, she had horrible dreams. She begged me to find the girl so she could ask her forgiveness."

"There wasn't much time," Nicole said. "Badger came to get me and explained it all on the way. My birth mother was bedridden out in Bell. There's a huge reception black hole out there. I lost my my mojo bag somewhere in the woods. I'd put my phone in it. We tried to text with Badger's phone but couldn't get reception. And there was so much going on, we kind of forgot. We were all there when she passed this morning." She looked to Badger and Running Deer. "I had no idea I had half-siblings or that my birth mother was so close by."

Badger said, "When I could finally get a signal, I saw that Dave, I mean, uh, Officer Marshall had texted me a bunch. So, we brought Nicole back. I'm sorry it looked like a kidnapping."

"When we saw it was you on the surveillance video--"

Dave began.

"What surveillance?" several people asked in unison.

"Well, I knew kidnapping was unlikely," Dave said, not explaining.

Dave, Iggy and Badger were exchanging knowing looks that I didn't understand.

I looked from one to another of them. Only Iggy would meet my eye and he deferred to Badger.

"What?" I asked. "There's something you're not saying."

Iggy said to Badger, "You might have to tell."

"Tell WHAT?" I asked. "I'm so done with secrets!"

"Yeah. Just don't go telling everyone. I'm a U.S. Marshall. I do witness protection."

Iggy said, "That's why he comes and goes. He relocates people all over the world."

Dave said, "That's why when I saw it was Badger, I backed off. He might have been working a case."

My brain did the weirdest thing just then. In the early days of computers, an operator had to load the machine with punch cards. The stack of punch cards I had on file in my vintage mind began to resort themselves. The ones relating to Badger shuffled. What did I know about him? He was buff, didn't talk much, hung out at the dojo, was friends with Joe Chow, knew martial arts. Was absent for weeks at a time. I'd thought he was shifty. Possibly a felon. At best a ne'er-do-well surfer of friends' couches. The cards settled. He was a highly paid, highly trained, bodyguard. Not a shifty drifter. He was a highly skilled and secretive Federal agent. Holy film noir and Ida Lupino!

Running Deer put a hand on Nicole's shoulder. Seeing them side by side, I realized who Nicole reminded me of—Running Deer! Yes! That's why she'd looked so familiar. Another small mystery solved.

"Okay, so let me get this all sorted in my head," I said, pressing my fingers to my forehead. "I feel like there's still something that we left out. The Bigfoot sounds were Urliss and Hollis traipsing around in fur suits. But something moved past that one camera that couldn't have been them because they were spotted elsewhere, right? So, what was that?"

The three men shared a look. Finally, Rebel said, "We aren't sure."

"And all of the weird noises were Urliss and Hollis, right?"

Rebel scratched his head. "Well, there was that last one. The creepy one you commented on, sounded like a horror movie laugh. Don't know what that was."

Nicole's face lit up, "Did it sound like this? She leaned back, hands on her hips and let loose a shuddersome laugh, exactly like what we'd heard. "MoooooOOOAAHH -ha-ha-ha!"

We all answered in unison, "Yes!"

"But it couldn't have been you, you'd left already," I said. "Oh, my head hurts. I'm so confused."

"It wasn't me," she said laughing, "it was Sonny, the bird!"

Dave looked at his watch and grumbled, "I've got a game to watch and some beer to drink. Anson, thanks for your help. You are free to go." He nodded to just about everyone while not acknowledging me.

I followed them outside. "Thank you for coming."

Dave got into his vehicle, gunned his engine and shot out of the parking lot. As Anson was getting in his car, he waved to me with a distracted, "See you, Ms. Haint."

"Are you okay, Anson? You look a bit peaky."

"Aw, no ma'am, I'm just puzzled," he said, scratching his head. His forehead seemed weighted down by the effort of his thoughts. "I was just thinking over my interviews. Here I was asking them about where they were and what they were doing, and they kept asking *me* questions like if I liked track lighting or if I loved the Oscars. One guy asked me about how I wanted my groceries delivered." He shrugged. "Nice bunch though."

"Yes, they are." I said, as he closed his door. I suppressed a smile. The Burlie Boys had been using code to see if Anson was available and it had swooshed over his head like an F-16.

I watched him drive away relieved that the long arm of the law would no longer be reaching into my camp.

Afternoon and Evening

After all the excitement, the rest of the day was blissful. The Burlie Boys checked out. Chet and Aubrey thanked me for a terrific time and promised to give The Lotus Lodge rave reviews on social network. My fears that the partiers would trash my cabins were unfounded. All was in order, the trash even bagged neatly on the porch.

The Gators crushed the University of Georgia in a game that was exciting even for a non-football person like me. Dinner was easy. The Take It Off ladies minus Prudence enjoyed Nicole's yoga class then went off to Lake City to go bowling. The Wiccans enjoyed their soul class at the Emporium and were making kitchen witch dolls in the evening.

Rebel and Shane were crashing in on the prepper's evening plans and Buster and I had the evening all to ourselves. The hesitation and self-checking of the previous evening was gone. I felt relaxed, safe, wanted and buzzy with new love.

We went to bed early.

Sleep came much later.

Felicific Fall Back Sunday

Word of the Day: Felicific [fee-*luh*-**sif**-ik]
Adj: causing happiness.

What an extra gift after such a strange week to have Fall Back Sunday. It was dreamy to open one eye, see the clock and not have to leap up to go make breakfast at the retreat. I moaned in contentment and spooned against Buster.

"Woman? Izzat you lickin' my toes?" he drawled.

"Hmm-Mmm," I answered in the negative.

"It's the weirdest damn thing," Buster continued in a sleepy voice, "someone's lickin' my toes on the right foot an' I've lost the feelin' in mah left leg. Sugar, I'm havin' a most peculiar kind of stroke."

I rolled over and opened an eye. Mischief was asleep on the back of Buster's knee and NB was licking his toes as if he'd stepped in a can of high-grade dog food.

"Welcome to my world," I said and kissed him on the forehead.

"I like your world except when you find yo'self wakin' up to the sheriff bangin' on the door."

He cradled his head on one arm and traced his fingers over my shoulder and back. "Haint Blue. You are quite somethin'. I hoped but never really—" He didn't finish the thought. His magnetic hazel eyes were deep with emotion. "Izzat your real name? Haint?"

"No. You just slept with Helena Bluszczski."

"Are you a Russian spy?"

"No, I just have a last name that most folks find unpronounceable. How about you? Were you born Buster?"

"No. You just spent the night with George Burgwyn Shadetree the Second."

"Oh my. Sounds like landed gentry."

"I'as named after ma great-great uncle George Burgwyn. He was a Brigadier General. My dad always called me Buster. It stuck."

"Can we just stay here forever?" I asked.

"Mmm-Hmmm. Got no choice. Cain't move mah leg, no how," Buster said, kissing me back.

"I'm not ready for you to leave today, George Burgwyn." I said.

"Well, 'ats good. Shane's gotta install them locks and they won't come 'til tomorrow.

"Do I get you all day today? What have you boys got planned?"

"We'll see."

Once Mischief was convinced to relocate, Buster proved that he could move just fine. Just fine indeed.

Consequently, we were a bit late getting to the dining hall. When we arrived, Jim had the day's agenda on the whiteboard.

Communications

- ✓ Radio options
  - ★ FRS, MURS, VHF, HAM
- ✓ Gunshot/air horn/knocking/whistles
- ✓ Visual --flares
  -mirrors
  -gestures

Essential Ditch Medicine

- ✓ **Likely scenarios**
- ✓ **Essential supplies**
- ✓ **Makeshift supplies**

"Hey, sorry I'm a bit late, I'll have breakfast going in a sec," I said, beginning the usual routine. The breakfast buffet was coming together. I was just setting out bacon when Prudence rushed in.

"I've got to dash. I'll just grab a smoothie and some coffee. Ooh! Is that bacon? I'll take some of that too. Today's the Harvest Festival at church. I'm late."

I poured her a smoothie in a to go cup.

"Thank you, Haint. We had a successful event here. And it's quite pretty and relaxing. I'm so glad that your missing person wasn't missing. I don't often see Dave in his professional capacity. It seemed so strange him asking me questions just like on a television program! Kind of exciting. Anyway, must dash, but the ladies all had a good time and I think I even lost a pound!"

"Well thank *you* for choosing the Lotus Lodge, Prudence. It means a lot." I countered. "I hope your Harvest Festival is a success, too. Here, let's put all that in a bag. Make it easier."

"Oh, thanks. I know it will be," Prudence said, allowing me to bag her breakfast. "Bye now!" she said, backing out the door.

Julie was tidying the mini bookstore. A pale blue book with a skull and a yin/yang symbol caught my attention. It was called, *The Tao of Survival* by James Morgan Ayres♥—a slim volume, subtitled, *Skills to Keep You Alive*. I liked the feel of the paper cover and began flipping through it.

Julie glanced over and said, "You might like that one, it's got a lot about how the art of survival is mental. Since you're a Buddhist, you might like it. There's even a chapter on self-healing by way of visualization."

"Oh?" I flipped through with care. There were lots of short exercises for being more aware of your surroundings, honing your senses, even managing pain.

"It's my favorite book; I take it everywhere and do the exercises. You know, survival doesn't always have to be about dire situations. It's about being present in whatever circumstances...like reading people, noticing exits, even super simple stuff like checking your gas gauge and rearview mirror more often."

♥published by Gibbs Smith 2013

"Huh. I lingered over a section called "Tao Space" that talked about centering attention…sitting space…standing space...breathing space. "How much is it?" I asked.

Julie smiled. "Please take it. My gift to you for having us."

"Really? I don't mind paying for it. I mean, this is a bookstore, right?" Below the promotional comments on the back jacket, the price was listed as $18.99.

"Really. This was a great weekend. We had a great time."

"Well, thanks," I said, "I'm touched. This is the first gift I've ever received from a guest."

And I'll bet you never guessed the first gift would be a prepper guide, did you? chortled the Inner Critic.

I realized that my ideas about the preppers had gone from wary and skeptical towards acceptance. Their focus on dire possibilities made me uneasy but on the flip side, they had skills and plans, unlike the younger generations that seemed to only have cyber skills but couldn't cook or sew a button.

We all have our niches, don't we?

Soon I was hugging my guests goodbye and watching the parking lot empty out. Serena's theatrical departure of Marilyn Monroe waves and blown kisses was marred by the lack of paparazzi vying to photograph her; Maggie Beth and Shane shared a long hug and goodbye kiss; Theadora hugged me with a whispered, "Be well, Honey, and good luck with that Scorpio"; Sonny shrieked, "See ya, Toots!" and "Let's ride!"

Nicole apologized repeatedly for the missing persons drama.

"Oh, don't sweat it! It's fine. No harm done and you got to meet your real mom and find out you have siblings!" I said hugging her.

"I'm getting certified in yoga nidra. Please call me anytime you need a yoga teacher, I'd be more than happy to come."

"That'd be terrific, I will." I had only a vague idea of what yoga nidra was, but with Lorraine out of commission for some time, this was great news.

"You are very understanding," she said, closing her car door and firing up the purple Element.

The preppers were the last to check out. I still couldn't get their names right, but they all expressed that they'd had a great experience. The Calhouns weren't huggy people but they thanked me profusely and said they enjoyed their retreat and that they'd book with me again perhaps in the spring.

The cryptozoologists were the last guests remaining. I had assumed they go galivanting off somewhere and I'd spend the afternoon cleaning cabins. I was wrong. They found me cleaning the kitchen and insisted that we all had to go to the Suwannee River State Park for a late picnic. It was dog friendly. I could bring NB. We spent the rest of the day and evening in Live Oak. They treated me to dinner at an outdoor café. It was a welcomed indulgence after the long weekend.

Buster came home with me that night. Our last night together. I tried not to think about the future. When would we see each other again? Seeing him stretched out naked in my bed wearing only the dvarapala necklace that I'd given him and a bit of covers, he looked like a page from a sexy, rugged men calendar. It hadn't occurred to me that the little guardian dude figure was protecting his heart as well as his body. Buster's eyes were dark with emotion as he patted my bed inviting me to join him. I was wearing a black, antique silk kimono. I imagined that my luminous white skin would contrast dramatically with the black. I sank into his embrace. His generous kisses became urgent and exploratory, heading down my neck. I straddled him, covering both of us in the thin silk. The jumble of thoughts in my head vanished like ghosts as he said with a husky whisper, "Oh, my magical Moon Eyes, come here you. I been waitin' all day for this." And oh yes, there was magic.

We'd all agreed on a late and leisurely breakfast Monday morning. The men were quiet as they attacked their waffles and sausage. Buster leaned back and asked Shane, "Did your nightly visitor make an appearance las' night?"

Shane swallowed and pointed his fork at Buster, "A man should neva kiss and tell. But yes, she did come."

"It's true," Rebel said. "I saw her meself, standing by his bed. He told her very gentlemanly like that she needed to go on to the white light. She's beautiful, but I sure had a hard time sleepin' after that. She skeered me half to death. I don't know how you do it, man."

Shane shrugged. "Guess I'm used to it."

A delivery truck rolled into the retreat shortly after breakfast with a large package for Shane. The men disappeared to install locks and collect their cameras while NB and I cleaned cabins. In what seemed like no time, Shane was handing over a booklet.

"And here are the instructions about how to set the codes.

Do NOT lose this."

"How much do I owe you?" I asked.

"*Phhppphh*!" exploded Shane. "It's no-ting."

"Oh, come on, I can't let you—"

"*Cher bebe*," Shane said, flaring his eyes. "There is no discussion here. It's nothing. Trust me. I write it off." He demonstrated how easy the lock was.

"I can't thank you enough. I was resistant, but this is super. I'll feel better and so will my guests." I gave Shane and Rebel big hugs and thanked them for the locks, the food and the great company.

"I can't believe Max kept you all to himself for so long. Wish I'd met you years ago."

"Me too, Honey, me too," Buster said, sweeping me into a hug. "You know, in many cultures, they don't even have an expression for goodbye, they just say until next time."

"Mmm-hmm." I mumbled into his neck.

There was so much I wanted to say, to ask, but I knew if I started talking, it would come out as nonsensical babble. I stepped back and watched him get into the driver's seat of the Roamer. I was torn between envy for his adventures and a clinginess wishing he could stay.

In my wildest dreams, I'd never pictured myself getting misty while waving goodbye to three cryptozoologists. Shane was heading back to New Orleans. Buster and Rebel were driving out to Washington to a Sasquatch Summit in Ocean Shores, Washington.

I stood in the driveway waving until they were out of sight.

Chapter 34

Tuesday's Scatology Lesson

What a weekend! With all the guests gone, a down day with no agenda was welcomed. I slept in, wrote in my journal and didn't even change out of my pajamas until afternoon. NB and I went for a long walk over to the retreat and back, ending up at my own meditation circle. Tying Naughty Britches' leash to a tree and telling her to stay, I began walking the circle.

Like its counterpart next door, my meditation circle is incomplete, mapped out with sticks and some rocks in an asymmetrical pattern spiraling to an opening in the center. Standing on the rim of the entrance, I set my intention.

"Dear Divine Universe, thank you for this day and all the blessings in my life, the ones I'm aware of, and the ones I am not. As I greet this day, may my mind receive your emanations, may my soul receive your blessings and my heart receive your love. May everyone I meet or even think of on this day be blessed. Thank you especially for the safety of my guests this weekend, for Nicole and the wonder of her finding another family. Forgive me my mistrust and misunderstanding of Badger. Bless the Three Investigators as they go on to new adventures and thank you for bringing Buster...George Burgwyn Shadetree into my life. Amen.

I was exhausted but felt a sense of peace settle around me as I began walking slowly, focusing on my steps and my breath.

Deep breath in with OM. Hold. Exhale with AH. Pause with HUM. Deep breath in with OM. I lost track of time, engrossed in my breathing, until an unpleasant smell broke my mindfulness. As I passed close to the left side of the center, the odor intensified. Something dead, something musky.

I looped away and back again, this time entering the circle.To the left of the water bowl I leave as an offering for animals, was an area of matted down grass with a dark mass in the center: a generous pile of fur-filled poop. My hand flew to my nose as I turned to backtrack, but something pale blue in the center of the pile caught my eye. And a sparkle caught sunlight. I walked straight out of the circle to find a long stick. Returning with a slim branch, I poked at object. Purple lettering and faux diamonds.

"Poopsie..." I whispered.

I ran out of the circle to Naughty Britches, unwrapped her leash and trotted her back to the house. I snatched the phone, my fingers a little shaky, punching buttons.

"Buster?"

"Well, hey, Sweet Moon Eyes, I was just thinkin' 'bout you. You in that black kee-mono--"

"Hi, uh, Yeah, me too. Thinking about you. Uh, this may sound stupid, but I just found a great big pile of furry poop with a dog collar in it in my back yard. It's a big pile. I mean...*big*. What was that word Shane used that meant heft? Averdoosomething?"

"*Avoirdupois*."

"Yeah, it's got that. Tell me it's a bear or a coyote or something, okay?"

"Well, has it got scratches all 'round it like a cat does in kitty litter?"

"No, it's in grass."

"Okay, well, not bobcat. Is it kinda all over the place like? Some here, some there?"

"Nope. It's all in a pile and the grass is matted down around it."

"Not a bear. A bear just goes as he goes. Doesn't slow down or stop."

"Like Naughty Britches."

"Yep, like that."

"It's got a lot of fur in it."

"One big pile, or more like little baby Lincoln logs?"

"One big pile."

"Hmm. Not coon then. Could be coyote, but their poop ain't much bigger'n a dog, and it's real sim'lar."

"This isn't anything I've seen before," I said, feeling mighty uncomfortable talking about types of poop with Buster, and even more uncomfortable that he was eliminating (subliminal pun, sorry) my hoped-for suspects.

"How fresh is it?"

"Ah…pretty recent."

"Hold on a sec," he said.

I could tell he was on the road; there was a steady hum in the background and some upbeat music playing.

I heard him relaying my part of the conversation to Rebel and a "Well now!"

Buster came back, sounding excited, "Can you talk a coupla pictures of it and send it to me? And put a coin next to it for a size reference."

"Uh, I can try. I'm not sure how to send pictures with this phone. Haven't really tried."

There was a heavy sigh and then Rebel said, "I can talk you through it. Don't get nervous, it ain't goin' anywhere."

"Okay. It'll take me a minute to get a coin and go back out there. Lemme call you back."

Walking back out to the circle, I had to laugh at the bizarre turn my life had taken lately. A few years ago, wrapped in grief, I had few friends and stayed home most days. Now I was running a meditation retreat, oh yeah, a *haunted* meditation retreat. I was meeting new people, getting exposed to new social worlds, and had fallen in love with a guy who had trained with a guru in Tibet and chased mythical beings around the countryside when he wasn't teaching fly fishing and making big bucks with videos.

NB whimpered as I re-entered the circle. I reached the unpleasant pile and stared. It was supersized. Strategically placing the quarter next to the pile, I stood back and called Rebel. This was a painful process, as I couldn't keep the line open and take pictures and mash buttons. After several fails, I hit 'send' and waited. Buster called me back.

"You got a Fed Ex office close by?"

"I am not sending poop via Fed Ex, Ups or U.S. mail. Sorry. I'm pretty sure there are laws against it."

"Why? It's not liquid, perishable, hazardous or flammable. Besides, how would they know what it is?"

"Well it was kinda liquid. And don't they make bombs out of manure? It might be flammable, and I think it qualifies for biohazard."

"Cheese 'n crackers got all muddy!" Buster yelled.

Cheese and crackers wasn't quite the expletive blast I'd expected. I'd been fearful I was about to see a big red flag regarding his temper; this non-threatening outburst made me giggle.

He took a big breath and exhaled. "Okay, hon, fine." He exhaled again. "Lemme see here. If ya could put it in a Tupperware and freeze it, Rebel could pick it up." His voice was less distinct as he asked, "Don't you have some barbecue cookoff in Georgia in a coupla weeks?"

"Yeah, week before Thanksgiving."

Buster's voice was clear again, "I think he's gonna be that way in about two weeks. He could swing by an' pick it up. Will 'at work?"

Ew. I hesitated. I wasn't keen on using my Tupperware for this, but I'd think of something. Maybe a box. Triple wrapped in plastic bags. Still, he was so excited, what if this really was a Bigfoot poop? Real evidence? Naw. Ridiculous. But the least I could do was to save it for them.

"Yeah. Of course." I stared at the rabies tag sticking out. Poor Poopsie. Guess I have to tell Mrs. Bunderbridge she should stop searching for her dog.

Buster said, "That's great, hon. Sorry if I lost it there, but this could be the real deal. We'll have to get it DNA tested."

"I'm on it," I said, mentally scanning my closet for a good box. How about a cake box? I was sure I had some Art of Tart cake boxes in the recycle bin.

I heard Rebel in the background saying, "This is it. Turn here."

Buster said, "Whoop. Gotta go. Love you, Moon Eyes. And thanks for your help. See you soon."

He said he loved me. Just like that. Hoo-boy.

You're in deep, said my Inner Critic.

Yeah. I was.

I stood there, disconnected phone in my hand, staring at the furry mound. Feeling a heart pang from the abrupt disconnect, vaguely annoyed at the disrespectful deposit in my sacred space, uneasy about how to 'collect' and store it, I stood there, taking it all in.

Then I realized with a jolt that at this very moment, I was voluntarily assisting in cryptozoological research. Ridiculous. And yet, I was kind of excited, and it felt…right.

I looked up at the sky, yelled, "Holy crap!" and cackled like a tenured asylum patient.

Chapter 35

Vanity and Jealousy

A little later, back in the circle with the accoutrements for the job, namely a resuscitated cake box and a handheld gardening shovel, I carefully scooped the scatological treasure and placed it in the center of the container. I wrapped it in five red plastic bags from Whatcha Need and scribbled, "For Buster" across the top. As an afterthought, I added a little heart underneath. I traipsed back to the garage, hung up the shovel, and set the box carefully in the freezer, away from all other food items. Then I called Lorraine.

"How're ya doing, Gimpy?" I asked when she answered.

"Don't saints usually get tortured before they become saints?" she asked.

"Usually. I don't think Mother Theresa was tortured; she died 'cause she was old. And, Saint Theresa of Avila died of some lingering illness. No torture."

"Crap. Saint Eleanor is healthier than I am. I foresee she might die from misadventure."

"Oh, she loves you. She just wants to help."

"Yeah. Her love is killing me."

"Oh. Isn't that a song by that Russian band you like?"

"Yes! The Red Elvises. So, what's up with you?"

"Funny you should ask. I just put some Bigfoot poop in the freezer in my garage."

"What *are* you smoking? Did that hot guy get you on *flakka*? That stuff'll kill you."

"I'm serious!" I said, not believing I was having this conversation, "I found this huge heap in my meditation circle. Buster asked me to preserve it for DNA testing. Isn't that cool?"

There was a pause. "Well. Won't that just be a boon to your business, your picture on the internet next to a pile of shit with a caption: 2014: Haint Blue, of Catfish Springs discovers 'evidence' in her back yard. Oh! I've got it! You can start a blog page: Meditate with a Skunk Ape: clear your mind and your bowels--"

"Yeah, okay, thanks for that."

"Hope you took a good selfie of you and the poop. Too bad you don't have video. Could've gone viral. Still, no tellin' who all this information will attract. You'll be famous. Of course, they'll prove you're a fraud, but not before you can do the talk show circuit. How does one get to be an authority on Bigfoot feces, anyway?"

"Stop!" I yelled. "Forget it. Sorry I mentioned it. Uh, and there's a problem."

"I can't wait."

"The poop was, well, let's say that Mrs. Bunderbridge isn't going to find her lost dog. Poopsie's collar was in the poop."

Lorraine is not one to bust out laughing, but I had to hold the receiver away from my head. Naughty Britches and Mischief, sleeping on the couch jolted awake, bleary eyes looking around for the source of the distressing yowling.

When the cacophony settled down to a conversational level I asked, "I'm not looking forward to telling her. I'm afraid she'll blame me somehow. She's not exactly the nicest woman."

"No, she's horrible. I'm not sure I'd tell her."

"I couldn't stand to see the missing dog signs all around town knowing she's got false hope he'll be found. No, it's the right thing to do. If she blows up at me, she blows. But she might not. No point in anticipating possible outcomes."

"I guess so. Wait! Oh my gosh, problem solved! Yes, tell her the bad news, but also tell her about Lullabelle's puppies! They'll be available in just a couple weeks! Once she sees them, she'll have to have at *least* one."

This was a solid idea. I wasn't about to tell her that her beloved Poopsie was eaten by a Skunk Ape. I'd just tell her I found the chewed-up collar. It was probably a coyote.

"Oh, hey! Speaking of pictures. Lerlene called."

"Yeah?"

"The article about her art with the picture of your sign is in the paper."

"Yeah?" That reminded me I had to talk to Lerlene about a new sign and go clean up the wreckage. I'd forgotten all about that.

"I haven't seen it yet. She's over the moon about it."

"Yeah?"

"Says the interview takes up the whole page. And the sign looks dazzling. The sun was hitting it just right."

The sign that was now all splinters. I remembered the sun in my eyes. "Oh, good."

She's got a bunch of copies. I'm sure she'll get you one."

"Okay, great."

"So, aside from Bigfoot poop-scooping, what're you doing today? Wanna come over?"

"Sure."

"I got bored and made a batch of cookies for us plus some less sugary ones for NB for when she comes over."

"I dunno… I'll have to brush her teeth again. She got into something in the yard. Her breath is awful."

"Oh! That reminds me! Saint Eleanor! You'll die, wait 'til I tell you!"

"Oh?" Saint Eleanor stories tended to be epic.

"Saint Eleanor was a wee bit tipsy the other night and told me this story. She's got an ancient Airedale with chronically bad breath. She claims she gets its teeth done regularly… I don't know if I believe that. She said the vet recommended chlorophyll tablets. Well, the dog sleeps next to her, so she as keeping the chlorophyll tabs on her nightstand. She'd give the dog a tab once in the morning and once at night. Apparently, the dog's pill bottle and Mom's pill bottles are in the same kind of brown plastic bottle. Mom took her pill as usual with water and noticed that something didn't taste right. There was a sort of earthy aftertaste."

"Uh-oh," I said.

"Well, she'd already swallowed the darned thing, and she wasn't about to make herself upchuck, so she put on her reading glasses and read the label to see about side effects."

"Uh-huh," I said, knowing Lorraine wouldn't be telling this story unless there was something crazy.

"She started reading the directions…ha-ha-ha…two tabs daily for dogs with breath odor..ha-ha, oh, hee-hee… or for…ah-ha-ha or for…BITCHES IN HEAT!!! Ah-ha-ha-ha-ha!"

I could tell she had dropped the phone. I could picture her rolling on her bed in hysterics. I laughed too, but more at her than the chlorophyll tab story.

"Oh, ow, that hurts!" She laugh-wailed. "I moved my leg wrong! Oh! ah-ha-ha, ow!"

"Well, I'll be over soon. I'll do what I can about Miss Foul Breath."

Naughty Britches bounded into Lorraine's house, rushing to greet her and readily receiving the offered home-made treat.

"Don't worry, I've got goodies for us, too," Lorraine said, hugging me. Lerlene just left. Told me to give you a couple copies."

"Oh, shoot. Sorry I missed her. I need to ask her about doing a replacement sign."

"She says she's already working up some sketches for it. Here, have a look. She looks great, and the sign looks, well, as good as a psychedelic whatever-it-is can look, but you—"

"What?" I asked.

I picked up the paper. Despite the bold font, I missed the headline, my eyes going straight to the dazzling photo of the cosmic lotus. Brilliant color, as Lorraine had said. Lerlene looked terrific: confident, perky, well-groomed, professional. I on the other hand, did not. I set the paper back down. "Well, Lerlene looks good, and the sign looks great, or should I say, looked great. That's all the really matters," I said, hiding my face in my hands.

"She said the sun was in your eyes…"

"Yeah, it was."

Your outfit looks great. Have you lost a little weight?"

"Oh, who cares? Look! My face is all mushed up like a Sharpei!" I wailed.

"Oh, not quite that bad…"

"Well, it's probably just as well! Who'd recognize me anyway? I have cornstalks sprouting out of my head! I look like an eight-foot-tall alien!"

"Here… Saint Eleanor made cookies," Lorraine said, trying but failing to hide her laughter. "And it's not like it's the *New York Times*. It's just *The Chatter*." She pushed a plate of cookies toward me.

"I know it's her artwork, but it's still *my sign, my business*…or it was. And that's *me* looking like a freak."

"I think she's already working on the replacement. You'll see. It'll be even better. Have a cookie."

"Where is Saint Eleanor?" I asked.

"Grocery shopping. I've got her running to three different

stores. She should be gone for a while," Lorraine said with a wicked smile.

I noted that the article was written by Wynnter Grahame. I pointed and chuffed, "Oh, Pity and Al Pacino… doesn't that make you nuts? Why can't she just spell it like the dang season? Look at that: W-*y*-*n*-*n*-t-e-r. No wonder people can't spell anymore."

"Right. Crazy," she nodded with a sassy smile. "Helena."

"What?"

"Isn't that your real name?"

I squirmed, "That's different."

She raised an eyebrow. "Oh? I see. So, a completely wacky nickname is okay but a non-standard spelling for originality is taboo?"

I made a face and reached for a cookie. So much for my high horse.

"Speaking of names, where's your man George Burgwyn?"

My man. Hmm. "He's off to the Sasquatch Summit in Ocean Shores, Washington."

"Sasquatch…Summit," she said, biting her lip.

"Yup."

"All righty then."

"Apparently its huge," I said.

"Oh, I'm sure. And what are you doing with yourself?"

"Decompressing. Cleaning rooms. Laundry. A great big nap."

"And storing poop, don't' forget that," she added.

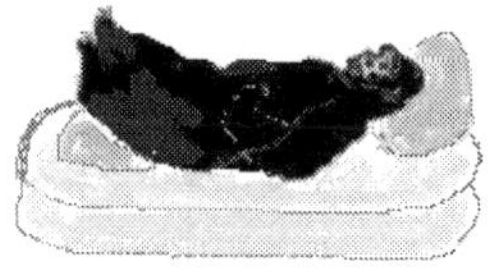

That evening, after a luscious nap and a turn in the hot tub, Mischief, Naughty Britches and I were lounging on the couch. I was reading a story in *Best Buddhist Writing 2013* when a song came on the radio called, "She Left on a Monday♥." It was beautiful and moody, about a man who lets his woman leave and maybe he should go after her. "Go to her, foolish man," the refrain advised. It made me relive every moment with Buster over the past week. His smile, his smell, our intimacy. What was it about the Thunderbird again? A symbol of renewal and destiny. I picked up the phone to call.

Don't be that needy girl, the Inner Critic advised.

I set the phone back down.

I'll just keep it light, I thought picking up the phone.

Don't do it.

I put the phone down again. I *could* call Iggy. I picked up the phone, scrolled for Buster's number and let my finger put pressure on his name. It rang three times. I was about to set it down when there was a blast of noise and a woman's voice giggled, "Hello?"

I punched the red phone icon to hang up. "Who was *that*? Had I dialed a wrong number? No, that was the right number. It sounded like an underage girl in a honkytonk bar. *Who was*

♥ Artist: Bic Runga from the album *Beautiful Collision*

that?

I dialed again.

She answered before the second ring, still giggling, "Yo, hello? He-hee." Pounding music and clinking glassware.

"Hello. This is Haint. I was looking for Buster, have I got the correct number?"

"Oh, yeah!" she shouted. "I'll tell him you called when he comes back. What's yer name?"

"Haint."

"Ain't?"

"NO, HAINT, H-A-I-N-T. Who are y--"

"Okay, bye!" Click. Sudden silence.

Ironically as hell, the song on the radio was advising, "All I need is to get on the phone and call." Yeah, I did that. And some perky young thing just answered Buster's phone. If my heart had a nose, the heady rose scents of first love it had been enjoying were jolted by a whiff of ammonia.

I knew he was eccentric, but player hadn't occurred to me. My mind raced. There was probably a very reasonable explanation for why this other woman was answering his phone in a bar. Probably. Stick to facts. Don't let your imagination go. My head got it, but my heart was trudging along like a blind person with a broken walking stick. Who was she?

I am too old for this shit, I thought.

Ah, so you say, Moon Eyes, but you have a poop sample in your freezer, Sweetie, the Inner Critic said with a chuckle.

THE END

We sure hope you enjoyed this book. If you did, would you do a quick review on Amazon or Goodreads to keep us here in Catfish Springs alive? We'd sure appreciate it!

What's going to happen with Haint and Buster? What kind of holiday mayhem is cooking at Blue's Lotus Lodge? Will Haint be alone in a

Stay in touch!

Please visit my blog at : **https://haintsretreat.com/** It's got recipes, Florida stuff, favorite movies and more. Please explore!

You can also check in with my publisher at:

https://hedonistichoundpress.com/

Until next time, wishing you abundance and peace,

--Haint Blue